THE
DREAM CRYSTAL

MARK O'BANNON

Published by MEOw Publishing.

Visit our website at: www.MEOwPublishing.com

First published in 2011

ISBN 978-1-933888-11-8

Printed in the United States of America

This book is dedicated to the
finest man I have ever known:
My father, Maurice Edwin O'Bannon

Books by Mark O'Bannon

IMPERIUM PREQUEL SERIES
(May be read in any order)
Pirates of the Imperium
High Salvage
Touching Infinity

IMPERIUM SERIES
Imperium – Return of the Archons (Coming in 2026)

SHADOWS & DREAMS SERIES
The Dream Crystal
The Dark Mirrors of Heaven (Coming in 2026)

AIA THE BARBARIAN SERIES
Aia the Barbarian – The Fallen God

WHISKERS
Whiskers (Coming in 2026)

CONTENTS

Notes

Aisling is pronounced, "ASH-ling."

Faerie, Fairy – The term "faerie" is used for mythological beings. The term "fairy" is used for modern types of fairies, brought into existence by the imagination.

Tuatha Dé Danaan – A race of people defeated in battle by the Milesians (Irish) and driven into another world, said to live inside hills or mounds of earth.

Sídhe (Shee) – The term is the plural form of Síodh, and it means "mound" or "hill." The term, "Sídhe" is used loosely to refer to the people of the Tuatha Dé or to the communities they live in. So a "Faerie Sídhe" is a town, and the "Sídhe" are faeries. The modern form is "Síthe" (plural) or "Sí" (singular).

Rath – A Faerie Fortress, usually seen in the Milesian world as a circle of stone ruins.

Milesians – A race of Celtic people that invaded Ireland and conquered the Tuatha Dé. The Milesians are the Irish people, but most faeries refer to all mortals by this name.

Síofra (SHEE fra) – A Changeling faerie, exchanged with a human child.

Áit Thanaí – Thin Place – A magical place where the "veil" between worlds is "thin," which means that it is easier to move between worlds where one is found.

Ley Lines – An ancient road system lying underneath Bealach an Rí (The King's Road). Movement along these roads are incredibly fast. Ley Lines connect Vortices, which are sacred sites on the earth, usually surmounted by standing stones. The ancients were said to be able to travel instantly between the vortex sites.

Maps

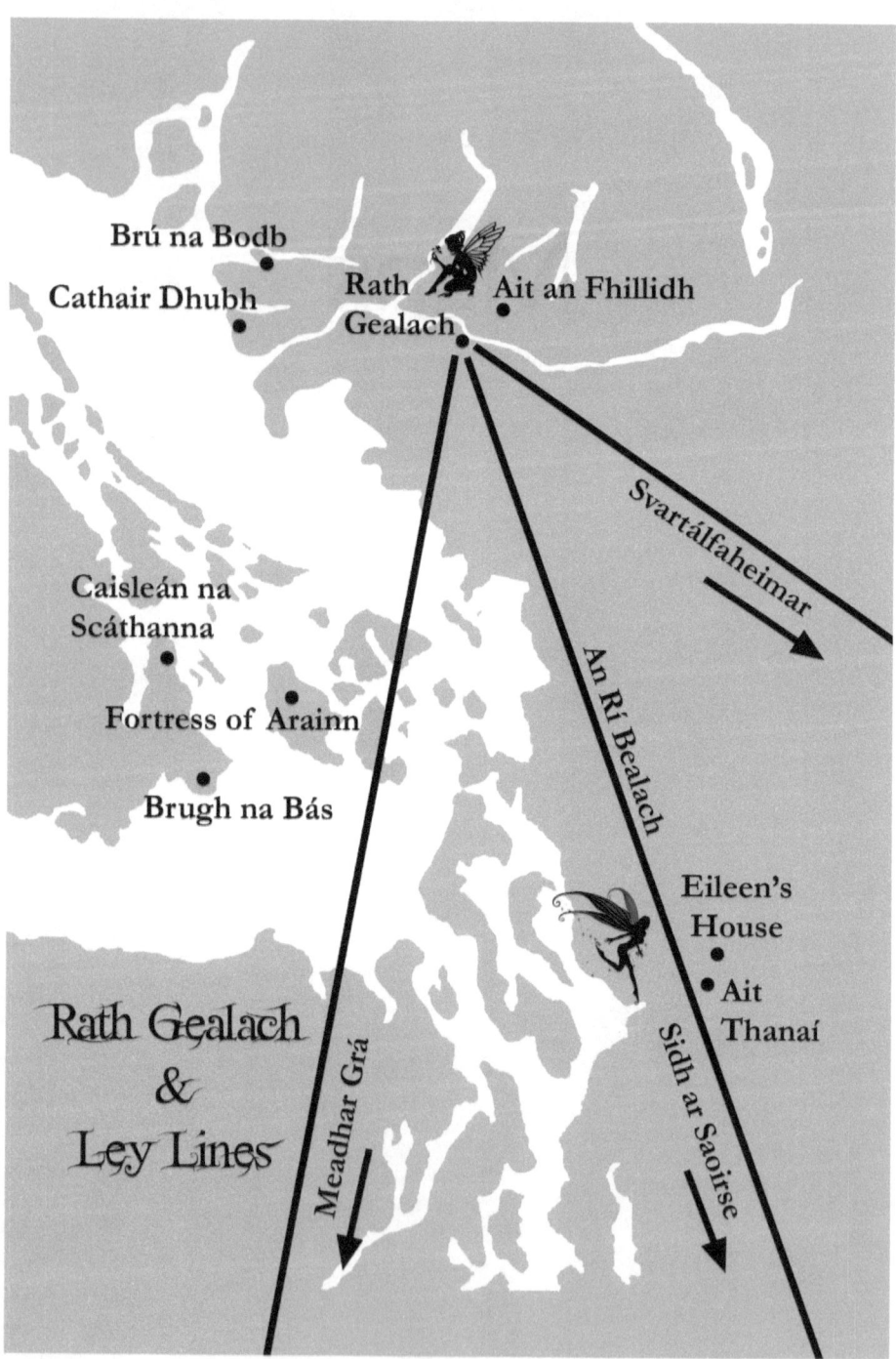

Brú na Bodb

Cathair Dhubh

Rath
Gealach

Ait an Fhillidh

Svartálfaheimar

Caisleán na
Scáthanna

Fortress of Arainn

Brugh na Bás

An Rí Bealach

Eileen's
House

Ait
Thanaí

Rath Gealach
&
Ley Lines

Meadhar Grá

Sidh ar Saoirse

Tír na nOg

Rath Gealach

Svartálfaheimar Measarthachtshee

Síd Imreas

Meadhar Grá Sidhe an Domhan

Roth Cinniúint Lismore

Sidhe ar Saoirse

Cnoc Síoraíocht

Na Teach Cúirtéis

Slieve Críonnacht

Capall Bán Cnoc Firinn

Brí na Slieve

Faerie Sídhe & Ley Lines

"What we achieve inwardly will change outer reality."

— Plutarch

Chapter One

Shadows & Dreams

They whispered to her sometimes, from the darkness, but she had never seen one of them before. No more than a quiet breath against fallen leaves, their murmurs taunted her about the futility of dreams. Cruel things always happened to those around her when she thought she could hear their voices.

Erin O'Neil sat like an alabaster statue, poised gracefully in thought, at the corner table of the café, dreaming dreams of beauty and letting those fantasies spill out onto her drawing pad. Twirling a pencil around fingers that longed to rest on the keys of a piano, the music of Beethoven began to fill her imagination. A dark rose fell into her thoughts, and she picked up a red pencil, using it to color the dress she was creating.

A quiet whisper lingered someplace near.

Erin looked across the café and noticed a girl, shivering in the sunlight. Dejected, she sat in a pool of sunshine that seeped into the café. Long blonde hair, slightly tousled, framed clear blue eyes, that dripped with sadness. She wore a white dress littered with little red flowers, and a white jacket. Steam rose from a cup of coffee in her hands. Erin remembered the girl had just dropped out of fashion school. Her name was Brigitte.

Despite the sunshine, there was a long shadow next to Brigitte. Erin stared at the black silhouette for a moment, wondering about the play of light inside the room. The shadow seemed out of place, as if it had a mind of its own.

A waitress came by and began to pour coffee, but Erin placed a hand over her cup. The waitress withdrew the coffee pot, irritation spreading across her face. "Don't you want a refill?"

Erin shook her head, wondering what was wrong with the waitress's nose. "I'm drinking peppermint tea."

The waitress, who could have been beautiful, was now marred by large tattoos, multiple body piercings, and excess body hair. It was as if she had worked hard to become as ugly as possible. "Look, you can't bring stuff in here."

Erin brushed a strand of long dark hair out of her eyes. "Excuse me?"

The waitress glanced over her shoulder and lowered her voice. "You have to order something. You wouldn't want me to get fired, would you?"

Erin glanced down at her cup, which was identical to all the other cups in the café. "I didn't bring this in here," she said. "You brought it to me."

"No I didn't," said the waitress. "We don't even serve peppermint tea."

Erin smiled. "Don't be silly. This cup didn't just appear out of thin air."

A slight breeze slipped through the café, and it seemed to carry a whisper of something along with it. Focusing on the sound, Erin thought she heard Brigitte's name called out, echoed in a distant murmur.

Erin glanced back in the girl's direction. The sunshine had quickly faded away into a pool of shadows. One moment, Brigitte was sitting there, wrapped in the darkness of abandoned dreams. The next instant, she was gone.

Erin frowned, disbelieving what she had seen.It had taken a long time—yet only a heartbeat—for the blackness to swallow Brigitte. Sunlight began to intrude upon the darkness again, as if the girl had never been sitting at the table. But curls of steam ascended from an abandoned cup, a lonely reminder that she had indeed been there.

A tingling sensation crept up Erin's spine.

"Don't you like coffee?"

It was an unpardonable sin for anyone living in Seattle.

"No."

"You're always alone when you come in here, aren't you?"

Erin looked down at the floor. "I have friends."

Not really listening now, the waitress moved off, trailing a bouquet of coffee.

Erin stared at the empty table where Brigitte had been and tried to forget what she'd seen. Sunlight covered the table now, washing the shadows away.

A flash of light made her blink.

The tiny sphere of brilliant blue light scintillated in the morning gloom outside the café. Then, a bright silver flame swept out from its core, searing a hole in the gray light that filtered down from the overcast skies covering the city. The little ball seemed to hover there for a moment, and then it winked out with another flash.

Erin blinked again, wondering if she would have seen such a thing if she had been drinking a caffeinated beverage. "I'm still asleep," she grumbled.

There was another wink of blue light, and then it was there, floating right next to her. It was like a small blue soap bubble, hovering over the table that held her latest drawing. It seemed to be examining the picture, flickering brighter for a second. Sensing that it was a delicate thing, like a dream, she held her breath and cautiously raised a hand. The pretty globe of light drifted down to barely touch the tip of one finger. It felt warm, like a smiling angel. She smiled back, but it disappeared, winking out in another flash.

After a moment of stunned silence, she glanced around the small café. It seemed that no one else had seen the glowing ball of light. She knew that everyone was still trying to wake up, but someone should have seen something! Erin shook her head, wondering if she had been losing too much sleep lately. Rising from her seat, she picked up her drawing pad, and went to her pattern making class, sensing that today would be different from any other day she had spent in college.

The morning mist ascended from the wet ground, seeping into the sky. Her boots echoed against the damp pavement, bringing a smile to her face. She loved noisy shoes.

As she was crossing the street, her smile began to fade. There was a prickling sensation crawling up her back, as if someone was watching her. Something dark lurked in the corner of her vision too, and she glanced around, half expecting to see the little ball of blue light, but there were only a few students around, walking to class.

Just before she reached the other side of the street, a truculent dog stood in her way, growling. She stopped a moment, recognizing the dog, who had become something of a school mascot. Memories of his wagging tail and his playful antics filled her thoughts. For an instant, she thought the dog was growling at her, but she quickly realized that he was looking at something else, behind her. *But there isn't anyone there*, she thought. With tail between its legs and ears flattened down, the dog began to bark, obviously terrified. With a quick glance at the approaching cars, she chose to walk around the dog, angling towards another section of the sidewalk. Just as she reached the other side of the road, she heard a car race by, followed by a thump and the dog's yelp.

As she spun around to look, Erin saw the shadowy figure of a man standing near the dog, which lay dead. Gasping, she stood there, staring at the shadow. A cold wind blew over the roadway, scattering papers into the sunshine. The shadow man turned his head in her direction. Darkness covered his face, obscuring his features.

"Hey Erin!"

Turning back towards the school, Erin looked at the concerned face of her friend, Genevieve, who came running over. "I heard the car. You okay?"

she asked.

Erin glanced back at the dead dog, trying to push away the shock of what she had just seen. There was no sign of the Shadow Person now. She just barely managed to keep her voice steady, "Yeah."

"That's what you get for wearing a sexy dress today," said Genevieve. "The driver was staring at you."

Whispers drifted by, and Erin knew that it was *their* fault. She glanced down at her orange velvet mini dress, black fishnets and patent leather boots. "There's nothing wrong with what I'm wearing," she protested.

Shading her eyes from the morning sunlight, Genevieve watched the car fade away down the road. "Isn't it illegal to just drive away like that?"

Sadness fell over Erin like a fine mist. "I don't know."

The sensation of being watched returned. A look around the area didn't make the feeling go away either. "Come on, let's go. You don't want to be late for class, do you?"

On the way to their pattern making class, Erin couldn't shake the idea that someone was looking at her. As they walked through the hallways of the fashion school, Erin kept looking over her shoulder. Several times, she thought she saw something dark out of the corner of her eye, but when she turned to look, there was no one there.

Erin entered the classroom ahead of her friend and took a seat by a large table that held a sewing machine, tools, scissors, and a few empty rolls that had once held yards of blue and white cotton for her latest project. She picked one of them up, and shot a glance at her friend. "Hey Gen, did you see who took my material?"

Genevieve was taking off her leather jacket. She looked up and ran a hand through her long chocolate colored hair. "You used it, didn't you?"

"No." Erin looked over the table, noticing that everything else that she had placed there yesterday was missing too. "Not again," she grumbled. Irritation began to creep into her voice, "Where's all of my stuff?"

Her eyes turned to the dress form standing by the work table. It held a beautiful blue dress, completely finished. It had three layers of white and blue cotton, and it matched the drawing that she had made for it exactly, to the last stitch.

"There it is, silly!" said Genevieve. "Hey, did you come in late last night to finish your project?"

Erin's mouth dropped open. "No!" She raised a hand to touch the dress, as if she wanted to make sure it was really there. "I didn't finish this."

"Then who…?"

Just then, Miss Bentley, the instructor, came over with a stiff expression on her face. Looking down her nose at Erin's attire, she said in a 'how-dare-you-wear-that-in-public' tone of voice, "Nice dress."

Erin crossed her legs. "Well, tomorrow is Halloween, isn't it?"

Miss Bentley noticed the completed dress next to Erin and she raised her eyebrows. "Working overtime again, Miss O'Neil?"

Erin tried to avoid looking into the instructor's eyes. "Not really, no."

She wondered if someone had been playing a strange joke on her. For the last several days, every new dress that she had designed was finished the next day, putting her far ahead of the others in class. There were over a dozen outfits standing by her work area now, all of them completed by some mischievous person.

Miss Bentley examined the new dress, her face full of wonder at the exquisite design. After a moment of devouring it with her eyes, she turned back to Erin. "You know that you're not allowed in this room after the school closes at night?"

Apparently, Miss Bentley wanted to take Erin down a peg. It was obvious to most of the other students that Erin's designs were far better than anyone in the school. Erin wasn't sure how to respond, so she simply nodded.

Miss Bentley frowned and shook her head. She raised a hand to touch the dress, but dropped it away just as quickly, as if she was afraid of it. "I suppose we can talk about this later, but for now, you're wanted in the director's office."

With a glance at her friend, Erin picked up her bag and left the room.

After she had gone through the door, she heard someone whispering over her shoulder. She stopped and looked around. The hall was empty. Frowning, she walked down the hallway that led to the staircase.

The gray-paneled walls were interspersed with smoky glass that looked into various classrooms. She marched past them all, listening to the echo of her boots bouncing off the walls and not wanting to hear anything else.

As she turned a corner, a dark movement from somewhere made her jump, but when she turned to look, the hallway was empty. "What a curious day," she muttered.

Erin climbed the staircase that led up to the third floor. The cold air filling the passage made her shiver as she reached the top of the stairs. Down at the end of the corridor, silhouetted in shadow, was a tall man wearing one of those short Victorian top hats. She squinted at him, but couldn't make out any of his features, since he was entirely covered by shadow. She was briefly reminded of the shadow standing by the dead dog, but this person was entirely different.

There was something mysterious and alluring about him, like a beautiful piece of music. He tilted his head slightly, admiring her. Smiling, she had an urge to say hello, but a shyness inside held her back. He reached out, offering his hand. She began to walk down the hallway, feeling her breath quicken with excitement.

A quiet something followed her down the hallway, whispering louder with each step she took. Something moved out of the corner of her eyes, but she couldn't take her sight off the man with the hat. He just stood there, waiting, with an outstretched arm. Then his eyes began to shine red, a pair of burning embers.

A small flash of light came, and the tiny blue ball of light reappeared. It moved off down the corridor in front of Erin. Distant laughter came from the Hat Man at the end of the hallway. The shadows faded away.

The tiny sphere remained, hovering in the corridor.

Erin was trembling. After a few shaky exhalations, she opened her mouth to speak, but the tiny ball of light vanished too.

"Erin O'Neil, isn't it?"

Erin glanced at the woman appearing in a doorway. "Yes."

The woman motioned for her to go inside. Erin stole another glance down the empty hallway and went in, taking a seat in a nice looking office with a window. Gray clouds smothered a city outside where people went about their daily lives in servitude. It felt good to be in fashion school, a refuge against the cold, dreary world. As the woman sat down gracefully, Erin noticed a bowl of candy sitting next to a placard that read: Mrs. Whitaker—Fashion Director.

"Miss O'Neil, why are you attending this college?"

All of her life it seemed that she had lived in another world part of the time—with one eye on the real world and the other eye looking—elsewhere. It was a world filled with glamour and refinement and charm . . . and terror. Because beauty was the greatest form of power, beguiling and enslaving. Its artistry covered the natural world and it filled the heavens above with cold fire, bathed in darkness. Beauty came to the earth like an angel sent down to annihilate the wicked. The ability to control it was an attempt to command the heavens.

"Miss O'Neil?"

Erin blinked. It was a simple dream, really: to fill the world with pretty clothes of her own designs. Erin gazed outside at the dead gray world, dreaming of one day filling it with color. "I'd like to become a fashion designer."

Mrs. Whitaker folded her hands in front of her on the desk. "Your instructors tell me that you've created some very charming designs, but that you need to exercise more restraint. They say that your clothes are too—enchanting."

To bring forth such elegant beauty, wreathed in pretty clothes, took more than imagination: It took the courage to fight against those that dared to stifle its creation. It took passion to overcome those that tried to control it too.

Erin sighed. "Oh why do people hate beauty so?"

"What was that?"

Erin raised her eyebrows. "Isn't that the point of being a fashion designer—to fill the world with magic?"

Mrs. Whitaker leaned back in her chair, looking down her nose. "Your designs would never make it in the real world of fashion. Look at any fashion show—"

Erin chuckled. "Take the most beautiful people in the world and dress them in the ugliest clothes you can imagine. Fashion shows have become a circus—a clown show."

"If you believe that, then you don't really know much about fashion."

Erin smiled. *Another shallow one.* "Like modern art, fashion has become an exercise in vanity and a distortion of the truth."

"What truth is it distorting?"

"Beauty."

Mrs. Whitaker looked down at the tight dress that Erin wore and she shook her head, sighing. "You should really learn to control your pride."

Erin's face burned. She felt like she was the recipient of one of those 'dumb blonde' jokes. The darkness that surrounded the city must have seeped into the school. She frowned. "Why is it that people always try to stifle the beautiful?"

Mrs. Whitaker crossed her arms. "Sometimes, you need to repress your passions."

It was as if it was a crime to be pretty, or an offense to make something that delighted the senses. Erin crossed her legs. "What's the use of being beautiful if you don't flaunt it sometimes? My designs make a woman more attractive, that's all."

Mrs. Whitaker lowered her voice, as if she were afraid of her own words. "Some people are offended by such beauty."

Erin was just beginning to realize that people were afraid of her. But the idea of repressing anything beautiful was really a weak, silly idea. She adopted a smile to take the sting out of her words and looked Mrs. Whitaker in the eye. "I never listen to those with inferior attitudes."

* * *

Erin had always thought her parents' house had too many windows. Instead of inviting plenty of light in, all it really accomplished was to give her the feeling of being exposed. She sometimes wondered if her father's job as the chief ophthalmologist at the university made him more prone to looking out of those windows. It was as if he had wanted to use his eyes as much as possible in a world of grays.

Erin walked into the entry foyer and paused to listen to the sound of a piano coming out of the music room. It was Mozart's Piano Sonata No. 11. Turning aside, she stepped up to the closed door, shutting her eyes. Knowing that her mother did not want to be bothered while she was playing—especially by her, she didn't go in. At one time, she had tried to get close to her mother, learning to play the instrument with the skill of a concert pianist, but nothing seemed able to please her. Sadness always lingered in both her parents, permeating everything they did. Nothing seemed to explain it. Erin had worried about them most of her life, but there didn't seem to be anything she could do.

Her father was sitting in his office, gazing out of the large window. All of the furniture was upholstered in white, except for his chair, which was made from black leather. A silver Kung Fu trophy stood on a black marble base on his desk, along with an iMac computer and a few papers. Pausing at the open doorway, Erin knocked on the door frame. His smile was polite and formal. "Hello, Erin."

"Hello." She stepped inside, feeling like an intruder. She could see herself reflected in the glass window behind his desk. The image intensified the feeling that someone was watching her, a notion that had followed her around all day. She sat down opposite her father, not sure where to begin.

"What can I do for you?" he asked.

Erin brushed a strand of dark hair out of her face and the motion made her more uncomfortable. Since both of her parents had blonde hair, she never liked to play with hers around them. "I've been kicked out of school. I was hoping you could speak with the Fashion Director. . . ."

Her father leaned back in his chair, considering her words.

Reflected in the glass, Erin saw a girl, about the same age as she was, standing in the doorway. She had long silver hair, a black sleeveless shirt, and a silver locket on a chain around her neck. She carried a doll in one hand. With an angry, lost expression in her eyes, she just stood there, watching them. Erin glanced over her shoulder to look, but no one was there. When she turned back again, the reflection in the glass had gone. Wrinkling her brows, she was interrupted by her father before she could ask about the girl.

"Why can't you study something more practical?" he asked.

Forgetting the girl for the moment, Erin ran her hand along the arm of her chair, feeling no warmth there. She could see that her entire life was beginning to fade away. She didn't respond, and the room filled with silence.

There was a dark movement out of the corner of her eye. And then, like the quiet sound of rustling silk, she began to hear a voice, whispering. Too faint to make out clearly, it surrounded her father, who began to shake his head. "I won't support something as useless as a fashion degree. Now, if you—"

Erin wouldn't let him finish. "You know it's my dream to become a fashion designer!"

Her father turned away from her, and began to look through the window, as if he was searching for something. He murmured, "Dreams are for children."

*   *   *

Erin ran upstairs to her room, furious. "What kind of parents are you, anyway?" she shouted. Throwing herself onto her bed, she clutched a rose-colored pillow, feeling the pressure inside her mind, which came from the images there—dreams waiting to be born. There were so many things she had wanted to create—no, so many things she had *needed* to create. To ignore the images was unthinkable. She knew they would soon slip away into oblivion forever if she abandoned them. But her father had refused to help her get back into school, and she knew that she would never be able to go back.

Glancing around her room, she looked at the cool white walls, the rose-colored bedspread and the white furniture sitting in the fading sunlight that drifted through the window. It had all been there since she was a child. Everything seemed to go together, complementing each other, except for one thing that had always stood out: A large mirror with Celtic knotwork running around its edges. A pair of dragons sat on the top edge of the frame, their tails trailing down into the maze of twisting designs. She had always liked the mirror, gazing into it when she was feeling sad or troubled.

But now the mirror reflected something strange. Erin sat up and stared into it, searching. The room had changed. Cold moonlight fell through white drapery onto a dark hardwood floor. A white crib sat on one side of the room, and a child lay there, sleeping.

Erin was trying to understand how the mirror could show the reflection of something that wasn't there when a pair of tiny spheres of light—one of silver, the other gold, drifted in through the open window.

Erin moved her eyes over to her window, but nothing had changed. Sunlight filtered in through the sheer white curtains. She looked in the mirror again, wondering at the reflection there.

The balls of light floated over to the white crib, remaining there for a heartbeat. There was a silver flash and a man appeared, looking down at the sleeping child. He had long blond hair, a gold torc around his neck, golden bracelets, a white tunic and a cape, embroidered with yellow thread. He carried a gray box in one hand. The gold ball of light hesitated a moment, its color draining away until it was a faded bronze. Then there was a bright flash and the ball was replaced by a tall woman with dark hair. She wore a green gown embroidered in white, and carried another child in her arms, surrounded in a pale blanket.

The man reached into the crib and picked up the sleeping child. He gave the woman a stern look. Reluctantly, she placed her own child into the crib. They both stood there a moment, gazing down at the crib, and then the man handed the woman the stolen child. He picked up a doll lying in the crib, and replaced it with the gray box. The woman began to cry, and kissed her child on the forehead. There was another flash and both of them were gone. Two balls of light hovered there for a moment, and then they floated out the window, leaving their own child behind.

Erin blinked and the reflection in the mirror changed to show the room she was in. She shook her head, wondering why she had been seeing so many strange things today. Getting up, she walked over to her night-stand, and sat down. "I must be going crazy."

Then a memory began to drift into her mind. She stood up and went over to her old toy chest. Hand crafted from birch and alder, it was painted in white and had a hinge at the top. A whiff of cedar greeted her nose as she opened the chest, and she began to rummage through it.

Down at the bottom of the chest it lay there, forgotten. The small, gray stone box had always been a source of curiosity for her as a child. Erin picked it up and brought it over to her nightstand, looking down at the Celtic knotwork designs in gray marble. A large dragon, spreading its wings, was carved into the top, and a dragon head looked out from the front too. It was a curious box, without any apparent hinges or way of opening it. After trying to discover its secrets for many years, she had given up on it.

Erin left the box and walked over to the mirror, tracing the silver drag-ons there. Then, the reflection inside the mirror changed again, causing her to step back a pace. This time, she was looking at a completely different room. A large fire burned out of a black stone fireplace. The room was surrounded by black pillars, which were connected to a wood latticework which ran between them. Several long wood tables stood around the fire-place, and a group of tall men sat at the tables, eating roasted meat and coarse bread. A girl approached one of the men, carrying a pitcher made of glass.

Erin recognized the girl as the same person she had seen reflected in

13

the window of her father's office. The girl wore a white peasant's blouse, a black vest, dark leather pants, and tall, thigh high boots. Her silver hair was a wild entanglement that fell down to her shoulders. She poured water from the pitcher, but it changed color as it fell into the glasses, turning deep crimson, as if it was being changed into wine. The man picked up the glass and tasted it. A bitter expression covered his face and he shouted at the girl. He threw the glass against the wall, shattering it, before striking the girl in the face. As she fell to the floor, Erin noticed that she was wearing a black metal collar around her neck with a large ring attached to it. Erin narrowed her eyes at the sight of the captive soul bound in iron and silence.

Erin stepped back another pace from the mirror, her mouth open. "What's going on?" The reflection in the mirror changed back to a view of her room, refusing to answer her question. Erin sat down onto her bed, holding a hand up to her forehead, bewildered. "Lights and shadows and strange visions in the glass."

Footsteps appeared in her doorway. Erin looked up to see her father standing there. "Erin, how long will it take for you to clear out this room?" he asked in a polite tone.

Erin dropped her hand down to the bed, where she gripped the rose-colored pillow. *First, he tells me that he isn't going to help me get back into school, and then he asks me to leave the house,* she thought. But her parents had already asked her to leave a month ago, when she had started school. Her father had wanted to turn her bedroom into a study. Feeling like an abandoned orphan, she looked out of the window, watching the sun set over the trees. Darkness seeped into her room. "I'll be out by this weekend," she replied.

He smiled and nodded and then he was gone.

"I suppose dreams really are for children," she whispered.

*   *   *

Chapter Two

Dancing Lights

Erin took a deep breath and began to strike at the wooden dummy, first slowly, with deliberation, and then with more force and speed. After a time, it sounded like a drum roll. She felt herself begin to slip into a state of intense fury.

Her life was a smoldering ruin. The helplessness at seeing her world fall apart fed a cold rage inside. The beauty filling her imagination would never again rise out of her dreams. Erin despised the idea. Hoping to control the ferocity building up inside, she thought she could work it off at the Kung Fu studio where she had spent so much of her youth.

The studio, part of a Shaolin temple, was constructed out of wood and stone. At one end, there was an area for students. This was connected to a central courtyard, open to the sky, where competitions were sometimes fought. Dark clouds gathered overhead, covering the courtyard with gloom. A large brazier to one side held a fire, which cast a red glow over the area.

A roof of stone covered dark hardwood floors, which surrounded the central courtyard. Long mirrors ran along the west wall. A shrine stood at the other end, flanked by a dozen candles. Thin banners depicting Chinese characters and artwork guarded the weapon racks along the north wall.

On the south side, a group of students, wearing green, rested after a long workout. Many of them were watching Erin with wonder in their eyes, and something else. Was it fear? For years, people had always tried to avoid being around her. Sometimes, she felt like a foreigner in an alien land.

Fury transformed into delirium, and she felt herself striking the wooden dummy with such vehemence that she would have knocked it over if it wasn't designed to withstand such treatment. A gust of wind from the courtyard blew hair into her face.

Laughter brought her frenzy to a halt. Erin looked into the arrogant eyes of Jason, one of the best fighters in the school. He had always covered his face with a façade of decency, but she knew what kind of monster he really was. He had always been an oppressor, and enjoyed intimidating people when no one was looking. While this kind of behavior was never tolerated by Sifu Yuen, the Shaolin master that ran the studio, Jason had managed to conceal most of his cruelty. His skill as a fighter was considerable and his arrogance unchecked. Erin had thought that Sifu Yuen was working to change him into a better person, but he hadn't improved much in the time she'd known him.

"Why don't you tie your hair back?" taunted Jason. He shook his head. "No discipline at all."

Erin narrowed her eyes. "I like to keep it free," she said. Returning her attention to the wooden dummy, she said under her breath, "My hair may get in the way, but I can still see what kind of person you are."

Jason only smiled, and he went back to instructing one of the younger students.

Erin began to train again on the wooden dummy, but the fire inside wanted to break free, to roar across the world. After a few minutes of crazed aggression, she found herself standing motionless, staring at it, unsatisfied.

Like a poke in the side, an odd sensation came on—of someone watching her. Something dark shifted at the edge of her vision, and a whisper brushed her shoulder: a cruel voice, hissing, "Break him."

"Yaw!"

Erin turned around and saw that Jason, wild-eyed, had just thrown the student down onto the mat with more force than necessary. Glancing around the studio, she noticed that none of the senior instructors had noticed. Putting her hands on her hips, she looked into Jason's cruel eyes. "What were you saying about discipline?"

A black shadow hovered behind Jason, whispering, but when Erin looked at it, the shade slipped away. Jason stood up and stepped close. "Girls like you are always causing trouble, flaunting their looks around," he said. "You're such a tease."

Erin smiled, knowing that he wanted to bully her into keeping silent. Another day, she might have allowed him to do so, not wanting to cause trouble, but this day, the fire inside her heart wouldn't go away. Fully expecting to lose, she said, "Care to have a go?"

Moments later, Erin stood to one side of the courtyard, dressed in a white suit embroidered with a gold dragon, with anger seeping into her skin like a heat wave. The frustration at seeing her life unravel began to mix with the dislike she had always felt for Jason. She murmured to herself, "I really hate bullies."

Jason moved into the fighting area, flexing his neck and cracking his knuckles. Brian, the instructor overseeing the fight, stood between them with a flag on the end of a pole raised above his head.

The candles surrounding the stone fighting area flickered as if a slow breeze was tickling them, but the air inside the temple was still. Erin placed a fist inside an open palm in a salute as she bowed to Jason, who returned the gesture with an air of contempt. A bell rang and Brian announced, "Begin!"

Erin took up a fighting stance, waiting.

Jason lunged forward, throwing three punches in rapid succession.

Erin just managed to dodge the first two by retreating a few steps, but she had to duck under the third strike. She spun around into a new position and took up a defensive stance, feeling a hollow fire starting to ignite.

Jason seemed to sense the ferocity in Erin but her restraint just made him angrier. He brandished his fists and wound up for another attack. "Yaw!"

As he charged, he threw a pair of punches. Erin dodged them both, looking for an opening and trying to keep herself centered. He punched again and she dodged it, moving around into a new position. She dodged his fourth attack and backed off.

Erin tried to shake off the wildness that dripped off of her like a cold sweat, but it spread throughout her body anyway, until her fingers tingled. He was trying to intimidate her, but she refused to let it happen.

Jason threw two more punches.

Erin dodged them both, stepped back and looked for an opening. She whispered to him, so that only he could hear, "This is the last time you bully anyone."

He narrowed his eyes. "Don't you like discipline?"

He stepped back and, angrily baring his fists, Jason wound up for another attack. "Yaw!"

This time, Erin caught his punch with a circular block and counterattacked, smacking him in the face three times. Then she delivered a body punch, which threw him back a few paces.

The candles seemed to flicker and grow brighter. While she maintained a calm, focused expression, she could feel an inferno rising around her. It felt like a hot breeze blowing against her face.

Jason seemed to sense it too, and he attacked again, swinging wildly.

Erin blocked the first two attacks and ducked under the third.

His fourth punch missed entirely.

The strange sensation spreading through her body was igniting her reflexes. Erin stepped back a few paces, hoping to gain a measure of control over the storm that was threatening to break. Resisting an urge to shake her head, she chose to focus on her opponent.

Jason put his fists up in determination and rushed forward in a fresh attack, throwing a series of quick punches. "Awwwr!"

After dodging the first attack, Erin blocked the following strikes, stepped inside his reach, and whirled around to deliver a backhand punch to his face. She threw a body blow with her elbow, causing him to bend over in pain.

Brian shouted, "Stop!"

Overwhelmed with passion, Erin spun around, jumped up into the air, and delivered a blow to the back of Jason's neck, knocking him onto the floor.

While Erin looked down at her defeated opponent calmly, she was anything but relaxed. It was like a fire had finally ignited inside of her, and it seemed to be drawing others into its conflagration too. The flames surrounding the arena were now blazing brightly, as if they had been feeding off of her energy.

Jason rolled over and stood up with a painful, shocked expression.

Erin saluted him with some surprise, since she had never before defeated Jason in a fight. Brian's expression caught her gaze and she looked into his smoldering eyes. The passion spilling out of her seemed to have ignited something inside of him too.

Furious that she had ignored his command to stop, Brian threw the flag down and walked over to the weapons rack. She could hear something whispering to him in the shadows. Erin just stood there, dripping fury, not caring that he was picking up a sword. He walked over and offered the sword to Erin, and then went back to the weapons rack and retrieved two more for himself. She looked at the curved sword, noticing that it was not one of the usual practice weapons. This one was a real Dao sword, with a slightly curved handle bound in black leather. Its edge was as sharp as a razor. As he stepped back into the fighting area, she saw something dark out of the corner of her eye, watching them. Although she couldn't see its face, she had the impression that it was grinning. She chose to ignore the shadow and turned towards Brian, bowing in a salute.

Erin could feel her heart bathed in fury, beating fire. She took up a fighting stance, holding the sword out in front with the blade pointing up, and with her other arm upraised, palm-up behind her head. While Brian was the second best sword fighter in the temple, Erin felt a strange confidence that spread out from the tingling sensations that washed over her body. It was like a steady breeze, fueling her reflexes and heightening her senses. The fires around the arena were now brighter than ever and the candles were flaring hotly.

Brian moved forward with a double spinning sword attack. Twirling the swords out in front while advancing, he struck four times, twice with each sword.

Steel flashed—too close. For an instant, she felt the bite of the blade in her mind, sharp and real. Erin stepped back and parried.

Then he lunged forward, aiming the point of a sword at her face.

Erin parried the attack and stepped closer so that she could strike him on the head and shoulder with her free hand.

Brian recoiled and brandished his swords, a fierce expression filling his eyes.

Erin raised her sword, standing ready. She said in a coy voice, "Come on!"

"Awwwrrr!" He ran forward, aiming a dual overhead strike at her head.

Her reflexes afire, Erin stepped out of the way of one of the sword strikes and parried the other with her sword.

Brian lunged forward, fully extended this time.

Parrying upward, Erin stepped inside and grabbed him by the wrist. Striking him across the back and front with the flat of her blade, she moved closer and then struck him across the chest several times. Then she stepped behind him, pulling his arm back.

Brian struck out with his remaining sword and missed.

Erin stepped in front, pushed her elbow up against his neck, grabbed his other arm and then forced it behind his back.

With a cry, Brian dropped the sword from his free hand.

Erin pushed him out of the arena and saluted. "Nice try."

Silence descended over the temple. The group of students on the south end had drawn closer to watch, but now they seemed to be holding their collective breaths. Brian cursed and walked away, humiliated. Jason was nowhere to be seen.

Erin stood there, feeling a rush of energy and fury wash over her. The tingling sensation rippled through her body, and she could tell that all of her reflexes and senses were at the highest she had ever experienced. She was now an unquenchable fire—the center of all energy, ready to tame the fates.

In the shadows, she heard whispers mingling with the crackling of the fire. The candles all around the area had almost consumed themselves. Sunshine fell through a space in the clouds overhead and washed the courtyard with its bright radiance. The fire in the brazier had grown into a furious pyre, casting red light onto the stonework.

Erin glared at the onlookers, spotting Luo, the best fighter in the school, among them. Only Sifu Yuen had ever beaten Luo before.

It was increasingly more difficult for Erin to restrain herself. It was like trying to stop a firestorm sweeping over a forest.

A dark silhouette moved through the crowd, unnoticed by everyone except Erin. It approached Luo, whispering angry words.

When he stepped into the courtyard, Erin smiled and bowed in a salute. Rather than use the sword, she placed it in her left hand, resting the weapon against her shoulder. She could feel a shimmering power rippling along her skin. It was like being bathed in resplendent fire.

Luo yelled and attacked, throwing three rapid punches towards her face.

In the past, there was no way she could ever have stopped an attack delivered with such speed, but today, it seemed like he moved in slow motion. There was plenty of time to counter his moves. Erin blocked all three attacks with her free hand.

Luo struck again, aiming for her throat.

This time, Erin dodged to one side and grabbed his wrist, breaking it. She then kicked him in the chest while holding his arm. Finally, Erin released his arm and kneed him in the chest, causing Luo to fall to the stone floor of the courtyard.

Out of somewhere came a whisper, "Destroy him!"

Having abandoned all restraint, Erin switched the sword to her right hand, spun around and swung it down at Luo, aiming for his neck.

Clang!

A sword had appeared from the side, blocking her strike. Erin looked up into the face of Sifu Yuen, who was now standing in the courtyard. He wore a black cotton suit. Although he was in a fighting stance, his eyes were like a calm mountain lake.

Erin could feel her heart beating rapidly. An intensity she had never experienced before fed off the fury that had grown from dark embers into a raging storm.

She took up a fighting stance and readied an attack.

And then it was over. Sifu Yuen was faster than she was. With three swift moves, he had disarmed her and thrown her to the ground.

The light that had been shining down onto the courtyard went out as the clouds overhead moved in front of the sun. Erin felt something hot rushing out of her, and lay on the ground with her palms resting against the cold stone, panting like an angry tiger.

* * *

Some time later, she looked up and saw Sifu Yuen maneuvering around the courtyard gracefully, making circular motions with his hands and practicing moves that she had never seen him use before. Erin found herself staring at him in wonder.

All of the flames surrounding the courtyard had gone out, and a cool breeze washed over the area. Erin could hear the trees outside swaying above the roof of the temple. Sifu Yuen finally stopped. With a calm glance, he dismissed all of the onlookers, and they melted away from the courtyard.

Erin was shaking. "My God! What have I done?" she whispered. Never before had she lost control of herself while fighting. Continuing to brutally strike a helpless opponent, or to exhibit any kind of merciless behavior was the trait of a barbarian. The memory of trying to strike her opponent down with a sword still lingered in the air, like a fresh wound.

I could have killed him!

What happened? One moment, she was simply fighting, trying to work off some frustration. The next instant she was trying to kill someone.

Sifu Yuen looked down at her with some concern. He gestured for her to get up. "Come with me, please."

Not daring to speak, she got up and followed him into the temple. As they walked, she could feel the fire inside of her bleeding away. It was as if the further she moved away from the fire and light in the courtyard and into the dark recesses of the temple, the weaker she became.

They went down a wood paneled hallway to a meeting room with a few couches and chairs. The only illumination was a pair of candles which made shadows dance across the walls. A small window opened up onto a garden outside the temple where a fountain brought the sounds of falling water into the room. It was soothing, but it didn't wash away the shock at what she had just done. She took a seat on the edge of a chair while he busied himself in the adjacent kitchen. Erin rubbed her hands together and closed her eyes. But the memory didn't go away. She had to fight off an urge to run away and forced herself to sit there on the edge of the chair. She felt like a balloon that had lost all of its air. She had disgraced her teachers. How could she have let this happen?

He walked into the room carrying a tray that held a tea pot and a pair of cups. Sitting down opposite to her, he began to pour the tea, and offered a cup to her. Erin took it numbly but didn't drink.

"How long have you been coming to the temple, Erin?"

Erin didn't look up. "Thirteen years, ever since I was six."

Green tea scented the air, and he took a sip before continuing. "I've always thought that you were better at Kung Fu than your father, but I've wondered why you never entered any competitions."

Erin shook her head, her mind drifting back. Originally, she had joined the school because of her father, hoping to prove herself to him. But after a few years, when she had become good at Kung Fu, he had quit altogether, leaving her with the feeling of being abandoned. Ever since then she had thought of the temple as a second home. "I was never really interested in fighting."

He nodded and set the cup down on the table between them. "Have you ever been afraid of hurting others?" he asked.

For the first time, Erin looked into his eyes. For several years now, he had taught her what Kung Fu was all about: Courtesy, consideration, bravery, and loyalty. While a few people interested in martial arts were motivated by a desire to hurt others, here at the temple they had always taught gentleness and the love of life first. Compassion and wisdom were the twin pillars of the Shaolin philosophy.

There had always been the fear of hurting someone deep down inside her—somewhere. She dropped her eyes. "Forgive me, sir, for bringing violence to this place."

Sifu Yuen leaned back in his chair, looking at her with calm eyes. "I have never seen anyone do what you have done here today," he said quietly.

Erin bit her lip and looked away. This was worse than she had imagined. She wondered what he would have said if she had actually hurt someone. The shame of what she had done made her want to hide. But it didn't sound like disappointment in his voice at all, and so she looked back, curiosity overcoming pain.

His voice turned thoughtful. "There are legends of course, from a long time ago, but to see it happen in one of my students . . . was a bit of a surprise."

Erin narrowed her eyes. "Sir, what did happen to me?"

The candlelight reflected in his eyes. He paused a moment as if considering what to say next. "An elemental spirit, probably one of fire, attached itself to your psyche. It gave you great powers—swiftness, strength, and power—but then it tried to control your actions."

24

Erin raised her eyebrows. "I was possessed by a—a candle?" she asked.

Sifu Yuen laughed. "A spirit of fire."

"How?"

"Every elemental spirit is different. In this case, passion, fury, or anger could have done it. But not everyone is capable of summoning such beings."

"But I didn't do anything."

"Your passion attracted this elemental."

"So now every time I feel passionate about something, one of these . . . spirits will try to possess me?"

He shook his head. "Sometimes, but other kinds of elementals may be attracted to different traits. Anger, tranquility, sunshine, darkness, thunderstorms, or even the wind could attract different kinds of elemental spirits."

Incomprehension made her frown. "Where do they come from?"

"They are created by your own psyche, or by the echoes of strong emotions or conditions in an area. These beings can exert their power within their domain, but they lack individuality, remaining dormant until something brings them forth. Elementals can be seen in the wind blowing across a field of grass, in a waterfall, in lightning, in the trails of smoke floating through the air, or in sheets of drifting rain. When summoned, they can enhance your abilities, but they can also influence your thoughts, actions, and desires."

Erin remembered how good it had felt to defeat her opponents—to destroy, or even to kill. Part of her still wanted to slash out with the sword, to taste blood—

Her eyes drifted outside, where the fountain played in the diminishing light. "I can't stop how I feel—"

Sifu Yuen leaned forward. "You must remain neutral."

What did that mean? She shook her head. "I don't know how to do that."

Sifu Yuen leaned back in his chair, his eyes fixed on hers, but he remained silent.

Erin leaned forward, resting her elbows on her knees. "Sir, I have been seeing some . . . curious things today."

Sifu Yuen didn't answer. He poured another cup of tea for himself.

Erin began to rub her hands together. "I saw a ball of light floating outside of my school today and two more of them reflected in a mirror." She swallowed her uncertainty and continued. "I've seen shadows—people in the shadows, whispering . . . things."

Sifu Yuen looked at her for a long time. "The lights are spirit beings. Take care. Not all of them are friendly."

Erin nodded and looked into his eyes. "What do you know of the Shadow People?"

He shrugged. "Who can say?"

It was like staring back into a whirlwind, reliving the fight she had just endured. Fire and shadows and disturbing voices pulled at her memory. Erin licked her lips, thinking of the fighters she had just beaten. The shadows whispered to them—and to her.

Sifu Yuen interrupted her thoughts. "You're not like any student I've had before. Too long, you have been hiding out in this temple."

Erin slid back into the chair, pressing her back against the dark wood. What was happening here?

He put the teacup down and looked into her eyes. His gaze made her feel naked and exposed, and so she looked away.

"You have a destiny to fulfill."

Erin shook her head, hoping that he wouldn't continue.

Sifu Yuen stood. Sadness dripped off him like the water falling from the fountain outside. "Tonight, you must leave this place. You will not be allowed to return until you have done what you were meant to do."

* * *

The world was bathed in a soft whisper. It had begun to rain softly. Erin walked down the stone steps of the temple, glancing at the pair of stone dragons on either side. A numb emptiness fell onto her cold skin, mixing with the drizzling rain, spreading misery. It was like falling down a

26

deep well into chilly darkness. She walked through the garden in front of the temple, breathing in the last scents of the flowers there and choking on tears that mixed with the rain. Her entire world had collapsed. Unable to take another step, she sat down on the side of the path, hugging her knees, shivering.

Erin thought of her father, gazing out of his tall windows, sad faced, alone. It was as if he had always wished for something—something that he wasn't even aware of: the love of a daughter truly his own. She wished she could give him that—bring back someone he could love.

A tiny brightness floated out of the trees. Erin pushed a wet strand of hair out of her eyes and blinked away water. It was the same blue-silver ball of light she had seen that morning, coming closer. Not wanting to look at it anymore, she dropped her eyes down to the gravel. A moment later, the ball of light was hovering there, bathing her face in warmth. She looked up.

A tiny whisper washed away in the rain.

Erin pushed her dark hair out of her face again, listening to the blue sphere.

Something twinkled silver inside, echoing out another soft whisper: "Aisling."

Erin whispered back, "What did you say?"

A final echo came from the blue ball of light, more definite this time: "Aisling."

Erin licked her lips and raised a hand, feeling the soft rain pepper her palm with dampness that reflected the blue-silver light twinkling from the sphere just inches above it. The sphere touched down, spreading friendliness through her hand, up her arm and into her heart. It made her smile.

Awash in a sea of despair, she had found a lifeline. The name resounded in her mind: Aisling.

The little ball of light drifted away, towards the pine trees at the edge of the garden surrounding the temple. Erin watched it go but it stopped just before going past the trees, as if it was waiting for her to follow. Smiling, Erin stood up and walked towards it.

The ball of light slipped away through the forest, followed by Erin. After a few moments, Erin saw several other lights through the trees. The blue ball of light rushed forward to join them. Erin counted over two dozen of the tiny lights, all different colors, dancing around a clearing. But she stopped just outside of it, afraid to take a step into the glade. Content to simply watch the spirits, Erin stood there, one hand resting on the bark of a pine tree.

Finally, Erin couldn't resist the temptation to join the tiny lights, which seemed content to simply dance around the flowers and over the grass covering the glade. She stepped into the clearing.

All of the lights went out.

A cold moment passed while she listened to her startled breathing and peered through the darkness. The rain that covered the world whispered softly through the pine trees overhead. Erin glanced back over her shoulder from where she had come, but she couldn't see the temple.

Then, a single ball of light appeared on one side of the clearing, flashing red and purple. The orb hovered for a moment, and then went off through the trees. Erin tried to follow it, but it kept moving out ahead of her, just out of sight, dodging behind trees and shrubs, always poking out from somewhere, playfully. Finally, she stepped out onto a road and saw the little light floating there just on the other side. It flashed purple, and then faded into a transparent red color, waiting there.

Just as Erin began to cross the road, white light washed over everything, and she heard the horn of a car that froze her heart. Erin jumped back, acting on instinct, and landed on her back just as a speeding car shot past.

Erin lay there for a time, listening to her rapid heartbeat and looking for the tiny ball of purple red light.

It had gone.

Erin had been kicked out of fashion school, kicked out of her house, and then kicked out of the Shaolin temple. She was going crazy too, seeing lights and shadows and hearing voices. After taking a few slow breaths to calm down, she muttered to herself, "What a day!"

Another car shot past, followed by a rushing wind that blew wet hair into her face. "I can't wait to see what happens tomorrow!"

*　*　*

Chapter Three

Cold Steel

Fading dreams whispered from the darkness, like the last breath of a concerto, expiring with soft susurrations. Erin awoke, breathing in the aroma of lavender smoke from a pair of burning candles on the coffee table. The unmistakable presence of someone lurking close by pulled at her senses.

Faint illumination came through the closed curtains, blocking out whatever sunlight that still remained from the last embers of the day. She lay on Genevieve's white couch, with her book of fashion illustrations clutched in her arms. An endless supply of books lined shelves on the walls—abandoned memories of forgotten times and places, books on the occult, and an occasional romance novel. A line of target shooting plaques and trophies stood on the mantelpiece.

The house seemed to be empty, but she couldn't shake the idea that someone was there, watching her as she lay sleeping. Erin sat up quickly, nearly dropping her book of illustrations. Swinging her legs out onto the floor, she put the book down on the coffee table and raised her hand to her forehead. "I can't believe I fell asleep," she muttered. Brushing dark hair out of her face, she looked out into the hallway. Glancing up the stairs, she called out, "Gen?"

No answer.

Sighing with black thoughts, a gentle breath of air blew across the side of her head, pushing hair into her face. Dark movements danced at the corner of her eye, mingling with a hateful malevolence.

Erin's heart froze.

Slowly, she turned her head around, scanning the room.

Under the archway leading into the hallway stood the shadow of a man, barely discernible. Silently, he watched her. Erin had the impression that he wanted to let her see him staring at her.

Jerking her arm, she stood up, knocking one of the candles over. Narrowing her eyes, she looked at the shade. It was a tall, cloaked figure, with the shape of its head hidden in folds of the hood. Tingling sensations—pins and needles, like when an arm or leg had fallen asleep—dribbled over her entire body. For a heartbeat, she was unable to move. A pair of red eyes emerged, smoldering, from the darkness within the hood, and she heard the thing laughing.

With a whoosh, a wave of heat washed over her side, as the crackling sound of fire erupted. The shadow backed away, swirled into a blurry streak and then whisked out of sight down the hallway. Instantly, Erin was able to move. She looked down at the coffee table and saw her portfolio of fashion designs burning, set alight by the candle.

Cursing, she picked up her book of illustrations and rushed into the kitchen. Tossing it into the sink, she turned the water on. Smoke billowed up, filling the air, and she ran over to a window, opening it. A red sunset spilled into the kitchen, bathing the room in furious splendor. She whirled round in shock. All of her fashion designs were destroyed!

With a shout of rage, Erin ran out into the hallway, looking for the Shadow Person. But the house lay empty.

No one was there.

The gloomy day had emptied into night. Rain had fallen earlier, clearing the air and spilling dampness over the dark earth. A cold wind blew russet leaves over the ground in front of the coffee house, which stood next to a large oak tree. Here and there along the ground, the yellow flowers of St. John's Wort could be seen. Farther off, dark pine trees reached into the night sky, standing at the edge of a forest, like a tall curtain veiled in green.

Candlelight flickered out of the grim masks carved into a pair of pumpkins which stood on either side of the doorway, their glow holding off the darkness. The coffee house was always full of people just drifting through life. It was a place for insomniacs and those that never truly did anything. Now, it called out to her seductively, as if she were about to enter its domain and never escape again.

Erin's short black boots echoed off of the wood planks that covered the entryway. As she approached, a scraggly man with a long gray beard shambled out of the shadows, hand out. "Got any spare change?"

Wrinkling her face, Erin shook her head and tried to move around the beggar.

Dissolution shrouded the man. It was as if he had been fading away for a long time and was now struggling to hold on, ready to disappear entirely if he didn't get help soon. His words were past the point of desperation. "I'll take anything," he said.

Shaking her head, she replied, "Sorry."

He stepped aside, but pointed a finger at her. "What you do every day," he said, "echoes throughout eternity."

Ignoring the beggar, Erin opened the door and went inside, hesitating at the entrance to look around for her friend. The overwhelming aroma of espresso confronted her. It felt like she was being smothered in coffee. Taking a deep breath to clear away the sensation, she plunged inside, walking over to the counter to order a cup of tea.

The coffee house was full of people, some of them clad in Halloween costumes. Candles had been set out on the tables, giving the place a medieval look. A cute guy sat across from a girl, deep in conversation, their hands clasped together. Noticing Erin's stare, he looked up.

Unable to resist an urge to flirt, she smiled at him.

He released the hands of his girlfriend, and smiled back, entranced.

Coyly, Erin turned her back on the couple and looked around. She spotted Genevieve sitting at the table, wearing jeans, black leather boots, and a t-shirt. Wrapped around her neck was a long knitted scarf, a good luck charm. A leather jacket hung from the back of her chair. Genevieve smiled as Erin approached. "I love that dress."

Erin glanced down at her outfit. She was wearing an anime style black and white dress over tights striped in black and purple. But the compliment only made her think about school. Her smile faded just as quickly as it appeared. She hung her bag over the back of a chair and sat down. "Hi."

Genevieve glanced towards the door. "So how much did you give him?"

Erin glanced outside where the beggar lurked. He was now hiding in the darkness, just outside the entryway. "What, him?" She shook her head. "Nothing."

Genevieve was shuffling a deck of tarot cards. "You know, not everyone—"

"I won't help anyone that's given up on life," she explained.

For a moment, Genevieve looked softly into Erin's eyes. She went back to shuffling her tarot cards and then began to lay them out on the table.

Erin looked over at the couple and she managed to catch the cute guy's attention. Brushing a strand of hair out of her eyes, she smiled boldly. Just as he returned her smile, Erin noticed the silhouette of a man lurking behind the girl, leaning over close to her ear. Quite suddenly, the girl slapped her boyfriend, got up and went outside. Erin reached up to touch the cross around her neck, holding her breath. The Shadow Person looked in her direction just before it turned into dark specks, vanishing entirely.

"You shouldn't have done that," said Genevieve. "Just because you're desperate doesn't give you the right to flirt with every cute guy you see."

"It's not my fault he flirted back," she said. Shaking off the surprise at seeing the Shadow Person, she added, "Besides, you're one to talk. How many guys are you dating now?"

"None at the moment," said Genevieve. "But I don't toy with men like you do."

"I wish I had somebody to toy with," complained Erin. "Most guys treat me like I'm from another world. Sometimes, I hear someone whistle at me but when I look over my shoulder, they just turn green and run away."

Genevieve giggled. "Maybe they're afraid you'll turn them into a toad or something."

Smiling, Erin closed her eyes and breathed in the peppermint aroma as she waited for the tea to cool down enough to drink. Opening her eyes again, she began to pour sugar into the cup.

"Where did you get that?"

"What?"

"The sugar!" said Genevieve. "It wasn't here a moment ago."

Erin laughed softly. "Don't be silly!"

Genevieve frowned and went back to her tarot cards, but Erin looked at the container of sugar with suspicion. Had it really appeared out of nowhere? Shrugging, she put it down and tried to forget the strange things happening around her.

Erin sighed. Inside, she was trying to fight off a sense of desolation. It was like standing on a beach as the sand slipped away with each successive wash of the waves. Everything in her life was sliding away and she was sinking down.

"There's a Halloween party at John's house tonight. Want to go?"

Genevieve's question brought Erin back to the present. But the stain of what she had done still burned in her memory. "You know, I almost killed somebody in the temple yesterday."

Genevieve chuckled and flipped over another card. "You always were a bit wild. I guess your parents aren't going to help with school, are they?"

Feeling like an orphan, Erin looked away. A shadow moved in the darkness behind a red-haired girl. For a moment, she forgot everything, concentrating on the shade, but Genevieve's expression drew her attention.

"You're serious, aren't you?"

Erin nodded and crossed her arms. "I got into a sword fight with Brian and then I broke Luo's wrist. Sifu Yuen kicked me out."

A silence stood between them.

A girl's voice interrupted, "Excuse me."

They both looked up at the red haired girl. She was wearing a short green skirt, black tights, a white peasant blouse and a green brocade corset. Her long hair fell in russet tangles around her shoulders.

"I lost my purse while I was sitting here earlier. Have you found anything?"

Erin didn't answer.

Genevieve pointed under the next table. "Is that it?"

A smile lit up the girl's face. "Yes! Thanks."

As she went off, Genevieve whispered, "In Ireland, they say that girls with red hair are magical." She leaned close. "I love the corset!"

"Yes." Erin watched the girl go outside. A light mist was rising, and it parted out of the way as she moved through it. The girl got into her car and drove away.

Erin looked into Genevieve's blue eyes. "Do you believe in fate?"

"I believe in destiny."

The Shadow Person had disappeared, but Erin felt it there still, watching. Shaking off the strange sensations, she tried to ignore the thing. "I suppose the world will remain a gray place forever," she said. "You know, I could have changed the world with my fashion designs."

"You still can!"

"No I can't," said Erin. "I fell asleep on your couch this afternoon, and when I woke up, I accidentally knocked over a candle. My portfolio caught on fire. All of my designs are gone."

After a moment of silence, Genevieve said, "So make new designs."

Erin didn't answer. Her life had changed overnight. The strange vision in the mirror troubled her even more. "I just don't know who I am anymore, Gen."

"But you can't quit school!"

"Why not?"

Genevieve put down the deck of tarot cards and leaned forward. "Because you're the best there is."

Ignoring her friend's comment, Erin turned around and reached into her bag, withdrawing the gray box she had taken from her old toy chest. She placed it onto the table between them.

Genevieve ran a hand through her long dark hair and looked down at the intricate carvings. "What's this?"

Still haunting her thoughts, shining spheres of silver and gold had been reflected in the mirror in Erin's room. She wanted to know if they had been real. Erin looked down at the box. "It's something I've had since I was a child. I've never been able to open it."

Genevieve ran her fingers over the dragon. "These are Celtic designs." She felt along the edges and then withdrew her hand. "And there's something else." Leaning back in her chair, she looked up, a distant expression in her face. "I sense something, something dangerous about this box."

Erin glanced at the tarot cards sitting on the table. Smiling, she said, "Your intuition bothering you again?"

Genevieve didn't respond. She gathered up her tarot cards and handed them to Erin, who reluctantly began to shuffle them.

The feeling that someone was watching her didn't go away. Erin glanced around the coffee house, into the dark corners and along the walls, but didn't see anything. She put the tarot cards back onto the table and her friend began to flip them over.

Genevieve said, "You're represented by the queen of pentacles. The hanged man covers you." Brushing long brown hair out of her face, she continued, "You come from a place of abundance, but everything is chang-ing now."

Erin huffed. "Your psychic powers are awesome."

Instead of replying, Genevieve flipped over a card.

Erin looked down at the figure of a person lying on the ground with ten swords sticking out of her back. Erin said, "The ten of swords."

"There is violence in your distant past."

Erin thought of the sword fight. "Don't you mean yesterday?"

"No." Genevieve flipped over three more cards, placing them around Erin's card in the pattern of a cross. They were the six of cups, the hermit, and the sun. Genevieve had a faraway expression in her eyes. "You are haunted by memories of your childhood, but you will soon get everything you desire, if you use discretion."

Erin crossed her arms, wondering if her friend was simply trying to talk her out of quitting fashion school.

Genevieve placed the last four cards onto the table. They were the queen of swords, nine of swords, ace of swords, reversed, and the world, reversed. Genevieve said, "Sorrow surrounds you, and a disaster is coming which will destroy what you hope to achieve."

"I know," said Erin. "It's already happened."

"No. Something else," said Genevieve.

Erin frowned. "Gen, I know you're trying to help—"

"Tss tsst!" Genevieve raised a hand to silence Erin, and then tilted her head, as if she was listening to something. "You are being protected by a powerful curse, and this curse is bound to your fate."

Erin wondered what her friend was talking about and looked down at the cards, trying to discern where the idea of curses had come from. She smiled. "You mean my *destiny*."

A whisper drifted by on a cold draft, "You'll never be any good at this..."

A loud noise brought her attention to the man sitting at the next table. He had just slammed his laptop shut in a huff of anger. As he got up, he muttered, "This isn't for me. I'm dropping this class." In a cloud of frustration, he left.

Seeming to come out of her reverie, Genevieve watched the man go. "I know that guy," she said. "He's always telling other people what to do, as if he's smarter than everyone else. I'm surprised he has that attitude." She looked down at the candle on the table. "I guess he's just another loser."

Ignoring the barb, Erin looked around the coffee house, into the shadows. She wasn't listening to the conversations in the room anymore, but to the silences in the darkness. But there was nothing there this time.

"Have you heard?" Genevieve asked. "Nobody's seen Brigitte since she dropped out of school."

Unwilling to bring back the memory of what she had seen yesterday, Erin didn't answer. Instead, she picked up the box, and placed it in her lap. Tilting her head slightly, she looked down at it, whispering softly. "Somewhere, there is a place full of sunshine and flowers. It's a place full of pretty clothes and friendly people—a world of fantastic beauty. It's a place where dreams come true." She looked away outside where the darkness began to cover the rising mist. "But it's just a silly fantasy. Wouldn't it be great if such a place actually existed?"

Genevieve looked like she had been slapped in the face. "You're not quitting."

Erin sighed. "Gen, I've just looked into the mirror and I've seen that I'll never have what I want. I'll never become what I want to be." It felt like she was dying inside. "There's no use in lying to myself anymore."

Reaching out, Genevieve took Erin's hand. "But you don't live in the same world as everyone else. You live in a world of beauty and refinement and courtesy. In your world, there is no jealousy, no tyranny... no hate." Genevieve withdrew her hand and leaned back in her chair, sensing the emptiness around Erin. "I much prefer the world that you live in."

Something malevolent came into the room on a slight breeze, murmuring dark words. Erin was straining to hear the voices when her friend cut in.

"You once talked about filling the world with beauty. Think about how you can change things, Erin."

"It's just a dream, Gen."

"But you—"

"It's over!" The darkness began to close in, embracing Erin in an icy blanket. "None of it makes any difference."

Erin looked through the dimly lit coffee house, feeling an oppressive weight on her heart. From now on, the world would be filled with grays. "Perhaps it was meant to be this way," she whispered.

Something lingered close by, waiting. Erin could see it out of the corner of her eyes, but didn't turn to look at it. It just stood there, watching. There was a sense of happy malice—like cruelty, emanating from it. She closed her eyes for a heartbeat, hoping it would go away, but it remained where it was.

Erin looked over at her friend, who had become silent. Genevieve was looking down at her cup, preoccupied. "What?" asked Erin.

Genevieve raised her eyes. "Oh," she smiled a little. "It's nothing. I was just... thinking about the future."

Erin remembered the tarot cards, but her friend wasn't looking at them.

"I guess college is just a place to hide out until the real world forces you to get a life." Genevieve looked down, avoiding Erin's eyes. "I suppose dreams really are silly fantasies."

The exquisite designs in Erin's mind would soon fade away. Sadness began to seep into her soul. She wanted to look away, but was afraid of seeing the Shadow Person. Erin shook her head and whispered, "I think I'm going crazy, Gen."

"What do you mean?"

Erin bit her lip. "I've been seeing things, and hearing voices, well, whisperings really." She glanced to the side where the Shadow Person was, but it had vanished again. Breathing a sigh of relief, she continued. "Have you ever seen glowing balls of light?"

Genevieve didn't answer.

Erin smiled pensively. "It's just a question. I'm not suggesting that—"

"No." Smiling, Genevieve tilted her head a little. "I've heard of some odd things, but that's probably just imagination."

Leaning back in her chair, Erin placed her hands in her lap. "Yes, of course."

But she couldn't get the little lights out of her mind. There had been so many of them yesterday, dancing over the grass. Sifu Yuen had said that the lights were spirit beings. She thought of the blue sphere, and wondered what kind of spirit it was, and then she remembered what it had whispered.

Genevieve was looking into her eyes. "What?"

"I wonder." Erin looked down at the gray box. The Celtic designs surrounded a dragon. She placed her hands on either side of it and said quietly, "Aisling."

It may have been her imagination, but Erin thought she saw a silvery light trace itself along the Celtic knotwork. Gently, she pushed up against the edge of the box and a hidden lid opened with a click.

"I thought you said you've never been able to open it?"

"This is the first time I've been able to," Erin explained. Holding her breath, she opened the lid wider, and looked inside.

Lying on top of the purple velvet lining were three objects: A gold medallion on a chain, a silver ring, and a small crystal that glittered like a diamond. Erin picked up the ring, letting it rest in the palm of her hand. The delicate tracery of designs echoed those of the box it had rested in: Celtic knotwork surrounded a dragon, whose eyes were a pair of blue sapphires.

"Wow!" Genevieve raised a hand. "You mind if I look?"

Erin slid the box over to her friend, but didn't give her the ring. Instead, she slipped it onto her right index finger. It fit perfectly.

The ring glinted in the illumination of the candle resting on the table. It was cold against her skin. She turned the dragon around so that she could look into its watery eyes. A thought, like a distant memory, began to

41

stir within her mind.

It was cold. The night sky was full of stars. Silver moonlight reflected off a sea that was as smooth as glass, but something moved out on the water, coming closer. It was a silver ship. Tall men with proud faces moved about on the deck. At the prow stood a blonde haired man with a gold torc around his neck.

It was the same man that had appeared in the mirror hanging in her room. Someone touched her on the shoulder. The memory faded away. She shook her head. *Who would want to talk to me?*

She turned around to see who it was, but there was no one there.

Genevieve noticed the look on Erin's face. "What is it?" she asked.

Erin leaned forward, placing her hand on her forehead. She wondered if she was going crazy. "Nothing. I just thought someone was trying to get my attention, that's all."

Genevieve reached her hand out, putting it on Erin's shoulder and smiled reassuringly. "Hey now, I'm here. It'll be okay. Listen, I'll follow you wherever you want to go."

Smiling at her friend, Erin took her hand into hers.

Genevieve looked down and slid her hand back. She picked up the gold medallion, turning it over in her hands. The engraved dragon had its tail woven into an intricate Celtic knotwork design. On the other side, there was an inscription of some kind, but Genevieve flipped it over and Erin didn't get a good look at it.

Erin looked away. "Gen, I think I'm losing my mind. I've heard these... whispering voices. I've felt someone watching me too. Also—" She wasn't sure if she should continue, and she looked out the window of the coffee house. The flickering candlelight from the pair of pumpkins made the white curtains glow. It was like looking at a distant firelight through a veil.

"So, you've heard them too?" Genevieve asked.

Erin was too stunned to respond.

Genevieve explained, "I heard quiet voices while we were in class yesterday, when you were leaving the room."

A cold breeze drifted through the coffee house. No one else noticed, but Erin heard something whispering in the darkness. Then it was gone.

Erin glanced around, her voice quiet, "You've heard them?"

"Yes, I have."

Something inside Erin found strength from what her friend had just told her. "Just now?" she asked.

Genevieve narrowed her eyes and nodded. "Yeah," she said, "a few seconds ago." Sighing, she brought her hands up to her forehead. "Maybe I'm just going wacky here."

This time, the touch was definite. Erin felt a hand on her left shoulder, and she felt what must have been the sharp edge of a knife placed coldly against her throat. She inhaled the dark scent of musk, cinnamon, moss and musty flowers. Dimly, she could hear a multitude of quiet screams, no louder than a faint echo of a whisper, emanating from the curved blade, as if the pain it had caused was so intense that misery had begun to seep out of it.

Something whispered very quietly in her ear, "Keep silent about us, Exile."

Erin froze.

Genevieve looked around, as if she heard the whispering shadow. She stood up, and then noticed the look on Erin's face. "What is it?" she asked.

Erin could feel the sharp edge pressing against her throat. "Nothing," she said. "Sit down, please. You're embarrassing me."

Genevieve blushed and sat down. "Sorry."

Erin tried to smile, but the cold edge was still pressed against her throat. She could feel the sting where the knife cut into her skin.

"I could swear I just heard it again," muttered Genevieve, glancing around the room. She shrugged and began to examine the medallion again.

The hand on Erin's shoulder went away and the sharp edge of the weapon was taken from her throat. The whisper was just a tiny breath of coldness in her ear. "We are around you in the darkness."

Genevieve looked up, her eyes searching. "So, I've heard these whispering voices sometimes, but I can't understand them. It's like some language, so beautiful, but so mysterious too."

Erin saw something moving next to Genevieve. At first she thought it was just a play of the candlelight, but then she noticed what looked like a human shaped shadow standing next to her friend. It was getting colder. Red candlelight glinted off something in its hand. After a moment, the shadow moved off. Erin was too terrified to react and so she remained silent.

Genevieve giggled and waved her hand in front of Erin's face. "Hey there!" she said, smiling. "You look like you've just seen a ghost."

As the shadow moved through the wall of the room, the coldness went with it. "What's that?" Erin looked at Genevieve. "Oh, well, it's probably just Halloween jitters."

Her friend didn't respond.

Reaching up to touch her throat, Erin looked down at the slight trace of blood on her fingers. The Shadow People were real. The shock of it sent a chill up her spine. Erin hugged herself, shivering. Some of the cold lingered. She looked down at her striped tights, wondering aloud, "Why is this happening to me now?"

The smile that appeared on Genevieve's face made her dark eyes look prettier. She said, "Probably just the time of year. Halloween used to be called *Samhain*, you know. This is the time of year for the manifestation of Thin Places."

"Thin Places?"

After asking permission with her eyes, Genevieve put the medallion around her neck. "Celtic holy places," she said. "It's where the barrier between the physical world and the spiritual world becomes weak."

A little blue ball of light appeared in the roadway outside. Erin looked at her friend, whose mouth had dropped open. "Is that one of those balls of light you were telling me about?"

Erin nodded.

Genevieve stood up, and put on her jacket. "Let's go take a look."

Still shaken by the threatening shadow, Erin remained where she was. Genevieve walked outside where the blue sphere hovered. No one else in the coffee house seemed to notice it, but Erin could see its light shining onto her friend. Genevieve took another step closer, and then it winked out. For a moment, Erin couldn't see her standing there.

A lonely noise came from outside. It sounded like a galloping horse, approaching the coffee house. Erin stood up, feeling a growing sense of apprehension in the air.

Galloping out of the darkness, a black horse came. Sitting on top of the horse was a headless man. Genevieve screamed and fell down, as if she had just fainted. Everyone in the coffee shop looked outside. Some of them laughed, thinking it was some sort of Halloween gag, but most of them kept silent.

Erin ran outside and shouted, "Genevieve!" The cold night air surrounded Erin, giving her the impression that she had just jumped into an icy lake.

The headless horseman remained still for a moment, facing her, holding the unconscious Genevieve under his arm like a rag doll. In his other hand was a pumpkin head, carved with a menacing face, and lit with a red light. The horse reared up and the headless man threw the pumpkin head at Erin.

Erin leapt out of the way.

There was a crash as the pumpkin head shattered into pieces. The headless horseman's laughter filled the roadway. He reared up on his horse again and then sped away up the road through the forest.

Mist parted out of the way as the black horse galloped off into the darkness.

Erin shouted after it, "Genevieve!"

There was no answer.

The horse faded away. The sounds of its hooves retreated into the gloom.

"Genevieve!"

But her friend was gone, carried away into the night.

*   *   *

Chapter Four

Thin Places

Cold wind blew over the trees, parting the mist that clung to the roadway like a giant hand pushing aside a veil. Erin strained to hear the sounds of the horse, but there was nothing there, except darkness spilling out into the night.

The shadows began to gather around Erin, whispering. Out of the corner of her eye, she could see one of them. It had a clearly defined outline, and a dark transparent body, silhouetted against the wall. Candlelight glinted off something sharp in its hand. In its eyes, a cruel light smoldered. Then, like a light shutting off, it disappeared.

The impulse to run away mixed with an urge to go after her friend, and so Erin jumped into her BMW. As she stepped onto the accelerator, she sensed that the Shadow People were following her. She could see several of their murky images in her rear-view mirror, flying through the air, arms outstretched, reaching out.

A wall of trees surrounded by wispy trails of mist flew by as she accelerated down the dark forest road, leaving the shadows behind. It seemed incomprehensible that a lone horseman could outrun a person in a speeding car.

Erin began to wonder if she had imagined the entire affair when she saw a tiny blue light up ahead in the middle of the road. She stepped on the brakes and swerved to miss the ball of light. The car slid into a ditch at the side of the road and came to a halt.

Erin got out of the car and moved into the road where the light hovered. It blinked twice and moved to the other side of the road where someone lay in a ditch.

"Genevieve!"

Erin ran past the light, and knelt down next to her friend.

"He threw me," she said, sitting up.

"You okay?"

"Yeah," Genevieve said, looking around. "Where are we?"

Frowning, Erin glanced at the unfamiliar road. Autumn leaves covered the pavement and mixed with rocks and debris that had blown in over the years or had fallen from out of the trees that arched over the roadway. "We're on the road to nowhere," she whispered.

"Since when have you driven a BMW?" asked Genevieve.

"What?"

Erin paused. It was true—she didn't own a car. Needing one, it had simply been there. She glanced at the ditch where it rested, half-wondering if she had stolen it.

As if aware of her gaze, the car vanished.

In its place sat a large pumpkin.

Erin swallowed hard. "Did you see that?"

Genevieve stood up, rubbing her shoulder. "I'm not sure what I saw."

The tiny blue ball of light drifted in front of them, flashed with silver light and winked out. In its place stood a tall, thin woman, with long milky blonde hair and eyes the color of a deep mountain lake. She had sharp, delicate features. Blue and white flowers, along with oak leaves, were woven into her hair. She wore a long white dress embroidered in blue, and a silver belt which held a sword in a black leather scabbard. She was the most beautiful girl Erin had ever seen before. A friendly, but serious expression filled her face. "Dia daoibh," she said.

Genevieve moved out in front of Erin. "Who are you?"

With a smile touching her lips, the girl said, "My name is Eileen."

Erin put her hand on Genevieve's shoulder and whispered, "It's okay." She stepped around her friend. "What—"

A cold wind blew through the trees, scattering leaves and bringing with it a trail of whispering voices, rising in intensity. The chill reached inside Erin, freezing her heart. She could feel icy tendrils creeping up her spine. Then a scent touched her nose. It was a mixture of musk, cinnamon, moss, and musty flowers.

Eileen glanced over her shoulder down the road from where they had come. She pointed towards a path into the trees. "If you want to stay alive, you should get away from here."

Erin and Genevieve exchanged doubtful looks.

Eileen drew a long Celtic sword with a twisted gold handle. Its silver blade was engraved with ancient Celtic symbols that glinted in the moonlight. She turned around slowly and walked into the road. "There's no use in standing there."

Erin didn't move. "No. I can fight."

"You cannot harm them. Now, please go!"

"Who are you talking about?" Genevieve asked, but Eileen ignored the question.

Their voices were like an angry sigh. Erin could just spot the outlines of shadowy figures coming up the road. In front of the rest was a shade with a curved knife, glinting in the moonlight. She touched Genevieve on the arm. "Come on!"

They ran up the trail as fast as they could. The sounds of a fierce sword fight erupted behind them, but they didn't look back. Tall trees blocked out the stars that shone down on the wild forest.

After a time, the sound of the sword fight began to fade. As they moved through the dark trees, the silence became overwhelming. Everything gave way to the quiet—the insects, the night animals, the birds, and even the wind in the trees drifted away, until only silence remained.

The path rose up a sharp incline and by the time they reached the crest of a hill, they were both winded. Erin leaned against the smooth bark of an ash tree, panting.

Genevieve sat down on the path, which was mostly obscured by ferns and flowers. "Tell me, what just happened?"

Bewildered, Erin shook her head and glanced back down the vanishing trail. Inhaling deeply to steady herself, she stood up straight and looked down into the forest below them. She was trying to figure out where they were when she heard the sound of a horse approaching. She looked over her shoulder warily, but there was no sign of the headless horseman.

Instead, a white stallion emerged from the darkness a dozen yards away, awash in the blue moonlight that fell through a gap in the trees. The horse tossed his head and neighed. Genevieve stood up. "He's beautiful, isn't he?"

Erin simply smiled and began walking towards the white horse. Peacefulness washed over the animal, but just as they drew near, the horse turned around and trotted off along an unseen path that twisted through the trees. Erin wanted to follow, but she felt Genevieve's hand on her arm. "Why are we following him?"

Erin bit her lip, watching the white horse vanish through the trees, just out of reach. "Where else have we to go?"

"Back to the road?" Genevieve looked through the trees with some uncertainty on her face. "If we can find it," she muttered.

Erin shivered, thinking of the dark shadows that pursued them. The idea of those things, surrounding her for such a long time, always watching, and whispering poison, terrified her. "I don't really think it's safe, Gen."

They followed the horse for some time as it traveled through the forest path overgrown with bushes and wildflowers. The horse remained ahead of them, but just out of reach, until they descended into a moonlit valley. Once it had reached the bottom of the hill, the horse galloped off and vanished into the trees leaving a dreamy silence behind.

Erin began to hear a soft melody drifting over the wind. The quiet music mingled with a cascade of tinkling sounds that reminded her of a wind chime. At first it was so quiet she wasn't sure it was real at all, but as they descended into the valley it grew into a definite melody that floated by on the breeze.

They came to a large clearing surrounded by oak, ash and hawthorn trees. The trees were full of birds, and their songs joined in with the distant music. A large ring of red-capped mushrooms formed a circle in the middle of the clearing, and hundreds of tiny lights danced in the air, flashing every color of the rainbow. It was like watching fireflies dance in the moonlight, tossing tiny fireworks.

The music had grown louder as they approached, but it was muffled, as if it was coming from a place nearby, but through a body of water or some other kind of obstruction. It was lively and inviting, but something else made them stop when they reached the edge of the glade.

It was a strange sense that was both inviting and forbidding. Peace echoed against a wall of beauty. It was like standing next to a still lake that echoed the twinkling stars above it. Unwilling to break its still surface, it was too compelling to resist doing anything but stare at the reflections.

They stood there for a long time, straining to hear the merry music that was still only a whisper on a cool breeze. Finally, Erin shook herself awake and touched her friend's shoulder. Genevieve murmured as if she had just awoken from a dream. Erin felt an urge to whisper her words, like being in a library and not wanting to disturb anyone inside it. "Come on," she said.

The moment they stepped into the clearing, wild Celtic ballads filled the air with the sounds of flutes, drums and lutes. The inviting scent of food—roast beef, potatoes, turkey, grapes, plums, wine, sweet cakes and pumpkin pie stirred a hunger inside of them unlike anything they had ever felt before.

All of the little lights changed into a parade of beautifully clad people who were laughing, eating, dancing and drinking. They all appeared to be quite young, and Erin found herself staring at them. Exquisitely beautiful, they wore a bewildering variety of gorgeous apparel: Long elegant dresses and black tuxedos and short, tight skirts with spidery tights and peasant blouses and bright tunics and shiny rings and necklaces of gold and silver and boots and strapped sandals and bare feet adorned with silver bells. They had an air of both nobility and playful abandonment.

Erin shot a glance at Genevieve as one of the young men approached them. He had sharp features, bright blue eyes, dark brown hair, and he wore what looked like a Greek tunic embroidered in blue over an athletic body. Leaves and flowers were woven into a crown around his head. He wore a short sword on a scabbard hanging from his belt. He smiled at Erin and took her hands into his. Without a word, he drew her away into a wild dance around the circle. Erin laughed, unable to resist the urge to participate. They swirled away in a whirlwind of dancing. Dozens of friendly, laughing people surrounded them. After dancing around the entire clearing, the man brought her back to where they had first met.

Erin was too breathless to say anything but he spoke first anyway. "Fáilte ar ais!"

She dropped her hands from his and smiled shyly.

He laughed. "Sorry, I forgot you don't speak Irish. Welcome home, Aisling!"

"What did you call me?" she asked.

"That's your name, isn't it?"

"No," she said uncertainly. "My name is Erin O'Neil."

He laughed. "Not your Milesian name," he said, "your true name."

"Milesian?"

He wrinkled his face as if he had just tasted something sour. "Ah yes, you've spent most of your life among them, haven't you?" He smiled again.

"The Milesians are simple mortals, but you aren't one of them."

Erin glanced at Genevieve, who was just standing there, gaping. Genevieve raised a hand and brushed it through her hair. Suddenly the man noticed her. His mouth dropped open and his eyes shone with un-veiled appreciation. "I'm so sorry my dear! I didn't see you standing there!"

He flourished his hand and a red rose appeared out of nowhere. He took a step towards Genevieve and offered the flower while taking her other hand into his. He gazed steadily into her eyes and smiled. "Alas, you are an enchanting girl!"

Genevieve gave Erin an amused look and then dropped her eyes. "Thanks."

The man reluctantly dropped her hand and looked at Erin again. "I am Fintan Mac Bóchra." He raised his eyebrows and glanced sideways. "What is your name?"

"Genevieve Sully."

There was a moment of silence as Fintan looked on, apparently too enthralled to continue. So Erin asked, "Did you say my real name was Aisling?"

Fintan pulled his gaze away from her friend as if he was coming out of a trance. "Yes." He motioned for them to follow and he led them into the clearing towards one of the tables laden with food. It stood next to a silver fountain that splashed clear water into a basin. People walked up and dipped goblets into it and came away with wine, beer, ale and other kinds of beverages.

Fintan motioned for them to sit down. "You are a Síofra."

"A shee—what?"

"A Changeling. Your true parents exchanged you for a mortal child when you were young."

Erin shook her head, and wondered if she was having a rather unsteady dream. "That can't be true."

"It is."

Sadness began to seep into her thoughts. "My parents—aren't my real parents?"

Fintan sat next to Genevieve, placing an arm behind her. "No."

Long memories of her parents began to make sense to her—her father, sadly gazing out of the tall windows of her house, her mother, wanting to be alone, and a certain emotional distance that made them as empty as their house. Erin asked the question that had begun to trouble her. "They know, don't they?"

He picked up a bunch of grapes and began to eat. "No. They are under an enchantment that clouds their minds, though they might still sense something is amiss."

Everything was starting to make sense now. She looked out over the field of merry people. "And my real name is 'Aisling.'" It wasn't a question any longer. She began to accept it.

Fintan nodded.

Genevieve looked around the clearing, which was aglow with the lights coming from the merrymakers. "But who are you?"

Smiling, he stood up and swept his arm out towards the others. "We are the dreamers of dreams. We are the music makers, the poets, the wanderers, the hidden people lost in the ages of history."

Fintan picked up a silver goblet, and filled it with a dark red wine from the fountain. He whispered something over the cup and then offered it to Genevieve. She took it and looked down into the dark liquid.

He continued, "We collect the dreams of mortals and help make them real. We give power to a single man to change the world. We curse the fortunes of those that displease us. We are the guardians of riches and the earth's hidden secrets. We dance under the moon and shine in the sunlight."

He winked, as if sharing a secret. "We catch the stars and run like crazy."

Genevieve giggled. "You're a Faerie!"

"I prefer the term 'elf,' if you please."

It was just then that they noticed that Fintan had pointed ears. Genevieve ran a hand through her hair and began to take a sip of wine.

Eileen's voice pierced the lively music around them. "Now Fintan, you know better than trying to enchant our mortal guest."

Aisling—she had begun to think of herself by that name—turned around and saw the beautiful blonde girl they had encountered in the forest. She had the look of one that had been walking in the sunshine all day. There was no trace of her having just been in a fight.

Genevieve stopped herself from drinking and put the goblet down. She looked suspiciously at the red liquid. "What would have happened if I drank it?" she asked.

"I daresay you would never have seen your home again." Eileen walked around to the fountain and dipped a cup into the clear water there. She whispered something and the clear liquid changed into a golden amber brew that had an aroma of cloves, cinnamon and apples. She handed it to Genevieve. "How long would it have been before you would have tired of her, I wonder, Fintan?"

Fintan turned towards Eileen. "What is she doing here, anyway? I thought you were guarding Aisling." He glanced at Genevieve and swiftly added, "Not that I mind. She has the eyes of Queen Nefertiti."

Eileen sat down and picked up a nectarine. "The Shadow People were only watching them, but when these two opened that enchanted box, they took a more . . . active interest."

Genevieve shuddered. "That headless horseman was terrifying."

Eileen laughed. "You shouldn't have stepped on that flower, certainly."

Genevieve frowned in irritation. "What flower?"

"St. John's Wort," she said. "Didn't you see those little yellow flowers growing around the coffee house? When you step on one at this time of year, a Dullahan is almost certain to appear."

Genevieve raised her eyebrows. "Dullahan?"

Fintan explained. "He's a Faerie that likes to take Milesians for a ride sometimes—especially on Samhain." He motioned towards the faeries dancing and singing and partying in the clearing. "That's why we're here tonight—to celebrate the New Year."

Eileen began to eat the nectarine. "I daresay it's a good thing the Dullahan appeared. I wasn't sure how I was going to get you two away from there."

Aisling didn't want to talk about the Shadow People just yet. Stifling dark memories, she glanced at her friend and then wrinkled her face. "So I'm a... faerie?"

Fintan sat down again next to Genevieve. "Yes, we are known as the *Tuatha Dé Danaan*—the people of Danu."

Eileen interjected, "Oh please, Fintan! Nobody calls us that anymore."

"The 'Tuatha Dé' then."

An extremely beautiful woman came over to their table. She wore a long, tight dress the color of wine, which accentuated all of her curves. Her arms were bare, except for a pair of long purple gloves made of silk. Her black shoes laced up her ankles. She had long black hair curled about her shoulders, and captivating eyes that echoed the darkness around her. A silver handled mirror was tucked into a purple belt around her thin waist, and she carried a goblet of wine in her hand. Looking down disdainfully at Aisling, she said, "Who cares what the Milesians call us?"

Fintan leaned back against the table and looked up at the newcomer. "Dia duit, Morrigan. This here is Aisling, and this—"

"Keep your filthy changelings to yourself, Fintan." Morrigan wrinkled her nose. "And kindly remove this," she gestured towards Genevieve, "*Milesian* from our presence."

Eileen stood up. "That's quite enough, Morrigan! They need our protection."

Morrigan smiled derisively. "Now, now, Eileen—this is a party." She laughed and glanced around the clearing where dozens of people continued to dance. "You wouldn't want to upset Gentle Annie, would you?"

Eileen didn't answer. After a moment, Morrigan shrugged. "Suit yourself then." She walked off to join another group of people.

Fintan smiled. "She must have been looking into her magic mirror again." He stood up and offered his hand to Genevieve. "It shows the image of the most beautiful woman in the land. When she doesn't see her own reflection, she gets jealous."

Genevieve took his hand and stood up. She was blushing, but said nothing. He said, "You will stay with me tonight, won't you?"

"Oh, you wicked little thing!" Laughing, Eileen stepped between them, breaking their contact. Genevieve looked like she had just awoken from a trance. "They'll stay with me, Fintan." She motioned for them to come with her and they left the disappointed elf at the party.

They walked to the edge of the clearing and followed an overgrown path into the forest. A group of faerie lights lit the way, dancing along in front of them. After walking for half an hour, Aisling realized that she was very tired, but it didn't stifle her curiosity. She asked, "If I'm a Faerie, why don't I have pointed ears like you?"

Eileen had an amused tone in her voice. "Don't you?"

Aisling reached up and ran a finger over one ear. To her astonishment, it was indeed pointed. "How did this happen?"

Eileen giggled. "You can change your appearance, becoming just like a Milesian when you want."

Genevieve looked at her friend and remarked in an irritated tone, "Just my luck. You're the faerie—not me."

Aisling whispered back, "I'm not too sure I like all of this, Gen."

Eileen said, "Don't be silly! There's nothing wrong with being one of us." She added quickly, "—or a Milesian either, I suppose."

Not bothering to stifle the annoyed tone in her voice, Genevieve asked, "Are all *normal* people called Milesians?"

Eileen sounded like she was irritated too. "The Milesians are what you call the Irish people, but we've taken to calling all of your people by that name."

Aisling pushed her hair over her ears, not sure if she really liked the change. "I take it that Milesians aren't too popular around here?"

Eileen stopped, tossing a shy expression over her shoulder. "No indeed. They were the ones that invaded Ireland and defeated us in battle.

Ever since then, we have lived here in exile. Even after so many centuries, many people are still angry about it."

"How old are you?" Genevieve asked.

"Me? I'm just nineteen, like you two." Eileen's voice dropped to a whisper, "But some of us are very old. Fintan Mac Bóchra is one of the most ancient among us."

Aisling laughed. "He doesn't look older than twenty."

"Of course he doesn't." Eileen looked at the faerie lights, which had just passed out of sight beyond a grove of pine trees. "We're immortal."

Before they could reply, Eileen went after the lights. As they walked, they heard a few night owls and squirrels moving through the forest. After a time, Eileen stopped at the edge of a clearing.

A garden of stars grew around the moon's reflection on the still surface of a lake. A European-style house stood a stone's throw away, its inviting windows aglow with flickering lights. They could smell smoke from the chimney and perfume from flowers growing in the garden. "This is my house. Stay here as long as you like."

Aisling and Genevieve hesitated, exchanging glances. Genevieve said, "Sorry, but I wasn't really expecting a house like this."

Eileen's laughter filled the clearing. "Why, did you think we all lived inside of giant mushrooms?"

Genevieve crossed her arms. "No. It's just that—"

"We're not all little frivolous faeries you know."

"Of course not," said Genevieve. "I just thought—"

"We're not all the same. There are sprites and flower faeries and hobgoblins and elves and gnomes and tree spirits and trolls and even a few giants around these hills." Eileen huffed out irritably. "I really hate Milesian stereotypes."

Genevieve stepped back a pace, and nervously brushed a strand of hair out of her face. "I didn't mean anything. I was just surprised not to see—"

"A house inside a tree?"

A flash of light appeared out on the lake, and they saw a white horse galloping across its surface, carrying two people. Eileen went down to the edge of the water, followed by the others. Aisling could see the horse's hooves just touching the surface of the water, but not sinking in. It was surreal. When it arrived, the horse, bearing two riders, leaped onto the ground in front of them. Aisling found herself looking into Fintan's bright eyes again. "Dia daoibh, hello!" he said. "I've got another one for you, Eileen." He motioned to the girl sitting behind him. "This here is Aoife Kippen."

To her surprise, Aisling recognized the red haired girl from the coffee house. Although she was holding Fintan tightly around the waist, she was smiling.

Eileen smiled at Aoife and asked, "Another changeling?"

Fintan nodded. "I also caught a pair of shadows trying to slip through the Veil when she crossed over." He called over his shoulder in a quieter voice, "You'll be safe here."

Genevieve stepped forward to help the girl off the horse. She had some trouble getting off, since she was still wearing a corset. When she reached the ground, she smiled breathlessly. "Hello again. Are you a faerie too?"

Aisling spoke before her friend could answer. "I am—yes." She noticed that Genevieve was trying to avoid looking at Fintan, but he was studiously ignoring her this time. Aisling wondered if he was trying to make her friend jealous.

"Slán agus beannacht leat," said Fintan. He looked into Aisling's eyes and added, "I'll see you all later then."

Fintan rode off across the lake, shooting across the water, breaking a line in the moonlight's reflection. For some reason, Aisling was sad to see him go.

"Well then, please come inside." Eileen brought them up to the house.

They made themselves comfortable in the sitting room, which was filled with potted plants and flowers. The room had hardwood floors, covered with a red throw rug, earth-toned furniture and a blazing fire set in a stone hearth. Eileen waved her hands as they walked in and a dozen candles ignited, providing illumination.

Genevieve looked darkly at Eileen, who went over to the fire. "I wonder if I'll remember this wacky dream in the morning?" she mused.

Aoife laughed. "I sure hope I do! This is unbelievable." She moved a hand over her green corset and wondered aloud, "It would be great to be able to change my clothes with just a thought."

Eileen sat in a tall red leather chair, and crossed her legs. "I can show you how to do a few things, but most of your abilities will have to be discovered by you—through trial and error, I'm afraid. Everybody here has their own kind of magic, you see."

Aisling looked into Eileen's blue eyes. "We can do magic?"

"Of course," said Eileen. "I daresay you've been using it all of your life without even noticing it."

Aisling remembered the cup of peppermint tea in the café, sugar appearing out of nowhere and the BMW which had turned into a pumpkin. Was that why people had always avoided her?

Aoife asked, "So how does magic work, anyway?"

Eileen laughed. "Just close your eyes and imagine what you want. At first, you'll need some kind of triggering mechanism to make it work—like snapping your fingers or whispering words of power."

Leaning back in her chair, Aoife closed her eyes. A moment later, she opened them and looked down at her green skirt, black tights, white peasant blouse and green brocade corset. "Nothing happened."

"You forgot to trigger it. Snap your fingers."

When Aoife did so, her outfit changed completely. Now she had on a long green silk nightgown, and furry slippers made to look like a pair of white rabbits. She laughed.

"After a little practice, you won't have to close your eyes or snap your fingers," Eileen said. She waved her hand and all the candles in the room went out, leaving the fire as the only illumination in the room. "There are all kinds of magic," she said. A rainbow of sparkling lights glittered where the candles had burned just moments before. "Ritualism, conjuration, summoning, enchantment, black magic, sorcery, mysticism, runes, elementalism, alchemy, spiritualism, divination, extra-sensory perception, glamour—" The flames ignited, filling the room with soft candlelight again. "I'll show you more about it tomorrow."

Aisling couldn't resist smiling. But she didn't want to try any magic. She was still wondering if this was some kind of schizophrenic episode. Finally, she asked the question bothering her, "Who are the Shadow People?"

Eileen stood up, walking to the window that looked out on the moonlit garden. Silence covered the room, broken only by the crackling of the fire. Blue moonlight mingled with the fire at her back. Finally, she spoke. "No one knows for sure."

"What do they want?"

"We are at war with them."

Reaching up to touch her throat where it had been cut, Aisling wondered if she should say anything else. Summoning up the courage, she said, "One of them held a knife to my throat last night."

Genevieve gasped. "What?"

Eileen turned around, her face bathed in red fire. "Which one did this to you?"

"I'm not sure," said Aisling. "It was a curved knife." She could still remember the faint cries emanating from it. "I heard screaming voices coming out of the blade."

Eileen scowled. "That particular weapon is called a 'Jambiya.' It steals the souls of those it kills. That was the Hat Man's Lieutenant, the cruelest among them. His sword is called a 'Shamshir' and it also steals souls."

"Hat Man?" Aisling thought back to the hallway at school. "I saw a Shadow Person like that. He had one of those short Victorian top hats."

"Yes, I was there," said Eileen. Her voice dropped to a whisper. "The Lord of Shadows. He's their leader."

Aisling wondered what he would want with her. "The one with the knife—the Hat Man's Lieutenant, warned me not to speak of them." She looked over at Genevieve.

Eileen sat down again. "They want to keep their existence a secret among the Milesians. You can speak of them here, though."

Genevieve asked, "Where is 'here' anyway?"

Smiling, Eileen said, "This is Tír na nÓg—The Land of Eternal Youth, but most people just call it The Land of Dreams."

Aisling wondered about the Shadow People. "I've heard their whispers for years." She looked into the fire, lowering her voice. "Yesterday, I saw them for the first time."

"Why didn't you tell me?" Genevieve asked.

"I thought I was schizoid, Gen."

"You're not crazy!"

"What would you call it? I've been hearing voices and seeing things." Aisling raised a hand to her forehead. "I ought to get myself to a psychiatrist when I wake up from this dream."

Eileen said in a quiet voice, "Yesterday was the first time you noticed me, too."

Aisling smiled, remembering all the little balls of light. Eileen was the pretty blue orb she had encountered in the café. Then a realization struck home: Someone had been finishing her school projects. Crossing her arms suspiciously, she asked, "Have you been visiting my school?"

"I'm sorry." Eileen looked down, guilty. "But your designs were so beautiful. I just had to see what they looked like!"

*   *   *

Warm rays of light flooded into her face, melting away a dozen lonely dreams: Of gray skies and sheets of drifting rain; of a desolate city where people walked about aimlessly, without hope or promise of a better future; of dreary people, content to wear uninteresting, ugly clothes; and of her father, gazing out of a tall window, into the gloom.

Erin opened her eyes, momentarily blinded by sunshine falling through the window. Inhaling the bright air, she spent a moment listening to the birds outside.

Sitting up onto her elbows enough to get out of the beam of light, she blinked away the night. Frilly curtains surrounded the four poster bed. She was covered in white blankets decorated with little blue flowers. At the foot of the bed stood a large oak chest bound in brass. The Japanese-styled dress and striped tights from the previous day lay on top of it. Reaching up to touch the smooth nightgown she was wearing, her fingers caressed the silk for a moment, remembering a dream that had seemed so real. Sitting up fully and crossing her legs, she pulled the covers up, breathing in lavender and fresh linen. She grabbed a pillow and held it closely, eyes shut, hoping this impossible dream would never fade away.

Erin—no, her name was Aisling, wasn't it?—opened her eyes again. This was the same room Eileen had brought her to last night. Was that from a dream? She sought an answer outside the window. Cool lake waters sparkled in the morning sunlight. She smiled. It was real! At least part of it was. The idea of being a Faerie couldn't really be true, of course, but some of it had happened. Getting up, she went over to look outside. Tall pine trees surrounded Eileen's house, and there was a fantastic garden all around it too. Closing her eyes again, she inhaled jasmine, rose and hyacinth while the sunshine warmed her face.

Something struck her on the nose and she was splashed with cold water. Stepping back, she reached up to wipe the water out of her face to the sounds of laughter coming from outside. She was just blinking away the water in her eyes when she caught the sight of something bright being tossed at her again. The object exploded, splashing icy water all over her face. Another round of giddy laughter lit the scene outside. "What—?"

This time, she saw the object—blue, being thrown at the window, aimed squarely at her nose again. She ducked out of the way just in time as water sprayed the wall behind her. An accusing voice called out, "Ha! You missed her!"

Aisling peeked outside and found a dozen tiny faeries flying through the air, carrying water balloons. They were all so terribly small that it was amazing to see them carrying such large, heavy objects. One of them slowed to a hover and aimed at her steadily, throwing his balloon with such speed that she barely dodged it this time. It struck the bedpost, spraying water all over her clothes.

Narrowing her eyes in fury, Aisling felt an urge to sweep all of the little faeries out of the air. Impulsively, she waved her hand and was surprised to see a huge gust of wind whoosh outside, blowing the faeries away into the distant trees. Dozens of angry cries fluttered in from outside. Aisling walked over to the window and placed her hands squarely on the windowsill, looking out. The little faeries had dropped their burdens, splashing water all over the garden.

"It wasn't a dream at all," she whispered.

*   *   *

Aisling had settled on a pair of black leggings, a bright turquoise peasant blouse with a white belt, and a pair of short black boots. All she needed to do was close her eyes, imagine the outfit in her mind and it had appeared on top of the chest.

When she met her friend that morning, Genevieve whistled. "Hey, Erin, where did you get the new clothes?"

Aisling ran a hand over the material of her blouse, feeling the softness of fresh cotton against her fingertips. "I just imagined these clothes and there they were."

Shaking her head, Genevieve sat down in a chair. "I still can't believe it all. I thought for sure I'd wake up to dark, gloomy Seattle, but when the sun hit my face, I realized that this was all real."

Aisling laughed. Sunshine and Seattle did not mix well in November. "So, what do you want to wear today?"

"What?" Genevieve looked down at her clothes. "Hmm, how about a new pair of boots?"

Frowning, Aisling said, "Easy to please, aren't you?"

"Boots are expensive, Erin."

Aisling seemed to have no trouble adapting to her real name, but her friend still hadn't done so. Biting her lip, she said, "I suppose you should call me 'Aisling' here."

Genevieve smiled conspiratorially. "Hey, I'll call you anything you want if I get a new pair of boots out of it."

Aisling closed her eyes, letting images drift into her mind. A moment later, Genevieve was wearing a pair of blue jeans, a black belt with silver studs, a red cotton blouse and a pair of tall brown boots with buckles down the side. Aisling hadn't touched her friend's scarf, however. She knew Genevieve would never forgive her if she had removed her favorite accessory.

Genevieve stood up, looking down at her new set of clothes. "Coolio."

Aoife came in, wearing a floppy green hat. "So if we're faeries, where are our wings?"

Aisling crossed her arms, remembering the field of dancing lights. "I thought we just changed into those little balls of light."

"Balls of light?" asked Aoife.

Shaking her head, Aisling said, "Never mind; I have no idea how to fly."

Eileen came in and smiled. "I'll show you how to fly, if you want."

"Great! I've always wanted to fly," grumbled Genevieve.

Aisling hoped her friend wasn't getting too jealous. "Can we do anything we want here?"

"If you can dream it, you can do it," said Eileen.

"Do we really have wings?" Aoife asked.

"Yes, but only when you want to fly." Eileen turned around and walked out the front door, heading for the garden in front of the house.

They followed her and found themselves basking in the morning sunlight amid a garden full of flowers and little birds. Aisling looked around suspiciously and noticed one of the small faeries hiding under a rosebush.

Eileen gave them all a demure look. Instantly, a large pair of beautiful blue transparent wings appeared, sprouting out of her back. She swished her wings a few times, blowing air into their faces.

"Wow!" Aoife took off her hat and threw it into the flower garden. Smiling, she closed her eyes in concentration for a moment. And then a pair of brilliant emerald dragonfly wings appeared, coming directly out of her back, through her clothes. The wings sparkled in the sunlight.

Eileen gave Aoife a look over, nodding with appreciation. "Very nice!"

Aisling hesitated. "I'm still not sure I believe all of this."

Eileen laughed. "Don't be silly! You have to *believe* if you want it to work." She leapt into the air, beating her wings wildly and flew to the top of the nearest pine tree. "Come on!"

Aoife launched herself into the air and flew towards Eileen, but didn't stop when she got there. She shouted as she went by, "How do I stop?"

Eileen called back, "Just lean backwards."

But it was no use. Aoife shot straight into another tree, crashing against the branches and spilling pine cones onto the ground. "Oh fiddle!"

Eileen flew over to catch her, laughing.

Aisling looked over at Genevieve pensively. "Maybe we should forget about all of this, Gen. I'm sure there's a way back home."

"No way!" Genevieve crossed her arms. "I swear, *Aisling*, if you say you want to go back to Seattle after all of this, I'll go find Sifu Yuen and have him beat the—"

"Okay, okay!"

Unsure whether it was the mention of her Kung Fu master's name or her own real name, Aisling looked up into the trees, inhaling nervously. "All right then."

Closing her eyes, she imagined having a pair of wings. For a moment, nothing happened. She was just about to forget it when she felt something twitch. The sense of something large sprouting out of her back made her gasp. The extra weight caused her to teeter backward, but she managed to regain her balance by leaning forward slightly.

"Wow!" Genevieve shouted. "Your wings are beautiful, Erin—Aisling!"

Aisling glanced over her shoulder, and saw a pair of white wings, embellished in silver. They were nearly transparent, but they glittered in the sunlight. She noticed too, that holes had appeared in her clothes to accommodate the wings. "Convenient little detail," she remarked.

There was a shout from the treetops. Aisling looked up and saw that Aoife had extricated herself from a tangle of branches and was now hovering there next to Eileen. She looked at her friend again, still hesitating. "But what about you?" she asked.

Genevieve waved her on. "Go on! I want to see you fly!"

Aisling nodded and looked into the treetops, spotting a distant pine tree taller than the others. With a quirky smile on her lips, she leapt into the air.

It was exhilarating. Her wings easily carried her upwards, and she shot past the other two, aiming for the distant trees. Like a fresh breath of cool mountain air, or a cold drink of spring water, she could feel her entire body tingling with excitement. Before she knew it, she had reached the tallest tree and was circling around it in a wide arc. Her eyesight, too, was sharper now, and she could make out small details below like never before: A small fish jumping out of the lake, tiny dragonflies sweeping across its surface, a squirrel racing up the scruffy trunk of a tree.

The feeling was almost too intense to describe. It was like the first time she had listened to Beethoven's Moonlight Sonata. Aisling found herself overwhelmed by the beauty of it all. A gentleness that she had never known began to mingle with tremendous sadness—sadness at never having experienced this, sadness that her friend would never know what it was like to fly, and the sadness that comes from joy.

Aisling landed gently back in the garden, while her friend looked on. As her feet touched the ground, her wings vanished in a huff of air. Tears streaked her cheeks, but she wiped her face before Genevieve could see.

Genevieve ran over to where she had landed. "Hey! That was fantastic!"

Aisling felt her friend's hands on her shoulders, turning her around. "Well, it looks like your blouse is still intact," Genevieve said.

Aisling laughed.

*   *   *

Chapter Five

The Dispossessed

They spent several weeks in that place, overdosing on the many simple pleasures to be found there—flying, walking in the garden sunshine, creating new clothes to wear, and learning how to use magic.

According to Eileen, not all fairies were alike, and none of them shared the same kinds of magical abilities. Aisling had discovered that she was good at Elementalism, being able to throw gusts of wind or ignite fires. She could cause it to rain, and she could sense things moving about the earth, either in the trees or underneath them. Being able to create clothes was another great delight, but Aoife had trouble mastering the skill.

Genevieve had discovered a large library in Eileen's house and spent much of her time reading books containing old tales, legends, and the occasional book on magic. One day she had taken out her tarot cards and they had fascinated both Eileen and Aoife. They spent an entire day having their fortunes told, but her friend later told her that it was extremely difficult to discern the future of fairies. Nothing spectacular was due to happen around them, it seemed, though she did sense something very dark in Aoife's future. Aoife tossed away Genevieve's warnings with a laugh.

Mostly, Aisling spent her time around Eileen's house or exploring the forest. She hadn't encountered many kinds of fairies yet, except for the elusive and rather annoying flower fairies who had thrown water balloons at her that first morning.

In fact, ever since she had swept a group of them away so violently, the flower fairies had taken it as their mission to try to disturb her life as much as possible. They were always playing tricks on her, hoping to catch her off guard, and Aisling had found them to be quite an annoyance.

One day, as Aisling flew over the forest, she spotted a huge oak tree guarding the top of a hill. A dozen tiny fairies were flying around it, darting in and out of its golden leaves. Curiosity drew her closer, and after wondering what they were doing, she decided to investigate.

Aisling wore a green blouse with flared sleeves, a thick white belt with a silver buckle, white tights and a pair of shoes, also white. Topping off her outfit, like an accessory, were large wings, now stretched out in alabaster brilliance, and bathed in sunshine. She smiled at the idea of designing outfits that matched her wings.

A golden circle of fallen leaves covered the ground around the top of the hill, and a gust of wintry air scattered a handful of leaves from the place where she landed, just as her wings faded away. The oak stood sentinel over the hill, its limbs stretching out some fifty feet in all directions. Most of its orange leaves had fallen to the earth, carpeting the ground. She had never noticed how powerful oak trees were. Drawing strength from the earth, its branches stretched horizontally, defying gravity unlike most other trees.

With a sense of trepidation, Aisling looked up into the leaves, hoping to spot the tiny winged fairies playing there, but they seemed to be hiding. Another cool breeze swept over the hill, pulling dozens of leaves off the tree and swirling them into little circles. The wind brought with it a faint whining sound too, a soft echo, like words. It was as if the tree was lonely, calling out to her. As she walked up to the trunk, a gust of air swam through the tree, blowing more leaves off the cold branches. There was a quiet sound that seemed to whisper softly, "Aisling."

She stepped up to the tall oak, walking around the trunk, running a hand along its rough bark. She began to sense an exciting presence living inside the tree. It was as if someone had just kissed her hand, and then blew softly up her arm until it reached her neck—but the wind died down just as it got there, leaving her tense with anticipation.

Holding her breath, she closed her eyes and breathed in the sense of the oak, leaving her hand touching the coarse bark. There was an alluring scent that she hadn't noticed before, coming from the tree. It was an earthy, woody aroma, mingled with the regal power of something dark, and it was old, like patchouli, mixed with a hint of something spicy. Ideas began to flow into her mind: thoughts of power and command. It was strangely alluring. Another gust of cold air brought leaves with it this time. As one touched her high on the shoulder, it seemed like someone had just dropped a gentle kiss onto the side of her neck.

Aisling opened her eyes, enthralled by the beauty of the moment. The tree dripped liquid sunshine. Orange and yellow leaves were falling out of the branches, whirling about for the time it took to take a breath, and then gently landing on the ground.

Something struck her painfully on the head.

"Ouch!" She pulled her hand away from the tree to rub her forehead.

Laughter fell down out of the tree, along with a flurry of acorns. Raising her hands to block some of the projectiles, she noticed several small winged fairies hiding among the golden leaves. Aisling backed away from the tree hastily, looking into its branches. A squirrel appeared along one branch, bearing a rider on its back. It was a tiny faerie girl, brown haired and grinning. She held an acorn in her hand. The squirrel stopped, the girl closed one eye, took aim and threw it.

Dodging the acorn, Aisling shook her head in exasperation. These fairies were cute but they were annoying too. Catcalls and taunts came out from behind leafy hiding places up in the tree. Aisling retreated away from the oak tree and a windy gust swept over the hill, carrying with it a disappointed whisper.

Noticing a path leading down the side of the hill, she began to follow it. After a long descent, she found herself in a stone amphitheater set into the side of the rock. A white marble stage faced several rows of tiered seats, and a row of Greek styled marble pillars ran across the back of the stage. A cool gust of wind brought a groan, followed by another whisper.

In the center of the marble flooring, a circular basin—almost like a baptismal pool, held clear water. The groaning sound came from the pool, and for a moment she thought she could see a face there, forming out of the water and then swirling away.

Aisling stepped onto the marble stage. Clicking the heels of her shoes against the marble, she walked over to look inside of the pool, and saw a clear night sky reflecting a field of stars above her head. She glanced around, perplexed, since it wasn't nighttime at all. The cold sun shone down on the amphitheater, spreading rays of warmth like a thin blanket.

Looking back into the basin, she saw a house in the distance, its windows aglow. She noticed a pair of lights, one of gold, the other silver, drifting in front of the house and then going inside, through a window. For a brief moment, the glow inside the house held an aura, and then the pair of lights went out, replaced by firelight rippling against the windows.

Something stirred in the darkness. She felt a presence, standing in the starlight. Although it didn't seem to be paying attention to her, she knew the feeling when a Shadow Person was near. She could hear several whispering voices moving away, getting softer, as they approached the house. They grew quieter and quieter, until the sounds were only an echo among the trees.

A woman screamed.

A cool voice broke into the scene. "What would a miserable thing like you be doing here, I wonder?"

Aisling looked up from the vision into the blinding sunlight. For a moment, she was only aware of her loudly beating heart. It took a few seconds to calm down and focus on the present. She knelt by the side of

72

the pool, trembling.

The voice had come from the dark haired Morrigan, who was standing by with a large group of people. She had on a short black skirt, a black turtleneck sweater, white tights and black shoes. She wore her straight black hair in a ponytail this time. A mirror was tucked into a white cloth belt around her waist. When Morrigan saw the expression in Aisling's eyes, she laughed.

More than two dozen fairies had arrived, sounding like a scattering of hailstones. Some of them were still landing by the amphitheater, their butterfly wings vanishing as they touched the white marble. They wore a wide variety of clothes, from short skirts and blouses to long Victorian dresses to tunics and capes to modern styled shirts and pants. There was even an occasional leather jacket among them.

One man, wearing a black tunic, embroidered with Celtic knotwork in silver, white tights and a green velvet cape, came forward. "Is this one of the new changelings, Morrigan?"

Scowling, Morrigan nodded and turned round to walk over to one of the stone benches. She sat down, crossing her legs. "I don't know why the queen lets them wander about so much. They should all be confined to one place."

Ignoring her remark, the man walked forward. He had short dark hair and a goatee. "Hello, my name is Fáelán Anluain."

"Hi." Taking his hand, he helped her stand up. She could feel some of the jitters fading away, but her voice was still shaky. "I'm Aisling."

Fáelán smiled, and out of the corner of her eye, Aisling noticed Morrigan staring at him darkly. Was that an envious look in her eyes? Before she could make up her mind, Morrigan looked away.

The others began to take up seats in the amphitheater, while a few remained on the stage near the pool of strange visions. Aisling glanced down at the water. "I saw a house surrounded by shadows—"

The smile on Fáelán's face faded. "It shows you a vision of something you are meant to know." He looked into the water suspiciously. "We call it, 'Linn na Cinniúna,' the Pool of Destiny."

Another faerie, wearing a dark Victorian suit, with a high collar, came over to the basin. "That's the old name. I call it the 'Party Pool." He put his hand on Fáelán's shoulder. "Do you really think its visions are that important now?"

"This is ancient magic, Laigne," said Fáelán. "We shouldn't play around with it."

But Laigne wasn't listening to him. He moved around to the other side of the pool, dropping a curious gaze into it. "Come on. Let's see what fun it reveals to us today!"

Laigne glanced down into the basin, and Aisling followed his gaze. The still water began to ripple, as if a gentle breeze washed over it. Settling down to clear glass, the water reflected an image of pink clouds covering a sunset over a large field, bordered with pine trees. There was a ragged girl, wearing a green dress, striped black and green tights, and combat boots. Long brown hair framed blue eyes and a straight nose. If she hadn't looked like she was starving, she could have been pretty. In her hand, she held a bow. Something dark stood off to the side, whispering. The girl tilted her head, as if listening, and then she raised the bow, loaded it with an arrow, and took aim, directly at the viewer.

Fáelán tossed a coin into the pool and the image rippled away.

"Hey! I was watching that!" protested Laigne.

Ignoring his friend, Fáelán turned to Aisling. "So where are you staying?"

Laigne, with a knowing smile, went to sit down next to Morrigan. Aisling caught off guard, ran a hand through her hair before answering Fáelán. "I'm at Eileen's house, over by the lake."

"Eileen Bisset from Cnoc Firinn?"

Aisling shook her head, unsure of herself. "I don't—"

Fáelán smiled. "From the clan of Donn?"

Morrigan called out coyly from the stone bench, "Fáelán, you should

74

get away from that girl. She still stinks with the stain of the Milesians."

Feeling more assured now, Aisling glared at the dark haired faerie. "You're no better than anyone else."

Morrigan's eyebrows shot up. "Did I give you permission to speak, changeling?"

Cold fury ignited. Despite the wintry air surrounding the amphitheater, Aisling felt something hot against her skin. Out of the corner of her eye, she saw steam rising from the pool.

Fáelán whispered, "Take care Aisling. She's more dangerous than she looks."

Ignoring his warning, Aisling glared at Morrigan. "I'll speak whenever I like, to whomever I like."

Smoothly, Morrigan stood up, moving like a panther stalking its prey. She walked around to the other side of the pool, glancing down into it offhandedly. For a moment, her eyes were transfixed there. Then, with obvious effort, she wrenched her view away from the enchanted water. For a moment, Aisling caught a trace of fear there, but then it was gone, replaced by a look of contempt. "So Fáelán, you think this changeling is pretty, do you?"

"What?" He looked into Aisling's eyes. "Of course she is." Quite suddenly, he turned around and walked over to the other side of the amphitheater, taking a seat a few rows back.

Morrigan tilted her head, musing aloud. "What would it be like, I wonder, cut off from everything you know? To be abandoned—cast aside. To know that your own, true parents had never wanted you?"

Although Aisling didn't turn as Morrigan spoke, she kept an eye on the girl as she walked around the pool. The air had grown still, and all of the sounds coming from the wilderness around them had ceased, as if the world was holding its breath. Angry steam continued to rise from the enchanted water.

Since she had lived in this world, Aisling had sometimes wondered why her real parents had abandoned her, and why she had been given away, to live in such a dreary place as Seattle. The strange visions from the mirror haunted her too, and she wondered about the girl reflected in the glass window of her foster father's house.

Aisling looked away towards the path leading up to the oak tree. She had an urge to walk away, up the path, to get away from everyone and go hide in the forest. Instead, she turned to face Morrigan, recalling what Fintan had said about her magic mirror and how Morrigan had reacted to the sight of Genevieve. "What's wrong," taunted Aisling, "not the most beautiful girl anymore?"

Morrigan ignored her comment, but Aisling noticed her brushing a hand against the mirror in her belt. Morrigan glanced down at the pool again, avoiding looking directly into it this time. She said, "Not an easy thing to look at, your own destiny—especially for one of the dispossessed."

Morrigan looked up, directly into Aisling's eyes. It was like being watched by a black raven, who, patiently waiting, circling overhead, in search of death. It was strangely unsettling.

Fáelán's plea for restraint broke the silence. "Morrigan—"

Although there was no wind, Aisling felt a whirlwind beginning to form around her. The steam drifting out of the pool faded away. Aisling felt an exhilarating strength building up inside. With the wave of her hand, a huge gust of wind shot out towards Morrigan. It was like the blast of a hurricane, and some of the other fairies were knocked to the ground. Morrigan swayed on her feet.

But then, the winds faded away, being funneled around Morrigan, who had raised a hand, seemingly to control it. Then she rotated her arm and made a pulling motion, and Aisling felt herself falling forward onto her knees, while all of the power was siphoned away. Where there had been strength before, now there was only an echo of energy. Like a wilted flower, Aisling fell onto her face, completely drained.

Morrigan laughed, looking over at Laigne and the others. "Not very adept at controlling elementals, is she?" She glared at Aisling with pity and taunted, "You're just—so *unimportant*, aren't you?"

All of the life inside had gone. The fury inside had been replaced by an oppressive loneliness, which made Aisling want to hide. It was like being discovered, naked, in a crowd. Her hair had fallen into her face and she looked up through a dark strand at her tormentor.

Morrigan began to laugh. "Come on Laigne, let's go somewhere else," she said, wrinkling her nose. "Let's get away from this changeling creature."

Most everyone in the amphitheater began to laugh. Some of them looked at her with pity, but most of them sprouted a pair of wings and flew away. A few of them changed into little balls of light. Aisling noticed that Morrigan had changed into a shining sphere too. It was red and purple, just like the one that had drawn her into the road in front of a speeding car.

*   *   *

Aisling felt the cold marble against her cheek. Like a shattered jar, she lay, broken. Completely drained, she was unable to move at all. Aisling felt her body tingling all over, like a limb which had fallen asleep. Gasping for air, she closed her eyes, hoping the onslaught of dizziness would go away.

Empty sunlight blew away on the breeze, and Aisling shivered. Along the wind, a disembodied voice came, rising out of the Pool of Destiny. Taking a deep breath to gain some of her strength, Aisling sat up. She brushed hair out of her eyes and saw a face forming out of the water in the pool.

There came a whisper in a watery voice, "Glory to the queen, whose beauty shall restore the Land of Dreams."

Silently, the face returned to the water, which rippled and danced and then returned to clear glass reflecting the blue sky overhead.

Like a spark ignited from dying embers, Aisling drew strength from the hopeful words. The tingling dizziness faded away, and she got to her feet. Without another glance, she went back up the trail, still unsteady on her feet.

The tall oak tree was shrouded in the fading sunlight. A cool breeze swept past, bringing with it an inviting whisper. The tree was a beacon of strength and power. Aisling approached, scanning high up into the branches, but none of the little fairies were in sight.

Her eyes fell down, and she saw a tall, bare-chested man leaning against the tree, smiling. An overwhelming desire clouded her mind. The memory of the touch she had felt while standing under the oak tree still lingered against her skin. She could almost hear a soft voice on the wind, calling her name.

As she reached the man, he brought his arms around her in a warm embrace. Aisling closed her eyes, basking in the strength and power radiating from him. He breathed over her neck, and she felt life tingling over her skin. It was like jumping into a cool lake on a hot day, refreshing and exhilarating at once. She heard her name whispered into an ear, and she opened her eyes. With tongue on her lips, she began to kiss the man.

Just before their lips touched, strong hands grabbed her shoulders and Aisling found herself pulled back, away from the man. The dizziness returned, and she fell onto the ground, blinking. Golden leaves fell from the branches around her, like tears in the sunshine. The man was gone now, and he was replaced by a pang of loneliness, which fell out of the branches and blew away on the wind.

Tearing her gaze away from the strong trunk of the oak tree, Aisling noticed Fintan, looking like a Greek god, standing by, his hands on his hips. He shook his head. "You shouldn't hang around this tree."

Aisling shook her head, hoping to clear away the dizziness. "Why not?"

Fintan laughed. "How will I ever seduce your friend if you're inside a tree for a century or more?" He walked over to her, extending his hand. "You'll put in a good word for me with her, won't you?"

Smiling, Aisling took his hand and got to her feet.

A trio of lights came down out of the sky. Aisling recognized the blue-silver orb of Eileen. The others were blue-green and pink, tinged with white. When they came near, they changed into her friends, led by Fáelán. Aisling raised her eyebrows. "How can you do that, Gen?"

Eileen giggled. "She can travel this way if a Faerie helps her do it."

"Oh." Aisling sat down on the ground, with her back to the tree. Lonely whispers still beckoned to her out of the leaves.

Genevieve asked, "What's wrong?"

"Nothing," said Aisling. She didn't want to talk about Morrigan. "I've just had a bad day, that's all."

"I didn't think there were any bad days here," Genevieve said.

Biting her lip, Aisling looked away.

"Fáelán told us about your affray with Morrigan," said Fintan. "You shouldn't let her trouble you, Aisling. Normally, she's very kind. Morrigan is a great healer."

Aisling began to feel a little better. She dropped her gaze down into her hands. "Does everyone here abuse changelings so badly?"

Fintan nodded. "Most of the Tuatha Dé treat changelings like they're diseased animals."

Aisling's curiosity perked up. "Why?"

Fintan looked into the oak tree. "Since the war with the Shadow People began, faeries have been hiding their children in the Milesian world. But when changelings return home, their parents are usually missing or dead. This stifles their magical energy, leaving them weak. Also, without a clan, you're vulnerable."

Taking off his green cape and laying it over the ground, Fáelán sat down next to Aisling. "Anyone can cast a hex or curse on you with impunity because there is no one else, no clan, to protect or avenge you."

Aisling began to shiver. "But why are changelings so weak?"

Fintan looked at Aisling. "Because magic works better here than it does in the world you grew up in, where it takes considerable effort to manifest thoughts into reality. Those who live in the world of the Milesians tend to lose their ability to use magic. Changelings are mostly numb to it when they get here."

Aisling raised her eyebrows. "Numb?"

Fintan nodded. "They stop believing, you see."

Aisling leaned forward, causing a strand of hair to fall into her face.

She brushed it out of the way. "Is that the reason why you call this the Land of Dreams?"

"Yes. The Land of Dreams is the land of loves, passions, and desires." Fintan looked at Genevieve, who was unresponsive. "But you have to be careful because things tend to happen instantly here. One careless thought and—"

Aisling began to wonder if that was how curses worked. "So whatever you think here comes to pass?"

"Mostly," said Fintan. "But you have to develop your skills to be more effective. Everyone has their own kind of magic, too." Rising from the ground, he walked over to the tree and placed a hand on the trunk. "Fate also has a hand in what you can do. Some are destined for greater things than others."

Fáelán smiled. "See, not all changelings are losers."

Aisling had never felt so helpless.

Fintan continued, with a trace of remorse in his voice. "Most changelings don't survive long if they come back home. There are a few that do, but they're treated like outcasts by most of the Sídhe."

Unable to continue listening, Aisling got up and ran down a path through the trees. Hoping to outrun the black thoughts swirling behind her, she ran on and on, through the fading sunshine.

After a time she came to a clearing covered with flowers. A stone sundial stood in the center of the glade, washed in the fading sun. Winded, she dropped down into a patch of lavender, feeling the desolation of her life. Who were her real parents? Why had they hidden her among the Milesians?

Several minutes later, Genevieve sat down beside her. "It's alright Erin."

"Aisling is my name, Gen."

Her friend didn't answer.

"It's just hard to realize that I'll never be anything more than I am now."

"But you're a Faerie! That's something that I could never even imagine being."

"It doesn't change who I am."

Genevieve ran her hand through a patch of lavender, inhaling the perfume on her fingers. "But you can make whatever clothes you like. You can be a real designer now."

Aisling smiled. "Yes. But there's no point of it here." She looked up into the trees where a black bird had landed. This world was already a beautiful place. There were no gloomy skies, no shabby buildings, and the people here weren't all lost and dreamless.

"Maybe you do have a real purpose, but you just haven't discovered what it is yet," Genevieve said.

"Why am I here, Gen?"

Her friend shook her head. "Who can say?"

The phrase reminded Aisling of her Kung Fu teacher:

I think you have a destiny to fulfill.

The idea of it seemed to go against everything Aisling had experienced, although she was now living in an entirely new world, doing things she had never imagined.

Genevieve broke into Aisling's thoughts. "Do you want to go home?"

Aisling shook her head. "No."

Now that she knew the truth, Aisling didn't think she could face Erin's parents. The thought of living among them now was unbearable. She didn't want to lie to them. She dropped her gaze down into the flowers. "I wonder what happened to the real Erin?" she whispered.

Genevieve reached down and brought up the gold medallion, which still hung around her neck. She traced a finger along its surface until she reached the dragon's head. "Perhaps this belonged to her."

The image from the mirror still haunted Aisling. She shook her head. "No, my father left that for me after he took Erin."

Flipping it over, Genevieve began to examine the other side, which contained writing in an unfamiliar script—if it was writing at all. "I wonder what this says?" she whispered. "You know, I haven't been able to find this kind of writing in any of the books in Eileen's library."

81

Eileen and Fáelán came into the clearing. Genevieve glanced around suspiciously and asked, "Where's Fintan?"

Eileen giggled. "He took off, but I can go get him if you want."

"Please don't!"

For the first time in a long while, Aisling smiled. "Anyone know what time it is?"

"Why don't you look at that sundial," said Eileen.

Aisling stood up and went over to it, but the stone pillar wasn't a sundial at all. At the top, it flared out into a bowl. Strange writing surrounded it, and a pair of carved dragons encircled the pillar, their heads touching the underside of the basin. Unable to decipher the carvings, she noticed a circular depression inside the center of the bowl, but it was nearly covered in oak leaves. No water stood in the basin, and she noticed a pair of holes set into it, just above the dragon heads. Traces of dirt and moss streamed over the carvings where rainwater had drained out through the holes.

"Gen, can I have the medallion?"

Her friend handed it over, and after Aisling cleared away the leaves, she placed it into the depression, where it fit perfectly. Aisling held her breath and took a step back.

A gust of wind sighed through the trees.

Nothing happened.

Genevieve said, "Well, that was anti-climactic."

"Where did you get that medallion?" asked Eileen.

"It was inside a stone box that my father left with me." Aisling looked at the stone basin, wondering.

Fáelán was thoughtful. "Maybe you need to fill it." He held out his hand, conjured up a pitcher, and poured water into the basin. After a few moments, it was full, but the water drained out through the holes in the bottom, washing the dragon heads.

Aisling stepped closer, gazing into the water that covered the medallion. The surface grew still, and then she saw the same house that she had glimpsed in the Pool of Destiny. Impulsively, she leaned close and whispered, "Aisling."

The world seemed to spin about them, and it made her dizzy. A line in the air appeared, and the clearing expanded, like a piece of paper being unfolded. A secret path lay before them.

Genevieve whispered, "Glorioski!"

Eileen looked into the magic doorway and said, "This kind of magic is unknown to me. I doubt even Fintan could hide another world this way."

Aisling held her breath, too excited to speak. Her true parents had made this path. At the end of it, she would meet them. It was the same path that she had seen reflected in the Pool of Destiny.

The solitary vision of her parents in the mirror of her room was the only memory she had of them. She wondered what they were like. She remembered that her mother was tall, with a noble bearing. Her father was a complete mystery to her. She had wondered about the silver ship, and where it had come from. Was that her mother's vision she had seen when she put on the ring? She found herself looking at the ring, still around her finger. Did it belong to her father? The idea of getting answers to all of her questions filled her with excitement. But the pain that they had caused Erin's parents still burned in her mind, and she wanted to ask them about this most of all. She still cared about them and hoped that she could make things right. Maybe Erin, if she was still alive, would want to come back with her?

"Let's to it," said Fáelán.

He stepped forward.

Genevieve shouted, "No, wait!"

Aisling looked at her friend, who had turned pale. "What's wrong, Gen?"

Genevieve had a faraway look in her eyes. "Don't go down that path, Aisling."

"Why not?" asked Aisling.

Genevieve's voice had dropped down to a whisper. "They're waiting for you."

"Who?"

"Who do you think?"

A cold memory tingled against a place on her throat, where the Hat Man's Lieutenant had once pressed a knife. But Aisling had no intention of quitting. With a sidelong glance at her friend, she stifled a giggle and said, "Your intuition is bothering you again, isn't it?"

"It's not funny, Aisling!"

Aisling closed her eyes and imagined a steel Dao sword. She reached out and the Chinese weapon appeared in her hand. "I'm not afraid of the shadows anymore, Gen."

"You should be," Eileen said. She put her hand on her own sword belt, which she wore all the time, and grumbled, "What a way to waste a perfectly good night."

Fáelán shook his head. "Whatever." He stepped onto the dark pathway, which wound into the trees. With a wave of his hand, a ball of light appeared in front of him, and it lit their way.

They walked for several hours, into the darkening night. It had begun to snow, and they found themselves traveling through a silent world surrounded by whitening trees. At one point, Genevieve asked why they didn't travel the same way they had before; as balls of light, but Eileen had told her that it was safer to travel on foot.

Aisling had decided to turn her shoes into white boots. She made a leather jacket for Genevieve to ward off the cold, and a white shawl for herself. Eileen wore a long dress, striped in blue and white, along with a light blue scarf. Fáelán hadn't changed his clothes, apparently not being bothered by the cold.

They came to a house covered in snow, standing by a grove of trees. It was the same house that Aisling had seen in the Pool of Destiny, except for the snow. There was no sign of either the Shadow People or the pair of glowing lights.

Their sounds were swallowed up by the snow, and the moon had come

84

out, bathing the clearing in a white light. Quite large, it was an impressive building, made in the fashion of an old manor house. A lonely willow tree, overgrown with moss, stood in front of the house. A sturdy oak door arched across the entrance, flanked by flower gardens, now unkempt. The door stood ajar, and with a sense of trepidation, Aisling pushed it open, holding her breath.

An empty foyer stood before her. Aisling heard Fáelán whisper something and all of the candles in the house lit up, throwing flickering light onto the walls. Slightly unnerved, Aisling stepped inside. *Where were her parents? Why had they abandoned her? Where was Erin?*

As the others followed her into the foyer, Aisling found a large mirror hanging on the wall. It had a pair of dragons engraved on the frame.

The glass was cold to the touch.

"What is it?" asked Genevieve.

Aisling whispered, "This is just like the mirror in my room."

Tracing a finger along the edge of the frame, Aisling felt the chill of silver. In the mirror, a vision took shape: a barren stone chamber, bathed in moonlight. The silver-haired girl she had seen before sat on the bed, cradling a doll. A leather collar circled her neck, a heavy chain running from its ring into the wall.

Fáelán came over to the mirror and looked into it. Aisling looked away, into his eyes. The friendly mask covering his face dropped away, and she thought she could see directly into his soul. He stood there, transfixed, gazing into the glass.

Aisling looked back at the mirror, wondering. She stepped back, whispering, "I know this girl—"

Fáelán glanced at Aisling and then reached up to touch the mirror. When his finger touched the glass, the image vanished. He stood there for a moment, hand remaining on the glass, staring into the reflection of the foyer.

Next to the entryway, a staircase led up to the second floor. Aisling looked into the rooms on either side of the foyer, which appeared to be a

85

small dining room and a sitting room. Genevieve and Fáelán walked into the dining room, while she and Eileen went into the sitting room.

The cozy room was dominated by a large golden harp next to a huge fireplace. A brown leather couch stood in front of a low oak table. Another pair of comfortable chairs, made of leather and wood and bound in brass, sat along one side of the room next to a large bookcase. A rocking chair sat next to the fireplace. Eileen pointed to a long wood box on top of the stone mantle.

Aisling took it down and brought it over to the table. Kneeling down, she examined it. Made of dark cherry wood, and carved with an intricate pattern of Celtic knotwork, the box was nearly three feet long. A pair of gold latches held it shut.

Eileen ran a hand over the box, without touching it, and then leaned back onto the couch. "This isn't mine to open."

Aisling raised her eyebrows. She ran a finger along its surface, feeling the intricate designs like it was a puzzle to solve, and picking up a thick layer of dust. Wrinkling her nose, she looked up at Eileen, who smiled and waved her hand over the box. The dust vanished and the wood was now polished clean.

"Thank you," said Aisling. Unfastening the latches, she opened the box.

Black velvet lined the inside. Upon it lay a Celtic styled sword. Its golden handle was carved into ridged oak for a better grip. A gold pommel arched out from the grip around a small gold ball. The gold crosspiece inclined out towards the blade, which was made out of the finest metal she had ever seen. An exquisitely made black leather scabbard, with Celtic knotwork and strange inscriptions in silver was also in the box.

The type of weapon was heavier than Aisling was used to, but when she picked it up, she was surprised at how light it was. Its balance was perfect, and when she gripped it, she could feel something tingling in her hand. She knew that Sifu Yuen would have said it enhanced her Chi, since she was more focused while it lay in her hand. Moonlight streaming through a window mixed with flickering candlelight, shimmering off the blade in blue and red. A long pattern of leaves was engraved in the blade. Resisting an urge to wave it about, Aisling reverently placed it back inside the box. "This must have belonged to my father."

An empty hole opened up in her heart, casting her into oblivion, and for the first time, she knew what Erin's parents had lived through for so many years, even though they were unable to understand why. Aisling wondered why her real parents had done such a cruel thing. Looking at the sword that had once belonged to her father made her realize just why they had needed to take such an extreme action: to protect her, while a war raged around them. Leaving the sword, Aisling stood up and went out of the room.

When she stepped back into the foyer, she felt a cold sensation sliding up her spine. Out of the corner of her eyes, she saw something dark, by the open doorway. The Shadow Person didn't vanish this time. Even though it was a shade, it was not the same kind of shadow that would be reflected on a wall, but it was three-dimensional, with detailed features and volume to it. Moonlight filtered through its semi-transparent form, bathing the hallway in a blue halo of darkness. For a moment, the Shadow Person just stood there, watching her.

There was something terrifying about seeing a shade where moments before, nothing had been there. Nevertheless, Aisling drew the curved dao sword out of the scabbard at her side, and took up a fighting stance.

The dark thing drew its own blade, which captured the moonlight. Its eyes began to glow red with menace, and she could hear its heavy breath. Hatred, mingled with hunger, seeped out of the darkness.

It moved closer slowly, and Aisling struck it with her sword, but the blade swept through its body as if nothing was there. For a tiny fraction of a second, she froze, too shocked to comprehend why her sword failed to touch the shadow.

The Shadow Person reached out with a gloved hand, shoved her against the wall, and pointed the tip of its sword at her throat.

Before it could strike, Eileen's blade appeared, cutting into its dark form. The creature blinked out, shrieking. It faded away, sword clattering to the floor, leaving the hallway covered in abandoned moonlight.

For a time, the only thing Aisling could hear was the loud beating of her heart, and the cold silence that covered the foyer.

Eileen put a hand on her shoulder reassuringly. "Stay here."

She went away, searching for shadows.

Aisling narrowed her eyes, furious that she had made such a stupid mistake, one that could have cost her life. "Never again," she whispered.

Eileen came back into the foyer, sheathing her sword. "I don't think there are any more of them in the house."

Genevieve appeared in the doorway. "We should get away from here."

"Not yet. "Aisling sheathed her ineffective sword and went upstairs. Where were they? There was no sign of her parents anywhere. She walked down a hallway lined with pictures of places she had never known. At the far end of the hall, there was an oak door, bound in iron.

Silently, the door opened to a chamber filled with white furniture, a small bed, and blue-white curtains. Stuffed animals and toys lay on the bed or on top of shelves that lined the walls. Aisling walked up to one of these, a stuffed puppy, and ran a hand along it, picking up a layer of dust. A window overlooked a garden below, now fallen into darkness. The bed covers were thrown about, as if someone had been sleeping in it just moments before, except that it too was covered in dust.

Aisling began to feel emptiness in the pit of her stomach. Turning round, she walked down the hallway, where another door lay, slightly ajar. As she approached, Aisling noticed a dark stain on the hardwood floor. Cold gripped her heart, and she found herself holding her breath as she pushed the door open.

The body of a woman lay face down in a dried pool of blood. Aisling recognized her at once—the woman from her visions. Her mother.

Beside her was a man, once handsome, with blond hair. Black burn marks marred his white tunic. Her father, lying there next to her mother.

Aisling stood frozen, unable to breathe. A cold numbness rushed through her body, and she choked back tears.

When she came back to herself, Genevieve was kneeling at her side.

Aisling didn't remember falling to the floor. She looked into her best friend's eyes. "Who did this?"

Genevieve shook her head. "I don't know."

Aisling closed her eyes, trying to shut out the pain. "I don't even know their names."

Dimly, she could feel Genevieve's hands squeezing hers.

"Shadows," said Eileen. "It was the Shadow People."

Aisling stood up. Supporting herself with a hand pressed against the wall, she felt a cold fury inside. With a final glance at her dead parents, she looked into Eileen's eyes and said, "Tell me about your war."

Eileen had a look of both shock and understanding, as if she had expected this. She said, "The Shadow People come, murdering some, and taking others away."

Genevieve asked, "Where do they take them?"

"No one knows." Eileen turned her back on the grisly scene. "Perhaps back to where they come from. We call their leader 'The Hat Man' because he always appears with a hat, unlike the others."

All of the emptiness and frustration and desolation inside Aisling began to form into something, hard, at the pit of her stomach. She said, "I want to learn the ways of magic. I'm going to defeat them. I'm going to destroy the Hat Man."

Eileen was silent for a moment before she spoke. "You can't learn much magic from me. You'll have to ask the queen for help."

Fáelán said, "The queen won't talk to changelings, Eileen."

Aisling began to walk down the hallway, away from her past. "She'll talk to me."

* * *

Chapter Six

Tír na nÓg

Aisling sat, arms around her legs, gazing into the light of a lone candle that she had conjured up. It stood on the stump of a tree, which served as a makeshift table. Stars decorated the heavens, and the trees surrounding the clearing were covered with snow, which had been falling all day long. The road they had been traveling on was now covered in white frost, but the banks on either side of it were piled with snow.

Today, Aisling had created a blue and white striped dress, white stockings, tall black boots, a warm white coat, and a pair of off-white ear-muffs. Despite the snow, she didn't feel the cold at all.

Eileen was wearing a long yellow dress, tied tightly with a white sash, and a pair of white boots. It was as if she were daring the cold to touch her. Her blonde hair fell about her shoulders, and it complemented the color of her dress beautifully.

Glad to have made the dress, Aisling smiled. She had just been playing around with ideas, but Eileen had insisted on wearing the yellow dress. *It's really more appropriate for the spring.*

Still, she gave it to her anyway.

Genevieve, on the other hand, sat against a pine tree, shivering and hugging herself closely. She grumbled, "Why can't we have a fire, anyway?"

Eileen didn't look away from the candle's flame, which sparkled against the snow in the trees. "I told you, this is a magic candle. It will keep us warm and safe from the Shadow People tonight."

Undeterred, Genevieve grumbled, "Magic candles—right. Just give me a decent fire and a shotgun."

Eileen chose a condescending tone for her reply, "Shadow People are non-corporeal. A shotgun won't harm them, remember?"

"No," said Genevieve. "I've never seen the things, supposing they really exist."

"You shouldn't want to see them—ever." Eileen said.

"Did I say I wanted to see them?"

"Is anyone thirsty?" Aisling decided to interrupt before they got too embroiled in one of their arguments again.

Genevieve continued to complain, ignoring Aisling. "I still don't see why we have to sleep out in the cold."

"I'm not cold," Eileen said, and then she laughed. "Oh, but I forgot, you're such a *delicate* Milesian girl, aren't you?"

Aisling stood up, walking to the edge of the clearing to look down the road. "How long did you say it will take us to reach this place?"

Eileen stopped needling Genevieve and answered the question. "We're headed for Brú na Bodb, the king's palace, which overlooks the Milesian town of Vancouver in Canada. It's near a Sídhe called Rath Gealach. We'll be there sometime tomorrow."

"If I had my car, we could have been there by now," complained Genevieve.

Eileen laughed. "The roads are blocked by snow, but we can always travel along Bealach an Rí—the King's Road. Besides, what's the point of traveling if you don't get to see the countryside?"

"I've seen it before," grumbled Genevieve.

"Not along this road, you haven't. Only the Tuatha Dé can move along the Ley Lines that are under this road. If a Milesian—"

Aisling interrupted again. "Do you have anything to eat? I'm starving."

Eileen shifted onto her knees, drawing out a large tablecloth from a bag she had slung over one shoulder. She picked up the candle and spread the cloth out. "Table, be covered."

Instantly, the cloth was covered with a plate of roast beef, red potatoes, corn on the cob, pumpkin pie and a set of silver goblets, all full of clear water. Genevieve stared at it, eyes wide. "Okay, I take back everything I said."

Aisling laughed, and returned to sit next to the others. She picked up a goblet and took a long sip of cool water. "Why didn't Aoife want to come with us?"

Genevieve was already eating. "She said she wanted to finish making a dress to wear at court. Fáelán is bringing her down tomorrow."

As they ate, Aisling noticed that the food never seemed to diminish. All of the plates kept refilling themselves. The goblets provided whatever beverage they desired. It just took a moment's concentration to make something appear. She wondered if Eileen had made the magic tablecloth, or if she had found it someplace else.

Another strange thing happened. Aisling found herself becoming more sensitive to the chill around her. Inside her heart, she could feel the cold, the snow, and even the tiny ice particles blowing by on the wind. She noticed frost forming along the sides of her goblet, and the world around her felt like it was becoming entombed in a tall clear crystalline icicle. For some reason, she was incredibly thirsty, too. She drained the water from the cup, feeling a comforting coolness sweep down her body.

Eileen smiled the smile of someone hearing an inside joke. "Summoning another elemental? What kind is this one, I wonder?"

Aisling didn't get a chance to respond.

A woman's voice called out from the edge of the clearing, "What a pretty tablecloth it is, don't you think, Siri?"

A high pitched laugh followed, like a half-mad hyena, ready to devour a lion. Aisling stood up, carrying the goblet in her hand, and she found herself facing a large group of about thirty or forty faeries. None of them had wings, and they all wore ragged clothes. They had an air of insane desperation, mixed with hunger. It was like being confronted by a pack of wild dogs in the wilderness.

Genevieve whispered, "This candle isn't very magical, is it?"

"It only works on the Shadow People," Eileen said, wrinkling her nose, "not against changeling outcasts."

A tall girl with straight black hair came forward, dropping out of a tree. The wild look in her eyes was mixed with dark humor. She giggled, and tilted her head sideways, as if she was looking at the world through a skewed angle. She had a knotted, twisted stick of wood in one hand, and she began to twirl it in her fingers. "Do you think they'll share with us, Siri?"

Next to the woman was a half-starved girl wearing a ragged green dress, striped black and green tights, and combat boots that laced up the front. Aisling noticed a vacant expression emptying out of the girl's eyes. She murmured, "I want it, Báirbre. Give it to me."

Eileen began to stand up, but Aisling waved her back.

Although Aisling had put her dao sword down next to the table, she didn't retrieve it. Instead, she moved to the center of the clearing where the intruders were gathering. They quickly surrounded her, moving around in a circle.

The snowstorm was getting stronger, and more of the tiny white flakes were drifting down out of the sky, devouring the warmth. Aisling was getting thirstier, too. She drained the goblet and tossed it over to Eileen, who caught it with a suspicious look.

They didn't seem to care about the magic tablecloth at all now, but were intent on something else entirely. Báirbre stood back from the rest of them, and now Aisling saw that she wore a black gothic-styled dress, with several layers of cloth, and a brown cloth belt. Autumn leaves were woven into her dress, and vines encircled her bare arms.

Eileen said, "Please, there's no reason at all to—"

The girl Siri hissed, "Sssssss! Don't interrupt!" She sat down next to a tree, and waited, while the rest of the outcasts closed in.

Aisling breathed in a scent of pine. The woody aroma was tinged with an echo of the food still on the table, with the chilly air, and with the scented candle, still burning. A clump of snow fell off one of the pine trees, bringing with it a long white trail of cold, icy mistiness.

They attacked.

Aisling kicked forward and then back, knocking down two of the changelings. She delivered a spinning kick to the side, knocking another one out. Then she jumped up and kicked out in two directions, knocking another pair down on either side.

The fight only made them wilder. They devoured the cold like a pack of wolves.

A tall man punched out, and Aisling blocked it and counter-punched, knocking him down. She dodged down under another attack and kicked her opponent in the chest knocking him to the ground.

Another pair of faeries, holding knives, moved forward.

Sweeping out with her leg, Aisling knocked one of them over and then she delivered a forward chest kick to the other one.

Báirbre began to giggle. "This one knows how to dance!"

There was a slight pause—no more than half a second—but she sensed something in the darkness, just out of view, in the trees, watching. It seemed to be staying out of the candlelight, but the hair on the nape of her neck stood up.

An attack from behind brought her back to her senses, and she turned, striking one down, and then turned around again to face an attack aimed at her face. She blocked it, grabbed the faerie's arm, pulled him off balance, put her hand on the back of his neck and pushed him down, into the snow. As she straightened up, she struck another attacker in the side of the face, knocking him down too.

A shout from over her shoulder caused her to turn, and she kicked a Faerie in the chest, knocking him away. He fell backwards, knocking down another one.

Over the sounds of the fight, she could hear Báirbre's taunts. "Ooh, this one fights like a tiger. Take her down! Kick her in the head!"

Two strikes came at once, but Aisling blocked them both. She delivered an elbow blow to each of the faeries in turn, knocking them out.

Then, out of the corner of her eye, she saw a shadow, standing next to a tree, watching. She turned to look at him directly, but it vanished.

A woman kicked, and Aisling blocked it with her leg, knocking her to the ground. Turning around again, she kicked another assailant in the chest. Another attacker tried to strike her. Aisling blocked it and elbowed him in the face.

Eileen stood up and drew her sword.

Báirbre raised her knobby wand and shouted, "Sioc!"

Like a cool wind, Eileen dissolved into a thousand tiny icicles that scattered into the air. Genevieve screamed.

Siri giggled. "They don't want to play nice, do they Báirbre?"

Aisling's heart was gripped with the shock of what had just happened. The cold began to seep out of her body, forming stillness around her. All of the falling snow seemed to be suspended in the air for an instant. Aisling's breath began to mist over.

Her attackers began to slow down, struggling against something in the air. It was like they were trying to keep from being frozen in place. One of the changelings jerked and broke free of the enchantment, charging forward.

"Aieeee!"

The shout alerted Aisling to a high jumping leg kick, aimed at her face. She blocked it with her leg, and then swept low in a spiral kick, knocking him down.

The stillness covering the clearing had been shattered. The changelings that remained now swept forward with renewed vigor, but she could feel a cold exhalation around her as she fought.

A skinny brunette girl swung and missed.

Aisling stepped inside her reach and struck the girl in the face, knocking her out. She fell to the ground, covered in frost.

A faerie wearing a black tunic punched.

Blocking the attack, Aisling grabbed his wrist and forced him back, and then kicked him in the chest. He, too, fell down. Ice covered him as he struck the ground.

The shadow was back, just out of view. For a second, Aisling wondered if they were drawing energy from her, or if the shadows simply liked getting others into trouble.

A tall, thin faerie wearing a leather jacket stepped close to deliver a punch.

Still distracted by the shadow, Aisling stepped aside while blocking; then pushed the thin faerie in the back, out of the clearing. She kicked another advancing opponent in the chest and he fell backwards. Then she turned to face a high leg strike, blocking it with an arm and stepping close to her attacker, kicking him down. As each of them hit the ground, they froze in place, enshrouded in ice.

The next opponent moved forward, aiming a punch at her face.

She turned towards him, blocked his punch and then elbowed him in the chest, knocking him down. A cold wind blew past him as he fell. Aisling turned and kicked another attacker in the chest. He fell down and was entombed in ice.

The last faerie changeling to attack her threw a punch at her chest.

She blocked the strike and punched him in the face, breaking his nose and knocking him out. She could see the ice forming on his face as he fell down.

Three dozen unconscious changelings lay in a wide circle, their bodies now covered in ice and frost.

Aisling turned to face the changeling leader.

The smile on Báirbre's face went away, and she pointed her wand at

Aisling.

Thump!

A snowball knocked the wand out of Báirbre's hand.

Aisling turned to where it had come from. Genevieve stood there with tears, dripping anger and sorrow. She picked up the sword and tossed it.

Catching the Dao sword, Aisling quickly moved over to the change-ling, pointing it at her. In the back of her mind she was a little surprised that Genevieve cared so much for Eileen.

Báirbre giggled and fell down into the snow. She began to crawl back-wards until she bumped into a pine tree, just out of the candlelight. The dim moonlight reflecting off of the snow was the only illumination in her face. "You're going to kill me now," she whispered.

A frozen stillness had descended over the clearing, and frost began to form over the rest of the unconscious changelings. A trace of icy particles remained suspended in the air where Eileen had been standing.

Aisling placed her sword at Báirbre's throat. "What did you do to her?"

In a misty voice, Siri called out from under the pine tree, "She's part of the snowstorm now."

Aisling glanced around the clearing, which was slowly filling up with snow. The changelings had all formed an icy covering around them. The ef-fect startled her. The ice particles in the air began to settle onto the ground, where she had last seen Eileen.

Shaking her head, Aisling turned back towards Báirbre. "Bring her back!"

Báirbre raised a trembling hand towards the blade at her throat. "My wand—"

Genevieve retrieved the knobby wand and pointed it at Báirbre, who had a strange combination of amusement and terror on her face, as if she didn't really care what happened to her. Genevieve lowered the wand, ex-amining it closely. "I wonder if this thing has an 'undo' function?" she mused.

Báirbre looked warily at Genevieve and said, "Transformation spells last until they are withdrawn."

Aisling pressed the sword against Báirbre's throat, gritting her teeth. "*Then withdraw it!*"

It looked like all the motivation had drained out of Báirbre. She simply lay there in the snow, as if she had forgotten how to live. Her eyes grew wide and her voice dropped down to a whisper, "Oh, no. That can never happen now—"

Looking over her shoulder, Aisling found that all of the changelings were now enclosed in frozen tombs. Eileen also lay there now, wrapped in ice. It was as if she had just formed out of the air. Frost was still collecting on her body.

Siri was now standing at the edge of the candlelight, her voice edged with excitement, "You've summoned a Frost Elemental!"

Both Aisling and Genevieve walked back into the candlelight, and looked at Eileen, who lay there next to all of the other changelings. They exchanged bewildered glances.

The feeling of being watched returned. Aisling whirled round, and saw a Shadow Person bent over Báirbre. The moonlight covering the changeling had gone now, plunging her into darkness. Báirbre began to fade away, transforming into a dark mist that seeped into the ground. A moment later, Báirbre was gone.

Aisling stood there, mouth agape, staring at the shadow.

It gave her one last look with its glowing red eyes, and then it, too, faded away.

"What just happened?" Genevieve asked.

A sad voice drifted over from where Siri stood. "Lost—" She echoed all of the loneliness Aisling had ever felt before. Siri began to cry. "She has fallen into shadow."

All of the anger Aisling had felt towards their assailants had gone now. The changelings were much like the homeless people she had seen all of her life: distant, faded shades of humanity, they covered themselves with the pain of losing everything they could have been. Loneliness was their only companion.

Aisling never understood how they could have given up on life. Her anger turned to a kind of contempt. She turned her back on Siri, and sat down next to Eileen's cold form. Dozens of changelings remained frozen in the clearing, too, but she found herself uninterested in helping them.

Siri was sitting down under the pine tree again. Her voice was a plaintive whisper, "We have abandoned hope. One day, I too, will fade away."

Aisling knew that she was also a changeling, and wondered if she would share their fate someday. She looked down at Eileen, and placed a hand on her arm. She felt the burning sting of ice where warmth should have been. Shaking her head, she said, "Just tell me how to reverse this."

Siri tilted her head, intent on the falling snow, but she didn't answer.

Silence came down, blocking out the night.

Aisling remained where she was, unable to move. All motivation had drained away. Though it had stopped falling, the clearing was now covered in snow. Genevieve sat next to the candle, watching it glow. Siri sat outside the clearing under the pine tree, as silent as the snow. For a time, it seemed that all of creation lay suspended in a single moment of clear silence.

Time passed while the world grew colder.

Then a distant song came down out of the windy skies—a faraway melody that lingered over the pines before settling gently in the clearing. Aisling began to make out words as beautiful as a nightingale's song on a spring day. Inside, she felt a powerful force resisting the song, but the simple melody cut through the ice like a ray of sunshine.

Aisling stirred, having just awoken from some kind of dream.

Something fluttered up in the treetops, knocking off the snow clinging to the pine needles and sending a cascade of white powder down onto the earth. The movement was eminently disturbing, like a scream inside a quiet library. Aisling looked up into the flickering candlelight and saw a blue and white ball of light descending. The sphere touched a branch, scattering snow. The icy mist fell away, and the light was replaced by an exquisitely beautiful faerie, borne upon sapphire wings. She hovered for a moment, looking down, and then she landed on the snow. "Why have you summoned a Frost Elemental?"

Trapped in a frozen vision of perfection, Aisling had to fight to wake up. Shaking her head, she ran a hand through her hair and looked at the newcomer. She wore a short black dress in a modern cut with a white belt, blue tights over slender legs, and short black boots. Long blonde hair fell down to her waist. Her blue eyes held a distant, yet friendly expression.

Aisling explained, "I'm not very good at controlling elementals."

The tall faerie laughed. "I'm Trista," she said. With a shrug, the girl's blue wings vanished. Spotting the goblet on the table, she went over to it and began to pour out its contents. "If you want to de-energize an elemental, you need to stop doing whatever you did to bring it to you."

With a wave of her hand, she cleared off the magic tablecloth and folded it up into a small package. "Pleasure, plenty, abundance, cups—and especially water—nourish these kinds of elementals." She looked into Aisling's eyes. "Think of something active or exciting. All of those quiet thoughts are keeping it around."

Aisling closed her eyes and began to think of running through a field of grass before a thunderstorm. Warmth tingled through her body, causing her fingers to twitch. She opened her eyes and all of the snow covering the clearing had vanished.

The changelings lay on the ground, still unconscious, but many of them had disappeared. Aisling wondered if they, too, had fallen into shadow. Siri was still there, and she lay sleeping alone under the pine tree, covered in frost.

Eileen sat up and ran a hand through her hair. "What happened?"

Genevieve stood up, shaking herself awake. She tossed the rugged wand over to Eileen. "She got you with this."

Picking up the wand, Eileen held it in her hands for a moment, probing its magic with her thoughts. "Probably a wand of transformation," she muttered. She tossed it away like a broken toy.

Aisling glanced at the other changelings, feeling a pang of remorse for them. The shock at having seen one of them falling into darkness remained in her thoughts. She stood up. "Let's get away from here," she said.

Trista had trouble containing her excitement. "Come home with me! We can have a party!" Her sapphire wings reappeared, and she flew off into the sky, knocking snow off of the nearest branches.

Turning into balls of light, they followed her home, and spent the night listening to Trista's enchanting songs.

* * *

The sun shone down on the white valley. Just around a bend in the road, they came to a view of Vancouver, which was surrounded by mountains on three sides, and the ocean on the other. Instead of the modern city, Aisling looked down on a medieval town, with a snow topped castle down by the water.

Almost too bright to see in the sunshine, hundreds of little lights sped through the town. In the distance, Aisling caught sight of faeries flying through the air too. A wide variety of wings, shaped like dragonflies, butterflies, bees, or even hummingbirds, could be seen. With a glance at her friend, whose face was frozen into a state of unbelief, Aisling asked, "Ready for this?"

"Okay, I've put up with traveling inside a ball of light, and giving up a nice ride in my car and everything, but—" Genevieve looked down at the medieval town full of flying faeries, "Just where is Vancouver?"

Eileen and Trista laughed.

Eileen pointed down at the castle. "That's Brú na Bodb—the Palace of Bodb Dearg, King Artrach's father. He brought us here from Ireland."

Trista said, "This isn't the same town you've known. Remember, we're in another world—Tír na nÓg, the Land of Eternal Youth."

Genevieve gave Eileen a wry smile, unable to resist taunting her. "Is that why everyone here looks like a little child? Everyone here is so—thin."

Eileen raised her eyebrows. "You're skinny, too." She glanced at Aisling. "Not much larger than a size six, is she?"

Holding up her hands, Aisling said, "Don't get me into this."

102

Eileen put on a sad face, unwilling to stop teasing Genevieve. "I just thought you knew your friend's dress size, that's all."

Aisling felt a need to defend Genevieve. "I'm smaller than her. I'm a size zero."

Trista giggled. "Well of course you're smaller, silly! You're a Faerie, like me!"

Eileen pointed. "There's a good spot, just outside the main gatehouse."

"Why not land inside the castle?" asked Genevieve.

Trista giggled. "Ooh, that would be impolite!"

"Shall we?" Eileen said, and offered her hand to Genevieve, but she took Aisling's hand instead.

Aisling closed her eyes and imagined herself surrounded by a bubble of light. Brightness surrounded her, and she felt herself floating. She opened her eyes and saw that she was inside a tiny sphere of silvery light, touched off with gold. She flew down towards the castle, accompanied by Genevieve, who was surrounded by a ball of pink and white light. They landed on the bridge leading over the moat.

The clippety-clop of galloping horses approached from behind, and Aisling felt herself being pulled out of the road by Genevieve. A dozen centaurs shot past, tossing up clumps of snow as they went. They disappeared inside the castle.

Genevieve was astonished. "Okay Erin, tell me we're not dreaming."

"If we're dreaming, we'd be in a coma!" said Aisling. They had spent more than a month here already, and any reservation she had had about it not being real was gone.

Aisling looked up at the tall battlements, wondering what the faeries would need a fortress for. Eileen had said they were at war with the Shadow People, and she wondered if they could move through solid stone walls. Whatever the reason for its existence, this castle housed the most powerful faeries in the kingdom. Suddenly nervous, she looked at her friend. "We should change our clothes before going in, don't you think?"

Trista began to hum an enchanting melody from the other side of the road. Birds began to gather around, landing on the bridge and swirling around, singing along.

Eileen broke into the song, "Trista, you know the queen doesn't like songs of enchantment out here in front of the castle. It impedes the traffic!"

True enough, there were already several faeries standing by, or sitting on the wall of the bridge, listening. "I can't help it if people like my songs. But I can't stop singing them either!"

Eileen's voice dropped to a whisper, "Trista! The queen is watching!" She pointed towards a square tower rising high above the castle, where a pair of stone gargoyles were perched.

Trista laughed, but relented all the same. Her sapphire blue wings appeared and she took off. Trista called out from high above, "I'll see you later tonight! I can't wait to see what kinds of designs you come up with Aisling! Make me something too!"

As Trista ascended into the sky, they heard another song, but it faded away, leaving a lonely silence behind.

Genevieve watched her go, and whispered, "I really like Trista."

"Me too," said Aisling with a smile.

They turned away from the castle and went into the town, exploring. Shops and taverns and coffee houses filled the streets, with faeries walking, singing, drinking, and dancing while others flew overhead.

Unlike the Milesian world, everyone here wore different kinds of clothes. Some favored renaissance or medieval fashions, some preferred Victorian or gothic clothes, and others wore modern styles. Many faeries wove natural elements into their clothes, like Eileen had, and Aisling stared at them in wonder: Flowers woven into the hair, leaves, vines or even cobwebs made into dresses. Sometimes she noticed something quite silly and outlandish, like large mushroom hats or feathered masks. It felt like one of those parties where no one cared what people did or wore, and the effect was quite exhilarating.

Aisling went into a large fabric shop, running her hand along the different kinds of materials. Ideas flitted through her mind with each touch of silk, every caress of cotton, and with every new color.

A tall, blonde haired fairy approached. She wore a tight black dress, gold bracelets, rings on her fingers and she had little spiral earrings. Black stockings woven into a cobweb pattern adorned her legs. Her black shoes had a sparkle of diamonds on the sides. She had a dreamy, wistful expression on her face. "May I assist you?"

Aisling was too stunned to respond for a moment. She loved the idea of attaching gems to shoes and her mind was whirling with ideas.

The girl ran a hand through her long hair, and the echo of a smile touched her lips. "Well, if you need any assistance, just ask for me. My name is Alaiya, but people like to call me the 'Style Fairy.'"

Aisling found her voice, "Yes, alright."

She continued on, letting her hand slip along each roll of material as she passed, and when she did so, it ignited a flash of ideas in her mind. At the end of one row of silk brocades, Aisling came to a stop.

The scent of lavender, patchouli, musk and just a hint of vanilla brushed against her nose. Something tickled against her skin, and she had the sense that someone was watching her. Turning around, she found a man standing at the end of the row. He was quite tall. He wore black leather pants, boots, a white t-shirt, and a black motorcycle jacket with chains attached to it. Rings were on his fingers, and a large silver cross hung around his neck. But what struck her most of all were his warm brown eyes, framed in the coolness of innocence. They held a dark youthfulness that spilled mystery into the air like a perfume. They were the most beautiful eyes she had ever seen before. A look of wonder and surprise filled his face. When their eyes met, she felt a jolt like an electric shock run through her body.

Before she could say anything, he took several steps backwards, out of the light that fell through the tall windows. He stepped into the shadows, and Aisling's heart skipped a beat. He looked just like one of the Shadow People now.

A flash of light made her blink—then he was gone.

Moments later, Genevieve ran up to her, carrying a bolt of fabric.

"Hey, Aisling! Check out this material! Isn't it—"

The look in Aisling's face stopped her friend short. Aisling stamped her foot in exasperation. "Ooh, I wish they'd stop doing that to me!"

"What happened?"

Aisling bit her lips, not wanting to say anything about the shadow. He was the most gorgeous man she had ever seen, but wasn't he a Shadow Person? This was the first one whose features she had seen. Even in direct light, they had always appeared as a patch of darkness. Turning to her friend, she said, "Nothing. I'll tell you about it later."

Genevieve gave her a suspicious look, apparently trying to decide if she should pursue the matter any further. But the Style Fairy came over again, deciding the question for her.

Alaiya asked, "What materials would you like?"

Aisling frowned. "I don't really have any money."

A familiar voice cut in, "I've got you covered."

Aisling turned around and saw Fáelán standing there, offering a bag to Alaiya. Presumably, it was full of coins. Alaiya smiled and said, "Very well. Just let me know when you're finished."

Aisling had never felt kindness like this before. "Thank you, Fáelán."

"You shouldn't look like a—" he stopped himself from saying the word, "changeling." Fáelán continued without missing a beat, "I mean, you should look good when you meet the king and queen."

Genevieve asked, "Where's Aoife?"

Fáelán looked outside. "She's talking to the Chocolate Fairy."

Aisling raised her eyebrows and she noticed that Genevieve looked equally surprised. Both of them said at once, "Where?"

Several hours later, after getting a facial, manicure, pedicure, and a new hairstyle, they lay on a row of massage tables overlooking the ocean. The warm sun was starting to go down, and a chilly wind blew over the marble floor of the resort they had discovered. Piles of materials lay on a nearby table, along with a set of drawings of Aisling's designs.

"So why not just snap your fingers and make the clothes like you've done so far?" asked Genevieve.

Looking out over the water, Aisling wrinkled her nose. It was like asking a chef why he didn't microwave his creations. "Something is lost when I do it that way." She turned towards her friend, smiling. "Trust me."

Aoife sighed longingly. "I love being a Faerie."

Genevieve chuckled, "You don't have to be a Faerie to enjoy this place."

The tall faerie that was giving her a massage said, "That's true. I'd be happy to show you around town later, if you like."

Genevieve turned her head to face Aisling, grinning. It seemed that every male faerie they encountered wanted a piece of her. Aisling wondered if it was because she was so beautiful or if it was because she was simply a Milesian. For once, she wanted to look into Morrigan's magic mirror and see for herself if Genevieve was the most beautiful girl in the land.

Aisling smiled back, but she couldn't help but wonder why no one here was interested in her. Fáelán had shown some interest, but after they had met, he had become distant. Maybe he was hanging around Aisling to get back at his friend Morrigan, who seemed to be interested in Laigne. She sighed. "I wonder if the spirit from that old oak tree is still around?"

Eileen giggled. "Watch out Brian. If you try to enchant this Milesian girl, you'll find that she has her own set of tricks to contend with."

"Yes, but it would be fascinating to find out what they are, wouldn't it?"

Much to Genevieve's chagrin, Eileen didn't give in. "I'm sorry, but we really do have to attend the party tonight."

The pounding on her back knocked the wind out of her as Aisling talked, "What party?"

Eileen said, "The Yule Ball. It marks the winter solstice."

Aisling's groan was a loud one. "Oh no!"

Aoife asked, "What's wrong?"

Aisling closed her eyes, hoping the massage would remove the stress she was suddenly feeling. "Now I have to redo all of my designs."

Laughter drifted up into the darkening sky.

107

They walked up into the stone courtyard through the gatehouse and looked at the arched stone roof of the tall castle, which had a flight of stone steps leading up to the front door. Faeries were walking in or dropping down from the sky, some of them trailing sparkling lights as they landed.

Tonight, Eileen wore a long elegant sleeveless dress made from white silk embroidered with gold flowers, a white silk brocade corset, black boots, white silk gloves, and she had bluebells and marigolds woven into her long curly blonde hair.

As they reached the stairs, Eileen tripped. She put a hand out on Genevieve's shoulder and raised her foot. The tall laced black boot had a broken heel. "Where's a leprechaun when you need one?" With a wave of her hand, the boot was repaired and she started up the stairs again.

Aisling wore a pair of black leggings, short gray ankle boots, a thin, white cashmere turtleneck sweater, and a black leather belt with a silver buckle. On top of everything she wore a short silver jacket. She had on no jewelry, except her father's ring and a pair of silver dragon earrings.

As she stepped onto the staircase, she hesitated. Doubt twirled in her mind. What if the Queen wouldn't listen to her? What if she refused to teach her advanced magic? For an instant, she thought how audacious her idea was. How could she ever hope to defeat Ith?

Fáelán put his hand on her shoulder. "What's wrong?"

Aisling looked into his dark eyes and whispered, "Oh Fáelán, what if I fail?"

He chuckled. "You can't fail. This is the Land of Dreams."

She wrinkled her face. "What do you mean?"

"Anything is possible here." He dropped his hand. "You should be asking yourself: What would I do if it was impossible to fail?"

She raised her eyebrows as a pair of tiny faeries whisked past. "I've never thought like that."

Fáelán gestured, indicating that she should go up before him. "That is why Milesians never succeed at anything. You need to stop thinking like them Aisling."

Another lingering doubt touched her mind: What if Erin was dead? She wondered how Fáelán would react to the thought, but chose to remain silent.

Genevieve called down from the top of the stone staircase, "You coming?"

As they entered the castle, they were directed to the main hall up a flight of stairs. They entered a long hallway floored in blue veined white marble. Its white walls were completely bare of images, as if dreams were outlawed in this place. A long row of gold candelabras lined the hallway, and several chandeliers hung from the arched wood-paneled roof. To one side, a row of tall windows looked out over the town. None of the candles were lit, and the last drip of sunshine was just now slipping out through the windows. The hallway was full of the Sídhe, and they lined up along both sides of the long hall. At the far end a pair of tall thrones stood under a pair of pillars that were carved into oak trees.

Aisling and her friends stepped over to the side, alongside the rest of the faeries. Across the hall, she spotted Morrigan wearing a tight, ankle length black dress with a belt of rubies, a ruby necklace and long black silk gloves. She wore red shoes that had skull and crossbones designs. The slight smirk on her lips darkened her eyes when she caught sight of Aisling.

A familiar voice whispered, "There you are. I thought you'd never get here."

"Fintan!" Aisling turned towards her friend. "It's good to see you."

A herald's voice rang out, "All hail, King Artrach and Queen Annan!"

The king and queen appeared, and as they went by, everyone bowed.

The queen, who appeared to be no more than nineteen years old, wore a white renaissance gown, embroidered in gold and silver. A purple sash circled her waist, and she had a crown of golden flowers in her hair. She had soft, delicate features like a flower. Her brown eyes reflected the smile that was perpetually on her lips. But her eyes were also constantly searching, as if she was analyzing everything that one did. She held a gold scepter in one hand.

The king wore a purple tunic embroidered with gold Celtic knotwork, white tights and purple velvet shoes. He wore a crown of leaves and flowers. Tall and athletic, he had short, curly blonde hair, strong features, and a short beard. He also appeared to be quite young. Although he was smiling, his eyes were alert. He, too, held a gold scepter.

The queen stopped in front of Genevieve, smiling. "You are a Milesian, aren't you? We have no authority over you, so there's no reason to bow."

Genevieve said, "I'm happy to be here, your majesty, so I bow."

The queen laughed. It was a gentle sound. She turned towards Aisling and her friends. "Who is this?"

Fintan replied, "This is Aoife, and Aisling, Your Majesty. They've only just arrived. They have spent their entire lives among the Milesians."

It was a delicate way of saying that they were changelings.

With polite dismissiveness, the queen moved on, but she stopped when she came to Eileen. "What an exquisite dress!"

Eileen bowed low. "Thank you, your majesty. Aisling made it for me."

The queen's eyes were full of wonder as she turned to Aisling. "So, you are an Enchantress!" The queen gave Aisling a closer look. "I love the jacket, and the rest of your attire."

Aisling returned the smile. "Thank you."

While looking into Aisling's eyes, the queen called over her shoulder, "Now who is the fairest one of all, Morrigan?"

A dark scowl lit up Morrigan's face, but she quickly covered it up with a smile.

King Artrach chastised the queen with a laugh, "Now Annie, you shouldn't tease our subjects."

Queen Annan held Aisling's gaze for a moment longer and then turned away with a bright smile on her lips. "Yes, of course. Forgive me, Morrigan."

As they moved off down the length of the hallway, Aisling and

Genevieve exchanged glances. Genevieve whispered, "I think she likes you, Aisling."

Aisling whispered back, "She was talking about you, Gen."

Standing in front of the throne, the king said, "Welcome all. I hope you enjoy the party!" He clapped his hands and a table, laden with food, appeared. Celtic music played a cheery tune from an upper balcony and people began to dance.

Aisling found herself alone as her friends went about the party, eating, drinking, dancing and playing. Eileen was continually helping Genevieve stay out of trouble. It appeared that every man Genevieve encountered was completely enthralled. With a smirk, Aisling wondered if her friend really wanted Eileen's "help."

Aisling felt someone's presence nearby. She turned to see who it was and found the queen standing next to her. "This must all be terribly exciting and confusing to you."

Aisling ran a nervous hand through dark hair. "Not entirely, your majesty. But I'd like to learn more about magic."

Queen Annan looked into Aisling's eyes, swimming there for a time, but then she looked away at the dancers. "You know, that's the first time someone in your position has asked for assistance."

The haunted expressions of the changelings troubled Aisling's mind. More than anything, the terrible image of Báirbre fading away, into the shadows, disturbed her most of all. "Can you help the other changelings?"

For the first time, the queen stopped smiling. "We've tried to teach them magic in the past, but none of them has ever been able to adapt to our world." She picked up a red apple, indulging in its aroma. "They are beyond hope, I'm afraid."

Aisling picked up a goblet of wine. "I'm not sure I believe that." She refused to accept that the changelings—that she, was beyond hope.

Queen Annan turned towards Aisling. Her smile had returned. "Perhaps you can make me a dress? I'd love to see what kinds of enchantments you weave."

The queen's smile was infectious. Aisling grinned. "Yes, I'd like that."

"Fantastic!" Queen Annan placed the apple back onto the table with the other food. She began to move away, but she paused a moment, whispering a gentle comment over one shoulder, "I'm not entirely sure I believe it either."

Aisling took a sip of the wine, wondering if the queen was going to help her. She began to wander through the hall.

After some time, a voice intruded on her thoughts, "You're under a geis."

Aisling looked up and found King Artrach standing next to her. "Geis?"

"A taboo—a curse," said Artrach. "Did you know?"

"Excuse me your majesty?" Aisling wondered how he could have known so much about her. Genevieve had once mentioned something about a curse.

King Artrach smiled. He picked up a bunch of grapes. "It is an ancient curse: Very old magic. I haven't sensed this kind of thing for centuries."

It had been so long ago, the night where Genevieve was carried away by the Dullahan, but she had forgotten all about the tarot reading. Aisling frowned. "But I'm only nineteen, your majesty."

"I said that the magic was very old, but not the curse."

"How can you know this?"

"I'm the king of the Tuatha Dé Danaan." Artrach laughed. "Work it out."

"What kind of curse?"

"In some ways, this geis is a gift," said Artrach. "The curse also protects you, as long as you do what it requires."

The memory of a shadow, holding a knife to her throat filled her mind—a blade that screamed with the souls of those whose life it had taken. Now she understood why Ith's Lieutenant hadn't killed her. A cold sensation swept down her back, but she wasn't sure if she liked the idea of a curse protecting her. Taking a sip of wine to keep herself from choking on her words, she asked, "Do you know what this curse does?"

"Every geis is unique," said Artrach. "This one commands you always to use magic. So if you ever try to give it up, you will die."

"How can I give up what I don't understand?"

"Magic isn't so difficult, if you learn its secrets."

"How does this curse protect me?"

"While you observe the geis, anyone trying to harm you shall suffer a curse that will utterly ruin all that they love."

Aisling considered his words, looking out a window into the cold night. Little fires were appearing all over the countryside. "My friend, Genevieve told me that this curse is bound to my fate. What could that mean?"

King Artrach was silent for a moment, his eyes looking into a world of distant possibilities. "We are all enslaved by our destiny," he said.

"I'm not sure I like the sound of that," she whispered. Her eyes dropped to the blue tiled floor. "Majesty, did you know my parents?"

The king didn't seem to hear the question. "Tomorrow, I shall ask some of the clan leaders of the Sídhe to begin teaching you about magic."

It felt like a heavy burden had just been lifted from her shoulders. Aisling smiled.

"I have doubt that a Síofra can learn to survive here," he whispered, "but we shall keep an eye on you just the same."

*   *   *

Chapter Seven

Shadows in the Garden

Rose sunshine spilled through the tall arched windows of the castle, scattering faded light across the music room. The room sat high up in the castle, overlooking the ocean. Aisling was playing a wistful song that was like a leaf drifting in the wind—first one way, and then the other. The melody echoed throughout the tall chamber, sending warmth into all of the places that the sunshine could not reach.

Aisling had begun to play again after finding the piano in the music room of the castle. As a child, she had mastered the instrument, hoping to make her foster mother happy, but Erin's mother had a loneliness that Aisling could never satisfy. For a heartbeat, she wondered where Erin was, and whether she longed for her mother. Her music drifted off into near silence.

But she never knew her.

A pang of guilt at having grown up with Erin's parents burned in her heart. Shaking the dark thoughts away, she filled the silence in with music.

Usually, she enjoyed playing Mozart, Beethoven, or sometimes

Chopin, but today, she was inventing her own songs, which were an entirely different sort of music. These songs were a wistful sort of jazz. The Land of Dreams was saturated with inspiration and creativity, and all one had to do was to sit still for a moment and let the mind wander. Everything came easy here. It was as if an angel was always standing by, ready to give you whatever you wanted. Then she remembered Fáelán's enticing words: *What would you do if it was impossible to fail?*

Rapid footsteps echoed outside in the hallway as someone approached. Aisling continued to play, but she glanced up at the marble entryway as a woman entered. Tall, with straight blonde hair, wearing white pants, brown thigh boots, and a coffee-colored leather jacket, she strode into the room with a mischievous smile on her lips.

Aisling, too engrossed in her song to say hello, simply smiled.

The woman paused a moment, and then paced back and forth in the room in a kind of dance as Aisling played. The music of the piano drifted one way, and then another, across the room.

When Aisling stopped, the tall woman smiled. "I'm Rosheen. You play quite beautifully." Her sharp eyes glanced around the room, as a gust of wind blew through the chandeliers. "I see that you've attracted an Air Elemental."

Aisling began a new song. "Yes, they sometimes come in here while I'm playing," she said. "I'm Aisling."

"I'm the leader of the Luchtaine clan," said Rosheen, "from Capall Bán, a Sídhe down by Austin."

Aisling smiled, and noticed another faerie that had appeared, sitting up on top of the piano. She was all white, with blonde hair and pale, translucent wings. She had silver fingernails and a sharp, elegant face. A look of roguish mischief shone out of her eyes. She held a glass of milk in her hand.

Aisling teased the faerie: "You want some cookies with that?" Then she dropped her head, closed her eyes and went into a rolling, teasing, taunting melody. When she opened her eyes again, the little faerie was gone.

116

Rosheen laughed. "Sometimes, it can be dangerous to tease faeries, especially that faerie, whose name is Kylie."

Since Aisling didn't respond, Rosheen changed the subject. "Are you staying here at the castle?"

For some reason, the king had offered to let them stay in the fortress. Nodding, Aisling said, "Yes. My friends and I have been here for about two months now."

Rosheen walked over to the piano and placed a hand on it, feeling the music thrum through her fingertips. "How did you manage that?" she asked. "Brú na Bodb is no place for a Síofra."

Aisling wondered why the faeries thought so little of the changelings. "Oh, I made a dress for the queen," she said. "She liked it so much that she made me her dressmaker."

"Well, looking at your attire, I can see why Annie asked you to design dresses for her," said Rosheen. "You're quite lovely."

Today, Aisling wore a pair of black tights, a short, pleated red skirt in three layers, a white blouse, a black ribbon belt tied into a bow around her waist, a light brown jacket and short suede brown boots. Her hair fell loosely about her shoulders, but it didn't cover the smile she gave Rosheen. "Annie?"

Rosheen's laughter had a slight edge to it. "Everyone calls her, 'Gentle Annie.' Didn't you know?"

Aisling shook her head. Musing aloud, she said, "You know, in the Milesian world, there's a war against beauty. Attractive people are always the brunt of cruel jokes. They're never taken seriously, either. But here, everyone is beautiful."

Reading her thoughts, Rosheen asked, "Can't get a date?"

Aisling felt her face burning and it nearly disrupted her playing. "My friend, Genevieve never seems to have any trouble."

Rosheen laughed. "She's that pretty Milesian girl hanging around court?"

"Yes," said Aisling. She let out a loud sigh. "It's just that sometimes, I wish people didn't treat me like I have leprosy."

"Beware of the tyranny of jealousy," said Rosheen. "There was a girl, Macha, who was destroyed by her lusts for men. She used to lure them into the forest for trysts, and then she bound them to her will. Her sister, Morrigan is a lot like her."

Aisling wrinkled her nose. "Yes, I've met her. She's most unkind."

Rosheen laughed. "Anyway, the king has asked me to teach you about magic," she said. "Ooh, it's so exhilarating, summoning wind elementals to make you swift!"

Aisling frowned. "I haven't learned much so far. Lasarina taught me how to conjure up things besides elementals, and Irial says I have talent in enchantment, but I haven't been able to learn much else."

"As a Síofra, you shouldn't expect too much," said Rosheen. "But give it time. You never know."

The queen had said that changelings were nearly incapable of learning magic, but the king had said that if she gave up trying, the geis would cause her death. Feeling like a caged bird, Aisling didn't answer.

Rosheen whirled around and away. As she went out the door, she said, "I'll take you riding in my chariot sometime, if you like. That's the best way to hear them."

"Who?"

"The spirits on the wind," she called from the hallway.

Aisling watched her go out the door. "As long as there isn't any whispering," she muttered. Ever since the winter festival, she, gladly, hadn't seen or heard any of the Shadow People.

Another kind of marching sound, coming from the hallway, announced the arrival of Marcus. The leader of the Iucharba clan and Slieve Críonnacht—a Sídhe near Flagstaff, Marcus was one of her mentors. He strode into the room, wearing a short tunic, a breastplate and sandals. He had short black hair, and a thin mustache that swept down to a small goatee. Most of the snow had melted, but she wondered why he wasn't cold.

He does have nice legs, though.

Marcus entered the room, went over to the balcony and opened the bay doors. His only words were: "Come with me."

Aisling stopped playing the piano, wondering what he wanted to show her. Getting up, she went outside onto the stone balcony and peered down into the gardens below. Unfurling golden wings, he jumped off the balcony. She shrugged, opened her own silver-white wings, and dove off after him.

The sensation of falling would have been frightening if she had not done it so often. Almost every day, she practiced flying with Eileen, Trista or Aoife while Genevieve looked on from one of the towers. Today, she had to let herself fall quickly to catch up with Marcus, and so she kept her wings close together. He was plunging towards a bright light that she had never seen before. In the few seconds it took to fall towards it, she could see that it was some kind of pillar with a flame burning from its top. At the last second, she spread out her wings to break her fall and landed quietly on the ground next to Marcus.

They were in a rose garden, which was covered with frost. They stood on the white marble floor of a circular dais, with marble paths radiating out in every direction, through a garden of rose bushes. Trellises stood at the entrance to every path, and sycamore trees lined the way. In the center of the courtyard stood a pillar, which was made of red-veined black marble. The sharp odor of natural gas lightly simmered in the air, and it intermingled with the perfume from a few roses that bloomed in the winter. Aisling noticed that more roses bloomed closer to the pillar of fire.

Marcus raised his arm, sweeping it out in a grand gesture. "This is called the 'Bladhm Shíoraí,' the Eternal Flame. It has burned here for centuries. Today is the festival of Imbolc, where we celebrate the flame from which all inspiration, all poetry, all life is born."

Aisling had an urge to sit down. So far, she was unable to control fire elementals, though she could summon them. She kept silent.

Marcus put his hands on his hips. "Aisling, I haven't been able to teach you sorcery at all, but you do have talent with fire."

"It doesn't feel like it," she grumbled. She looked away into the garden, resting her eyes on a frosty rose. "To tell the truth, I'm afraid of what I might do with such power."

"Release yourself from your feelings. Loose and let go," he said. "Emptiness is where you need to come from if you want magic to work."

How fortunate the man with none.

Sifu Yuen had once spoken these words, but she had never understood them. Still, she had sensed that there was a silent power to be had in nothingness, but what this power could be had always been elusive to her. "I don't understand."

"Cleansing is the first step to learning magic," said Marcus. "You have to purify yourself, get rid of what you don't want in order to get what you do want. Magic doesn't flow easily into a cluttered, crowded state of mind. Magic is transmitted perfectly through emptiness."

Aisling frowned. "But how do I keep elementals from taking control of me?"

Not listening to her question, Marcus asked, "What do you sense when you look into the fire?"

Aisling ran a hand through her hair, and gazed into the flames, which spouted up from a gold censer at the top of the pillar. White fire seared a hole in the fading daylight. After concentrating for a time, she could hear the distinct sounds of whispering mixed in with the crackling flames. She took a step back. "Shadows," she said, "whispering shadows."

Marcus tilted his head slightly, as if he was trying to understand her words. "Yes, they are always there, just beneath the surface." He walked around the flame, and looked up into it. The light danced across his face, and as the sun went down, the clearing in the center of the rose garden also lit up with flickering reflections thrown out by the flames. "They seem to have an affinity for Fire Elementals."

Crackling flames whispered down from the high pillar, splashing the garden with a crowd of dark reflections. Aisling felt them watching, from inside the light. "What do they want?"

He shook his head and then grew still. Closing his eyes, he raised a finger, testing the direction of the wind. "They are taunting, mocking, jeering at us. Can't you hear it?"

Aisling began to circle the pillar. "Why have you brought me here, Marcus?"

"You're one of the most sensitive elemental summoners I've ever encountered. I need to know—" He turned his searching eyes into the fire. "Do you think they live inside the flames?"

Aisling looked into the flame, listening. They did, indeed, taunt her from the flames, but there was one other word, chanted over and over again: Freedom. Taking another step back, she shook her head. "I don't know, Marcus."

Perhaps he was influenced by the elementals around the fire. This was the first time she had seen him angry. "Aisling, try to concentrate. We're fighting a war!"

Like a warm summer breeze, she could feel a Fire Elemental seeping into her skin. Sensual and exhilarating at once, it tingled against her skin like a warm caress that threatened to become a firestorm. Aisling had to force herself not to shout. "Don't you think I know that? My parents were killed by the Shadow People, and my sister—"

Aisling didn't continue. Erin wasn't her real sibling, but Aisling had started thinking of her like a sister anyway.

Marcus stopped circling the pillar that supported the Eternal Flame and dropped his gaze into the frozen rose garden. He murmured, as if thinking aloud, "Fire Elementals are attached to sunshine, summer, warfare, fires, light, energy, passion, aggression, sex, confrontations and ambition."

Aisling felt her self-control begin to slip away, like flames spreading across dry grass. Fighting off an urge to walk up and kiss him, a question came into her mind. "So if I or my environment exhibits these traits, it will bring a fire elemental into existence?"

Marcus walked over to a rose bush, cupping a barren stem in his hands. A new rose appeared, growing rapidly until it was in full bloom. He didn't pluck the flower, but dropped his hand away. "Not always. But when one of these types of elementals does appear, it will enhance your magnetism, strength, speed, and vigor. But you have to be careful not to let it gain too much influence over you. Before you know it, you may find yourself hot tempered, angry, or aggressive."

Memories of elementals, summoned out of nowhere, forcing her to kill out of anger, or to freeze others to death, filled her imagination. Exasperated, she said, "That's what I've been trying to tell you. I can't control them!"

Marcus smirked, as if he didn't believe her. "Fire Elementals can make you magnetic, sexy. Even now, I can see that you're enjoying its power. These spirits are a fine way to become the center of attention."

For an instant, Aisling wondered if Genevieve had a Fire Elemental attached to her psyche. Shaking her head, she said, "I don't want that kind of attention."

"The Shadow People may have something to do with your lack of control," he prompted. "Do you always hear them around elementals?"

Memories of her fight at the Shaolin temple returned. She had almost killed Luo. Shadows had whispered to him there, but did they also whisper to her? "I don't know." She crossed her arms, not wanting to think about it. "I can't help you Marcus."

He looked at her for a time, and then, without another word, unfurled his wings and took off, flying over the battlements of the castle and out into the city.

* * *

Although the idea of listening to the shadows while they whispered from the Eternal Flame made her want to go away, there was something enticing about being able to listen to the Shadow People without actually meeting them. So Aisling remained standing in a garden full of frosty roses, next to the pillar, looking into the fire.

Inhaling the perfume surrounding her, she hoped to use the few roses blooming in the winter garden to temper the fear that came from listening to the shadows, but there was something else in the air too. A familiar aroma of lavender, patchouli, musk and vanilla, she remembered it from the day she had arrived at the castle, when she was looking at fabric.

A cool draft of air brushed against her hair, knocking it into her eyes, and she could feel that someone was standing behind her, watching. Aisling turned around, while brushing the hair out of her face and she found herself looking into a pair of warm brown eyes, full of curiosity this time. She had nearly forgotten him, but he remained just as he was. There was a hint of fresh leather that mixed with his cologne. He stood there, just out of the light, smirking.

She wasn't sure if it was from fear, surprise, or something else, but Aisling's heart skipped a beat. Such a gorgeous man he was, but there was something else around him, too: a sense of danger, lurking there, under the surface. She was wondering if he really was one of the Shadow People when he spoke. His voice was deep, and smooth like silk falling across cool skin.

"Hello."

Unsure how to react, she said, "Get out of my way."

He raised his eyebrows. "Are you going somewhere?"

"No—yes." She took a step forward. "I was just about to—" but she didn't finish. His beautiful brown eyes compelled her into silence.

The Eternal Flame burning up on top of the pillar flared, and the sudden sound made her jump. The light splashed into his face, and she could see a trace of concern there for a moment, but he stepped back into the darkness by a trellis overgrown with climbing roses. When he moved out of the light, he looked just like one of the Shadow People again. She could feel her heart beating out a warning.

He reached up to touch a rose, and a rich voice came out of the darkness that surrounded him. "It's amazing to see so many roses blooming so late in the winter. Such a beautiful thing, a rose, but they fade away so quickly, don't you think?"

Doubt surrounded her. Who was this man, standing before her? She squinted, hoping to see him better, and asked, "What do you want?"

He took a step forward, but stopped just short of the light. "Tell me your name."

"What?" Aisling looked around the clearing as if she expected a dozen Shadow People to step out from behind the rose bushes and attack her. But she had heard their whispers all of her life, and it was only until recently that they had become hostile. None of them had ever wanted to talk to her though.

"Your name—" This time, more than curiosity slipped out of his voice. "You don't mind telling me, do you?"

Her only answer was silence.

"My name is Keir." His hand crept up to the silver cross around his neck. He rubbed it between his fingers. "I have come to warn you."

Like a sigh exhaled by the world, a long gust of wind blew over the garden, causing the Eternal Flame to dance wildly. Aisling's hair blew into her face again. She brought up her hand to brush it away, but remained silent.

Undeterred by her silence, he continued. "Ith, the Lord of Shadows, is watching you. He will ask you to become one of his followers, but you should reject him."

The idea of going along with anything related to the shadows was a crazy one. Forgetting her reticence, she asked, "Why would I ever want to follow him?"

Although she could hardly see his face now, she could tell that he was smiling. "He can be very—persuasive."

Aisling wondered what the lord of shadows did to persuade people.

Keir stepped back into the light, and his warm eyes sparkled with eternal fire. "There's something else: He may offer you a gift. It would be unwise to reject it."

Aisling crossed her arms. "Why should I trust a shadow like you?"

His reply was a mystery. "We are all shadows, deep down inside."

Aisling went over to one of the blooming rose bushes and plucked a flower. The tip of her nose touched the rose, and the ice clinging to its

124

surface chilled her skin.   Inhaling its cold aroma, she hoped to obscure his scent, but his scent was the stronger. She looked up, rather coyly, and asked, "Why are you telling me this?"

For the first time, he hesitated. Keir looked away from her eyes, at the garden. Most of the snow had melted, but there were a few flowers still. His voice was a whisper, "I don't know, really."

Their eyes met again. Warmth and electricity flared between them, and Aisling had to catch her breath. All she could do was to listen to her beating heart over the sound of the Eternal Flame.

Another gust of wind blew over the garden, and Keir turned his head away. His beautiful eyes swept over the garden, where the final rays of daylight washed away. The wind died down, leaving only the crackling of the fire.

His voice became cold. "He is coming."

A tiny flash of light; and he was gone.

Into the silence, she whispered, "Aisling. My name is Aisling."

The fire laughed at the darkness. She remained there for a time, listening to the wind and to the fire, burning, thinking about Fire Elementals and shadows. Darkness began to surround her as the sun finally went down, but it was held back by the Eternal Flame, which illuminated the entire platform in pure white brilliance. Aisling wondered about the shadows inside the flame, whispering about freedom.

Footsteps, and something else, echoed down one of the paths. It was a metallic sound, as something touched the ground, between the steps.

Click... click... click... click...

The steps marched slowly forward, and the clicking sound came on too.

Click... click... click... click...

Just outside the firelight, she caught sight of a man, walking. He was using a silver-tipped cane, and this was the source of the metallic sound. He was completely covered in the shadows, but Aisling recognized the short Victorian top hat that he was wearing.

Click… click… click… click…

As he came into view, she could see that he wore a nineteenth century suit. And the scent of lotus flowers, exotic woods, mandarin, dark violet and musk surrounded him. The aroma was enticing. He moved with the steady grace of a man that had known authority all of his life.

Click… click… click… click…

As he approached, Aisling felt her resentment fading away. It was replaced with simple curiosity. He came to a stop just outside of the firelight. For a moment, they stood there, looking at one another.

He glanced up into the fire, but the light didn't touch his face. "Ah yes, the Eternal Flame." He had a high English accent when he spoke, and his voice rang with authority. "It is the source of life and inspiration for those who still dare to dream."

Aisling wrinkled her nose. "You don't believe in dreams."

"Ah, but I do. 'Follow your dreams' is my motto." He placed his silver-tipped cane in front of him with a click. "Do whatever you want, think whatever you like, follow all of your dreams, goals, ambitions and desires."

She remained silent.

He introduced himself. "My name is Ith."

Wishing she had her sword, she toyed with the idea of conjuring one up, but restrained herself. She remembered how her sword had passed through the shadow in her parent's house. "What do you want with me?"

A cool wind brought the salty scent of the ocean to the roses still blooming in the garden. "Follow me. I will teach you what true magic is all about. My magic is more powerful than anything you can learn here in the Land of Dreams."

Fighting off a desire to flirt with him, Aisling began to circle the pillar, keeping the Eternal Flame between them. She smiled, not bothering to keep the amusement out of her voice. "No, I don't think so."

The Hat Man turned around, and walked around the edge of the light, circling the pillar of fire too, in the opposite direction. "Do you believe in freedom, Aisling?"

Her heart jumped when she heard the Hat Man use her name, but she tried not to show her surprise. "Of course I do."

They were now both walking around the pillar of fire. Ith sighed. "They say that man is born free, but everywhere he is in chains." The metallic click of his cane was like a metronome. "What would you say if I told you that Queen Annan—" he paused and it sounded like he was smiling now, "—Gentle Annie, is the greatest obstacle to freedom the world has ever known?"

"I'd say that you were a liar."

Ith chuckled. "How long have you been here? How long have you known the queen?"

Aisling didn't answer. She continued walking around the pillar, keeping him on the other side of the fire.

Ith continued in a rich, authoritative voice: "I say, 'Live your life with pride.' She says, 'Live a life of mediocrity.' I believe in a life full of passion, while Gentle Annie will only offer you a life of escape. I say, 'Think and do whatever you want.' She says, 'Guard your thoughts and actions.' Here, in the land of dreams, the queen will only permit you to live a life of frivolity and indifference. Only pride, only passion, will lead you to freedom."

Aisling tilted her head, wondering if what he said was true. She came to a stop, and he stopped too.

Ith whispered, "Freedom is the greatest thing there is. Follow your dreams! Do not repress them, as the queen would have you do. To follow the queen is to live as a slave."

Not entirely sure how to respond, Aisling stood there, considering his words. What he offered was enticing. Was she to choose a dark world of freedom or a light world of repression? Then the image of her parents, lying dead, returned. In the end, she didn't care about Ith's words. He had killed her parents. That was all that mattered now. "What are you doing here?"

Ith continued watching her for a moment, as if he was trying to guess her thoughts. Then he said, "Helping a few friends that got too close to the fire."

He picked up his cane and pointed it at the Eternal Flame. The whispering inside the fire grew louder. There was a flash. A stream of darkness came out of the fire, pooling into a dark cloud and then forming into a tall woman. Tangled blonde hair fell down over her shoulders, and she had a lost expression. It was as if all the sorrow in the world had pooled there.

Ith said, "Welcome back, Maire."

The woman smiled slightly. She looked at Aisling, and whispered, "Does this one need instruction in the arts of love, master?"

Ith didn't respond, intent on another cloud of darkness that he had drawn out of the fire. It quickly formed into a tall man, bare-chested and muscular, with short blonde hair. He gave Ith a bow and stepped to the side.

Aisling thought of how Fire Elementals were drawn to thoughts of passion and she wondered if this same passion had drawn the Shadow People into the Eternal Flame.

She caught him staring at her, as if he were sizing up an enemy. She returned his gaze, calmly, wishing that she had a sword that could work against the shadows.

Ith whispered, "Hello, Sean."

At the sound of his greeting, Sean looked away from Aisling's eyes.

Ith twirled his cane and two more black clouds slipped out of the fire.

The first cloud materialized into a thin woman, with dark hair, wearing a red dress. She had an imperious expression in her face, and held a bow in her hand. Ith said, "Welcome Canlyn, it is good to see you again."

The second cloud became a tall man wearing a tuxedo, with short blonde hair. His face was passive, as if all life had been drained out of him. Ith raised his cane to the tip of his hat. "Bryce, I have a task for you and my lieutenant."

Aisling waited for Ith to say what it was, but he returned his attention to the fire, where two more funnels of smoke were now whirling around the pillar. Ith raised his cane over his head and they swept into pillars of smoke. Gradually, the smoke solidified into two women. One wore a black half shirt, black pants with a silver chain, and open toed shoes. She had long straight black hair. She raised her hands over her head, stretching, while the other woman appeared out of the dark smoke. She had brown hair, a delicate face, and an elegant, earthy dress with leaves and vines woven into it.

After they had appeared, Ith placed his cane down onto the marble. "Rhona, Ceridwen. I have need of you two also." He reached into his pocket and withdrew a small key on a silver chain, and he handed it to Ceridwen. The key faded into shadowy darkness when she touched it.

For an instant longer, each one appeared as a normal person, but then the light in their faces seemed to fade away into shadow. The Eternal Flame illuminated their faces for one moment, and then it was gone, as they became shadows. Rhona and Sean both had red glowing eyes now.

Unsure of how to react to so many Shadow People appearing in her midst, Aisling simply watched while the Hat Man finished drawing them out of the fire.

Ith stood there for a moment longer, whispering instructions to them. He waved his cane and then one by one, each of the Shadow People moved away into the dusky garden until Aisling couldn't see them anymore.

Aisling wondered what she should have done, but the Shadow People were already free of the fire. They ignored her, and she thought it best to return the favor for now. She realized that she had been gripping her fists tightly.

She forced herself to relax. Not knowing how to harm the Shadow People was infuriating. She looked at Ith defiantly and in a half-threatening tone asked, "What's to stop me from telling the queen about your friends here?"

Ith chuckled. "I believe you've met my Lieutenant—" He didn't finish.

The memory of a cold knife against her throat still lingered. "They're watching me," she thought.

Ith waved his hand and the Eternal Flame flared brighter for a second, and then a molten ball of fire appeared in his hand. He held his other hand over it, as if he was trying to contain its fury. At last, the ball cooled, and the red glow went out, leaving a black sphere of crystal in his hand, no larger than a few inches in diameter. As the light died down, she could see his eyes flash red. "My offer shall remain open— for now."

The Hat Man placed the sphere on the ground and turned to leave.

Aisling gestured towards the black sphere. "What is it?"

Even though he was made from shadows, she could tell he had turned. He looked over his shoulder. His red eyes reflected the fire of the Eternal Flame as he whispered, "Passion."

The light flared brighter as Ith walked out of the garden. She watched him leave, doubt shifting her thoughts around, until all she could hear was the sound of his cane.

Click... click... click... click...

Smoke climbed up from the black sphere. Aisling considered leaving it where it lay, but curiosity overcame her. She stepped around the pillar of fire, which now burned clean, without any whispering voices. She kneeled down next to the sphere. Carefully, she picked it up and looked into its glassy surface.

It was a semi-transparent ball of obsidian. When she touched it, a cool tingling sensation washed up her fingers, up her arm and through her body until it grew into a ruby fire inside. Strength, courage, and intense desire purred in her heart. A desire to create, a desire to exceed, a desire to dream; each held its own kind of fascination within her mind.

She picked it up, and watched black smoke evaporate from it. She looked through its murky surface and turned it around in her hand until she found a red translucence that shone only in one direction. The light would only appear when holding the sphere at a certain angle, and she experimented with it until she was sure of this.

Aisling put the obsidian sphere into the pocket of her jacket. Unfurling her wings, she flew up into the castle, landing on the balcony of the music room. As she stepped inside, she wondered if Ith truly was her enemy.

* * *

The sunlight had gone, and the room was now covered in cool darkness. Aisling waved her hand and all of the candles in the room ignited, spreading flickering light into the shadows.

Aisling walked over to the piano, running a hand along its surface. Melodies came into her mind, like hidden treasures given up by the ocean, washing up onto a beach. The globe of passion in her pocket tickled her imagination, and she could hear new songs rising up into her mind.

Something else tickled her, right on the nose. Chocolate and walnuts! The sweet aroma was beguiling. She looked over at a low table in front of a high backed couch and there was a warm plate of chocolate chip cookies sitting there, all alone.

Aisling raised her eyebrows and looked around the room. There was no evidence that anyone had been there. It was strange that someone would have come in and left a plate of freshly baked cookies here. She walked over and knelt down on the floor in front of the cookies, wondering if her friends had come in looking for her earlier. A warm thought occurred to her: "Perhaps Genevieve came by to give these to me?" Smiling, she picked one up and took a bite. Warm, gooey chocolate, walnuts and just a hint of vanilla, tingled against her tongue. The chocolate chip cookie was the best she had ever tasted.

A bucket of ice cold milk materialized above her and emptied itself onto her head. After a sharp intake of breath, she screamed. Aisling closed her eyes as the milk ran all over her outfit, ruining it. After the downpour had stopped, she wiped her eyes with both hands, pushed the milk soaked hair out of her face and looked around furiously.

Hysterical giggling filled the room. Aisling saw the white faerie sitting on the piano again, laughing. The mischievous faerie laughed so hard that she fell off of the piano and onto the floor. Aisling picked up a cookie, which miraculously hadn't been touched by the cold milk, and threw it at her.

The faerie, whose merry eyes were devouring Aisling's indignation, ducked the sweet projectile. The cookie struck the far wall with a thump.

Then the little faerie vanished from the room, giggling.

Aisling's anger spilled out onto the floor. "Ooooh!"

She sat there, bathed in icy milk, shivering. Aisling murmured to herself, "I'm going to get her back if it's the last—"

The door opened, and in walked the queen, followed by a trio of maidens, and Morrigan. Aisling was too embarrassed to speak, but they didn't notice her sitting on the floor, shivering, in the middle of a large puddle of milk.

As they came in, a Faerie that Aisling did not recognize said, "I don't understand why you banned Trista from attending the party tonight, your majesty. She was only singing in the garden, and her songs are so lovely."

What could possibly be wrong with a Faerie singing? Aisling wondered if Ith had been right about the queen. But he wasn't exactly trustworthy, was he? She wondered why Ith had taken the trouble to try to recruit her to his side. "Ith wants something from me," she thought.

Queen Annan walked over to the balcony, followed by the others. She looked down into the gardens. Aisling wondered if she was looking at the roses illuminated by the Eternal Flame, or if she noticed the Shadow People there. "Trista indulges in her passions too much," she said. "Pride is a deadly sin."

Aisling noticed a trace of something in the queen's expression—part resentment, part determination. But it fell away completely as she turned away from the balcony.

The queen opened her mouth to speak and then noticed Aisling sitting there, covered in cold milk.

Aisling wanted to slide through the floor, and for a moment, she wondered why she hadn't used magic to escape her predicament. Before she could make up her mind, the queen said, "What on earth are you doing down there, Aisling?"

As always, the smile in the queen's eyes was infectious, and Aisling found herself smiling back meekly. "I was—"

Morrigan was having difficulty containing her glee. "Changelings have always behaved so—erratically, haven't they, your majesty?"

Queen Annan glanced at Morrigan and said offhandedly, "Yes. Sometimes I wonder why I took the creature in, but she does make such beautiful clothes, don't you think?"

Aisling didn't bother to explain what had happened, preferring to remain where she was, swimming in shame.

Queen Annan giggled and the smile reappeared. She went out the door, saying over her shoulder, "Well then, if you want to come to the festival tonight, Aisling, you had better change."

Morrigan smiled coyly. "Yes, you wouldn't want to miss the Guardian of the Well of Living Water—" she looked down at the milky mess on the floor, "— and the gift of wisdom."

Aisling watched them leave, feeling sorrier for Trista than for herself.

*   *   *

Chapter Eight

The Mirror of Eternity

Tall red leather boots with buckles down the sides stood on the table next to dozens of other shoes. With a sense of awe, Aisling reached out, hesitating slightly, as if the glorious boots would disappear if she touched them. She picked one up and glanced over at Genevieve, raising her eyebrows.

Her friend was looking through several pairs of exquisitely designed shoes, but when she looked up, she nearly dropped the one in her hand. "Wow!"

"Hey there!" The leprechaun was sitting behind the worktable, working away obsessively on another shoe, but now he had stopped. He was pointing a stubby finger at Genevieve. "You break it, you buy it!"

Genevieve giggled. "I can't break shoes by dropping them."

The little leprechaun glared up at her, as if he was unaccustomed to dissent. "You could, especially if you drop it from way up there." He shook his head, muttering to himself, "Really, I don't know how such tall people like you keep from breaking things all the time."

Genevieve put the shoe down on the table, still smiling. "So, you're saying that you can't make durable shoes?" She shrugged. "It doesn't look like poor workmanship."

The leprechaun had had enough. He stood up angrily. "Get out!"

Aisling had been laughing, but now she stopped. "Wait! I wanted to buy—"

"You too! Take your Milesian friends and get out of my shop!" The leprechaun was now hefting a small mallet, gesturing with it as he spoke. "Poor quality indeed!"

Trista looked up from a wall rack full of shoes. "I'm not a Milesian."

"Everybody out!" The leprechaun hustled them outside, and then slammed the doors of his shop behind them.

Eileen flew down into the street. Blowing frost up into the air, she landed in front of them. Her blonde hair fell wildly around her shoulders, having been blown around in the wind. She looked at the trio standing outside the shoe shop. "It isn't usually this cold in February. Did you summon one of your Frost Elementals again, Aisling?"

Crossing her arms, Aisling said, "Not that I know of."

Eileen looked at the closed shoe store and laughed. "Aisling, you had better control your friend here, or all of the shops will be closed before we can do any shopping."

Aisling gave her friend a dirty look. "Gen, I wanted to buy those boots!"

"Why not just make your own?" asked Genevieve.

Eileen sighed, and explained, "Certainly, you can't copy another fa-erie's designs. We have laws you know."

Genevieve crossed her arms. "So change it a little bit."

Aisling shook her head. "Oh, never mind."

Aisling glanced down the street of the town, considering what shop to visit next.

Vancouver did, indeed look different with medieval style buildings lining the streets. Dozens of restaurants, pubs, coffee houses and shops full of curious faeries going in and out of them held her gaze. The Sídhe arrived inside tiny globes of light, by flying down from the clear blue skies overhead, or sometimes they just appeared out of nowhere in a flash of light.

There were more trees, flowers and plants than there were buildings, however, and the entire town looked like an intricate garden, covered in frost. She stood next to a tea garden, and the scents of peppermint, chamomile, green tea, lemon grass, and jasmine floated out of a shop that was built out of a grove of trees. A petite Asian girl walked out of the tea house, transformed into a red fox and ran off down the street.

For a moment, Aisling felt someone watching her. She glanced around, but didn't see anyone looking at her.

Genevieve watched the Fox Fairy disappear behind a tree. "Hey, aren't Leprechauns supposed to have pots of gold around?"

The odd feeling forgotten, Aisling said, "I have money, Gen." She hefted a purse full of gold and silver coins hanging from her belt, gratefully given to her by the queen for creating another beautiful dress.

Genevieve looked up and down the street. "You think they sell jeans here?"

Aisling shrugged. "Yeah, probably."

Genevieve frowned. "I wonder if they'll have anything in my size? Everyone here is so . . . petite."

Aisling sighed. "Gen, I know you're tall, but I can always use magic to adjust the clothes you acquire."

"Oh. I hadn't thought of that." Genevieve grinned. "I do so love it here!"

"Indeed? Just last night you were complaining about all the candles."

"It's not my fault they've never heard of electricity here."

"We have electricity." Eileen pointed across the street.

A willowy fairy with blonde hair stood in front of a small cart. She wore metallic blue pants, a white peasant blouse, a stormy colored sash and white heels. Dozens of small spheres lay inside a quartz bowl on the table. Little jolts of blue electricity shot up from them.

They crossed the street and Aisling brought her hand up to hover over one of the spheres. A slight hum came from it, like a purring kitten. Carefully, she touched it. Her finger tingled and a little blue tongue of electricity shot up into the air.

Long hair blew across the tall fairy's face. Not bothering to move it out of her eyes, she said, "They're Electric Elementals, contained inside a crystal matrix." She picked one up and held it out, palm up. "Just place this in a room and it will give you all the power you need for whatever devices you have."

Genevieve murmured, "All I need now is a computer with an internet connection."

"Computers?" The Electricity Fairy giggled. "Milesians have such strange ways to communicate."

Genevieve crossed her arms, but before she could say anything, Aisling said, "We'll take two."

The electric fairy smiled. "Two shillings apiece."

Aisling placed the silver coins in the Electricity Fairy's hand. Tilting her head slightly, she asked, "How do you catch them?"

Pouting, the Electricity Fairy said, "They are not *caught*. They come to me, during thunderstorms."

Aisling was reminded of how elementals came to her. It seemed to happen all the time, but she had never imagined trying to contain one inside a glass ball. Before she could ask another question, a fairy darted by, followed by a dozen laughing children, some of them carrying ice cream cones.

The fairy wore a chocolate-covered bodice over a white and pink striped peasant blouse and skirt, striped tights, and strawberry-colored shoes. A tiny top hat perched on her head, and her brightly colored wings shimmered in the sunlight.

The children—if they could be called that—were dozens of tiny fairies flitting through the streets, a blur of colors and laughter. Aisling blinked; sometimes it was hard to tell which was which. They shouted and giggled, waving arms and ice cream cones, all calling for the fairy to stop as she sped past them, top hat wobbling and wings sparkling.

Aisling was wondering why they were eating ice cream in February when she heard Eileen exclaim, "Ooh, the Ice Cream Fairy! I'll catch up with you later." Then, she flew off down the street, scattering frost in her wake.

Genevieve watched Eileen go. "It's too cold to eat ice cream, don't you think?"

Trista said, "I'm not cold."

Trista started to hum a song, and it was deliriously enchanting. While she hummed, the elementals in the cart started sparking and flashing.

Aisling thanked the Electricity Fairy and they went down the street.

After walking for a few blocks, she shook the hypnotic melody out of her head and said, "So Trista, how are you going to deal with the queen? She seems to have it in for you."

Trista laughed. "I'm not going to do anything. I haven't done anything wrong."

Aisling put her hands inside her fur jacket, feeling the obsidian sphere there. She had gotten into the habit of keeping it with her wherever she went. Absentmindedly, she grasped it with her left hand and felt a wave of inspiration rushing into her mind. A gust of wind knocked some of the snow out of the trees, spreading a fine white mist over the street. She could see a sparkling white dress, tied with light blue ribbons. She clutched the sphere tightly in her hand. "I heard her say that you're too . . . passionate."

"What a silly idea!" Again, Trista laughed. "Come on! I want to show you something."

Trista offered a hand, and Aisling pulled her hand out of her pocket. Trista looked down at the black stone. "What's this?"

Aisling looked down, realizing that she was still holding the stone. Like a gentle breath over an icy lake, whispers came from the sphere. "Oh, it's...it's nothing, I—"

A warm voice interrupted. "You mind if I ask you a question?"

Aisling looked up and saw that Marcus was standing there, next to another one of the Sídhe, who had Genevieve's hand in his. He was tall, blonde and gorgeous. He wore a modern white suit, and had a red scarf around his neck.

Genevieve seemed too entranced to respond, but she finally did so. "Okay."

The faerie released her hand. "Do you believe in magic?"

Aisling pocketed the obsidian and asked, "What kind of question is that?"

He turned his clear blue eyes toward Aisling and a slight smile touched his lips. "I'm not talking to you. Jeez!" He rolled his eyes playfully and whispered to Genevieve, "Does she always do that?"

Genevieve glanced at Aisling. "What?"

"Interrupt people when they're talking." He reached into his pocket and drew out a gold coin. "Watch!"

He flipped the coin into the air, and it turned into a dozen tiny flower petals that swirled around their heads. Gliding and twirling, the petals multiplied—first a dozen, then a hundred—dancing through the air. He clapped his hands, and they all fell to the ground. Aisling looked down to see they had turned into gold, coins littering the ground around their feet.

Genevieve gasped, but Aisling shook her head. "What use is fairy gold? It'll probably vanish soon after we spend it."

He waved his hand and a bag appeared, and all of the coins slid inside it. He picked it up and handed it to Genevieve. "This gold is real." He looked at his companion and said, "Introduce me to this girl, won't you Marcus?"

Aisling wondered why Genevieve always got so much attention. "Nobody would ever want me," she thought.

"This is Genevieve, a Milesian girl, and Trista, and Aisling," said Marcus. "There's a geis protecting Aisling."

The attractive faerie said, "My best friend, Cúchulainn, was killed by a geis."

Aisling felt a sinking sensation in the pit of her stomach.

Genevieve asked, "What's your name?"

He teased, "I'm not sure I want to tell you just now." Smiling, he turned his back on both of them. "Marcus here was just about to show me some fire tricks."

At the mention of fire, Aisling bit her lip, remembering his questions about the Eternal Flame. Not for the first time, she wondered if she should have told Marcus about the six Shadow People she had seen, and about Ith, wandering around the queen's garden. Shaking off her doubt, she asked, "Can I watch?"

With a glance at Marcus, he looked over his shoulder and smiled. "Alright. But you have to pass my test first."

His friendly reaction surprised her. Maybe he did like her after all? "Test?"

"A riddle." He walked over to a patch of flowers and picked one. "Three girls were transformed into flowers by one of the dark Sídhe, but every night, one of them changed back and went into her lover's house. In the morning, the evil fairy saw the three flowers, and she realized that one of them had spent the night indoors. How could she tell which one it was?"

Aisling thought about it, wondering if he was trying to tell her something about curses and dark faeries. She wasn't even sure if she believed in evil faeries.

He shook his head. "Let me know if you ever figure it out." He glanced at Marcus, who had a grin on his face. "Come on, Marcus."

"Wait." Aisling looked into his pretty blue eyes, smiling. "If you tell us your name, I'll answer your riddle."

He crossed his arms. "Give me the answer first."

With narrowed eyes, Aisling thought for a second. She imagined what it would be like to live as a flower outside all night long. It would be cold, dark, and . . . . Aisling smiled. "The flower that spent the night in her lover's house wouldn't be covered with dew, would she?"

He laughed. "That's right." He held out his hand, and Aisling took it.

Rather than shaking it, he bent down and kissed it. "My name is Conall Cernach."

Somehow, Aisling managed to resist blushing. Perhaps Genevieve was not the object of his affections after all?

Trista asked, "What happened to the girl?"

"The dark fairy seduced the girl's lover," Conall said. "So she remained in the garden forever after that, alone."

The idea of having to spend an entire life alone made her shiver inside. "That will never happen to me," she thought. Aisling had spent too many years among Erin's parents, unloved. Again, she wondered what had happened to her sister Erin. She began to think of Ith. They were all walking down the street now, but Aisling gently touched Marcus on the arm, pulling him back a few paces. "Marcus, can I have a word?"

Marcus waited until the others were out of earshot. "What is it Aisling?"

Biting her lip, Aisling considered the consequences of what she was about to say. She glanced around the street and noticed that Conall, Genevieve and Trista had just gone into a store that displayed skinny jeans in the windows. For a moment, she felt as if her friend was about to take away the one faerie that had shown some interest in her, and she had an urge to run after them.

Instead, she looked into Marcus's eyes and told him about the encounter she had had with Ith, and how he had drawn six Shadow People out of the fire. She didn't mention the part about how Ith had invited her to follow him, or about the obsidian sphere in her pocket.

Marcus had to restrain his anger. "Why didn't you tell me this before?"

"I was . . . distracted." Aisling looked down at the street. "I'm sorry, Marcus."

Marcus put his hand on her shoulder. "Never mind." He looked towards the shop they had just gone into. "You're new here." The excuse sounded hollow, but it was nice of him to offer it. "I'll take care of these shadows."

Marcus drew a sword. There was a flash and Aisling found herself looking at a blue sphere, with a gold fire burning inside it. Marcus whirled up into the sky and there was another flash and then he was gone.

A gust of wind blew a cloud of white ice out of the trees. Aisling watched a squirrel run along a branch and disappear behind the trunk of a birch tree. Next to the tree lay a courtyard with a fountain, now frozen into inactivity. The gray stone was carved into the statue of an angel, and it too, was covered in frost.

A chilly sensation ran up her spine, and again, Aisling felt the cold glare of someone watching her. She brushed a strand of dark hair out of her eyes and noticed, very clearly, a Shadow Person, sitting on the edge of the fountain. Although his body was transparent, he had a very clearly defined outline. She had the impression that he was smirking. His eyes were glowing with scarlet fire.

For a moment, Aisling was too terrified to respond.

The Shadow Person vanished.

Aisling looked around the courtyard, realizing that she had, indeed, been under surveillance. She listened for a sign of the shadow, but she could only hear the wild beating of her heart.

The sound of a weapon being drawn rang out in the courtyard.

Whirling around, she came face to face with Ith's Lieutenant. He was holding a long, curved sword. Aisling held out a hand and conjured up a sword of her own.

As he struck down, she brought her own sword up, striking it against his.

Ith's Lieutenant slashed out three times, and she parried each one while retreating.

A gust of wind blew through the courtyard and she felt quickness dancing around her heart. She tried a counterattack, but he parried her blows.

He tried to strike her again, aiming his sword at her head.

Aisling parried his sword, spun around in a circle and slashed out.

Ith's Lieutenant backed off and raised his sword in a salute. "You should have kept silent about us, exile," he whispered.

Aisling held her own sword straight out and her left hand up, two fingers extended, in a fighting stance. "Hello."

An angry shout came out of the darkness. "Haw!"

He struck several times.

Aisling parried each slice, while retreating.

Closing the gap between them, he attacked once more.

Aisling could see his shadowy form against the cobbled street, but it didn't look flat at all. She spun around and slashed in the direction of his steps.

He dodged her attack and lunged forward.

This time, Aisling had to dodge, but she struck out as she did so, wildly swinging her sword.

He parried her attacks.

Aisling could feel the electricity elemental inside her pocket growing warm. As her sword struck his, blue electricity shot out, splashing the courtyard in a series of flashing lights. When she swung her sword down, a blue arc of lightning swept down too.

Ith's Lieutenant blocked the attack, moved forward and slashed out at her legs.

Instinctively, Aisling jumped up into the air, over his attack, and she slashed down, through his chest, but her sword didn't seem to touch him.

Red eyes flaring, he stepped back as she landed on the ground.

Aisling held her sword up, pointing it straight out in a fighting stance. Electricity ran up and down her sword. "So, you're not worried about the curse protecting me?"

Ith's Lieutenant matched her stance, pointing his sword out darkly. He laughed. "I live in the Land of Shadows. Do you think your curse holds sway over me?"

Aisling lunged out, and he parried it.

He struck back several times, but she parried his attacks while lightning flashed across the street.

Aisling glared at him. "The curse held you back, before."

Ith's Lieutenant whispered out coldly, "Yes, but I would rather suffer a curse than to see you at my master's side."

They circled each other, swords up, looking for an opening.

He found one first and struck several times, but her parries held him back.

Aisling tried to take advantage of an opening, but he beat her away, chuckling.

Again, they both faced one another, *en garde*.

Aisling held her sword up, pointing at him, with her other arm up. His last words echoed in her ears, "*...at my master's side.*" Not sure she really wanted to know, she asked, "What does Ith want with me?"

His sword pointed down at the cobblestones. "What does it matter? Soon, I'll slay you—just as I killed your parents."

She knew he was trying to bait her into making a mistake, and so she waited.

Raising his sword, he lunged straight at her throat.

Aisling spun around out of the way with her sword behind her back and parried his attack. This time, she was baiting him.

Seeing her spin around, he lunged again.

Aisling parried his attack and struck again, aiming at his chest.

He blocked her attack and lunged out with his sword.

Barely blocking it, she found that he had overextended himself. Augmented by the elemental infusing her with speed, she slashed out at his head.

But he ducked under the blade.

She lunged at his throat and he parried it.

Ith's Lieutenant chuckled. "You're almost as entertaining as that Milesian girl I took from your parent's house."

Aisling gasped.

Erin is still alive?

The shock brought her to a halt.

Seeing the surprise on her face, he lunged.

Aisling parried the attack, knocking his curved sword out of the way.

Unwilling to give her a moment's rest, he slashed several times.

Aisling retreated, parrying his attacks, hoping that he would expose himself in his recklessness.

He did so. Ith's Lieutenant lunged out, slightly too far.

Ducking under his blade, she twirled her sword around and knocked his weapon out of his hand. It tumbled down to the cobblestones.

Aisling pointed her sword at his throat, hesitating. She had never killed anyone before. He had bragged about murdering her parents, and she had an urge to do it, but she held herself back this time, remembering the fire that had nearly engulfed her at the temple. Fear held her back: fear of what she would become if she let go. Would she become a slave to her passions? "I am not an animal," she thought.

Crimson eyes flaring, the Hat Man's Lieutenant laughed. "We shall have to dance again someday, exile."

Before she could do anything, he faded away into black mist.

Aisling remained standing there with her sword out, wondering if Erin had lived as lonely a life as she had.

* * *

The doors to the shop opened and her friends came out. Genevieve and Trista were carrying small shopping bags. Conall was telling an amusing story to them as they were coming out. Aisling closed her eyes and imagined her sword not being there, and when she looked up again, it was gone.

"Where have you been?" asked Genevieve.

Aisling walked across the courtyard towards the others. "I was . . . inattentive."

"Not a very good excuse," said Conall. He looked around. "Where's Marcus?"

"He had to leave," said Aisling. "So, did you get a pair of jeans?"

Genevieve's face broke into a grin. "Yes!" She held up the small bag in her hand. "This place is fantastic, Aisling! I didn't know there could be so many kinds."

"You only wanted one pair?"

Genevieve shook her head. "This shopping bag is magical, check it out." She held it up and waved a hand over it. The tiny image of a pair of dark skinny jeans appeared, floating over the bag. She waved her hand, and the image was replaced by another image, this one of a pair of white jeans. Genevieve continued to wave her hand a few more times, and Aisling saw that she had indeed purchased several pairs of pants. "Coolio, eh?"

Aisling smiled. "I see you're talking more like a Canadian now."

Genevieve pouted. "'Coolio' isn't a Canadian expression."

The four of them began to walk down the street. This time, Conall was talking to Trista. In fact, they were walking arm in arm. Aisling choked off a bit of irritation and tried to concentrate on the shops they passed by. The sun was beginning to sink, painting the sky with fire.

Out of the corner of her eye, Aisling thought she saw something. She glanced around but didn't see anyone. Dropping her voice, she whispered, "Gen, I think Erin is still alive."

Genevieve also lowered her voice. "That's what my intuition tells me, but how can we find her?"

Trista and Conall had stopped. Trista turned around and said, "Well, I have to be going now."

Conall looked slightly disappointed. "I'll see you later then."

Aisling didn't like the sound of that, but she waved goodbye to her friend anyway, feeling slightly relieved when Trista sprouted wings and flew away.

A dark-haired girl walking on the other side of the road paused to watch. For a moment, Aisling stared, wondering where she'd seen her before. Suddenly she realized that she was looking at Rhona, one of the Shadow People. Smiling, Rhona looked into Aisling's eyes and winked. Then she changed into a shadow, with red glowing eyes. She moved off

147

after Trista, darting away into the fading light.

"What?" Genevieve asked.

Aisling had her mouth open. The Shadow People were watching Trista too. *Was this one of the 'tasks' that Ith had given them?* "Did you see that?"

Genevieve raised her eyebrows, shaking her head.

"Well then," interrupted Conall. "It's Saturday night. I know this great restaurant. You two want to join me?"

Genevieve bit her lip. "Actually, I'm a bit tired." She looked at Aisling and asked, "Do you mind if I leave you? I want to go back to the castle and look through what I've bought."

Aisling held back a smile. "Okay. See you later."

Conall raised a hand and whistled. A coach drawn by white horses appeared from down the road. The coachman was an elf wearing an eighteenth century suit and a tricorn hat, all in white. Conall opened the door for Genevieve. "Have a good night."

"I love this place!" Genevieve got into the coach. "Goodnight Aisling."

Conall paid the coachman, and off it went, up the hill towards the castle. He turned towards Aisling and offered his arm. "It's so much more romantic to walk, don't you think?"

Forgetting the shadows for the time being, Aisling nodded and took his arm. It was hard to believe this was happening. They walked down the street while darkness settled around the town. Many of the fairies changed into the little globes of light. They twinkled like stars that had come down to play on the earth. Thoughts of loneliness began to fade away as she felt the strength of his presence at her side.

Aisling was curious to know if Conall was interested in Genevieve. "I wanted to thank you for giving money to my friend."

Conall didn't take the bait. "Ah, God shares with those who are generous."

He brought her to a sushi place overlooking the ocean. Candles cast a warm glow over the place. Aisling wondered why Genevieve would want to return to electric lights.

After they had eaten, Aisling looked into Conall's eyes and found that she had grown curious. "So, what do you do anyway?"

Conall leaned back in his chair and glanced out at the sea, which began to reflect the stars. A crescent moon cast its pale light over the water. "I serve the king."

"How descriptive you are."

He teased back, "I always endeavor to be thorough."

Not willing to let it go, she said, "Shining the royal shoes, that sort of thing?"

He chuckled. "The man with the boots does not mind where he places his foot."

She was still trying to figure out what he had meant by that when he asked quietly, "So, was this the first time you were attacked by the Shadow People?"

Aisling looked away outside, where dozens of fairy lights floated over the town. It seemed that the Shadow People weren't the only ones keeping watch over her movements. Her eyes dropped down into an ocean burdened by moonlight. "The first time in this world, yes." Aisling crossed her arms. "His majesty's intelligence service—is it?"

He nodded.

Aisling looked out the window again. "You could have simply asked. There's no reason to wander around town with me."

Conall laughed and picked up her hand. "You underestimate your beauty."

Aisling looked into his eyes. "Really? You weren't . . . assigned to me?"

"Eileen is your guardian." He caressed her hand gently, and she felt warmth tingling inside her heart. "I really am attracted to you, but I just happened to notice that you were pointing a sword at a shadow when we emerged from that shop." He let go of her hand. "Why didn't you . . . ?"

"Finish him?" Aisling frowned. "I've never done anything like that before."

Conall leaned forward and whispered, "You're a virgin!"

"What?" Aisling felt her face burning. "No I'm not! I've had plenty of—" Biting her lip, she looked down, away from his smiling eyes. "Yes I am, but no one's ever shown an interest in me before."

Conall picked up a glass of wine, twirling it around in his hand. "I should think that Milesians would be terrified of you." He took a sip. "It's difficult enough for a man to approach a pretty girl."

Milesians were frightened of her? Is that why she had so few friends? Her mind whirling around like the wine in his glass, she said, "You don't seem to have any trouble with girls."

"Well I'm not a Milesian, am I?" He put his glass down onto the table, frowning. "Well, that seems to decide it then."

"What?"

"I was going to invite you over to my estate, but now—"

He has an estate? Aisling raised her eyebrows. "Now?"

Conall picked up her hand again, squeezing it. "We'll see."

Aisling squeezed back. "Yes."

*   *   *

Cool mist rose over the field of grass overlooking the entrance to Conall's estate. The low sun was still behind the pine trees, but some of the sunlight peeked through the tall branches, throwing spotted light across the grass. Dozens of tiny fairies flew over the field, stopping over a wildflower for a moment and then whisking off through the mist.

Aisling stood on the front porch, one hand on the white wall. She let her eyes drink in the sight of the field. When she heard Conall approach, she turned to face him, smiling briefly. "I'm sorry about last night," she said. "I don't really know what came over me. I can't believe I fell asleep."

Conall held a cup of coffee in his hand. "You're such a tease," he joked. "Perhaps your life among the Milesians has made you weak?"

Frowning, she looked away, back over the grassy field in front of the forest. For some reason, she didn't want to look at his house. It was a large estate—white walls and high glass windows overlooking the ocean. But all she could see was her father staring out at the sea. It made her sad. "Your home reminds me of my foster parent's house . . . lots of windows."

Before he could respond, she saw a white unicorn emerge from the forest. It walked forward a few paces and then stopped to gaze into her eyes. Aisling gasped. "I can't believe it!"

"Oh yes—a unicorn. They live in the trees around my property. But they never come near me." Conall chuckled. "You know, they're said to guard the doorways that lead into other realms."

The unicorn came forward timidly. Aisling walked out to meet him. She raised a hand to conjure up a bit of sugar, and the unicorn came over to eat it. Gently, she placed a hand along his side, feeling soft power tingling against her fingertips. "He's beautiful!"

Conall laughed. "Go ahead. Ride him back to the castle. It's perfectly safe, unless you fall off."

Aisling grinned. "Alright." She closed her eyes and imagined herself in a riding outfit: White pants, black boots, a white blouse and a riding crop. She jumped up onto his back and ran her fingers through his mane affectionately.

"Wait!" he called. "When will I see you again?"

Aisling looked into his eyes coyly, but didn't answer him. She leaned against the unicorn's neck and whispered, "Take me to the castle, if you please."

It wasn't as cool as it was the day before, and all of the frost had melted. Aisling soon found herself fantasizing, but instead of Conall, she was thinking of Keir, the mysterious Shadow Person. She wanted to know why he had warned her about Ith and she wondered if the Shadow People were really her enemies. Shaking her head in irritation, she whispered, "Nonsense. They sure aren't your friends."

The unicorn brought her to the edge of the forest, and began to trot off towards the castle in the distance. But a tall gothic cathedral caught her attention, and she asked the unicorn to bring her there instead. Momentarily, she was sitting astride the unicorn, peering up into a high tower built into the front of the structure.

"Aisling!"

She saw Fáelán standing in front of the building next to Lasarina, who, for several weeks, had been teaching Aisling the skills of conjuration—materializing items out of the imagination.

Aisling waved. "Hi Fáelán, Lasarina."

Lasarina smiled. "You should come visit me in Na Teach Cúirtéis," she said, with a southern accent. "After all, the Aed Ernmas clan is well known for its courtesy."

Slightly embarrassed at not having visited the Faerie Sídhe, Aisling lowered her gaze. "I'm sorry, Lasarina, but North Carolina is so far away, just for a visit."

"Hasn't anyone shown you how to travel along the King's Road, An Rí Bealach? It only takes about four hours to get there." Lasarina asked.

Aisling was still uncomfortable using the magic road system. "I've been a bit busy," she said.

"How are your conjuration skills?" asked Lasarina. "Are you faring well?"

"Yes I am." Jumping off the unicorn, Aisling walked up the steps to the high arched doorway leading into the cathedral. She looked at the stone tower over their heads. "What is this place?"

"Isn't it obvious?" said Lasarina. "Or haven't you seen a cathedral before?"

"I..." Aisling bit her lip. "...never thought faeries were that religious."

Lasarina laughed. "Well, I'm off."

Aisling stepped forward, holding her back. "Lasarina, I need to ask you something."

Fáelán sighed. "I'll be inside when you're done."

After he had gone in, she said, "I had a run-in with a Shadow Person yesterday."

All of the mirth fell from Lasarina's face.

"I fought him with a sword that I conjured up. I'd swear I struck him once, but the blade seemed to pass through his body." Aisling had been wondering about this for some time. "Can't our weapons affect the Shadow People?"

Lasarina shook her head. "Conjured swords aren't too useful against such beings. You should acquire a magic sword."

Aisling pouted. "Where am I going to get a magic sword?"

"Your friend Eileen carries such a weapon."

Not knowing how this could help her, Aisling nodded. "Okay, thanks."

Lasarina smiled. "Take care of yourself Aisling, and come visit me soon." She unfolded her wings and flew off towards the castle.

Aisling walked under the archway of blue-gray stone and passed through the sturdy oak doors, which were open. As she walked inside, she could feel a presence, like a cold breath over one's shoulder, keeping watch. Frankincense and myrrh spiced the air inside the cathedral. A gentle glow came from the beeswax candles set into niches along the stone walls. Each niche cradled a small altar, adorned with flowers and flickering candles. A line of pews marched up the nave towards the chancel, where a sacramental lamp was suspended from the ceiling between a pair of tall candelabra. Six red marble pillars supported the white stone archways on either side of the hallway that led up to the altar. A large Celtic cross overlooked an altar stone, which was bathed in light coming through a series of stained glass windows.

For a moment, Aisling stood in the entryway, astonished. "So, the Tuatha Dé are Catholic?" she wondered. Just as quickly, she realized how silly it was to be surprised. After all, they came from Ireland, didn't they? Absentmindedly, she dipped a finger into the stoup by the doorway and crossed herself with holy water.

Aisling's footsteps echoed through the cathedral. Looking about, she didn't see anyone present, but then she noticed Fáelán up in a balcony over the entrance, next to another faerie. Unfurling her wings, Aisling flew up to the platform and noticed that a large pipe organ stood between two sets of pipework. A large stained glass window admitted light to the balcony, filling the area with warmth. In the center of the wall, under the window, was a large mirror inside an ornate silver frame.

The tall woman standing next to Fáelán wore black leggings, a black lace blouse with a high collar, black shoes, and a silver belt. She had short black hair in a wedge cut, and dark green eyes. Most of the light falling onto the balcony surrounded her. She was leaning over Fáelán, who was sitting at the organ, but she looked up as Aisling landed and said, "Dia duit."

Unable to take her eyes off the faerie, Aisling simply nodded. There was more than light flooding the balcony. She sensed a powerful presence, like a peaceful blanket, filling the area.

Fáelán looked up and smiled. "That's how you say 'hello' in Irish," he said. "Nel, this is my friend, Aisling."

Aisling found her voice. "Hello."

Fáelán said, "She's the custodian here."

"Yes," said Nel, in a mirthful voice. "I was sent down from Heaven to guard this place."

Aisling was wondering how serious Nel was when Fáelán asked, "You play the pipe organ, don't you?"

Aisling shook her head. "No, I play the piano, but it would be fun to learn how to perform Mozart on a pipe organ, or Bach."

"I'd like to see that," said Nel. "Feel free to come by anytime to practice."

A movement caught Aisling's attention, and she found herself looking into the tall glass hanging on the wall. It was a mirror unlike any other: Oval shaped, it stood over six feet tall. The silver frame had an intricate pattern of Celtic knotwork, along with detailed engravings of other things, less savory. Mixed into a pattern of leaves and flowers were bones and skulls. Looking at it was unsettling. A chilly breeze came from the glass, and it seemed to freeze the soul. There were faint voices too—whisperings that made her skin crawl. It reminded her of the Shadow People.

"I see that you've noticed the Mirror of Eternity," said Nel.

Aisling looked away from the mirror, into Nel's eyes. "What is it?"

Nel glanced at the reflection in the glass. "It's a window that looks into the realm of our enemies: The Land of Shadows."

"What is it doing here?" asked Aisling.

Fáelán said, "This is the safest place for it. After all, the cathedral is under God's protection. The Shadow People cannot use it to look into our world while it's here."

Aisling walked towards it, and raised a hand to touch the glass. But before her finger touched the mirror, Nel stopped her with a single word: "Please—"

Turning to look into Nel's eyes, Aisling dropped her hand away.

Nel explained, "It isn't entirely safe to touch."

Aisling glanced at her reflection, wondering what could happen if she touched it. She looked over her shoulder, down into the pews. It would be a strange thing, to sit there, praying, while such a thing as this stood behind you, whispering dark thoughts.

"How does it work?" she asked.

Fáelán said, "This mirror can only be used by the king, the queen or Nel here. It is forbidden for anyone else to use."

Nel turned her inquisitive eyes towards Aisling and asked, "Why would you want to look into the Land of Shadows?"

Aisling returned Nel's gaze. "Thrice before, I've seen the image of a girl reflected in glass. I want to know if it's my sister Erin, and where she is now."

"Very well." Nel moved behind Aisling and placed her hands upon her shoulders. Nel whispered, "Look into the mirror and concentrate on the one you wish to see."

Aisling looked into her own reflection, thinking about Erin. After a moment, she shook her head. "There isn't anything—"

The cold wind blowing across her face changed direction slightly and a lock of hair fell into her eyes. The whispering died down, and her reflection in the mirror faded.

The barren chamber appeared, and the girl too. She was sitting on a small bed, cradling a doll. Sunlight shone through a window high up in the stone wall. Her silver hair tousled, she wore a pair of thigh boots, black leather pants, a white peasant blouse, and a black vest. A chain ran from the wall through a ring attached to a leather collar around her neck. She was singing softly to herself, her song drifting through the chamber, carrying the weight of a world that had left her behind.

Aisling's mouth fell open. It was a lullaby sung by her mother. Almost forgotten, she hadn't heard it in years. But the song was lonely now, as if the love and comfort it might have once given had tumbled down into a dark well. Aisling whispered, "Erin?"

Erin stopped humming to herself and looked up.

The door to the chamber opened, and Erin recoiled. A tall man stepped into the room. He had wild red hair and a red beard. Aisling recognized him as the one that she had seen striking Erin. A voice called from the doorway, "Release her, Eochaid."

The tall redhead, Eochaid, walked over to the chain on the wall and unlocked it. After the chain had gone, a second man stepped into the room. "Come," he commanded.

Aisling's eyes grew dark. It was Keir! Was Erin his slave? Resisting the urge to smash the mirror, Aisling looked away. When she did so, she saw that Fáelán was on his feet now, looking into the glass. She whispered to him, "I've found my sister."

* * *

Chapter Nine

The Duel

Fáelán paced back and forth in her room, high up in one of the castle towers, while Aisling sat in front of a mirror, drying her hair. The whine of the hair dryer blocked out what he was saying. Aisling felt the warm air blowing across her hair while she combed it out. Nearby, the small electricity elemental sparkled in its holder. He said something else, and Aisling turned off the hair dryer. She gave him an irritated look. "What did you say?"

Fáelán stopped his pacing. "I thought you were in a hurry?"

Aisling turned away from him, to hide her smile. "He must really like Erin," she thought. Stifling a giggle, she said, "I had to take a bath and change my clothes, Fáelán. I don't want to smell like a—a unicorn all day, do I?"

Instead of picking up the hair dryer, she removed a brush from her makeup case. She looked into the mirror and pictured her makeup for the day. Gently, she swept the brush across her skin—and when she glanced back, her face was flawless, airbrushed to perfection, like a painting.

Turning to face him, she set the brush down. "Besides, this really doesn't take much time—you should see how long it takes me to do my makeup in the Milesian world."

Fáelán shook his head. "Women!" he muttered. Turning around, he moved over to sit down in a chair next to a window that looked out at the ocean beyond the castle. "I still don't know how we're going to rescue your sister."

"I have to get a magic sword before I can do anything, Fáelán." Aisling stood up and walked over to him, holding out her hand. "Ready?"

Taking her hand, he stood up suspiciously. "You're ready to go now?"

Giggling, she asked, "How do I look?"

He let go of her hand, as if the contact was too intimate, and actually looked at what she was wearing: a dark red sweater made out of slinky material, with a high collar and flared sleeves, black leggings and short red suede boots. He said, "You don't need to fish for compliments, Aisling."

Wrinkling her brow, she wondered if he thought she was pretty. Conall seemed to think so, however, but he never said it directly. Fáelán was presumably only interested in her sister. She was starting to feel like a rose dying in a desert. She sighed. "Come on, Genevieve is probably in the library at this time of day."

The library looked like a cross between the Roman Coliseum and a shopping mall in Las Vegas. As they landed on the walkway leading up to the entrance, Aisling watched several other fairies go in and out. A dwarf, carrying a stack of books higher than he was tall, nearly walked into her as she approached the doorway.

Once inside, Aisling looked up at the tall skylights and counted several stories filled with bookcases. "How are we going to find her?" she asked.

Fáelán reached up to a charm around his neck and whispered a few words. A small golden fairy appeared, hovering in front of him. He said, "Take us to our friend, Genevieve, please." The tiny fairy bowed and whizzed off into the building.

Aisling looked at Fáelán and asked, "What or who, is that?"

"That's a Finder Fairy," he said. "It's a charm used to locate someone nearby." He grabbed her arm. "Come on!"

Moments later, they found Genevieve sitting at a large oak table reading an enormous book. A charcoal gray cat lay sleeping on top of a pile of books. Fáelán hopped up and sat on top of the table, next to the cat. Aisling walked up to her friend. "Hey."

Genevieve looked up. "It's about time you came to visit me here."

Aisling glanced around the room full of ancient musty books. "With so many kinds of magic, what's the use of having all these books around?"

Genevieve smiled. "They say that books contain the greatest kinds of magic. Imagine it! A thousand years ago, a man wrote this down. Now I can see his words. I know his thoughts, his loves and desires. He speaks to me out of eternity."

Aisling wondered what kinds of knowledge could be found locked away in the library. "What're you reading?"

"It's called 'Lebor Gabála Érenn—The Book of Takings.' It's about the different groups of people that invaded Ireland." Genevieve glanced at Fáelán, who looked rather impatient, and then turned back to Aisling. "Did you know that the Milesians came from Spain?"

Aisling raised her eyebrows. "They're Spanish?"

"No, they're Celtic. Their realm was called, 'Celtiberia,' but that kingdom was founded after the Milesians invaded Ireland," said Genevieve. "I was just reading about a dark enchantress named Ceridwen who took over the Creidhne clan, which ruled over Sídhe an Domhan before the wars of the dwarves."

"So Aisling," Fáelán interrupted. "Are you going to ask her now?"

Aisling crossed her arms. "Hey, I'm just as anxious to rescue Erin as you, but I was curious—I've never been to this library before."

Fáelán crossed his arms. "Hey, I'm just trying to keep the dream alive."

"What's going on?" asked Genevieve.

Aisling sat down. "I found Erin. She's imprisoned in the Land of Shadows."

Genevieve raised her eyebrows. "Where?"

"It's where the Shadow People live," said Aisling. "After I left Conall's estate this morning—"

Genevieve interrupted. "What?" Her books forgotten now, she leaned forward. "You stayed with him all night? What happened?"

Fáelán's groan woke up the cat, which stood up and began to stretch. "We need to find Eileen," he muttered.

Genevieve ran a hand through her long brown hair, unable to stifle her curiosity. "I'd rather hear about Conall."

Aisling glanced in Fáelán's direction and then turned back towards Genevieve. "I had a fight with a Shadow Person yesterday. It was Ith's Lieutenant."

Genevieve leaned back in her chair. "Why didn't you tell me?"

"I didn't want—it doesn't matter." Aisling shook her head. "I conjured a sword to fight with, but it didn't affect him."

"Eileen told us that the Shadow People are non-corporeal—weapons go right through them." Genevieve crossed her arms. "I'd still like to get a shotgun though."

Walking on top of the table, the cat stepped in front of Aisling, who absentmindedly began to pet him. She said, "Eileen killed a Shadow Person at my parent's house, but she has a magic sword."

Genevieve looked at the cat. "Do you have any books on magic swords?"

Aisling and Fáelán exchanged doubtful glances.

The cat jumped off the table and ran between the aisles of books. Genevieve said, "That's Hieronymus. You should see where he goes."

"You want us to follow that cat?" asked Aisling.

Genevieve leaned back over her book. "He's the librarian. Hieronymus was cursed after losing a fairy duel. So now he's a cat."

Aisling got up and followed Hieronymus, who led her through the library. She was starting to suspect that Genevieve might be playing a joke—just as the cat leapt onto the table. She examined the book the cat was looking at, but couldn't read the title.

"Thanks Hieronymus." Aisling took the book off the shelf and brought it back to the table, dropping it loudly in front of Genevieve and sitting down. The cat, having followed her back, jumped up onto the table and hissed.

Aisling looked around the library, realizing how loud she had been. "Sorry."

Hieronymus sat down in front of her stiffly, flicking his tail.

Aisling opened the book. The paper felt old, and a musty scent came out of it. It was written in a strange script. "How am I going to read this?"

Genevieve reached over to a small crystal globe sitting in the center of the table, nearly hidden by all of the books. "Take this."

The sphere reminded Aisling of the passion stone, now hidden away in her room. But this one was different—more elegant, and mysterious too. It felt heavier somehow, and coolness emanated so strongly that her fingertips tingled. She had no idea what it was. "Oh, thanks," she said. "This'll really help."

Genevieve laughed. "It's a Fomorian reading stone," she explained. "The Fomorians were one of the first groups of people that lived in Ireland."

Fáelán interrupted again, "Take the stone and rub it against the spine."

Aisling closed the book and did as he said. The title on the spine changed into English: "The Different Kinds of Magic Weapons and Their Natures, and of Their Diverse Uses." Opening the book again, she asked in a defiant tone, "So who were the Fomorians?"

Genevieve answered before Fáelán could interrupt. "They were a powerful race that lived inside crystal spires in the ocean. Some say they were from Atlantis. They used a kind of magic that's forgotten now, but a few of their artifacts are still around."

Aisling began to read about charmed weapons, dream swords, symbolic weapons of ritual magic, elemental weapons like flaming swords, dragon slayers, and unbreakable rune weapons.

After some time, she leaned back, frowning. Afternoon light filtered down from the skylights, bathing the table in warmth. She noticed that Hieronymus was sleeping again. She wondered if life as a cat would be so bad.

Genevieve looked up from her book. "So?"

Aisling ran her hands along the cat's soft fur, and it woke up Hieronymus. He stood up and moved towards her affectionate petting. Aisling said, "It talks about different kinds of magic swords, but it doesn't say how to make one."

A friendly voice interrupted. "What would you need a magic sword for?"

A tall, smiling man had just walked up to their table, carrying an open book. Aisling recognized the faerie leader of Roth Cinniúint, a Sídhe north of Chicago. He was trying to teach her about mysticism, but she hadn't made much progress. Finnian had long blonde hair, a short beard, and a perpetual smile. He wore a nineteenth century suit.

She had taken his friendly disinterest in her as a challenge, which was why she was always flirting with him. Running a hand through her hair, she said, coyly, "What was that, Finnian?"

Finnian closed his book. "I asked why you're looking for a magic sword."

Aisling crossed her legs and let a lock of hair fall over one eye. "I'll need a weapon to fight the Shadow People the next time they come here, won't I?"

Ignoring her alluring behavior, Finnian said, "The Shadow People can't come into the Land of Dreams naturally, Aisling. They have to find a magic gateway. Gladly, all of the doorways are sealed with magic or they're well guarded."

Biting her lip, Aisling uncrossed her legs. Hieronymus jumped onto her lap and she began to pet him again. "I've seen a few shadows since I've been here."

Finnian was silent a moment before he responded. "Where?"

"I saw six of them coming out of the Eternal Flame."

The smile vanished. "Why didn't you report it?"

"I told Marcus about them," she said. "I wonder if they'll escape back to where they come from."

Finnian smiled again, and he scratched Hieronymus behind the ears. "There are still a few ancient doorways, but they're locked. Marcus will get them."

Aisling remained silent. Ith had handed Ceridwen a Shadow Key. She was about to tell Finnian about it when he said, "I'll make you a magic sword if you want."

Glancing at the open book in front of her, she asked, "What kind of sword?"

"A Shadow Slayer, perhaps."

"How long—"

Conall's voice interrupted her. "Hello Genevieve."

Narrowing her eyes, Aisling wondered if he was teasing her again, or if he was really more interested in her best friend. Unable to resist smiling, she said, "Hi, Conall."

Conall sat down at the table next to Aisling, but he turned towards Genevieve. "A library is a stimulating place, don't you think?"

Looking down at her book, Genevieve smiled and said under her breath, "I'm not the one doing the stimulating."

Aisling had an urge to punch her friend.

Conall chuckled and turned towards Aisling. "How are you today?"

Aisling gave him a doggy-dinner-bowl look and squeezed his hand. "Fine."

"Oh, please!" Finnian sounded irritated. "Don't tell me that Aisling is your newest conquest, Conall."

Conall's voice turned chilly. "I don't know what you're talking about."

Finnian chuckled. "I think you do."

Dropping Aisling's hand, Conall stood up calmly. He and Finnian glared at one another. Hieronymus jumped down to the floor and ran under a chair. Conall calmly peeled off one of his white gloves and tossed it onto the table.

Finnian narrowed his eyes and he picked up the glove. "Very well."

Fáelán stood up. "Conall, you can't!"

Conall said, stiffly, "This man has insulted the lady's honor, and that of my clan."

"Isn't the Iuchar clan known for temperance?" asked Fáelán. "What would your leader say?"

"Canlyn is at an archery tournament at the Hill of Allen," said Conall, "in Ireland."

"Since you are the challenger, the choice of weapons is mine," Finnian said. "I choose pistols at twenty paces."

Aisling couldn't believe it. Conall was going to fight a duel! But was it about her or about his pride? "Wait, Conall, you don't have to do this!"

"It's already done," said Conall. "At sunset, several other duels are taking place. I trust you'll be there?"

Finnian nodded. "I'll see you tonight." Then he exited the library.

Conall flashed a smile. "Don't worry. The loser will only suffer a curse."

Hieronymus crept out from under the table. Genevieve had said that the cat had once been a fairy, but he'd been cursed after losing a duel. Aisling crossed her arms and looked away, but she couldn't help from feeling excited about it.

Conall took off his other glove and put it into his pocket. "You'll act as my second, won't you Fáelán?"

"Whatever, dude."

Conall nodded and went away.

After he had gone, Genevieve punched Aisling on the shoulder. "Now look at what you've done!" she said. "When are you going to stop toying with men?"

Rather than defend herself, Aisling asked, "Why would Finnian agree to a duel?"

"I don't know," said Genevieve. "Fairies are all a bit testy, aren't they?"

"The Comhrac Aonair is illegal, but that doesn't stop people," said Fáelán. "The what?" asked Aisling.

"Single combat," said Fáelán. "The Crown has officially outlawed dueling, but it's still tolerated. There are rivalries that have gone on for centuries among our clans. Conall's clan has been feuding with the Éogan clan, where Finnian is from, for years." He looked into her eyes. "Its one reason that changelings don't live very long. The clans protect their own."

"And I have no clan."

"No."

* * *

Dark clouds covered the sunset, filling the rosy skies with gray. Pine trees lined three sides of the large field, but the fourth side opened up onto a cliff overlooking the ocean. The dueling field was obscured from view of the castle and any official eyes there. Next to the field was a large grandstand built into the trees, and it was full of excited faeries. Aisling sat, arms crossed, next to her friends.

A blue globe of light drifted into the stands and after a flash, Eileen appeared next to Genevieve.

Fáelán asked, "Where have you been? We've been looking all over for you!"

"I was helping Marcus chase down some shadows. They've been trying to make some kind of deal with the Goblins," said Eileen. "What are you three doing here?"

"Conall's fighting a duel with Finnian," said Genevieve.

Eileen looked over the dueling field, which was full of faeries. "Dueling is illegal. If the Queen catches them . . ."

Fáelán's voice cut in, "Is that Morrigan?"

Turning to look out over the field, Aisling noticed her rival walking out calmly, carrying a bow. To her surprise, Aisling saw that her opponent was Siri, the changeling who assaulted them earlier that year on the King's Road. Siri was also carrying a bow.

Genevieve murmured, "I wonder what their dispute is?"

Fáelán frowned. "Maybe Siri didn't show Morrigan *proper respect*."

The herald landed off to the side of the field, and both Morrigan and Siri took off into the air. Morrigan, quickly climbing higher, pointed her bow down and took the first shot, barely missing Siri. The arrow stuck into the wood railing in front of Aisling, who wondered if the arrow had been aimed at her.

The pair began to maneuver through the sky, taking shots at each other. After a few moments, Siri fell backwards into a sudden dive, shooting as she fell. Morrigan, unprepared for her opponent's quick reversal, changed into a black raven and the arrow whizzed past.

"Stad!" The herald flew into the air, waving his staff. "Personal transformations are not permitted," he said. "As a penalty, you are to remain a raven for three days."

An angry squawk rang out from Morrigan, who landed off to the side of the field next to a Faerie that Aisling recognized as Laigne. After a moment's discussion, Laigne conjured up a bow and took off into the air, taking Morrigan's place.

"What's going on?" asked Genevieve.

Fáelán said, "Laigne is acting as Morrigan's second. So he's finishing the duel."

Aisling looked at Fáelán, realizing that he would have to take Conall's place if something went wrong. It was at that moment that Aisling felt the prickling sensation of someone watching her. Out of the corner of her eye, she thought she noticed something, and she turned to look, but nothing was there. She felt the Shadow Person's attention on the duel and she returned her gaze to the skies over the field. The pair of duelists were flying in circles, shooting at each other.

Siri landed and Aisling saw a Shadow Person appear. It was the one that Ith had called Bryce. He whispered something into Siri's ear. No one else seemed to notice the incident, but the expression in Siri's face hardened. She raised her bow, taking careful aim. Laigne had taken a few shots at Siri while she was standing still, but he was moving so fast that he missed. Siri's shot hit its mark, and Laigne fell out of the sky, pierced through the heart.

A hush washed over the crowd. Morrigan screamed, flying over to her friend, who lay face down on the ground. The herald landed next to Laigne kneeling down to examine him.

Aisling put her hand on Fáelán's arm. "I thought you said that killing wasn't allowed in duels."

"It isn't," he said. "As punishment, Siri will have to bear a curse."

The herald stood up and raised his staff, pointing it at Siri, whose eyes had a glazed look. "I place the Friendslayer Curse on you."

Eileen gasped.

"What does it mean?" asked Genevieve.

"She's now fated to cause the death of a friend," explained Fáelán.

Genevieve whispered, "That's horrible!"

Aisling stared at Bryce, who remained still. She wondered why no one else had seen him. A tall faerie escorted a sobbing Siri off the field. Bryce smiled and then faded away. Morrigan flew off and vanished into the trees.

Finnian walked up to where they were seated. He held out a long leather case.

"What's this?" asked Genevieve.

"Open it."

Genevieve reached inside the case and removed a pump-action shotgun. It was finely engraved with Celtic knotwork designs. It had a leather strap.

Finnian smiled. "I heard you mention an interest in one of these."

Aisling asked, "Is it magical? Will it affect the Shadow People?"

"Yes. It's a Shadow Slayer." Finnian smiled at Aisling. "I should have your sword finished in a day or two." He turned around and walked over to the herald, who waited in the field next to another faerie—his second.

Genevieve called after him, "Thanks!"

Fáelán got up and went down to join Conall. The herald held up a finely made oak box. Opening it, Fáelán took out a pistol and began to load it while Finnian's second loaded another. They handed the nineteenth-century pistols to the duelists, and they took up positions with their backs to one another. Fáelán returned to his seat next to Aisling.

"Why flintlocks?" asked Genevieve.

"They're not flintlocks. They use percussion caps," said Fáelán.

"That doesn't answer her question," said Aisling.

"They're not too accurate, and sometimes they misfire," explained Fáelán. "It keeps things interesting."

Conall had been the only one among the Sídhe that had shown an interest in Aisling, but she needed the magic weapon that Finnian had promised to make. It seemed unreal that Conall would fight a duel over her. It sent a thrill of excitement through her, even though she hated the idea of it. She wasn't sure she wanted either of them to win.

At the herald's command, they began to walk apart, slowly moving away from each other with their pistols raised. Conflicting thoughts swept through Aisling's mind. How would she fight the shadows if Finnian lost? What if Conall was killed? She felt an urge to look away or run away, but she couldn't get herself to move. Genevieve reached out and took her hand and Aisling squeezed it.

At twenty paces, they both stopped and turned around. Finnian was to shoot first. He took aim and paused. Conall stood quite still, pistol raised, with a look of superiority on his face. It was as if he didn't mind dying for his honor. Finnian raised his pistol into the air and fired into the trees. The bang echoed out over the dueling field while a cloud of white smoke floated across the clearing. A gasp swept through the crowd.

Aisling looked at Fáelán. "What does it mean? Is he giving up?"

"Not at all," said Fáelán. "That's called a 'delope.' By firing into the air, he's saying that his opponent isn't worth shooting. It's the worst kind of insult."

"Not necessarily," said Eileen. "It could mean that Finnian doesn't want to fight."

"Why would he agree to the duel if that were so?" interrupted Genevieve.

Eileen explained, "It's a way of offering an apology without losing honor."

"He had to accept the duel," said Fáelán. "If he refused to fight, then Conall would be able to curse the entire Éogan clan."

Whatever the reason for Finnian's shot into the air, Conall's expression was cold. He raised his pistol, took aim and fired. Smoke flashed from his pistol, accompanied by a loud boom. Finnian crumpled to the ground, clutching his leg. The herald stepped forward, raised his staff and turned towards Conall. "Choose your curse."

Conall turned his back to his wounded opponent and took off his white gloves. "Since he's so fond of trees, make him an oak."

The herald waved his staff and Finnian began to transform into a tree. His body turned into a trunk, his arms stretched out into long limbs and his feet dug into the ground, changing into twisted roots. In a short time, a majestic oak tree stood in the field, surrounded by fading sunlight.

The shock at seeing what happened to Finnian struck a nerve. *How could he have done this to him? To me?* She needed Finnian to fight the shadows. Dimly, she noticed that the next pair of duelists were about to use swords.

Her anger bled into a whisper, "Perfect!"

Aisling stood up.

"Where are you going?" asked Genevieve.

Aisling glared at the oak tree that had been Finnian only moments before. Her hopes of having a weapon to fight Ith were now gone. "I'm going for a walk."

As she stepped down out of the grandstand, she heard Fáelán's voice. "Let her go, Genevieve."

Aisling walked away from the dueling field, her mind full of fury. "What am I doing here?" she muttered. "Field of honor indeed!" Why did Conall shoot Finnian after he gave him a chance to end things without violence? Again, she wondered if Conall was defending her honor, or his own pride.

Before she knew it, she was surrounded by tall pine trees. They were bathed in the dim blue light of a crescent moon. She came to a small clearing and stopped. An owl hooted from above, and she could hear the wind blowing across the tree tops.

The feeling of being watched returned, like a cold blanket. The first thing she thought of was that Conall had followed her. Someone was coming up behind her. Sighing, she whirled around. "Conall, what do you—"

Ith's Lieutenant stood there, eyes glowing red.

Before she could block it, his hand lashed out of the darkness.

A flash of pain ignited in her head. She felt herself falling backwards onto the forest floor. The sound of a sword being drawn sliced through the night sky. Dizziness made her head whirl round. Pain throbbed against her forehead and she felt something warm trickling down her face. She looked up at tall trees, and his sword, which was now pressed against her neck.

The Hat Man's Lieutenant smiled down at her maliciously. "I'm sorry, love. No dance tonight!"

The crude clanking of chains caught her attention. Something was passing through the trees. Dozens of figures walked by, quietly, just out of sight, dragging a line of people behind them. A tall blonde man wearing a formal tuxedo came up to Ith's Lieutenant. It was Bryce. His face expressionless, and Bryce glanced down at Aisling with indifferent curiosity. "*Have they found it?*"

The Lieutenant didn't move. "No."

Aisling wondered what the Shadow People were looking for.

Bryce was silent for a moment before he spoke. "I can't locate Ceridwen. Doesn't she have the key?"

Ith's Lieutenant continued to stare into Aisling's eyes. "We don't need it now. Take the captives to the gateway."

"What about the prize?" asked Bryce.

The Lieutenant chuckled. "No worries. Ceridwen and Rhona are watching her."

Aisling tried to blink the pain and dizziness away. Who were they talking about?

Darkness covered Bryce's face and his features faded away into shadow. His voice a whisper now, he asked, "Are you going to kill this one?"

The blade moved a tiny fraction, cutting into her neck. A cacophony of quiet screams leaked out of the sword—echoes of dying souls. "Where would be the fun in that?" he whispered.

Bryce seemed to inhale the darkness around him. He said, "A beautiful thing is never perfect." His eyes began to glow with an unearthly light. "You should kill her."

Several loud shots echoed through the trees, and Aisling realized that it was probably Genevieve's shotgun. The Shadow People had sent a raiding party into the Land of Dreams, but how did they pass into this world?

The Lieutenant said, "You know, Bryce, there are two kinds of people: Wolves and sheep. It's better to be a wolf, don't you think?"

Bryce's laugh crept into her soul, freezing it. "You're more like a black panther."

On the other side of the clearing, Aisling saw Eileen appear in a flash of blue and silver. Spinning around, Eileen slashed out with her sword and the shadows fell away from her, screaming.

The Lieutenant said, "No, exile, I'm not through with you yet!"

He kicked her in the side of the head, and Aisling saw no more.

*   *   *

A line of beautiful models, all wearing one of her creations, walked down a runway, paused near the end, twirled around and came back. Her clothes were a splash of color in a gray world dominated by restrictive, conservative styles. Not all fashion was so cold, but no one had ever seen such beauty as she had brought into the world. Aisling smiled. White dreams faded away into sunlight. A black raven flew out of pink clouds and landed on her shoulder, calling out, "I guard your death!"

Aisling wrinkled her brow. "What did you say?"

She opened her eyes and found herself lying in bed inside a large hallway, next to a row of beds with injured faeries. Light fell through a line of

171

high windows set into the stonework along one side of the hallway.

Fintan sat next to her, smiling. "Was it a pleasant dream?"

Aisling propped herself up on her elbows, but a wave of dizziness made her lay down again. Reaching up, she touched a soft cotton bandage wrapped around her head. Her smile, tinged with pain, returned. "Yes, but dreams are such frail things, don't you think?"

"Everyone's dreams are unique," whispered Fintan.

"My dreams are impossible," she whispered back.

"Aren't they all?"

Bird songs splashed into the hallway from an open window. She saw shadows dancing along the floor, breaking up the sunlight. "Do you have a dream, Fintan?"

He leaned back in his chair, casting his eyes outside. "I did, one time, long ago," he said. "I wanted to fill Ireland with people."

Someone laughed. "Is that why you once had seventeen wives?"

Aisling turned to see King Artrach standing on the other side of her bed. Before she could ask about his remark, he sat down and took Aisling's hand into his. "I'm sorry that our greatest healer isn't here at the moment," he said. "Morrigan seems to have gotten herself changed into a raven."

"She's always transforming herself into a raven," said Fintan.

Artrach chuckled. "Yes, but now she can't change back for a few days, or so they tell me." If he knew about the duelists, he didn't say anything. Artrach seemed to be preoccupied with other things—but what could be more serious than an attack of the Shadow People?

Aisling wasn't so sure she wanted Morrigan treating her injuries. "It's kind of you to visit me, your majesty," she said. "I'm still not sure what happened though."

"Sometimes the Shadow People come here, looking for slaves," said Fintan. "It was a raiding party, that's all."

Have they found it? Remembering Bryce's words, Aisling realized that they were looking for something else, but she didn't say anything.

Artrach looked down at the ring on Aisling's index finger with some curiosity. "What a fascinating ring," he murmured. "Where did you acquire it?"

"My father left it for me."

He paused a moment, lost in thought. He let go of her hand, smiling. "I'm glad you will recover, Aisling. For a Síofra, you have an uncanny ability to survive."

Aisling had almost forgotten the word: Síofra—a changeling. She wondered if he was trying to avoid hurting her feelings by using it.

Artrach stood up. Uncertainty and worry misted into his eyes. "People are disappearing," he whispered. "We believe they're falling into darkness. Already we have lost four Sídhe communities. The last was the Goibniu clan of Brí na Slieve."

"How is that possible?" asked Fintan.

"Pride," Artrach said. "As soon as a Faerie becomes too passionate or prideful, a pit of darkness opens up and they're never seen again."

Fintan tilted his head slightly, as he thought about the king's words. "What are you doing about it, Artrach?"

Aisling was surprised that Fintan would address the king without his honorific title. Not for the first time, she wondered about Fintan's status in this land.

The king shook his head. "On an unknown path, every foot is slow."

Shivering, Aisling thought of the changeling Báirbre, fading away into the shadows. The king got up and looked down into her eyes. "I'm very sorry about your friend, Aisling."

King Artrach went away then, stopping at beds to visit with some of the other faeries in the hospital.

Fully awake now, Aisling sat up onto her elbows, daring vertigo. She looked into Fintan's blue eyes. Dark images pooled there. "Tell me," she said.

"Trista has been arrested, along with several others."

"Why?"

"I don't know."

***

A sliver of moonlight shone down over the land. A short man, pale-faced and proud, stood by a hill. His white nose poked out of a bushy beard and mustache, and his black hair fell wildly about his shoulders. He wore a green tunic, dark pants, boots and a red cap. He held a spear in his hand.

As balls of light, they had taken a journey to the southeast along the King's Road. Aisling, accompanied by Genevieve, Eileen, Fáelán, Aoife and Nel, stopped in front of the hill. When they materialized in front of the man, he pointed his spear at them. Aisling brought her hand up in front of the spear tip and hastily withdrew it after touching the sharp point. She looked at Eileen dubiously, but it was Nel that spoke first. "Snorri, we seek entry to Svartálfaheimar."

The man was silent.

Nel raised her voice, "We're here for the . . . executions."

Eileen stepped forward. "Banishment," she corrected.

Nel raised an eyebrow. "What's the difference?"

The man removed his spear from their path and stepped back. With his other hand, he waved towards the rock face and a stone doorway appeared in the side of the hill. His speech was barren, "Go."

The door opened up to a tall hallway, lit with candles set into sconces along the walls. After walking down through a long sloping corridor, they came to a large domed chamber that held rows of tables and benches. Silver candelabrums lined the walls, providing cold illumination to the hall.

Genevieve asked, "Who was that guarding the door?"

Eileen said, "He's one of the Dvergar. They live underground, inside hills like this one."

"Are there many of these cities?" asked Aisling.

"There's a Dwarf city near Sídhe an Domhan, where the Creidhne clan lives, but I've never been there," said Eileen.

Several doors provided an exit, but the largest one was now open. A bright blue tracery of illumination in front of the arched doorway, created a pattern of symbols in the air. Raising her hand, Aisling touched the energy barrier with the tip of her finger. Tingling sensations washed over her arm. She gave Eileen a questioning look.

Eileen said in a distracted tone, "It's just a spell to keep out the Shadow People." Without another word she walked through the archway. Aisling watched her friend go, hesitating like a swimmer afraid to jump into a lake. She heard Eileen calling from beyond the doorway, "You coming?"

Aisling glanced over her shoulder at Genevieve, who shook her head. "No, no, no. You go first."

Taking a deep breath, Aisling walked forward. Stepping through the magic barrier made her skin tingle hotly, as if she had just gone through a fire without getting burned. Taking another deep breath, she looked around for the others, but they had already gone on.

Beyond the archway they found a long stairway, descending into the earth and lit with candles. The stones were roughly cut, and the walls were moist. Three times they came to a resting place with benches set into the walls.

As they went down, Eileen was fuming. "This is all your fault, Nel."

Nel and Eileen were in front of Aisling, but their words echoed against the walls.

"How so?" asked Nel.

"The Shadow People were seen all around the cathedral," said Eileen. "Didn't you try to stop them?"

"How could I?" said Nel. "I was alone. I was sent here to guard the cathedral, not to run around chasing after fallen beings."

"You could have done something," said Eileen. "Now several people are captives of the Shadow People and one of our friends. . ." her words choked off into silence.

Nel was indignant. "Their pride attracted the shadows. I didn't make them fight their *affaires d'honneur*."

Eileen protested, "But Trista wasn't involved in any duels."

Nel didn't answer.

Were the Shadow People drawn towards the prideful? Aisling felt a

175

dark hole forming in her stomach. Was she the cause of this? She wondered if the Shadow People would have attacked if Conall hadn't been motivated to fight a duel over her.

After more than an hour of descent, Aisling heard a soft sighing sound. The walls, floor and roof of the passage were now covered in moisture. After another few minutes of descent, she recognized the sound of a waterfall. At last, they came to a wooden landing built into the side of a cave. Reflected torchlight rippled against a waterfall emptying into an underground lake. Several hundred of the Aos Sídhe stood on one side, away from the dark water.

Queen Annan stood next to a dozen guards, all wearing swords and breastplates. The queen's eyes were filled with sorrow. Her lips still held a hint of a smile, however. It was as if she had difficulty feeling pain.

Next to the queen was a fairy that Aisling had never seen before. She was thin and tall, with long straight black hair, and an oriental face airbrushed in silvery makeup. She wore bright red leather pants, a white tunic with flared sleeves, and black boots. She held a black metallic staff in her hand.

Fáelán whispered in Aisling's ear, "That's Kusanagi Gin, the Inferno Fairy. She was brought here by the Dvergar King, Mótsognir. She's in the queen's personal guard."

"What kind of staff is that?"

"It's some kind of elemental weapon," he whispered.

Among the gathered faeries, Aisling caught sight of Trista in the dress she had made for her. Cobalt silk clung and shimmered, falling to just above her knees and leaving her back, neck, and shoulders bare. Her long blonde hair framed it perfectly. Aisling had never seen her look so beautiful. When Trista smiled, Aisling looked away.

A hushed silence covered the throng, leaving only the sound of the water echoing through the cave. Queen Annan said in a gentle, commanding voice, "Over three thousand years ago, before the invasion of the Milesians, Ith came to our land with new ideas about pride and freedom."

176

Follow your dreams. Ith's words about freedom returned. Aisling wondered if the words he had spoken to the Sídhe so long ago were the same as his appeal to her. A cold wind blew through the cave and something prickled against her skin. Although there were several hundred faeries present, she felt someone watching from the shadows.

Queen Annan's voice dropped to a whisper, "When he left us, we sent warriors against him, knowing that if he made it home, he would come back to us again, with more of these dangerous ideas. This would have destroyed us all. Pride and passion lead to slavery—a cruel way of living, where the weak are dominated by the strong. For this reason, I have commanded the Aos Sídhe to repress their desires. Guard your thoughts and actions. Pride and passion will only lead to jealousy, resentment, cruelty, and evil. Be careful what you dream."

Out of the corner of Aisling's eye, something moved. A Shadow Person stood near Trista. Aisling realized that Trista, with her beautiful songs, must be the "prize" they had talked about. Bryce had also mentioned a key. Was she looking at Ceridwen now? Aisling realized that her best chance of rescuing her sister Erin was to capture the key. She began to search for the other Shadow Person.

Turning to the accused, the queen said, "These people have all broken my commandment to repress their desires, their pride and their passions. Yesterday, while you were fighting duels, the Shadow People, drawn by this pride, attacked, taking some captive, and slaying others. So I am banishing these people to the darkness. If they remain here, their dark thoughts will infect us, and we will all fall into shadow."

Hushed voices filled the cave. The shadows forgotten for a moment, Aisling's mouth dropped open. How could pride be a crime here? Wasn't her life all about pride? "Doing the impossible" had always been her motto. Was that pride? Was she doomed to fall into darkness too? She looked at Trista, whose face was full of sorrow.

Queen Annan waved her scepter and a dark whirlpool appeared in the water. Several of the Dvergar, who had been standing by next to the walls, came forward, brandishing spears.

Aisling held her breath, looking desperately about for evidence of the other Shadow Person. The Dvergar began forcing the captives into the whirlpool of shadow.

Suddenly, Trista began to sing. It was a sad melody. More beautiful than any music Aisling had ever heard before. It was a song about cruelty and injustice. It was the song of an innocent person, unjustly condemned to a savage fate. The entire host of the Sídhe stood transfixed. Even the Dvergar stopped.

It was at that moment that Aisling noticed Ceridwen standing in the crowd, among the Tuatha Dé Danaan. She had taken corporeal form, appearing just as she had when Aisling had first seen her. Around her neck was the Shadow Key on a silver chain.

In a moment she knew that she would forever hate herself for, Aisling moved away from Trista and towards Ceridwen. As soon as she was behind her quarry, Aisling reached up and swiftly snatched the silver chain hanging around her neck.

Ceridwen spun around, fading into shadow. Her eyes glowed with red malice. Realizing that she had been discovered, both she and Rhona—the other Shadow Person in the crowd—turned away and leapt into the black vortex.

Trista finished her song and with one last look at Aisling, turned and fell into the whirlpool of darkness. As silence descended over the cavern, Aisling found herself sitting on the ground, weeping.

* * *

Chapter Ten

The Garden of Thought

Aisling lay on the earth, her face covered by a tangle of dark hair. As the night receded, she became aware of the cool grass pressed against her face. She inhaled the dawn air deeply before opening her eyes, and found herself surrounded by a cloud of mist rising from the ground. Sunlight poured down onto the earth, filling it with warmth and light and vitality, and she could feel the world waking up. Little white flowers were sprinkled all over the grass. She inhaled the sweet fragrance of gardenias and the spicy wisteria aroma of viburnums. Not wanting to move at all, she simply lay there, looking through the hair covering her face into the mist, and listening to the fluttering of insects and to the birds, whose songs drifted into the morning breeze.

She shut her eyes, and guilt burned through her stomach like a dark hole opening inside her. It was all her fault. The raid of the Shadow People had been caused by a duel fought over her. Her flirtatious behavior had inspired the pride which brought evil into the world.

Trista had covered the world with a kind of beauty that Aisling had never known before, songs of enchantment and love and happiness and resplendent power. Now Trista's songs would never return. Trista had been banished because of Aisling, who didn't even try to stop it.

Unable to bear the shame that covered her, Aisling had gone away into the wilderness for two weeks. Her friends hadn't followed her this time. She'd been left alone with the flowers, the birds, the trees—and her guilt.

Opening her eyes, Aisling saw that the sunlight had burned off some of the mist. Raising a hand to brush the hair out of her face, Aisling remained where she was, listening. Silence filled the clearing where she lay, except for the birds—and something else: like a soft whisper, the gentle sounds of trickling water came on, rising with the warm mist that drained away into the sky.

Aisling sat up, pulling her legs underneath her. She wore a long burgundy dress, now covered in dew, and simple black sandals. Eyes down, she reached up to touch the Shadow Key, which now hung around her neck on a silver chain. What door would it open? How would she find it? Was this key truly worth it? No, nothing was worth Trista's life. Without her bright songs, the world would forever after remain a dark place.

A gentle melody drifted by, mixed into the sounds of rushing water. Aisling looked up, wondering where it had come from. It was a violin, and it reminded her of Mozart, but it was more enchanting still. The music intensified her pain, and the songs of Trista returned to her mind.

Getting up, she followed the music and came to a riverbank. Next to a willow tree stood a very attractive man, with dark pants, a white peasant shirt exposing a strong chest, and a green hat. He was playing a gentle song on a violin, next to the water. Aisling, afraid of halting such lovely music, hesitated. She sat down by the river to listen, gazing down into the cool water, where white water-lilies floated. The man continued his song, and it brought out both sadness and loneliness such as she had never known before. Tears watered the ground at her feet, while he played. It seemed that the trees were dancing too, sadly swaying in the gentle breeze. When the music stopped, she felt a deep longing.

The man approached silently, a faint smile on his lips. He offered Aisling his hand, and she let him help her to her feet. For a moment he paused, and she felt a mysterious power flowing from him, like clear water tumbling over a waterfall. She met his eyes—blue as forget-me-nots, cold as moonlight on a river on a frosted river. His arm slipped around her waist, lifting her easily, his smile touched with sorrow. Breathless, she answered with a shy smile of her own.

The man turned towards the river and jumped into the water.

Plunging down, Aisling was too surprised to have taken a breath. She fought to break free of him, but he held her down with strong arms, embracing her in a cold grip. She looked into his eyes, which were now smiling, while the last air in her lungs emptied out. He held her tight in his arms, pulling her down with him into the cold depths of the river. Her resistance drained away faster than the remnants of air in her lungs, and she began to choke, while darkness began to overtake her.

There was a flash of golden light all around her and she felt the man's grip loosening altogether. Firm hands reached under her arms and pulled her up. The man continued to sink down, his arms now empty, and his face filling with sadness again.

Breaking the surface of the river, Aisling spluttered and coughed. Someone dragged her out of the water and back onto the riverbank. She found herself lying face down, gasping for air and coughing.

A familiar voice rang out, "Two whole weeks! You never call—you never write. Don't you love me anymore?"

Aisling looked up into Genevieve's face and smiled.

Eileen, dripping wet in a short white dress, sat down next to Aisling, placing one hand on her back. "Are you alright?"

Aisling nodded gratefully. "That man—he was playing the most beautiful music—who is he?"

Eileen smiled. "He's a 'Nix.' Women of their kind are called 'Nixies,'" she explained. "Strong emotions attract them. They're water spirits, capable of shape-changing into the most attractive—"

"He's gorgeous, I know!" Aisling interrupted. "—and his music! It's fantastic!"

"Want him to teach it to you?" Eileen asked. "I can call him back if you want—"

"Eileen!"

Rising into a sitting position, Aisling looked at her friends and chuckled. "No, I think I'm done with music for the time being."

Aisling looked down at her burgundy dress, now drenched with river water. She stood up, closed her eyes and tilted her head up into the sun, imagining it bathing her in warmth. When she opened her eyes again, she and her dress were dry. She asked, "Not that I'm complaining, but what are you two doing here?"

"We need your help, Aisling," said Eileen. "Morrigan has been insufferable ever since you left!"

"She's almost as bad as Eileen here," said Genevieve.

Eileen glared at Genevieve. Aisling's gold medallion still hung around her neck. For a moment, Aisling thought Genevieve was the most beautiful woman in the world.

Noticing that Genevieve was completely dry, Eileen dropped her voice to an accusing whisper. "I didn't see you leaping into the water to help."

Genevieve crossed her arms. "It's too early for swimming, don't you think Aisling?"

Aisling, noticing that Eileen hadn't dried herself off yet, used her senses to feel around for another fire elemental, but the one she'd used moments before had gone. Despite the fact that she was now dry, Aisling began to shiver. She asked doubtfully, "You need my help with Morrigan?"

Eileen smiled, and wiped a wet strand of blonde hair out of her face. "Morrigan is putting on a fashion show next week."

Aisling raised her eyebrows. "Really?"

Eileen nodded.

All three of them shared conspiratorial glances.

* * *

It was a small island, with a quaint cottage nestled next to a garden. Situated on a hill, the house held a commanding view of the heavens, and of Vancouver, which gleamed against the night sky. Irial, who used the house when visiting the royal palace, was the leader of Cnoc Síoraíocht, a Sídhe near San Francisco. She had offered the cottage as a secret meeting place for Aisling and her friends while they worked on a fashion show of their own. Burning logs illuminated the room from the fireplace.

Something moved in the twilight outside the cottage, just beyond the trees. Aisling, holding a colored pencil between her teeth, looked outside through the small window overlooking the front of the dwelling. She heard Genevieve and Aoife talking quietly together, while they approached. Aisling put the pencil down by a drawing, one design among hundreds, and stood up impatiently as the door opened. The two came in, followed by Hieronymus, who slipped through the doorway just before they closed it.

Aisling crossed her arms. "Well?"

Genevieve, carrying her shotgun, came in and sat down on the rustic couch. She placed the magic weapon across her lap, closed her eyes and sighed. "Well what?"

Frowning darkly, Aisling walked over to lean against the window, throwing a glance outside. Stars glittered in the ocean, down below the island. "I can't do this all myself, Gen," she said. "I need help finding models, hairdressers, stylists, makeup artists, dressers—"

Aoife lowered herself into a rocking chair, and Hieronymus jumped into her lap. "Relax, Aisling. We're working on it."

Wondering if it was a good idea to have tried to create a fashion show, Aisling didn't feel very relaxed. "No luck again?" she asked.

Aoife ran a hand over the cat and shook her head.

Aisling sighed. "We don't even have a venue."

Irial, who had been teaching Aisling the powers of enchantment, sat in front of a spinning wheel and a loom. She had long brown hair that framed dark eyes, and delicate features. She wore a long white sheer dress, bound with a gold belt, and silver sandals. She was turning out bolts of cloth by feeding the spinning wheel pieces of straw. As soon as it came off the wheel, the thread magically wove itself into fabric on the loom. Her voice was calm, "Patience, Aisling. I'm sure everything will work out."

Aisling bit her lip, not wanting to argue with one of her mentors. Hieronymus jumped off Aoife's lap and began rubbing against Aisling's legs. Sitting down, she sighed and leaned onto her elbow, face in her hand. "I should never have tried this."

Aisling leaned back in her chair and Hieronymus jumped onto her lap. She idly ran a hand across his back. "Everything is so different here," she said. "I should be working on a winter show, not one with spring fashions."

Irial stopped spinning out blue silk on the wheel and looked up. "But why make clothes out of season?"

Genevieve put the shotgun down next to the couch. "In my world, you have to allow time for manufacturing, distribution, advertising, promotion—"

Irial's soft laughter sounded like stardust settling onto the earth. "How silly you Milesians are!"

"Meow!"

Aisling picked up the cat and dropped him onto the floor. "I'm sorry, Hieronymus. I have to work."

But the cat wouldn't give up. He sat down and looked up into her eyes plaintively. He meowed again, more insistent this time.

A blue flash marked the appearance of Eileen, who hovered for a moment as a tiny sphere, and then flared again, appearing in the center of the room. She kneeled down next to the cat. "I think he wants something."

The cat began to rub his collar against Eileen's hand. She reached down and grasped a small gem that hung from it. "Hold still, Hieronymus." Eileen took off the cat's collar and held up the gem. Moonlight fell through the window, and washed over the blue sapphire. "This is a Transfer Stone."

Irial brushed hair out of her face. "Really?"

Aoife, Genevieve and Aisling exchanged puzzled expressions.

Eileen laughed. "It's a kind of psychic crystal that absorbs a targeted person's thoughts and memories, transferring them into the stone," she explained. "Hieronymus has been spying on our competition."

Irial went over to the kitchen, procuring a large bowl. Filling it with water, she placed it onto the dining room table, while the others gathered around it. Eileen walked up and dropped the sapphire into the bowl. Irial looked at the feline. "Hieronymus?"

The cat jumped up onto the table and looked into the bowl, concentrating on it. A light ignited, down in the water. It began to shimmer and sparkle and an image appeared in the surface.

The person whose eyes they were seeing through stood next to Morrigan, who stood by a long rack of Renaissance dresses. Morrigan was talking to Alaiya, the Style Fairy. "Is everything ready to go?"

Alaiya turned around and nodded. "I've heard that there's another fashion show being organized by the Síofra Aisling."

Morrigan laughed. "Yes, with no venue, no guest list, no models, no hairstylists, no theme—" Shaking her head, she said. "What a fool!"

Alaiya chuckled and walked down a long hallway full of people and out of sight. Morrigan glanced over her shoulder at the person whose mind the magic gem had invaded. "Come on, Kerrin."

They went through a large estate, ending up in a private dressing room. Morrigan sat down at a table next to a window looking out onto the garden of a large house while Kerrin picked up a hair brush and began brushing Morrigan's hair. Aisling could almost feel the texture of Morrigan's beautiful hair in Kerrin's hands.

"Do you know why I spend so much time on my appearance, Kerrin?"

Hesitating only slightly, Kerrin continued to brush Morrigan's hair. "To be the most beautiful one of all," she said.

Morrigan glanced out the window, where black birds swirled above the garden surrounding the estate. "There's a reason of course," she said. "One of the greatest sources of my magic comes from the admiration of others."

"I know you're an enchantress, mistress," said Kerrin.

"I'm more than a simple enchantress," said Morrigan. "I protect the kingdom, and so I must guard the sources of my power."

Kerrin stopped running the brush through Morrigan's hair, for a moment only, but she didn't answer.

"You certainly don't think I have any rivals?" asked Morrigan.

"Of course not, mistress," said Kerrin.

Morrigan glanced at a hand mirror lying face down on the table. Her fingers hovered over it, as if she was considering leaving it where it was. After a moment's hesitation, she picked it up and looked into her own reflection.

Kerrin's hand began to shake slightly.

Morrigan said, "Magic mirror, if you care, show me the fairest of the fair."

Expecting to see Genevieve's reflection in the glass, Aisling was shocked to see her own face appear in Morrigan's mirror.

Morrigan flinched, and Kerrin dropped the brush. Morrigan turned around and yelled, "Get out!"

The image swirled away and vanished.

* * *

Daylight fell down to the field in front of the cottage. Aisling stood, sword at the ready, facing Fintan, while Genevieve and Eileen looked on. Sparring had always been a way to vent her frustrations.

Aisling didn't know what to do. Perhaps it was all a waste of time, trying to organize a fashion show. It irked her that she could be so easily humbled by Morrigan.

Aisling had summoned an Air Elemental, hoping to gain the power and swiftness to overcome her opponent. She attacked with her sword several times, but every stroke was blocked by Fintan, who had demonstrated considerable skill with a sword. Instead of venting her frustration, the entire exercise had just made her worse. Seeing an opening, Fintan deftly disarmed her. Aisling screamed out in annoyance.

"Let's take a break," said Fintan. "You're quite good, but I've been using swords for centuries."

Aisling sat down in the grass, defeated. "Nothing works here," she said. "I can't even create the kinds of clothes I like. The queen is *very* particular with what she wants."

Since becoming the queen's dressmaker, Aisling had been stifled in her clothing designs. Anytime she wanted to make something really good, the queen had chastised her, as if *Gentle Annie* was trying to curb her passion. It felt like working in a straitjacket.

No one said anything. Silence began to settle into the clearing.

Aisling couldn't get the attack of the Shadow People out of her mind. "I was completely blindsided in that raid. I can't believe they surprised me so easily."

Eileen, who had been watching from the lip of a stone wall, jumped down and came closer. "The Shadow People are difficult to see, especially if you're looking directly at them. No amount of martial arts training could warn you of a shadow that appears out of nowhere."

Genevieve, still on the wall, glanced down at the shotgun which Finnian had given to her. "Why don't the Sídhe use firearms?"

Eileen turned around. "If you're confronted by two opponents, one with a knife, the other with a handgun, which one do you deal with first?"

Genevieve smiled. "I'd probably take out the one with the gun."

Eileen laughed. "You'd be dead," she said. "The person with the knife would reach you and cut an artery, and your blood would drain out in no time at all. But many people have survived gunshot wounds."

Genevieve, not willing to admit defeat, hefted the shotgun. "Not if I shoot them with this," she said. "I just don't see why the Sídhe refuse to use firearms. There's a reason no one uses swords anymore in my world."

"*This* world's conflict is a war of surprise," said Eileen. "Shadow People appear suddenly and then you have a sword at your throat. There isn't time for long range warfare."

Genevieve ran her hand along the shotgun, almost like she was petting

187

it. "You people aren't very good at fighting, are you?"

Eileen frowned. "The Tuatha Dé do not spend their time waging wars," she said. "Swords are easier to conjure up quickly—that's all."

"So instead of warfare, you fight duels?" Genevieve let out an angry huff. "I've seen the results of those."

"Duels are more civilized than warfare," said Eileen. "Besides, no one would bring a superior weapon to a duel."

"You're too trusting, Eileen."

"Am I?"

Aisling interrupted them. "How about a truce you two?"

They both became silent.

Fintan, stifling a grin, retrieved Aisling's sword. "Remember, if you would build something solid, don't work with wind: always look for a fixed point, something you know that is stable—yourself."

Reluctantly, Aisling took the weapon. The Chinese sword had taken years to master, but now she looked at it doubtfully. It was called a 'Liuye Dao,' which translated to, 'willow leaf saber.' Right now it felt more like a leaf than a weapon. "Lasarina told me that conjured swords like these won't affect the Shadow People."

Fintan held out his short sword, whose blade curved downward at an angle. Its hilt was hook-shaped, and the end of the handle was fashioned into the shape of a horse. "This is a Greek sword. It's called a 'Makhaira.' This type of weapon was used by Alexander the Great. The angle of the blade and grip places the weapon in a position like you have when shaking hands. The blade's mass will carry the weapon forward because of the inertia in the blade, but the curved grip will help you keep hold of it. It will deliver blows with the momentum of an axe, and the cutting edge of a sword. I've added some enhancements of my own of course. As you can see, this isn't an iron weapon—it's made from steel."

Aisling held the sword in her hand, feeling something stir inside. Her fingers tingled slightly, and she could feel awesome power in the weapon. It was as if she was holding onto a current of torrential water, slipping through her hands, threatening to pull along anything that dared to touch it. She handed the weapon back, wondering why the sensation had felt so familiar to her. "I don't expect you to give me your sword, Fintan."

"Why not use your father's weapon?" Eileen said. "Don't you remember it?"

Aisling felt like she'd just been struck with a thunderbolt. "I completely forgot about it!"

Smiling, Eileen said, "I'll go get it."

Eileen changed into a blue ball of light in a flash and then shot up into the sky.

Aisling pursed her lips, wondering if she could adapt to the style of the Celtic sword. It was much like the Chinese Jian swords, which were straight, but they took more time to master than the curved Dao sword, which she was well practiced with.

Fáelán flew down out of the sky, landing with a smile on his lips. "Good news," he said. "Nel has offered the clearing next to the cathedral as a place for your show."

Relief spilling into her thoughts, Aisling smiled.

Fáelán seemed to be holding something else back, and so she raised an eyebrow. "There's more?"

Fáelán nodded. "Yes. We've found some models. Their names are Maija, Paola and Siri."

"Síofra?" asked Fintan.

"Yes," said Fáelán. "They're all changelings, like Aoife and Aisling."

Aisling stood up, while excitement began to flow into her blood. Now she would find out if she could make something as grand as Morrigan had planned. Was she good enough? For the first time since she had come to the land of dreams, she felt the thrilling challenge of doing the impossible.

* * *

Aisling paced back and forth, down the aisle in the center of the cathedral. She wore a yellow dress with white polka dots, rose-colored shoes, and a wide-brimmed hat, which was now in her hand. Too nervous to stand

189

still, she continued to move about until Genevieve walked in through the side door. Aisling stopped in her tracks, looking at her best friend.

Genevieve wore a short black tunic with white pinstripes, a matching miniskirt, a white belt, and sandals that laced up to her knees. Aisling still wondered why Morrigan's mirror hadn't shown Genevieve's reflection instead of her own.

Genevieve leaned against one of the pews. "Nervous?"

Aisling smiled. "Not really," she said. "Morrigan's show was fantastic, but I think they'll like mine better."

"Then why are you pacing?" asked Genevieve. "Nel managed to invite the king and queen, and most of the leaders of each Faerie Sídhe. I think the fact that some of them are your mentors had something to do with them showing up."

Aisling crossed her arms. "You should be in the show, Gen. Aoife and the others aren't as tall as you are."

"No, we can't make any changes now."

A fairy flew into the cathedral, and he landed in front of the two of them. He wore a red tunic, white tights, and had a yellow cape. He held a purple velvet pillow in his hands, upon which rested a fragrant bundle of incense. "A gift," he said, offering the pillow to Aisling.

Raising an eyebrow at Genevieve, Aisling took it. "What's this?"

"Out of Ethiopia, this is the finest myrrh in the world, Madame," he said. "There is a message, too."

Aisling took the note, which read, *I send thee myrrh, not that thou mayest be by it perfumed, but it perfumed by thee.*

She looked at the signature, unsure how to respond to the gift. In a distracted tone, she thanked the messenger, who bowed and flew out the open doorway.

Genevieve smiled conspiratorially. "Hey, Conall must really like you."

"This isn't from him."

"Then who is it from?"

"Keir."

Genevieve raised her eyebrows. "Who's Keir?"

Aisling put the gift down on one of the pews, uninterested in it. "He's nobody," she said. "Come on, let's go to our show."

They walked outside the cathedral, which was bathed in the light of the stars. They found a large audience in the garden, mixed in with silver candelabrums full of flickering light. Fáelán and Nel went through the crowd, carrying trays of champagne. Nel seemed to relish the chance to help Aisling. *Perhaps she did so out of spite for the queen?* She too, had been devastated by the banishment of Trista. Aisling and Genevieve walked out in front of the gathering, and bowed to the king and queen. "Welcome to our fashion show," Aisling said.

A bright light flared up overhead, washing the crowd in a brilliant silver glow that gradually shifted into all of the colors of the rainbow. Instead of a line of models appearing at the end of the runway, which split the crowd in two, there were a series of flashes high up over the stage. These changed into radiant fairies, flying through the air and then descending down to the runway. They strutted to the end, twirled around, took off into the air, flew over the crowd and then vanished in a flash, reappearing again in a different outfit and doing it all again.

The models were all changelings, except for Eileen. This caused a collective gasp throughout the Sídhe. Changelings were considered to be second-class citizens. Aisling enjoyed sending this kind of jolt through the crowd, though she wondered if she would hear about it later. She'd considered using Trista's songs in the fashion show, but decided against it, choosing something more like the music played by the Nix.

Paola appeared first. She was a demure brunette with a face that was always pouting. She wore a sheer red dress with a bodice studded in rubies, a short black skirt underneath a long sheer scarlet skirt, and ruby slippers. After strutting down the runway, she soared into the air and flared out in a bright cherry light.

Maija, a blonde with a haunted expression, came down next. She wore a tight mini-dress with a gray and blue marble pattern woven into it, cobalt blue shoes and a short gray fitted jacket with a high collar. The pattern in the dress looked like clouds drifting overhead. When she reached the end of the runway, she twirled around and her dress changed into metallic blue material. She spun around, flying up into the dark sky while lightning flashed around her. With a thunderclap, she vanished.

Siri, the changeling Aisling had encountered on the road, appeared wearing a gold mini-dress, bronze bracelets and golden sandals. She held a bow in her hand and shot an arrow into the night sky, igniting a golden fireball that illuminated the runway with molten light.

When Siri appeared, Aisling noticed Morrigan in the crowd, scowling. The last time she'd seen Siri was when the girl had killed Laigne. For an instant, Aisling felt a wave of sympathy for her rival.

Aoife appeared next, her red hair flying behind her. She wore metallic silver tights, a pink dress and a short white jacket. She seemed to be having the time of her life strutting down the runway and flying over the crowd. Aisling noticed Aoife smiling at the queen. It was as if Trista had never been banished.

Finally, Eileen appeared at the end of the runway, strutting towards the crowd wearing a white mini-dress with spaghetti straps, and silver sandals laced up to her knees.

The show continued, with alternating types of clothes, first long dresses, then short mini-dresses, and then outfits with leggings in various patterns and colors. After the final run, all of the models appeared over the stage and twirled up into the air until they could no longer be seen. An explosion of color flashed overhead, and then it began to rain flower petals.

Aisling and Genevieve met the models on the runway, and they gave a collective bow to the crowd, whose uproarious applause filled the clearing. Aisling turned to Genevieve, who said, "Wow!"

Eileen whispered in Aisling's ear, "That was fun. Let's do it again soon."

Queen Annan approached, along with Morrigan and the Style Fairy, Alaiya.

Kusanagi Gin stood nearby, watching in silence.

Aisling consciously ignored the Inferno Fairy, and after bowing, greeted the queen as she came near. "Did you enjoy it, Majesty?"

Queen Annan's smile had always been infectious. "It was lovely." She said. "Morrigan here was just telling me how much she enjoyed your show."

Aisling, taken aback, raised her eyebrows, and looked at Morrigan. There was a malicious satisfaction in those blue eyes. "Really?"

With a face that reminded Aisling of a purring cat, Morrigan smiled. She ran a hand over her black tunic, as if she was petting herself. "No one could deny that your designs are beautiful—for a Síofra."

Alaiya chimed in. "Yes, if you were a normal Faerie, like Morrigan here, I'd register your designs so that all of our merchants could offer your clothes to the Sídhe."

Wrinkling her brow, Aisling knew there was a reason behind Morrigan's friendly demeanor. "I'm not sure I understand."

The queen, unable to stop smiling for even a moment, said, "Didn't you know? When a Síofra falls into shadow, all of their work—all of their designs and all of their dreams, fall into darkness with them. All evidence of their existence is utterly erased."

As a changeling, her designs would inevitably fade away.

Forever.

Why build a sand castle, knowing that it would wash away with the next tide? Aisling didn't know what to say.

Queen Annan laughed softly. "I'm not saying that I expect you to disappear soon, but we can't have clothes vanishing out of our shops, can we?"

The trio left Aisling standing there, stunned. The idea that everything she would ever do, every accomplishment, would vanish if she fell into the Land of Shadows, was more than unsettling. The news ripped through her heart like a hot arrow. What was the use of creating anything?

Aisling knew that she could beat Morrigan in a fair competition, but Morrigan seemed determined to win at any cost. Aisling went home to her room in the castle feeling cheated, and more useless than ever.

Aisling stood in the center of the courtyard, eyes closed, listening to a quiet song that blew through her soul. Trista's music was truly ingrained in her memory forever, yet her friend had been cast into the darkness. Aisling wondered why the memories endured. Could she have been only partially flawed, not really prideful at all? But why would the queen banish her if she wasn't guilty? What did it really mean to fall into the Land of Shadows? The idea of being completely, irrevocably erased from existence was more than unsettling, but Trista still remained, a tiny shadow of sunlight in Aisling's mind. Cool wind blew across her skin, scattering dark locks of hair across her face. She tilted her head, listening to the silence surrounding her.

Someone approached.

Opening her eyes to a courtyard bordered by a low stone wall that overlooked one of the palace gardens, Aisling noticed one of her friends approaching. Fáelán walked down across the flagstones, past a long row of poplar trees. As he drew near, she turned around and walked over to the low wall, where the long case containing her father's sword was.

The case, made from dark cherry wood carved with Celtic knotwork, had gold latches and it was lined in black velvet. Unlatching the case, she looked down at her father's sword. Not at all used to this type of weapon, she wondered if she'd really forgotten it, or if she'd been avoiding using it altogether. To touch it, to hold it in her hand, was to reach into the past where her father lived. Indeed, he'd held this sword in his hand, he had used it. At the same time, it was like listening to the quiet voices of her destiny. An unmistakable sighing sound emanated from the box when she picked up the sword. As she held it aloft, the world looked brighter, and the sun danced off the blade.

Just as it had been when she first examined the sword, she was surprised at how light it was for its size. She ran a finger down the blade, touching the engraving there, and feeling subtle, tingling sensations wash over her skin. She could feel the *Chi* flowing free and strong through her body, and it gave her an urge to move.

As Fáelán reached her, she was already executing Wushu forms that had been ingrained in her since she was a child. The sword made everything come alive inside, like the perfect dance partner, always knowing what direction you were about to take. It turned a dull exercise into an enchanting performance.

Fáelán's voice snapped over the quiet courtyard. "I just don't understand it."

Aisling continued with the circular ballet. He took a seat on the wall, looking rather perturbed. Knowing that he would explain his comment, she didn't bother answering him.

"You have a magic sword now, and you know where she is," he said. "So why don't you try to rescue Erin?"

Aisling shook her head. "It isn't that simple."

"It *is* that simple. Let's just go get her."

Aisling spun around in mock strikes against shadow opponents. "I still need to find a doorway to the Land of Shadows, and even if I knew of one, I won't be able to overcome Ith."

"It's more than that, Aisling," he said. "Ever since the show, something's been different about you."

The fashion show was a time when she'd felt free. Free to create whatever she liked. Free to express her dreams. Free to live. But it didn't really matter what she could create, since it would all soon fall away into oblivion. For the first time, she wondered if she should have taken Ith up on his offer: To live a life of unrestricted freedom. The queen offered a better life perhaps, but it was one of repression. Neither choice offered anything of interest to her. Narrowing her eyes, she remained silent.

Fáelán crossed his arms. "Pardon the pun, but it's like you've become a shadow of yourself."

Aisling smiled briefly. "I never fight a battle unless I know I am going to win."

"Sort of takes the fun out of it, don't you think?"

Aisling swept the weapon down in a low arc and then twirled around to face him. "I don't intend to lose."

"That's not the reason you're hesitating," he said.

"No?"

His voice dropped down to a cold whisper, "You don't think you can do it."

Fighting off a growing sense of frustration, she stopped practicing and looked into his dark eyes. Unable to bear his accusation, she turned away and muttered under her breath, "What does belief have to do with it? I'm just being careful."

Fáelán said, "Aisling, if you want to succeed at anything, you need to believe in yourself."

Aisling laughed. "Don't be a fool Fáelán. We're talking about the Lord of Shadows. It would be a miracle to defeat him."

"I thought one of your mottos was, 'do the impossible.'"

Aisling squinted into the sunlight. "That's different."

"Really?"

Queen Annan's voice rang out in the clearing. "It's a Celtic weapon, isn't it?"

They both turned to see the queen standing under one of the poplar trees, accompanied by the Inferno Fairy. Both she and Fáelán bowed, as Queen Annan came forward.

Aisling glanced at Kusanagi Gin, feeling slightly unnerved by her. With the aspect of a beautiful Japanese girl, she looked entirely normal, except for the cold stare in her eyes. She held the strange staff in her hands.

Queen Annan's voice broke into Aisling's unsettled thoughts. "I like the attire— so simple, yet functional for sword play."

Aisling wore a loose white blouse with flared sleeves, bound with a green cloth belt, purple and white striped leggings and a pair of black patent leather boots that laced up the front. Her response was quiet. "Thanks."

The queen raised her hand, "May I?"

Returning the queen's smile, Aisling handed over the sword. After examining it closely for a moment, Queen Annan gave it back. "This inscription along the blade is interesting, don't you think?"

With raised eyebrows, Aisling looked at the engraving. Mixed into the pattern of leaves was a style of writing that she hadn't noticed before, along with something else that was unnerving: Bones and skulls were woven into the pattern of leaves. "I've never noticed these words before, your majesty," she said. "What do they say?"

Queen Annan tilted her head coyly, and walked over to the wall next to Fáelán, taking a seat on the cool stone. "It says: 'I will slay and I will make alive. This is your life and the blessedness of your days.'"

Before Aisling could ask what it could mean, the queen said, "This isn't Celtic. It's a Fomorian weapon."

Aisling and Fáelán exchanged startled looks.

"Could you excuse us for a short time, Fáelán?" The queen asked. "I have something to show our friend here."

"Yes," Fáelán bowed, "of course, your majesty."

White wings, with exquisite purple designs, appeared on the queen's back and she flew up into the air, heading for a hill overlooking the bay. The Inferno Fairy sprouted black metallic wings and followed after. Aisling returned her sword to the box, handed it to Fáelán, extended her own white wings, and then followed after the queen.

They flew high up over the hill, which contained a picturesque garden. Flowers and trees grew in a wild arrangement, yet everything held together in a kind of formal confinement. In the center of the grove, at the very top of the hill, stood a tall white pillar, surrounded by a swirling mass of smoke. Occasional flashes of light came out of the small whirlwind. The queen landed a few paces from the edge of the smoke, while Kusanagi Gin continued to circle overhead. Aisling landed next to the queen, too curious to speak.

Queen Annan retracted her gorgeous wings and began to stroll in a circle around the smoky area. "How do you think magic really works, Aisling?"

Walking next to the queen, Aisling said, "You choose what you want, imagine it, and then trigger it."

The queen's laughter was like rain falling into a clear pond. "You forgot the last step: Suffer the consequences."

For a moment, Aisling wondered if the reason people called the queen, 'Gentle Annie' was because of fear. But the queen was always friendly—her smile so disarming. Gentle Annie's warm brown eyes were extremely beautiful, but one had the sense that the queen was always evaluating, always thinking, always judging what she saw. Unsure of how to respond, Aisling remained silent.

The queen continued. "If you really think about it, visualization is the beginning of creation. Everything has to be done first in the world of the mind before it can be created. Thoughts, ignited by words of power, form the world around us, as it was in the beginning, is now and ever shall be." The queen had closed her eyes, but opened them again. "The physical world is a reflection of what takes place in the world of the imagination."

Aisling licked her lips, wondering what the queen was trying to tell her. "So, thoughts are... *things*?"

"Yes."

The queen stopped walking around the pillar. Black smoke whirled around the column behind her. "And where do you think thoughts come from, Aisling?"

Aisling drifted to a standstill next to the queen. These ideas had never occurred to her. What did it matter, anyway? She raised her eyebrows and shook her head.

Queen Annan smiled the smile of one who was just about to reveal a surprise. She stepped through the whirling smoke and reached out. As soon as her hands touched the object resting on top of the pillar, all of the smoke dissipated. A rainbow of bright light shone out from the queen's hand, and for an instant, Aisling had to shield her eyes against the glare. Blinking, she focused on a small gem, no larger than a pocket watch, resting in the queen's hand.

"This is the Dream Crystal," said Queen Annan. "Given to us by God in the ancient days, this gem is a physical manifestation of the potentiality of thoughts. It is where dreams, hopes, desires and aspirations come from, or it connects with these traits in people and fulfills them with ideas, which it parcels out to anyone who is a seeker of such things."

The queen offered up the crystal.

Aisling took it gently, and cradled it in the palm of her hand. Sparkling rainbows spun around the Dream Crystal in a whirlwind, and for a moment, a million images, thoughts, dreams and desires swept through her mind. It was exhilarating, and she became unsteady on her feet.

Aisling pulled her attention away from the Dream Crystal and looked into the queen's warm brown eyes, which were filled with surprise. The queen must not have expected such a reaction to come from the stone when she touched it.

Aisling brushed away a strand of hair that had fallen into her eyes. "All of our thoughts come from," she looked down into the crystal, swimming in its crystalline ocean, "—from *this*?"

Now, the queen's eyes held a trace of serious tension. "Not exactly," she said. "Here is how we believe it works: Someone thinks, 'I want something,' and then this crystal creates specific things to give out as ideas, through thought. Thoughts become dreams, dreams become desires, and desires become goals which are then made solid through visualization. If one were to speak of one's desires, and then write them down, simple dreams are transformed into reality. When a person takes action to achieve their goals, their dreams are made real. This is what we call the 'Cycle of Creation.' It all begins with the Dream Crystal."

If you can dream it, you can do it.

Eileen's words came to mind, and for a twinkling, Aisling was filled with awe. But just as quickly, she brushed the thought aside. "This is a lie," she whispered.

Her hand held a dead thing—a piece of glass. The rainbow faded away. Aisling handed the Dream Crystal back to the queen. Her mind was full of the memory of her life back home, where no one ever got what they wanted. Her last words were an accusation: "Dreams don't come true in the real world."

Queen Annan took the crystal, and its color ignited again, but it wasn't nearly as bright as it had been while it had rested in Aisling's hand. The queen's smile faded slightly, and she looked into Aisling's eyes for a heartbeat. Then, as if she had understood something, she nodded very slightly. "Oh yes, I forgot," Annie said. "As a Síofra, you no longer believe."

Against the sadness in the queen's voice, Aisling turned away. She faced a sea of flowers, and their perfume surrounded the clearing like a wall of dreams. For a moment, she wanted nothing more than to run away from here, to go rise out of her fantasies, and touch the world of reality again. "Dreams are for children," she thought.

"This is what we're fighting for, Aisling," said the queen. "Ith desires the Dream Crystal above all things. Whoever possesses this stone will gain control over the power of dreams and also, everything that is created—both here and in the Milesian world."

Aisling said, "You would reduce all of my accomplishments to a piece of glass."

Queen Annan laughed. "How can you still be so proud?" Her eyes darkened slightly, and her voice dropped to a whisper. "You know where that path leads."

Aisling frowned. "Do you really offer freedom, or is your way of life just a form of slavery?"

The queen was silent a moment before she spoke. "The ultimate freedom is the choice between good and evil. What use is freedom if evil is chosen over good? What you dream here comes to pass, so if you think and do whatever you want, you can cause great suffering in others."

Aisling lowered her voice. "Maybe that's the price for getting what you want."

"You can't always have what you want, unless you don't care about hurting other people," said the queen. "Faeries are powerful. If they didn't repress their desires, they would dominate the Milesians, becoming cruel tyrants."

The words were like a knife cutting through her heart. Aisling turned around and began to walk away, into the garden, but the queen's words made her stop. "I had to banish them, Aisling. My people are falling into darkness. I have to try to protect them."

Aisling said, "Throwing people into the Land of Shadows can't protect anyone."

"If they had remained here, they would have infected others with their pride and their passions," said the queen. "Though some were not ready to fall…." Her words died down into silence.

Aisling glared at the queen. "What?"

Now, the queen had turned away. She was fingering the Dream Crystal like it was a talisman, ready to take away her pain and toss it into the sunshine. "In Trista's case, I had to set an example," she said. "Her music—many of the Sídhe were becoming too passionate, rebellious—"

Cold fury flared out of Aisling's eyes. The queen had lied about Trista being ready to fall and she had cast her away into oblivion, unjustly. In a quiet voice, she asked, "Why have you brought me here, your majesty?"

Queen Annan was gazing into the Dream Crystal. "I wanted to try to explain to you why I did what I did," she said. "I have to protect my people you see." Her voice turned to a whisper. "So, so many have already fallen into darkness."

Aisling stood there, surrounded by flowers. Perhaps the queen was right? A frown darkened her face. "You don't have to explain yourself to me, your majesty."

The queen began to speak, but then she stopped herself. She began to head back to where they had landed. Aisling glanced back at the white pillar, now shining in the sunlight. No dark cloud whirled around it now. "Aren't you going to put the Dream Crystal back in its place, your majesty?"

Queen Annan's voice was full of sorrow. "No, no. After that raid, I believe this place is no longer secure. I'm taking it away, to a safe place."

Aisling smiled at the queen, but her thoughts came out of a dark place:

This war is being fought over a lie. Today, she would follow the queen. She would discover the secret place where the Dream Crystal was being hidden. She would...

*   *   *

Chapter Eleven

The Place of Returning

The boat slipped quietly through the water. Tall trees lined both sides of the river, but an occasional opening would appear, revealing long fields of grass bathed in windswept sunshine.

Her dark eyes looked out on the river, unseeing the beauty of a thousand dancing lights swimming alongside their vessel. Aisling, untouched by the warmth of the day, watched the play of light as it fell across the bow of the boat, where Hieronymus sat looking straight ahead. Using an oar to propel the boat forward, Eileen sang a quiet tune to herself. But the melody only reminded Aisling of Trista.

A bouquet of wildflowers that she had received earlier that day lay in her lap. It bore the aroma of something dark, as if the flowers had been gathered at night from the wild, secret places of the earth. The gift had included an invitation too. Aisling wasn't too sure that she wanted to see Conall after his prideful display during the duel, but she had decided to go anyway.

After a time, they passed by a gentle hill in the distance, covered in tiny white flowers and washed by waves of cloud shadows. On the crest of the hill stood a mound of grassy earth, and a ring of low trees silhouetted in sunlight. Half a dozen high beech trees stood watch over the rest of the grove, and an ancient enchantment seemed to cling to the place. It was as if a thousand doomed souls sought refuge there in all the warmth and sunshine. Aisling wondered if she was feeling some kind of elemental spirit that lived there, lost in a field of whispers. Eileen stopped singing when the hill came into view. Stillness filled the space around them.

Aisling wondered if her friend was holding her breath. Her dreary attitude forgotten at the sight of the hill, Aisling said, "What a beautiful place."

"We call it, 'Áit an Fhillidh'—'The Place of Returning,'" said Eileen. "Long ago, a fierce battle was fought here between warring clans of the Sídhe. It's said that lost souls are seen sometimes near the barrow tomb at the top of that hill."

"What were they fighting over?"

"A cuilithe."

"A kind of bird?" guessed Aisling.

Eileen laughed. "No, silly. A cuilithe is an energy vortex—one of the Áit Thanaí—a Thin Place."

From what Aisling could remember, Thin Places were locations where the veil between one world and the next was 'thin'—easily penetrated. She and Genevieve had used one to enter the Land of Dreams. "So it's a doorway…" said Aisling. "Does it lead back to the Milesian world?"

"This one leads into the Land of Shadows," said Eileen. "But it has been locked and warded with spells of power, so the Shadow People cannot use it."

Aisling reached up to touch the dark key hanging from her neck, wondering about dreams and desires and pride and darkness. But before she could ask another question, a wall of trees blocked their view, and she felt uncomfortable speaking about the place.

Before long they came to a wide clearing where a dozen boats lay beached on the side of the river. Many people were lying about or sitting on top of blankets, next to baskets laden with food. They pushed their boat onto the riverbank, and Aisling looked up to see Conall, who offered his hand to help her out of the water.

Conall said, "Nach breá an lá é?"

Wrinkling her brow, Aisling asked, "Pardon?"

"You should really learn to speak Irish," he said. "I said that it's a lovely day."

Stepping up onto the riverbank, with her long skirt in one hand and a pair of white sandals in the other, Aisling smiled. He was so gorgeous! But it was like looking directly at the sun, and she had to turn away. She dropped his hand and gazed up into the clear blue sky, sprinkled with clouds. "Yes," she said. "It's a fine day for a picnic."

Moving onto the soft grass, Aisling resisted the urge to run barefoot and put on her sandals. She wore a royal blue gypsy blouse that exposed her neck and shoulders, with short puffy sleeves ending above the elbow, a dark blue four-point overskirt on top of a white three-tiered skirt, a fancy bodice with a floral lace overlay, a pair of white lace gloves, and white sandals. Silver anklets with tiny bells tinkled as she walked.

But it was the other accessory that drew Conall's attention. He glanced down at the Celtic-styled sword hanging from a black scabbard attached to her leather belt. "Not something very practical for a picnic, is it?"

Aisling laughed, wondering if he was teasing her again. After all, he had sent her the bouquet of flowers, along with the invitation, hadn't he? "Eileen has a sword."

His coy reply wasn't an answer at all. "Eileen is always wearing a sword."

"Then why'd you ask me to bring mine in your note?" she asked.

Conall chuckled, as if she was teasing him back. "How cute you are, to pretend that I sent you a message."

Aisling looked into his blue eyes, wondering if he was really serious. But then he smiled. Unable to bear the lure of his eyes, she turned away.

But she was smiling too.

Genevieve's laughter came down from a nearby clearing. Aisling looked up into the sky and saw dozens of fairies flying through the air. Genevieve was holding onto one of these, which flew over to the river. Once it was over the water, the fairy let go and she fell, screaming with delight. A red fox ran over to the river and jumped in, swimming out toward Genevieve.

The air was full of fairies flying around in an exhilarating aerial dance. "Hey, they're playing tag!" said Eileen. "Come on!"

Her friend ran up the hill to the picnic area, leaving their blanket and picnic basket in the boat, forgotten. Conall said, "Go ahead. I'll bring the basket."

Aisling smiled demurely and ran up the hill, bells jingling as she went, wondering if her loudly beating heart was from exercise or something else.

Aisling spotted Aoife flying up into the sky, chasing an astonishingly cute guy. Just as she caught up to him, he dove out of the way, but she managed to grab his arm and began pulling him down to the river. With a great splash, they plunged into the water.

Eileen flew into the air and joined the game. Hieronymus ran through the grass after her. Aisling was content to simply watch. Conall came up, spread out the large quilted blanket, and began sorting through the food inside. Aisling joined him, kneeling down by the basket. Conall found a pitcher and began pouring lemonade into glasses.

Aisling looked out at the fairies swirling through the air. In the trees, among the leaves, there were dozens of tiny sprites, intent on watching the aerial duelists from the branches. She sat down, swimming in disbelief. "I had no idea places like this existed."

Conall opened a knapsack he had brought and removed a golden bowl. He placed it onto the blanket and whispered a few words. Immediately it was filled with dark red fruit. "Have a cherry."

Ignoring his offer, Aisling watched the game, until she noticed Conall staring.

He looked into her eyes, and for a moment she was completely

206

transfixed. "I'm having a soirée at my estate next month. I'd love to see you there."

Aisling tilted her head until a lock of hair fell into her face. Smiling, she brushed it out of the way. It would have been superbly easy to have said what came to mind, but instead of agreeing, Aisling bit her lip and looked up at the sky. Eileen was being dragged into the river by a trio of fairies.

Aisling felt Conall move up close behind. Two different colognes mixed together, one light and sweet, the other dark and mysterious. She felt his breath on her neck, but he didn't touch her. Instead, he reached around to her front and held up a bunch of cherries. Their faint, fruity scent mingled with the light sweet aroma surrounding his wrist. "Don't you like parties?"

Aisling took the cherries, eating one without a word. She took the pit out of her mouth just as he moved away. Darkness covered her thoughts. "Trista liked parties."

His gentle laugh made her turn around.

Narrowing her eyes in anger, she said, "How can you be so... proud?"

He was lying on his back, propped up on one elbow, smiling. His attitude only made him more adorable. The tone in his voice matched his grin. "I was defending your honor, not my pride."

Aisling looked away, out across the river, thinking that her honor didn't need protecting. She shook her head. "What do appearances matter, anyway?"

Conall laughed. "As a fashion designer, you already know the answer to that."

Still irritated that he would laugh at the mention of Trista, she didn't answer. It was as if he was taunting her, looking for hot spots. She brought her arms up around her knees. "So, why two kinds of cologne?" she asked.

Conall came closer, kneeled behind her, and whispered in her ear, "There's this girl I'm trying to impress." He raised his right wrist to her nose and she inhaled sweet jasmine, mixed with a hint of vanilla. "What do you think, friendly and innocent..." He lowered his arm and his hand brushed against her thigh as he brought it behind her back. From her left side he raised his other hand until a dangerous, exotic scent touched her nose. "… or something spicy, rebellious?"

Forgetting her anger for a heartbeat, she murmured to herself, rising out of a daydream. "Mmm… I'd choose the spicy one."

He removed his hands and whispered, "The rebellious one?"

Warm sensations tingled down her neck. "The dangerous one," she whispered. Dropping her eyes down to the grass, she wished he would bring his arms up around her again, but he'd moved away. A smile touched her lips. "But the right kind of cologne isn't the only way to impress a girl."

"I'll take that under advisement," he said.

Genevieve flopped down onto her stomach on a blanket, dripping wet. A thin, Japanese man sat down next to her. He waved his arm, and a warm breeze whooshed through the clearing. By the time Genevieve's hair had flitted to a standstill, she was completely dry. Rising up onto her elbows, she said, "Aisling, this is Shiro."

Shiro kneeled down and began to massage Genevieve's shoulders. "Hello."

"Hi."

Feeling hungry, Aisling moved over to her picnic basket and opened the flap covering the top. A scaly purple something moved inside. Aisling shrieked and jumped back. Out of the basket, a small reptilian head rose up timidly. Imperial sunshine reflected off its scales. A pair of large purplish butterfly wings appeared, and then both head and wings dipped down out of sight. Aisling cautiously peeked inside. A small purple dragon, no larger than a beagle, looked up shyly. Eyes full of guilt, he swallowed a strawberry and then ducked under a napkin.

"What is it?" asked Genevieve.

"I'm… not sure," said Aisling.

A silver flash turned into a blue ball of light, which hovered a moment and then changed into Eileen, soaking wet. "Táim fliuch báite!" she said, laughing.

Eileen waved a hand, and a warm breeze whirled around her until she was completely dry. Brushing tangled hair out of her eyes, she calmly walked over to the basket, kneeled down, and reached inside. "No worries. It's just one of the Dragan Sídhe—a Fairy Dragon."

Eileen brought the little dragon, chewing on another strawberry, out of the basket and set it down on the blanket between them. Very gently, she whispered 'Hello' in Irish: "Dia duit."

Genevieve's voice rang out. "He's adorable!"

Cautiously, Aisling reached out with her hand. The Fairy Dragon sniffed her fingers and then screeched. She ran her hand over his head. "Yes, he's cute."

Eileen brought a silver brush out of her handbag and began to straighten out her hair. With suspicious eyes, she watched Shiro massage Genevieve.

Nel and Fáelán walked over, carrying a picnic basket. Aisling wondered if they were secret lovers. *But he liked Erin, didn't he?*

Nel wore a white pleated silk dress with silver embroidery, a silk belt tied with a ribbon at the side, lace gloves to the elbows, and a white cloche hat that drooped down around her ears.

Fáelán spread out a blanket and sat down. Nel carried a ring of wildflowers woven into a crown, with pink and white ribbons hanging from the end. Placing it onto Aisling's head, she smiled and sat down next to Fáelán.

Genevieve said, "That crown of flowers suits you."

Fáelán said, "I didn't know there were Fairy Dragons around here. I'll have to ask Nessa about it."

Aisling inhaled the sweet aroma and reached up to touch the crown of wildflowers. "Nessa lives around here?"

Nel removed her hat and inclined her head. A ring of red mushrooms encircled a clearing in the middle of silver fir trees across the water. Hundreds of faeries swirled around the trees. "That's her Sídhe. Rath Gealach—the Fortress of the Moon."

"That doesn't look like a fortress," said Genevieve.

"Not all fortresses are made out of stone," whispered Nel.

The Fairy Dragon climbed into Aisling's lap, and she began to scratch him behind the ears. She wondered if Hieronymus would be jealous.

Genevieve raised a hand to her neck and then stiffened. "Oh my God! I've lost your medallion, Aisling!"

"You probably dropped it in the water," said Shiro. "I'll go find it." He changed into a red fox and trotted off down to the river.

Eileen watched him go, apparently deciding whether or not to say something.

Genevieve groaned. "What?"

Biting her lip, Eileen said, "You should be careful associating with Fox Fairies."

"Don't tell me!" Genevieve rolled onto her back and covered her eyes with her hands. Shaking her head, she grumbled, "She's always so helpful, isn't she?"

Eileen wasn't deterred. "Fox Fairies have the habit of killing people after they seduce them—that's all."

Genevieve sat up and looked at the others. "Is this true?"

Still eating cherries out of his hand, Conall nodded. "I'm afraid it is."

"Argh!" Genevieve dropped back onto the blanket. "Why can't I meet a nice guy for a change?"

"I'm a nice guy," said Conall.

Fáelán chimed in, "So am I."

Choosing to ignore Conall, Genevieve sat up and looked into Fáelán's eyes. "Are you asking me out?"

Nel laughed and put her hand on Fáelán's arm. "I think she likes you."

The unmistakable howl of a cat rang through the clearing. A moment later, they saw Hieronymus running through the grass. When he reached them, he jumped into the basket. With a quick paw strike, he closed the lid after him. Moments later, a dozen angry sprites flew overhead.

Aisling resisted an urge to giggle, holding a straight face while the sprites searched the area. After they had flown away, she whispered, "It's all right, Hieronymus! They've gone."

But the cat didn't come out of the basket.

There was a whoosh of air, and three fairies dropped out of the sky, landing close by. One called out, "Fáelán!"

Aisling saw a dark-haired elf, accompanied by Morrigan and Kerrin— the woman Aisling remembered from the vision in the Transfer Stone.

Kerrin stood slightly behind Morrigan, with a large basket.

"Hey, Tommy," said Fáelán. "Want to join us?"

Aisling gave Fáelán a dark look.

Morrigan's nose twitched, as if she smelled something foul. "I have an idea," she said imperiously. "Why don't we go across the river, just next to those willow trees?"

Tommy sat down next to Fáelán. "Go ahead. I'll join you in a few."

Taking the basket out of Kerrin's hands, Morrigan said in an inviting tone, "Conall, come down and have a drink of wine, won't you?"

Conall looked into Aisling's eyes. "Perhaps later."

"Oh, come on," purred Morrigan. "Just have one drink with me. I promise to let you go. There's something I need to tell you." Glancing at Kerrin, she said, "In private."

Conall looked up at Morrigan and frowned, apparently debating the idea. He got up quickly. "Very well." Avoiding Aisling's eyes, he said, "I won't be long."

Aisling gave Conall a scathing look as he and Morrigan flew off across the river. Kerrin had remained with Tommy, sitting down next to him.

Genevieve said under her breath, "Morrigan is as sniffy as ever."

Tommy glanced at the girls sitting around his friend. "So, Fáelán, I see why you've stopped hanging out with me."

Fáelán chuckled.

Just then, Aoife flew over, accompanied by the cute guy Aisling had been admiring earlier. He had his arm around Aoife. In a tipsy voice, Aoife said, "Want to join us, Aisling? We're going to have a party in the woods."

Still irritated, Aisling considered it for a moment. But she shook her head. "Aoife, how can you—oh, never mind."

Aoife had a tone of defiance in her voice. "What's the problem?" The man kissed her on the cheek, and she smiled. "I'm not hurting anybody. Anyway, why should I care what anyone thinks? I'm just having a good time."

Aisling crossed her arms.

Aoife shook her head. "Oh, fiddle!"

"I guess she doesn't like to party," said the man, who didn't seem so cute now.

They flew off into the trees.

Aisling, fuming, opened the basket in search of something to eat. "Get out of the way, Hieronymus!"

The cat jumped out of the basket and looked suspiciously at the Fairy Dragon, who was now curled up next to Aisling. He turned around and walked over to Kerrin, and the girl began to pet him. Still wearing the air of an offended person, Hieronymus sat down and let out a grandiloquent, "Meow!"

A big, musty book materialized, and it opened up to where a bookmark lay. Hieronymus began to read. Astonished at the idea of a cat reading a book, Aisling momentarily forgot that Conall was having a quiet drink with her rival.

Shiro came back and sat down next to Genevieve, who wasn't as friendly as before. He asked, "Where did you get this medallion?"

Genevieve pointed at Aisling. "It's hers."

Turning it over in his hands, Shiro said, "This is full of very ancient magic. It looks like a Fomorian artifact."

Hieronymus looked up from his book, flicking his tail with interest.

Forgetting her irritation, Aisling said, "My father left it for me, but I don't know much about it."

Eileen put her brush back into her handbag. "I can't imagine why Fintan didn't tell you more about the Fomorians," she said. "He was probably too enthralled by you, Genevieve. You're still seeing him, aren't you?"

Shiro looked rather surprised and irritated together.

Genevieve was too stunned to speak.

Frowning, Shiro said, "Fintan is your boyfriend?"

"Oh, yes," said Eileen. "Didn't she tell you?"

Shiro stood up. "I'll see you later, Genevieve."

There was a flash of angry light, and then he was gone.

Genevieve found her voice. "Thanks a lot, Eileen!"

Eileen ran a hand through her blonde hair. "You should be more discriminating."

"Yeah, but it's my decision, isn't it?"

Eileen wouldn't back down. "You're always saying that I'm too trusting, but look at you! I told you, he was going to kill you. Fox Fairies are too dangerous to play games with."

Fáelán chuckled. "I don't understand why you're so upset, Genevieve. You can't lose what you don't have."

Kerrin said, "You mean you can't force someone to love you."

Aisling glanced across the river and then back at Genevieve, who lay in the sunshine, burning.

"I don't know," said Tommy. "'Love is something that you take.' That's what Conall is always saying."

Genevieve glared at Eileen. "Since you're such an expert, Eileen, why don't you have a boyfriend?"

Eileen sank into a pool of silence. She looked away into the forest of beech trees, covered in blue shadows.

Fáelán said, "She did have a boyfriend, Genevieve. His—"

Eileen shouted, "Don't say his name!"

Stunned into silence, everyone prickled with an uncomfortable memory, causing Aisling to wonder what it was.

A flash of silver and Eileen changed into a ball of light, glowing blue. Eileen shot up into the air and sped off into the trees.

Aisling stood up, about to go after her friend, when Fáelán stopped her. "No. Let her go."

"But what's wrong with her?"

"Morrigan has this magic mirror," said Kerrin. "It shows the most beautiful girl in Tír na nÓg. Eileen used to appear in that mirror."

Aisling sat down, wondering what Morrigan's handmaiden was talking about.

"There's something that Morrigan has never understood," said Kerrin. "True love makes a woman more beautiful than anyone."

Nel murmured, "A broken hand works, but not a broken heart."

Aisling tasted dust in her throat. She whispered, "What happened to him?"

Fáelán said, "He died."

"Did Morrigan…?"

Tommy laughed. "Hey, take a look," he said.

Across the river, Conall and Morrigan were lying on the ground, their arms wrapped around each other, kissing passionately. White fire stung Aisling, but she couldn't tear her eyes away from the two.

"Getting some of his own medicine for a change," said Tommy. "Though I wouldn't mind kissing a girl as hot as she is…"

"What do you mean?" asked Aisling.

Tommy reached over to get a cherry. "Conall is always slipping Potions of Seduction into girls' drinks," he said. "He especially likes virgins."

"Potion of Seduction?"

Nel said, "It's just like a Love Potion, but it wears off after a night of passion."

"Morrigan slipped a potion into that glass of wine," Tommy said. "I suppose she wants her old boyfriend back. Conall dumped her when she started seeing Laigne."

Aisling's mind was spinning. Everything was happening at once. Closing her eyes, she tried to focus, but all she could see was Conall kissing Morrigan. Jealousy and rage and a kind of lost innocence stirred inside her. Involuntarily, she could feel something drawing a dark power toward herself. Half expecting to see some kind of black elemental spirit arrive, she opened her eyes.

Nel had been looking across the river, lost in thought, but now she was looking into Aisling's eyes. For a brief moment, there was a connection between them. It was like two oak leaves from different trees falling onto the same forest floor. Getting up suddenly, Nel said, "I think I'll go say hello to Nessa."

Nel put her white hat on and said,

"By harebells and rue,

"And a heart that is true,

"Hie over to Nessa!"

Wild winds swirled up and Nel was carried away in an instant, flying through the sky over to Rath Gealach across the river.

"She could have just flown over there," said Fáelán. "I don't see why she needed to use a magic hat."

Tommy was still eating cherries. "I guess she's in a hurry."

Several minutes later, there was a silver flash out across the river and a purple sphere appeared near the place where Morrigan and Conall lay. As they looked on, the orb changed into Nel, carrying a small wicker basket full of oranges. All three of them began to talk, and eat.

A few minutes later, shouting erupted from the other side of the river. Morrigan was arguing with Conall and it looked like it was about to turn violent. Nel vanished with a flash and then reappeared nearby, carrying the empty basket. Quietly, she took a seat next to Aisling.

Morrigan stood up angrily and then vanished in a flash. Conall remained where he was for a time, and then he, too, turned into a ball of light and went off into the trees.

Kerrin got up. "I'd better see if Morrigan needs anything." Transforming into a pretty pink ball of light, she sped off after her mistress.

"Mission accomplished," said Nel.

"What happened?" asked Genevieve.

Nel couldn't resist smiling. "This here is the Basket of Arausio," she said. "I asked Nessa if I could borrow it."

Fáelán and Tommy both began to laugh.

Nel explained, "King Boiorix of the Cimbri clan gave it to Nessa. Nineteen centuries ago, his clan faced two Roman armies. As a gift, he sent this enchanted basket, full of Discordant Oranges, to their leaders, Maximus and Caepio. In no time at all the two generals were fighting amongst themselves. Boiorix was then able to defeat both armies piecemeal. It was one of the worst disasters ever to befall Rome. I think they killed eighty thousand Romans."

Tommy said, "A fine way to counteract a seduction potion, don't you think?"

Her jealousy abated somewhat, Aisling looked down at the seemingly innocent basket and smiled, glad to have a friend like Nel.

After a moment of silence, Genevieve looked up and gasped. Away off, next to the edge of the forest, a black unicorn had appeared.

Aisling felt the primitive, earthy gaze of the unicorn, and she closed her eyes against it. A wave of wild, dark magic began to flow into her, building up like water behind a dike. At once, dark thoughts began to stir in her mind: how to spread disease, how to cause an accident, how to give seven years of bad luck to an enemy, and more.

A hundred different worlds began to scintillate around the black unicorn too, and she thought that if she concentrated, she would be able to step into these places at a whim. It was like looking down a hallway full of mirrors and doors.

"I haven't seen a black unicorn in centuries," said Tommy. "I wonder if Morrigan brought it here?"

"Even Morrigan wouldn't dare casting a hex on Nel," said Fáelán.

But Nel wasn't listening. "Black unicorns—guardians of the visible world," she whispered. "Dark magic emanates from them, but Morrigan didn't summon it. An angry elemental led it here."

Avoiding Nel's gaze, Aisling shook her head, hoping to clear away the black magic spilling into her mind.

A dozen ugly creatures came out of the forest, not far from the black unicorn. They had long pointed ears and scraggly hair. Malicious eyes twisted their faces into sneers. No taller than a child, they moved with a jerky, loping gait. Dressed in green and brown, they held bows in their hands.

"Goblins," said Fáelán. "Foul creatures even on a fine day like this."

The goblins began to fire arrows at the black unicorn, which then bolted and ran off into the trees. The little men went after it, their shouts scattering into the forest.

The idea of destroying something so beautiful infuriated Aisling. She grabbed her sword and stood up, with a look at Nel. "Come on!"

* * *

A sea of tall birch trees lay ahead, covered in green. The forest enclosed a wild, gentle place, undisturbed by wind, rain, or sunshine. A thousand birds called out, like gentle ripples against a clear mountain lake. Sunlight scattered off the birch leaves, and the trees swayed slightly against a gust of wind. Mint green grass carpeted the earth, disturbed only by patches of sunlight and the path left by the unicorn.

Aisling and Nel, choosing not to disturb the grass, flew over it, in search of the black unicorn. They glided past hundreds of trees, following a path through the grass. Nel, slightly ahead, signaled a halt, and Aisling drew up beside her, hovering over the grass.   "What is it?"

"Shhh!" Nel pointed into a clearing a hundred yards away. Goblins stood around the body of the unicorn like phantoms in a graveyard. "Too late!" she whispered.

There was a shout from one of the goblins. Something whisked by Aisling's ear. A goblin raised a bow and fired another arrow. Quickly, she darted out of the way, behind a tree trunk just as the arrow shot past. Nel charged forward, sword in hand, unconcerned about the arrows.

Aisling flew up into the trees, approaching the clearing from above. Most of the goblins were shooting at Nel, but a few of them tried to get Aisling. Sounds of fighting greeted her as the grove came into view below. A dozen goblins lay dead already, next to the carcass of the black unicorn.

Aisling drew her sword, falling down into their midst. At the sight of her, the last remaining goblins scattered away into the trees.

The tiny bells around her ankles tinkled. Aisling landed next to her friend, who stood by the body of the black unicorn. Somehow, Nel's white dress had remained spotless in the fight. She held a bloody saber in her hand. The curved weapon reminded her of the Shamshir carried by Ith's Lieutenant. "Interesting sword," she said.

Still breathing heavily, Nel glanced down at her weapon and smiled. "It's called a Palarak," she said. "Hulegu Khan gave it to me after he conquered Persia."

Aisling frowned, never having studied much history. "Umm, right," she said. Tilting her head curiously, she asked, "Just how old are you?"

Nel's eyes darkened for a moment, as if her soul was in danger of being devoured by the past. "I was born in the city of Babylon, during the reign of Samsu-Iluna, nearly four millennia ago."

Biting her lip, Aisling looked around the clearing. A bronze cauldron lay next to the dead unicorn. Wrinkling her nose, she noticed that it was filled with blood. "What do you think they were doing?"

Nel looked through a gap in the trees, towards a hill, bathed in little white flowers—The Place of Returning. Blue clouds filled the sky, throwing dark shadows across the grass. A ray of sunshine found its way down to the trees on top of the barrow, bathing them in warmth. A bolt of lightning ignited a thunderclap, which tumbled down from the hill. Nel said, "Black unicorn blood can be used to open doorways to other worlds."

"Such as the Land of Shadows," whispered Aisling.

"Yes."

The grass began to sway with a thousand whispering voices that spilled down onto the hillside. Another flash of lightning reached down to the barrow. Thunder drowned out the whispers, and then everything was silent.

"We shouldn't leave this here," said Nel. She withdrew a small glass flask from her white purse. With a "Pop!" she opened it and a thousand tiny lights fluttered over the dead unicorn. For a moment, the animal was bathed in sparkling light, and then the unicorn was gone. Clapping her hands together, the cauldron disappeared too. The flask seemed to be full now, but before Aisling could ask about it, Nel placed it back in her purse. The feeling of being watched came from the hill, like a foul wind on a clear day. Nel frowned. "We'd better warn Nessa." "No, wait." Aisling put a hand on Nel's arm. "Can you give Genevieve your magic hat? She can't travel like we can."

"Aren't you coming?"

Aisling put her sword back in its sheath. "No."

Nel looked over the field of grass, awash with cloud shadows and into the sunlit trees at the top of the barrow. "Aisling, if you go up there—"

"Don't worry about me, Nel."

Nel looked into Aisling's eyes, displaying a trace of curiosity, but she didn't ask any questions. Nodding her head, she stepped back a pace. There was a flash of purple and gold and then she was gone.

Aisling turned towards the Place of Returning, fingering the key around her neck. If a doorway was now open, then perhaps she wouldn't need it after all? Images of her sister, enslaved, burned. She found herself looking down at the grass, wondering if Erin had ever run through a field of green on a sunny day.

The important thing now was speed. Could she get into the Land of Shadows before the enemy came out? She was about to change into an orb, intending on flying up the hill, in search of the open doorway, when something caught her attention.

It was a movement out of the corner of her eye. Drawing her sword, she turned to face the shadowy figure walking through the trees. But it wasn't a Shadow Person at all.

Long, tangled blonde hair fell about the girl's shoulders, and she wore a white dress sprinkled with little red flowers. Clear blue eyes, darkened by sadness, looked through the green forest of beech trees, utterly lost. She moved like she was walking in

her sleep. Gently, she placed a hand on the closest beech tree, as if she

219

wanted to make certain that it was really there.

Aisling remembered seeing the girl from the café on the day before Halloween. At the time, shadows had covered her, and then the girl had disappeared. Aisling put her sword away, and walked forward—her little bell anklets jingling with every step she took. "Brigitte?" she whispered.

At first, the girl didn't react. She was gazing up into the tree, one hand anchored firmly on the smooth trunk. The sound of Aisling's approach finally reached her, and she turned to look. A collar of black steel encircled the girl's neck, with a large ring hanging from the front. Her eyes began to focus. "You were in my school," she said. "Erin?"

Unaccustomed to her old Milesian name, Aisling hesitated. That was her sister's name. For a moment, she was lost in the past. "What are you doing—how did you get here, Brigitte?"

Brigitte's smile was like a distant ship, fading away on the horizon. "It is you, Erin," she said. Brigitte glanced around at the tall trees, dripping green sunshine. "Are you one of the fallen now?"

"What do you mean?"

A thousand whispering voices flew over the grass covering the distant hillside, crashing into the forest like a wave across a beach. Wind accompanied the sound, knocking hair into her face. Aisling brushed it out of her eyes and noticed that Brigitte was now looking up at the barrow like a lost dog searching for its master. She whispered, "We belong to them, you know."

Aisling opened her mouth to speak, but a shadow began to cover Brigitte, like a gentle breeze. A moment later, she had faded away entirely.

Cold chills dribbled down her spine. Aisling looked out of the forest, across the field of grass. A lightning bolt struck the earth, thunder rolling down the hillside after it. Reaching up to her chest, she wondered if she held the key to the Abyss around her neck.

Drifting into the forest, the scent of dark lotus flowers, violet, musk, exotic woods, and just a hint of mandarin touched her nose. Intoxicated, Aisling felt her skin tingle with excitement. Like silk brushing across skin, she found herself wanting more. She closed her eyes, drinking in the wild aroma.

Had Conall changed his cologne again? A warm breath fell across her exposed neck, and she opened her eyes slightly, breathless with anticipation. An inviting presence stood behind her. It wasn't really his fault, was it? Morrigan had used a potion to lure him away. Tilting her head, she closed her eyes again, reveling in the tingling sensations washing over her body.

A whisper: "Good afternoon."

Opening her eyes, Aisling whirled around and found herself face to face with Ith, the Lord of Shadows. A wraith-like figure with a top hat and cane, he stood just behind her, eyes burning crimson. Shaking herself out of the trance, she asked, "How did you—"

No longer a whisper, his voice rang out with authority. "King Skilia of the goblins was kind enough to open the door." Ith walked over to a tree, cradling the cane in the palm of his hand, like a nightstick. "Tell me, why do you let the queen tell you what to do—what to think?"

"I don't." But she said it too quickly. "Not really."

Ith shook his head. "I just don't see why you let her control you. Do you enjoy life as a slave?"

Aisling, whether from excitement or surprise, could feel her heart racing. Her words were a quiet echo. "A slave?"

His voice was like taking a warm bath—relaxing and enticing at once. "How can you stand it? A person like you—repressing her dreams and desires!"

"I'm not repressing anything."

Ith thumped the cane against his palm. "So, you can do whatever you want here?" His voice turned sarcastic. "And now you're living out your dreams?"

Aisling crossed her arms, but the gesture only reminded her of being tied up. "Yes—well, no."

"Playing with sprites!" Ith mocked. "Do you really want a life of such... *frivolity?*"

Aisling bit her lip, wondering about her destiny. All of her life, she had felt a power inside, like a force of nature, ready to come forth. Images of great beauty, wreathed in pretty clothes, had always lived in her mind, just under the surface. To ignore them was like trying to hold her breath.

But the queen didn't like dreams.

As if he could read her mind, Ith said, "Under the queen, your thoughts aren't even free, are they? Pride is against the law, isn't it?"

His words were enticing, but his last remark brought back haunting memories of Trista… and Erin. "Are you finished?"

Ith placed his cane on the ground and stared, eyes burning. "I require… an answer to my offer."

She shook her head. "Nothing has changed. I won't go with you anywhere."

Shadows moved in the trees, just out of view. For a heartbeat, the clearing was silent. His next words were tinged with disappointment. "What a pity." Taking up his cane, he touched it to the brim of his hat in a salute. "Farewell, then."

Ith turned to leave, murmuring to himself, "At last, the Day of Liberation has come."

Aisling threw a glance up the hill, and thought she saw a host of shadows whispering by. A cold wind washed over the clearing, throwing sunlight and shadows into a wild dance as the trees swayed overhead. When it had died down, Ith was gone.

*   *   *

Despite the sunshine, rumbling thunder rained down on the forest. Aisling saw flashes of light in the direction of Rath Gealach. For a time, she stood, transfixed, listening to the battle. Worried about her friends, she began to run. But the loud jingling of her ankle bells made her pause. Leaning against a tree, she reached down to remove the anklets. Quietly now, she began to move through a maze of green, towards the storm.

Mint sunshine filled the forest with quiet, except for the birds and the stiff sound of horses approaching. Peering through the trees, she thought she caught shadowy movement, but it washed away into a pocket of sunlight.

Closing her eyes, she took a deep breath, sensing the wind and the grass and the sunshine fluttering down through the green leaves, and the horses, which had come to a stop. She opened her eyes again, listening.

"Hoh!"

One of the horses began galloping towards her, but she didn't see anything. She took a step back and then heard another horse, charging from another direction. Unable to see her assailants, she turned away, and ran.

"Haw!"

Looking wildly around, Aisling sped through the forest, away from the sounds of her pursuers. Racing into a clearing, she heard horses galloping past her on either side, and she slowed down, whirling around. Shadowy riders, bearing spears, faded into the sunlight and were gone. She turned away and ran again, fighting off panic.

A horse leaped over a fallen tree just behind her. As she turned to face it, she saw a Shadow Person on a horse, aiming a spear at her throat. She knocked the spear out of the way and fell down. The rider shot past, withering away into the sunlight. Getting up off the ground, she ran through the grass.

Aisling came to another clearing, washed in sunshine. She stopped to listen. She heard one rider halt in front of her, and another behind. A moment later both horsemen galloped forward, from opposite directions. Squinting in the sunlight, she could just make out shadowy horses bearing down on her.

Aisling drew her sword, parrying one spear and whirling around to knock the other spear out of the way as both riders shot past. The "Ching, ching!" drowned out the sounds of her attackers for a moment and she had to concentrate to locate them. Smiling defiantly, she realized that she was outmatched. Unless—

One rider came to a stop under a beech tree. She could see the shadowy horse and rider, eyes glowing red. The horse rose up onto his hind legs, neighing loudly. The Shadow Person lowered his spear.

"Haw!"

The horse galloped forward, fading out of sight as it passed into beams of light.

From behind, she heard the other rider shout, kicking his horse into a gallop.

Nearly impossible to see, the shadow rider came on, and Aisling had to jump underneath it, knocking the spear out of the way with her sword.

"Clang!"

Aisling got up just as a second rider approached. Parrying the spear with two quick strokes, the blow knocked the rider off balance and he fell to the ground, along with his horse.

A third horseman charged. Aisling parried the spear wildly and waved her other hand to spook the horse, which whirled around, reared up, and threw off the rider.

Aisling heard the first assailant wheel about, and the Shadow Person charged from the rear. Spinning around, she barely moved out of the way. Aisling grabbed the spear shaft and pulled the rider onto the ground. She fell down next to him.

Aisling got up just as the Shadow Person came at her. With a swift kick, she struck the shadow in the head, knocking him down.

Aisling heard the horses running away as she got up. Sunlight scattered the shadows into a thousand pieces, disorienting her—time to run again.

Pursued through green trees, Aisling raced over the grass, heart pounding. Nearly out of breath, she fell over a root and landed on her face. Struggling to her feet, she found herself surrounded by three Shadow People armed with spears.

With a shout, all three lunged with their spears. Aisling parried them all, whirling around in a circle.

One shadow spun around and slashed out with his spear, causing her to retreat. Taking the bait, he moved forward. Aisling cut the spear in half and, stepping inside his guard, she slashed out with her sword. Screaming,

224

the shadow fell back and disappeared.

Turning around, Aisling saw the point of a spear aimed at her throat.

Unable to block it, she fell backward, ducking under the thrust. In the same motion, she kicked up into his neck. She heard a snap. The Shadow Person fell silently away, dead.

Rolling up onto her feet, Aisling glared at her final assailant, daring him to attack.

Shouting, he lunged forward.

Sweeping her sword around and down, she cut off the end of the spear and slashed out at his neck.

The shadow fell down, vaporizing before striking the ground.

Nearly out of breath, Aisling remained still, listening to the wind and the birds and to the distant thunder. The shock of having killed for the first time began to weigh her down. She wondered if she had been stained by the dark magic seeping out of the black unicorn.

Moments later, she saw Eileen, sword in hand, flying out of the trees.

Still breathing heavily, Aisling sheathed her weapon. "You're late."

Eileen put her sword away.

"Ith has brought an army this time," said Aisling. "I saw them coming down from the barrow tomb."

Eileen nodded. "Yes. Some twenty thousand strong, I should think. They've already destroyed Rath Gealach and have captured hundreds of the Aos Sí. Already they're taking them back to the Land of Shadows through the doorway."

A hole opened up in Aisling's heart. "Genevieve…?"

"She's fine. Nel returned in time to warn us. Fáelán took her back to the castle, though she wasn't too happy about going without you."

Aisling's smile exposed her relief. She walked over to a tree to place a hand on smooth bark. She could smell smoke on the wind. "This attack is only a diversion. Ith is headed for the Garden of Thought."

"How can you know?"

Aisling shook her head. "It doesn't matter."

A thousand whispering voices drifted through the forest, sounding like the ocean washing over a beach. The voices began to grow louder.

Aisling licked her lips, wondering how long it would take them to get here. "Is Nessa all right?"

Eileen's face darkened. "The fortress of Rath Gealach has been destroyed. But Nessa transformed her people into trees and birds to protect them from the shadow host."

"Yes, but is she all right?"

"No one's seen her."

Aisling was silent for a moment, lost in thought.

"We have to go," said Eileen. "Morrigan is about to destroy Ith's army."

Aisling turned towards Eileen. "Indeed?"

"She can do it with one of her magic poems," explained Eileen. "Then Marcus will reseal the gateway with a closing incantation and a dash of rose oil."

Aisling raised her eyebrows. "If only I had thought of that."

Eileen's musical laughter lifted up into the trees.

But Aisling had already started to form a plan in her mind. She would soon bring an end to this silly war. "Are you going to Conall's party next month?"

"Can you get me an invitation?"

"I think so."

Two orbs of light—one blue, the other silver—flashed silver and gold, and then the forest was empty, save for a host of whispers that were soon swept away with a poem.

* * *

Chapter Twelve

The Masquerade

To dream and then to be forgotten—was that all there was? Perhaps the Shadow People were better off, entombed in forsaken dreams, locked away in the Land of Shadows. What was the point of repressing desire if one's ultimate destination was simple oblivion? Better to live—to aspire to a life of passion and freedom. To live the lie that dreams always told.

A tall round mirror wrapped in silver cast whispers into the air surrounding the gallery where Aisling was seated. The music of Bach's Prelude in C Major flowed from her fingertips. Aisling had learned to play the pipe organ, though she still had a tendency to look down at the pedals underneath her feet. With three manuals of keys and nearly three thousand pipes, she was able to fill the cathedral with the majesty and power of the angels. Unsure if she had really meant to put so much emotion into the piece, she wondered if it was induced by the whispers, always there, telling of dreams and desires and dark furies. Not caring if she was influenced by the shadows, Aisling continued playing, remembering Trista's last song, and carrying on until the music ran out.

Sudden silence rang out in the cathedral. Aisling looked down into the crowd below her from a seat up in the organ loft, while dark words whispered. They caressed her back like feathers tickling against a dream. She didn't turn to look at the Mirror of Eternity, knowing that it was a window into the prison where Erin languished. Father Harrigan, a Milesian priest, led the ceremony below, but Aisling wasn't listening to anything said there, intent on tuning out the dark voices surrounding her.

Looking up into the high white arches where blue shadows pooled, she closed her eyes, inhaling frankincense, myrrh, beeswax and just a hint of smoke. Warm sunlight, stained with a rosy color, fell onto her face. When she opened her eyes, she was looking through the organ pipes at light filtering through the high arched windows. For a moment, she swam in helplessness. "What am I to do?" she wondered.

Several thousand of the Tuatha Dé had been captured, taken away into the Land of Shadows. Nessa's community around Rath Gealach had been pulverized in a fury of fire and ash and blood. Aisling wondered how a poem could have stopped the onslaught, and wondered more about Morrigan—how could she command such power?

Nel's voice came from the direction of the mirror. "Very nice."

Feeling that it was wrong to smile overmuch after such a tragedy as the destruction of an entire faerie community, Aisling tried to cover up the smirk inching into her face by looking down at the congregation. "Thanks," she said.

"You're better than Fáelán," said Nel. Her voice dropped to a whisper. "But don't tell him I said that."

Unable to resist the smile now, Aisling turned and saw her friend standing next to the Mirror of Eternity. A cool breeze came out of the mirror, brushing against Nel's short black hair.

"Do you mind if I ask you something?" asked Aisling.

Nel glanced down at the assembly. Father Harrigan was nearly finished with his sermon. "Not at all."

"Are you and Fáelán seeing each other?"

228

"No." Nel turned around to face the Mirror of Eternity, lowering her voice to a whisper. "You know, he comes here, sometimes—" She traced a finger along the silver frame, through engraved bones wrapped in leaves and flowers. "...to spy on *her*."

"Oh." Realizing that Nel was talking about her sister, Aisling bit her lip. How would Nel react when Aisling rescued Erin? She quickly changed the subject. "So what's tonight's festival all about?"

Nel turned around, as friendly as ever. "Beltane is the start of summer. Tonight's lighting of the bonfire is followed by the call of courtly love. The very air is filled with romantic promise. I'd watch out for the Seduction Fairy, Li Kyong, if I were you."

Feeling doubly uncomfortable now, Aisling was glad to get interrupted by Aoife, who appeared at the top of the staircase, looking like a peasant girl. In an urgent tone, she whispered, "Hey, Aisling! They're finished. Aren't you going to play?"

Quickly turning to the pipe organ, Aisling began to play Bach's Fugue in C Major. Both Nel and Aoife giggled, and Aisling nearly lost her place in the music.

After the service, Aisling turned to look at Aoife, who was sitting on the gallery rail, overlooking the room below. Wondering if it was a trick of the light, she noticed that Aoife was unusually plain looking today. Aoife wore a tan blouse with a dirty vest, a rope belt and worn sandals. Her dingy red hair was dulled by the sunlight coming through the stained glass windows over the organ loft. An atrocious-looking medallion, bearing an ugly face contorted into an impish grin, hung from a leather cord around her neck. But the most surprising thing to see was a large wart on the tip of Aoife's nose.

Aoife saw the look on Aisling's face and broke out into laughter.

Perplexed, Aisling glanced at Nel, who was trying to cover up a smile. "What?"

Aoife reached around her neck and took off the medallion. Gentle light bathed Aoife for an instant, and Aisling saw that her friend was wearing a pretty blue peasant blouse, a white vest with blue floral lace, white sash, white leggings and adorable blue shoes. She was more beautiful than ever now, and the wart had vanished.

"What happened?"

"This is a Talisman of Repulsiveness," said Aoife. "I'm going to use it to get away from here after the service. Li Kyong is in the woods outside."

Aisling raised her eyebrows, still not understanding.

Aoife laughed again, and Nel joined in this time. "Don't you ever get tired of men hitting on you all the time?" asked Aoife. "With this, I'm invisible to them until I'm ready for their attentions."

"Oh." Aisling wished she had that kind of problem. She wrinkled her nose.

"Aw, come on!" Aoife held out the medallion. "You sure you don't want to try it for just a little while?"

"I would never wear such a thing," said Aisling. "It's wrong to destroy beauty."

"That's the nice thing about this talisman," said Aoife. She put the medallion back around her neck and she became plain again. "It's only temporary."

Aisling felt like she was back in Seattle, where the war against beauty still raged. Her eyes dropped down to the floor, while she remembered her old plans. "Aoife, did you ever have a dream?"

Aoife nearly fell off the balcony. She giggled while her face turned pink. "I wanted to be a fashion designer like you," she said. "But I don't really care about my dreams anymore."

Aisling raised her eyebrows. "No?"

"You don't need them here," said Aoife, and then she smiled. "All I care about now is having fun."

Biting her lip, Aisling wondered if she too, had abandoned her dreams. It was difficult to forget everything she had ever wanted and just party—something that the queen encouraged. But maybe that's what it meant to be a fairy after all?

Aoife interrupted her thoughts. "Hey, at least your dream came true. Now you work for the faerie queen!"

Aisling crossed her arms, wrinkling her nose. Being the queen's dressmaker wasn't all that satisfying. It was like working from prison. She wondered if Gentle Annie would have gotten along with Miss Whitaker, the fashion director at school. "Working for the queen isn't my dream," she said. "She doesn't even like the dress I made for the Masquerade."

"Why not?" asked Nel.

"It's too extravagant," said Aisling.

Aoife leaned back precariously over the railing. "Ooh, just do what you like Aisling. Don't let the queen control you. If she doesn't like it—"

"Hello girls." King Artrach had appeared at the head of the stairs.

Aoife yelped and fell off the railing. Aisling and Nel stifled a giggle and stood up, bowing low. Aoife must have unfurled her wings just in time, because they didn't hear her crash into the floor below.

King Artrach went over to the railing and looked down into the cathedral. "My dreams stopped coming true a long time ago," he said. Turning around, he smiled at Aisling. "Perhaps you should embrace yours while they're still alive."

Aisling looked down at the floor, too embarrassed to respond.

Artrach glanced at the Mirror of Eternity. "Still peering into the Land of Shadows, Nel?"

Nel ran a hand through black hair. "I can't understand how they could have surprised us, your majesty."

"Oh I wasn't criticizing you," he said. King Artrach walked over to the mirror. "All of my doubts are held in this glass." His voice went cold. "I wonder sometimes, why we keep this thing."

Nel seemed to be shaken. "Command me, your majesty, and I shall destroy it."

King Artrach turned around. "I'm not sure I'm willing to take that risk."

Aisling looked at Nel, wondering if breaking the mirror would bring bad luck or curses or something worse.

"I loved the music, Aisling. Father Harrigan did too," said Artrach. "Have you met him? He's a Milesian."

Aisling looked down at her outfit. She wore pink and black striped tights, a black half shirt, mini skirt, and pink platform shoes. A short pink leather jacket lay on the bench next to the pipe organ. Even if she put on the jacket, her bare stomach would show. "I'm not really dressed to meet a priest, your majesty."

Artrach's laughter filled the gallery. "There isn't anything wrong with being beautiful, Aisling. Besides—" He picked up her jacket, offering it to her. "Many of my subjects don't even wear clothes."

With a final glance at Nel, Aisling accompanied the king down to the steps in front of the cathedral. Most of the faeries had gone already, flying away into summer warmth. Bright sunlight fell out of the turquoise sky, filling the world with mirth. In a delicate game of tag, tiny sprites chased butterflies across the gardens surrounding the cathedral. Father Harrigan, a thin, balding man wearing elegant robes of green and white, along with an ornate silver cross on a chain, smiled as they approached. After bowing to the king, he looked at Aisling. "I've always enjoyed Bach, though it's a bit gothic for a day like this, don't you think?"

Unsure if he was criticizing or complementing her, Aisling said, "I've only just learned the pipe organ. I'm better at the piano."

"Aisling is from Seattle," said Artrach. "She grew up among your people."

Father Harrigan glanced at the king. "Are your subjects still kidnapping children, your majesty?" he asked.

"Our own children are left in their place," said Artrach. "Besides, only the un-baptized are at risk."

"How many children have been murdered in your war?"

The king crossed his arms. "My people are still falling into darkness."

"Because of pride," prodded Harrigan.

"I'm not sure if pride is the only reason for it," said Artrach. "Two clans are still at risk: The Aoi clan of Meadhar Grá and the Iuchar clan of Measarthachtshee have both lost their rulers, Maire and Canlyn."

"There is no reason to worry about the others," said Harrigan. "Only those without faith are at risk."

"Faith in what?" asked Artrach, "dreams?" Artrach shook his head. "In any case, changelings are innocent."

"Yes, of course," Harrigan said.

During their exchange, Aisling had been glancing at the white stone walls of the cathedral. Blue cloud shadows began to drift over one of the towers. She couldn't shake the notion that she was somehow responsible for the kidnapped children. Erin's sad face filled her mind.

Father Harrigan asked, "Did you enjoy my sermon?"

"I wasn't really paying attention," she said. Then quickly, she explained, "I was concentrating on the music."

"That's alright," said Harrigan. "I've heard it can be difficult learning how to play the organ after the piano. Perhaps that's why it isn't as popular."

King Artrach interjected, "The Milesians aren't as religious as they used to be."

"They're not the only ones who no longer believe," said Harrigan.

Not wanting to get involved in their argument, she said, "I'm glad you liked my music. I'll continue to play here in the future, if you like."

"I'm sure everyone would enjoy that," said Harrigan.

An exotic looking fairy landed not far from the cathedral. She had long straight black hair, cream-white skin, and delicate Asian features. She wore a tiny red dress, white fishnets and shoes, and a cream colored satin corset with red rose embroidery. Her small white wings were edged in crimson. She was one of the sexiest fairies Aisling had ever seen. The girl raised a hand, and blew across her palm. Tiny red and white sparkling lights whooshed off towards a nearby couple, who began to kiss.

The king smiled. "I'd better go. That's the Seduction Fairy," he said. "I wouldn't want to start kissing you Aisling. My wife wouldn't appreciate it."

Father Harrigan laughed. "Goodbye your majesty."

Purple wings, edged in gold, emerged from the king's back and he took off into the air, flying towards the castle.

The Seduction Fairy was relentless, chasing down single faeries and throwing spells at them. Occasionally, a giggle or a startled scream would come out of the woods. Harrigan smiled at all the mischief.

A gentle wind blew through the trees in front of the cathedral. They stood breathing in the pine-scented sunshine for a time. "Sometimes I miss my Milesian parents," said Aisling.

Father Harrigan continued to watch the faeries darting through the trees. "Why don't you go visit them?"

Aisling had made a promise to herself not to return without Erin. Frowning, she shook her head. "They deserve more than me."

"You are all they know of," he said.

"They remember her."

Father Harrigan turned to look into Aisling's eyes—eyes that echoed the pain of a mother and father missing their child, long since forgotten but lingering still, as a whisper of sunshine.

After a moment's silence, Aisling asked, "Who are the Shadow People?"

As if darkness had suddenly descended upon him, Harrigan turned away. "Fallen beings," he whispered. "Sadly, the world is full of them."

"I've seen it happen. On the road, I saw a changeling fall into shadow, and before that, I saw it happen to a Milesian girl in Seattle," said Aisling. "She just faded away into darkness."

Harrigan's harsh whisper startled Aisling. "It's happening to *us*?"

Aisling nodded. "Her name was Brigitte, and she wasn't proud at all." Looking into the trees, she whispered, "They take them away to the Land of Shadows—to use as slaves, I think."

Father Harrigan was silent for a moment. Then he whispered, "This is an ancient war. Some would say that it's eternal."

"Tell me how to beat them," she whispered.

Father Harrigan looked into her eyes. "With faith, hope, and love."

Aisling crossed her arms. "Not very useful forms of magic, some might say."

His words were a gentle mockery. "Some might say that, yes."

*   *   *

Not far from the cathedral, Aisling came upon an ancient grove, with fir trees taller than any trees she'd seen before. Landing next to the largest one, she placed a hand on the trunk, which was over nine feet in diameter. Breathing in the earthy scent of the tree, she said, "Why haven't I seen you before?"

Hoof beats approached.

"Quite a tree, isn't it?"

Turning around, she looked into the dark face of a man with brown eyes, curly hair, a goatee and a hungry gleam in his eyes. Bare-chested, he wore only a pair of dark brown pants, but his legs ended in a pair of hooves. A pair of short horns came out of his forehead. "They say it's over four hundred feet tall."

Aisling could feel her heart beating. Like a hungry wolf, he approached. Suddenly wishing that she was wearing Aoife's medallion, she backed up until she bumped into the tree. "Hello," she said, nervously.

He reached up to touch her face, gently. "You've never seen a satyr before?"

She shook her head and moved away from the tree, hoping to get a little distance from him. "No."

"There's no reason to run." Quickly, he jumped into her path, forcing her to retreat back against the tree. His smile was too friendly. "How about a kiss?" he said.

Aisling smiled, preparing herself for a fight. With her back to the tree, she side stepped around the trunk. Several other satyrs came into view. One of them laughed. "What a pretty lass, eh, Nikolaos?"

Nikolaos didn't answer. Instead, he stepped over to Aisling and leaned close. She could smell his sweat breath, which reminded her of honey and wine. With one quick motion, she shoved him back.

The crowd of satyrs laughed and jeered. Nikolaos glanced at his friends, and then at Aisling. He whispered, "That's alright, I can wait. Li Kyong should be here soon."

Aisling considered turning into an orb or simply flying away, but then she heard another voice, darkly familiar. "If you want to play with her Nikolaos, you should first ask her to dance. She so loves to dance."

The Shadow Person, Sean stood by the group of satyrs, his arms wrapped around two girls, a bright smile on his lips. For a Shadow Person, he was as solid as anyone.

Sean's companions were two gorgeous fairies, one blonde—the other brunette. The dark haired girl whispered something in his ear and he laughed.

Aisling took a step towards Sean, but Nikolaos got in the way. "No, no. I found you first."

"I'm glad the Nix I sent to kill you failed," said Sean. "One day, I shall deal with you myself." Sean's laughter filled the clearing and to Aisling's astonishment, he changed into a glowing orb of scarlet and darted away through the forest, followed by the two girls, after they had changed into pink and silver balls of light.

Nikolaos drew near. Again, she shoved him back—to the amusement of the gathered satyrs. One of them called out, "Someone go get the Seduction Fairy!"

Nikolaos took another step closer but he was stopped by a javelin, which plunged into the ground in front of him. Blue electricity sparked up and down the shaft. The unmistakable sound of an approaching chariot grew louder. Nikolaos frowned with disappointment and then he ran off through the trees, followed by the rest of the satyrs.

Rosheen appeared, driving a golden chariot pulled by white horses. Halting the vehicle, she smiled. "They're really quite nice once you get to know them."

Aisling watched them vanish into the forest. "I wasn't interested."

Retrieving the javelin, Rosheen laughed. "I know," she said. "I thought I'd intervene before you hurt one of them. Come on, I'll give you a lift."

236

As they got into the golden chariot, Rosheen looked askance at Aisling. "You know, magic is simply having a vision, fueled by passion."

Aisling wondered what kind of passion Rosheen was talking about. She looked into the forest, but there was no sign of the satyrs now. "What were they doing here?"

"Oh, they like to chase the nymphs that live in these trees," said Rosheen. She looked up. "In the Milesian world, this tree was cut down a century ago."

"Whatever for?"

Rosheen shook her head. "They don't really care about trees. Sometimes I wonder why the king tries to protect them from the Shadow People."

Aisling remembered shadows whispering into the ears of people, just before they did horrible things. "Rosheen, I just saw a Shadow Person here," she said. "But he wasn't a shadow—he was solid."

"He was in corporeal form? What was he doing?"

"He, um… had two fairy girls with him."

Rosheen cupped her hands in front of her face. After whispering something, she breathed over the palms of her hands, like she was blowing a kiss. A cool wind rippled through the forest, carrying an echo of her whispered message along with it.

Aisling gaped. "What did you just do?"

Rosheen laughed. "Don't you know how to send a message? You just whisper into the wind, and an air elemental will take it to whomever you like. I just told Marcus about your encounter. As the leader of the Fianna, he's responsible for chasing down stray Shadow People."

Aisling joined her friend on the chariot. "The Fianna?"

"They're part of the military," said Rosheen. "They have three mottos: 'Glaine ár gcroí; Neart ár ngéag; Beart de réir ár mbriathar.' The words mean, 'Purity of heart, strength of limb, and deeds to match our words.'"

"Oh," she whispered. "It sounds like the motto I learned in the Kung Fu temple: Courtesy, consideration, bravery, and loyalty." Aisling began to think of how her best friend had mocked the fighting abilities of the Sídhe in front of Eileen.

Rosheen began to drive towards the castle. As if she had been reading Aisling's mind, she asked, "Where is Genevieve?"

"Where else?" said Aisling. "She's on a date, down at the beach I think."

"I'm surprised Eileen let her go," said Rosheen. "You don't have a date?"

Despite the wind blowing through her hair, Aisling felt her face burning. "No."

* * *

Aisling looked out of the balcony from her room high up in one of the towers of the castle, towards the ocean. What a strange world she had come to. A war was going on, but no one seemed to notice. It was as if the Sídhe didn't care about anything or anyone, unless it involved some kind of airheaded game or party. Ith's words had bitten hard. How indeed could she live a life of such frivolity? The queen was the worst one of all. Always smiling, always friendly, always ready to play a game or organize another party. But underneath Gentle Annie's smile lurked a cold ruthlessness. Aisling shook her head. The queen was only trying to protect everyone in the realm, wasn't she?

Something struck Aisling in the back, covering her in cold water. The impact knocked her over, and she fell off the balcony. For a moment, Aisling was too stunned to react. The stone pavement rushed up to meet her, but all she could think of was how freezing it was with the wind whipping around her. Then at the last moment, she had the presence of mind to unfurl her wings.

Momentarily, she returned to her chamber, soaking with irritation and icy water. Remnants of a water balloon covered the balcony. Walking forward cautiously, Aisling narrowed her eyes. Being doused in cold milk came to mind. The short silver-white fairy was fond of practical jokes, but Aisling didn't have time for her pranks. "Kylie, come out or I'll—"

There was a screeching sound, followed by a puff of fire and smoke. A small fairy, all white, with golden blonde hair and pale wings shot out from behind Aisling's bed, followed by a blur of purple scales, breathing a puff of fire. Both fairy and fairy dragon shot out through the window. Aisling shook her head, and called out, "Calix, it's alright! Come back!"

Aisling had wanted to name the purple fairy dragon, "Ti-Lung" after the Chinese Celestial Dragon, but Genevieve had found him hiding inside the picnic basket when they returned to the castle and she had claimed the right to name him. She had chosen 'Calixtus,' but Aisling called him Calix instead, to the consternation of her friend.

Shaking her head, Aisling closed her eyes and imagined herself dry, in a new outfit. When she opened her eyes she wore a tan blouse that flared at the elbows, leggings with a gray, white, and black diamond pattern, and comfortable gray boots.

Aisling sat down at the dresser and began to run a comb through her dark hair. She wondered if she would ever be really good at magic. "It all begins with desire," she thought. In the mirror, she looked at the reflection of the bouquet of dark wildflowers, which sat on a table by the couch, next to the invitation to the picnic.

Another invitation lay there, but it was entirely different, written in another hand and bearing the red wax seal of a tiger. Placing the comb down, she went over to the table and picked up the two letters. Did Conall send the invitation to the picnic? It read:

Come join me at the spring picnic.
Just take the river up to Rath Gealach.
Bring your sword.
I'll see you there!

Written on a small white card, it wasn't addressed to her, nor was it signed by anybody. Aisling raised it to her nose and detected a faint aroma of lavender, patchouli, musk and vanilla.

The other invitation, written upon tan parchment was entirely different:

Aisling,

I would be pleased to see you at a little soirée at my estate this Sunday evening. Bring your friends, will you? Dress to impress and make certain you wear a mask!

Conall.

Aisling sat down onto the couch, an idea forming in her mind. "Masks—how appropriate for a changeling," she whispered.

Calix flew in through the balcony and landed on the floor, dripping wet. He shook off the water, spraying the room with cold droplets. He walked over to the fireplace, puffed up a huff of fire and then curled up by it.

Aisling closed her eyes, and summoned an Air Elemental. A faint ruffling sensation washed over her skin. Raising palms to her lips, she began to whisper an invitation of her own. From the balcony, she blew the message out into the air and it was carried away on the wind. She began to think about magic, visions—and passion.

Returning to her room she walked over to the nightstand. Upon a small three-legged stand, the black obsidian stone remained, unused until this moment. Even before she picked up the Passion Stone, ideas began to form in her mind—costumes, masks and other things....

*   *   *

Four glowing orbs descended from twilight skies that reddened with the fall of the sun. One came down by a fountain, splashing green and white light over the sparkling water. Two more dropped down into a field of dark grass. One cast pink light over the earth. The other sphere glowed silver and gold. The last ball of light, blue and silver, hesitated to come down, hovering in the air in view of a large estate. The house was a masterpiece of beauty, all white and full of tall glass windows, overlooking the ocean. Merry lights sparkled from within, along with friendly music. Both sensual enticements, they lured one forward, like the promise of a kiss.

Aisling appeared next to the tall iron gateway, standing in the field of grass, and holding hands with Genevieve. The two went over to the fountain where Aoife appeared in a sparkling light show. Aisling watched the pretty lights flash and dance until they materialized into her friend. "You'll have to teach me how to do that some day."

Genevieve scanned the sky. "Where is she?"

A silver flash behind them threw light over the fountain. Eileen's voice announced her presence. "I'm right here."

Aoife giggled and spun around in front of the other three. She wore a white Greek-styled gown with three silver studded black belts around her waist, and thigh-high black boots with embroidered roses in red. She wore a white mask lined in red with rubies and diamonds. Her long red hair fell in curls about her shoulders. "How do I look?"

"I like the boots," said Aisling.

Genevieve wore a black and white checkered mask with a plume of feathers. She fingered her favorite accessory, running a hand over the white scarf nervously. "I'm invited to a party and for once I can't get a date. Do you think there are any cute, single guys in there?"

Both Aoife and Aisling laughed, but Eileen was silent.

Aisling turned to look at Eileen, who didn't seem interested in the party.

"Come on Eileen," said Aisling. "We did get all glammed-up for this."

"I'm not very good at this sort of thing."

Genevieve laughed. "You just miss your sword. Come on!" She turned away and walked towards the enticing house.

Aoife whispered into Aisling's ear, "You shouldn't worry about her. It's not your problem." Without waiting for a response, she followed Genevieve into the party.

Aisling watched the two go, but didn't follow. Eileen usually enjoyed parties, but this one held the promise of meeting men—something she seemed to shy away from. Aisling wondered what her boyfriend's name was but didn't have the courage to ask. She wondered more what the cause of his death was. Turning to look at Eileen, who appeared to be quite miserable, she said, "Eileen, you have to let go of him."

Looking down into the water of the fountain, Eileen didn't respond.

When Eileen had resisted going to the party, Aisling had said she wouldn't go without her. Now, in front of Conall's estate, it seemed that Eileen was ready to back out. Aisling said, "Look, I've never been in love, and I can't imagine what it would be like to lose someone—"

Eileen interrupted. "I said I'd come. There's no need to say anything else."

Aisling bit her lip. She glanced down at her own outfit. She wore a frilly dress of semi-transparent blue, white and purple, with several layers falling into a pattern that made it look like a flower. In one hand she carried a small blue and silver mask with feathers, attached to a stick. "Tell me," she said, raising the mask to her eyes. "Do you like my dress?"

Smiling wryly, Eileen raised her own mask to cover her face and said, "I'm sworn to protect you, not to tell you how beautiful you look." She walked over to Aisling and took her hand. "A job that's suited more for a man like Conall, don't you think?"

The night Aisling had stayed at Conall's estate was a foggy memory of white porcelain and tall glass windows overlooking the ocean. Mostly, she had slept through the experience, though Genevieve had refused to believe it.

This night, the white hall was lit with dozens of candles, reflected into ghostly lights against the tall windows. The rich flavor of one of Mozart's flute concertos swirled around the house, mingling with the sweet aroma of talk and laughter.

Aisling walked into the masquerade, weaving in and out of people, pulling a reluctant Eileen behind her. They found a place near the staircase that wasn't occupied. Aisling began to search through the crowd.

"Are you looking for someone?" asked Eileen.

"Hmm?"

King Artrach appeared, wearing a red-orange mask of fire and smoke. At his side, Queen Annan a mask with gold on one half and white on the other, with a blue Eye of Horus around one eye. They strode onto the floor and began a dance—a medieval-styled affair that swirled around in an intricate pattern.

Disliking the way the Queen's dress had turned out, Aisling looked away outside, but the large glass windows reminded her of her Milesian parents.

Aoife stood underneath one window, flirting with the cute guy Aisling had seen at the picnic. There was something strange in Aoife's expression though, as if she wasn't really interested in . . . anything.

Fintan, wearing a golden mask, walked over to the staircase.

Aisling looked at Fintan, feeling strangely attracted to him. She ran a hand through her hair, unable to look away.

But Fintan wasn't interested. He asked, "Have you seen Genevieve?"

Eileen crossed her arms. "You shouldn't be wearing that in here, Fintan."

"It's only the Mask of Desires," he said. "Where is Genevieve?"

Unknowing why she did so, Aisling moved closer to Fintan. She took his arm in hers. Something about him made her want to know him better. Pouting, she lied, "Genevieve isn't here."

"Aisling!" Laughing, Eileen snapped her fingers in front of Aisling's face. "Wake up!"

Unable to catch her breath, Aisling closed her eyes. Although she hadn't had anything to drink yet, she felt dizzy with excitement. Shaking her head, she saw that Fintan had removed his mask. They were both looking at her strangely. "What?"

Eileen gave Fintan a dirty look.

Reluctantly, Fintan said, "No, I suppose it isn't appropriate." He snapped his fingers and his mask changed into a black hawk-faced visage. "I'll see you two later."

"Fintan!" Eileen held her hand up. "I certainly wouldn't want to discover that you've taken advantage of Genevieve tonight."

Fintan, holding irritation at bay, handed over the golden mask with a sigh and then walked away through the crowd.

Feeling suddenly thirsty, Aisling reached out and grabbed a glass of wine from a passing fairy waitress. "Why are you always watching over Genevieve?"

Eileen explained, "She's a lonely Milesian girl in a world of dangerous faeries who will stop at nothing to seduce her with magic. Besides, I—"

A fairy wearing a jester costume and a fool's mask with a long nose walked up boldly to Eileen. "Would you care to dance?"

Eileen bit her lip, hesitating.

The jester lifted his mask, revealing Fáelán. "Hey, it's me."

"Oh." Relief covered Eileen's face. "Alright then, let's go."

Aisling couldn't resist smiling as the pair went off to dance.

Something whispered near, enticing and flirtatious.

Nearly dropping her drink, Aisling tried to hear over the crowd. There was a movement out of the corner of her eye. Aisling turned to look, but didn't see anything. She glanced down at her drink, wondering if it was really just wine. Then she heard it again. Like a breath of leaves over cool earth, promises and enticements whispered out of the darkness.

A woman giggled.

Aisling turned around and saw a Shadow Person holding hands with a fairy girl. Not at all afraid, the girl smiled at him. They turned away and ran outside. Aisling set her drink down and went after them.

Running through a long hallway, she caught a reflection in the shiny gray floor. It was an exquisitely made dress in two pieces. A long skirt made up the first piece, and a simple tunic worn over one shoulder topped it off. Both skirt and tunic were white, with gray swirling patterns near the bottom. It was simple and elegant. But the dress wasn't what surprised Aisling.

The woman had long blonde hair and black eye shadow around her eyes, which made them look dark and intense. Over her face she wore a mask of gray and white. As she passed by, she smiled. It was Maire—the Shadow Person that Ith had summoned from the Eternal Flame.

Maire, fully corporeal, came to a stop in the hallway. She had a dreamy, crazed look in her eyes. "Hello, Aisling. Have you found the one you love yet?"

Not knowing how to respond, Aisling simply stared.

Maire laughed and dropped her voice. "Don't worry. This is a party!"

Before Aisling could say another word, Maire faded away into shadow, laughing.

Aisling stood listening to her heartbeat in the empty hallway.

The steady drumbeat of footsteps approached, and Aisling saw Nel walking down the far end of the corridor. In one hand, she held a white angel mask with diamonds around the eyes, attached to a stick. Nel came slowly to a stop. "What's wrong, Aisling?"

"There are Shadow People at the party."

"Of course there are," Nel said sarcastically. "You haven't seen Fáelán around, have you?"

Aisling shook her head.

For a moment, Nel's eyes were covered in loneliness, tinged with a kind of desperation. She smiled, and looked at the Shadow Key hanging around Aisling's neck. Raising a hand to touch it gently, Nel whispered, "To everyone is given the key to heaven; the same key opens the gates of hell."

Reining in her surprise, Aisling stepped back a pace until Nel dropped her hand away. "Seriously, I just saw two Shadow People."

Frowning, Nel said, "Really? I'd better go tell the King." At a quick pace, Nel continued on her way, cultivating a new sense of urgency with each step.

Aisling went outside through a set of large glass doors. Next to a large pool, a low glass wall overlooked the sea. Inhaling the cool summer air, she looked out on the ocean, wondering. A gust of wind arrived as a Faerie landed behind her. A spicy, exotic scent touched her nose just as she felt someone put a hand on her waist.

Conall breathed against her ear, "I'm glad you came to my soirée."

Aisling dropped her eyes into the sea, smiling. "How could I resist?"

Gently, Conall spun Aisling around and stepped back a pace. As he did so, Aisling had an urge to move into him, but she held herself back. Conall wore a white Victorian suit and a tiger mask striped in gold and black. Raising the mask off of his face, he said, "I saw a few of your friends around here someplace. . . ."

Shaking herself out of a trance, Aisling said, "I've seen Shadow People here."

Conall walked over to the wall overlooking the ocean, and he leaned onto it. "Yes, they sometimes come to my parties, especially when I gather together the wit, wisdom and beauty of the land. They are bound through magic not to harm anyone here, so don't worry about it."

"What are they doing here?"

Conall smiled irresistibly. "It's a party!"

For a moment, Aisling wondered how effective a spy Conall would be if he never associated with the Shadow People. Before she could respond, he lowered his tiger mask. "I'll see you later tonight, when things quiet down."

Aisling watched him walk away, towards the house where Morrigan stood in a doorway. Morrigan wore a short metallic silver dress with a long semi-transparent skirt of gray, a sterling necklace with a ruby, and silvery stilettos. A mirror-like mask covered her face.

Forgetting the Shadow People for the moment, Aisling watched Morrigan take Conall's hand and walk inside the house. Tonight, who was the fairest of the fair? Crossing her arms, she turned away to look at the sea, burning with the last embers of sunset. "I don't care," she murmured.

Another breeze swept over the pool, throwing hair into her face. Reaching up, she shoved it out of her eyes. When the wind quieted down, she breathed in lavender, musk, and patchouli. She turned around and saw him standing by the pool, water reflections rippling against the black mask covering his face. He wore a white peasant shirt, leather pants, black boots and a scarlet cape. He came forward like a dancer gliding across a ballroom floor.

Inhaling cold air into her lungs, Aisling tried to remain calm.

Keir's warm brown eyes drank in the sight of her, and spilled out mystery. He stopped three paces away. "Thank you for the invitation. I've never been to a party here in the Land of Dreams."

Smiling, Aisling ran a hand through her hair. "I got your note, along with the wildflowers," she said. "I'd like to thank you for the warning, too."

Keir moved to stand by the glass wall beside her. "I knew of my Lord Ith's attack of course, so I wanted you to bring your sword."

"Why?"

Keir gazed out into the ocean. The sea had devoured the sun, leaving golden embers burning out against the darkening sky. "It's so beautiful here, like in a dream," he said. "Did you know that if you die dreamless, you become a shadow?"

Chilly air blew away the warmth covering her heart, leaving it naked and empty. "Who are the Shadow People?" she asked.

Keir turned to face her. "Tell me your name first."

A smile slipped across her face. "Aisling."

"Dance with me, Aisling."

His touch was gentle. Into a sea of beautiful music, bathed in silver moonlight, they danced. Wild wind curled around them as they danced. It was like being swept away in a summer storm, fresh and clean and sad and warm all at once. They danced forever in breathless abandonment.

And then the music stopped.

Reluctant to let go of him, Aisling stood, looking into his gorgeous eyes, dreaming dreams of love and passion. But a cloud covered the moonlight and the illumination filling his face went out. Behind his mask, darkness grew.

Releasing her, Keir stepped back. He began to fade into shadows. Answering her question, he whispered, "We were like you once, full of dreams and passions and pride and frivolous games. Now we're only the echoes of forgotten dreams."

"You're faeries?"

Keir turned away, facing the darkening water where blue moonlight fell into the deep. "We were, once, long ago," he said. "The first ones were the Milesian warriors guarding Lord Ith. But after that, the Tuatha Dé Danaan came to us, forgotten, even among their own kind, or they were cast out when they began to change."

Were the Shadow People just good fairies that had fallen into darkness? Aisling thought of Trista and the others that had been thrown into the black whirlpool. But Trista, innocent, had never started to change into a shadow. For a moment, Aisling wondered if her lost friend had possessed some kind of resistance to the fall. Perhaps that was why the Shadow People had called her "the prize."

Keir smiled with longing, as though he would never be happy again. "Thank you for the dance, Aisling." Darkness surrounded him.

"Wait, don't go," she said. "I want to come see you."

Keir held corporeal form a moment longer, and she could see that he was concentrating. "I command the Fortress of Árainn, in the San Juan Islands, but you cannot come to the Land of Shadows."

Aisling licked her lips, fighting off a last wave of resistance. It was time. "Keir, I wish to end this war. Can you deliver a message to Ith for me?"

His warm, brown eyes faded into black, and his body turned to shadow. "Do not play games with the Lord of Shadows," he warned.

"This isn't a game," she whispered. "Do you know the square tower that guards the upper courtyard in Brú na Bodb—the king's castle?"

"Yes. What of it?"

Aisling glanced around the pool, making sure the area was empty. "The Dream Crystal is hidden in a chamber at the base of the tower. Guarded by a magic doorway, a person may only gain entry to the vault at the hour of twilight. The next opening will be tomorrow night."

"Why are you telling me this?" he asked.

"As I said, I wish to end this war."

Keir was silent a moment, hovering between a corporeal existence and shadow. "Very well, I shall inform him." He waved his hand and a scroll appeared, along with a red candle. Dripping wax onto the scroll, he stamped it with a signet ring on his index finger. "Show this to the men at my fortress, if you like. They'll let you inside."

Aisling took the scroll, resisting an urge to kiss him. For an instant, she thought of going to him, in the Land of Shadows, and remaining there forever. But that was impossible—especially since he was Erin's master. When she looked up again, he was gone. She whispered, "Now I've done it. I've betrayed the Queen."

Inside the house, the party had changed into an opulent expression of ecstasy. Most of the faeries, drunk with passion, were kissing and caressing one another. Shadow People were everywhere, making out with faeries.

Wondering where her friends were, Aisling went into a side room and stopped cold. Genevieve had her arms wrapped around Conall. They were dancing. It was like bathing in white fire. Aisling began to tremble, just as they kissed. Turning around, she ran outside, onto a small balcony, leaned against the glass door and fought off the pain of what she had just seen. "How could she do this to me?"

Aisling shut her eyes tight, holding her breath. All friendship, all hope, all of the love inside, began to drain away, into the ocean. Struggling to hold back a tsunami of pain, she turned away from the water, where elementals had begun to stir. She felt a watery spirit reach out, whispering of revenge, but she shook it off and opened her eyes.

A dreary motion drew her attention. Aoife sat in a chair, listless. She held a glass of wine loosely in one hand, over the edge of the chair. Aoife looked up into Aisling's eyes, with indifference. She dropped the glass and it shattered on the floor. Shadows surrounded Aoife, and she began to fade away, like a dark fog, blowing into the night.

Forgetting Genevieve and Conall, Aisling called out faintly, "Aoife?"

But her friend was gone, fallen into the Land of Shadows.

* * *

Chapter Thirteen

The Rescue

A cold wind blew Aisling's hair across her face. Looking up the gentle slope of the hill, she shielded her eyes against the sunlight. Her thoughts drifted to her sister. How much had Erin endured? Locked away from her own dark dreams, without even the hope of freedom she had suffered and survived in the Land of Shadows. A war of lies had trapped her there.

Little white flowers, with an occasional purple harebell, reflected the sunshine spilling down over the windswept hill. A ring of trees stood in front of a ditch encircling the hilltop, where a barrow tomb rested under a dozen tall birch trees. Next to the tomb there was a tall cairn of stones. Beyond the circle of trees was a low stone wall, pierced on one side with an opening. A pair of tall gray stone pillars stood on either side of the entryway next to the wall, like grave markers. Bereft of hope, pale globes of light drifted aimlessly about.

Aisling, wearing a peasant shirt, leggings and knee-high boots—all white, along with her father's sword on a leather belt, and a satchel hanging from her shoulder, stepped up to the entrance and inhaled the morning air, tinged with the sweet aroma of flowers. Áit an Fhillidh—the Place of Returning, seemed a perfect name for the barrow mound. No signs of the recent battle were evident, and all appeared as it had been on the day she first caught sight of the hill. Fingering the Shadow Key around her neck, she moved forward.

"Where are you going?"

Aisling turned at the sound of Eileen's voice, behind her. Her friend stood with her hands on her hips and a carefree smile on her face. She wore a red shirt with large sleeves, black leggings, belt and boots. Red and purple geraniums were woven into her hair. A holly leaf with red berries hung from a necklace. She carried a pack, slung over one shoulder, and her sword. Aisling returned the smile. "That's an interesting necklace."

"It's a magic talisman," said Eileen. "You didn't answer my question."

"I'm going to get my sister."

Eileen raised her eyebrows. "Without me?"

"Well—"

"You shouldn't try it alone," Eileen said. Taking her sword out, she walked to the edge of the stone wall. Pointing to the ground between the two gray pillars, and then along the wall, she said, "This place is protected by a Circle of Containment."

"Oh," mumbled Aisling. "I knew that."

Eileen laughed and sheathed her sword. "If you were to step across the line of the magic circle, I daresay it would kill you."

Aisling glanced at the innocent looking wall, and trembled. "Well then, I suppose you should come with me. I wouldn't want to die alone."

From the midst of the tall gray birch trees on the crown of the hill, came a fairy, flying towards them. She wore an exquisite dress with a short layered black skirt over a longer purple skirt, a black corset with purple ribbons over a gray blouse, striped black and purple leggings, and combat boots with buckles up the sides. Her blouse exposed an ample bosom and bare white shoulders. A black cross, edged in silver hung from her neck. Her wings were black. Pale faced, she had straight black hair bound with purple ribbons. In a gloomy voice empty of dreams, she said, "Who's there?"

"This is your party, certainly," whispered Eileen.

Aisling said, "I need to enter the Land of Shadows."

Sounding like waves crashing across a beach, a cold wind blew through the trees, scattering the pale balls of light. The fairy landed in front of them. "What errand could take you to such a place?"

"My sister is a prisoner there."

"There are many slaves in the Land of Shadows," said the fairy. "Besides, there is no way to open the doorway inside the barrow tomb."

Aisling touched the Shadow Key around her neck. "I can open it. Will you allow us to come inside the circle?"

A whoosh of air blew hair into her eyes. Aisling turned to see Fáelán. He carried a sword in a scabbard at his side. To allow them to travel together, he was holding hands with Genevieve. She carried her shotgun in a leather case slung over her back.

Fáelán said in a sarcastic tone, "Thanks for waiting for us."

Aisling frowned at Genevieve, who didn't have a trace of guilt in her face.

Ignoring Aisling's dark expression, Fáelán asked, "So, who's this?"

The fairy in the dark dress said, "My name is Sinéad. I guard this place."

"I guess that explains why your face is so pale," muttered Fáelán. He glanced at the tomb. "So, you're the Goth Fairy?"

Ignoring him, Sinéad looked into Aisling's eyes. "I cannot allow you to pass."

Aisling crossed her arms and asked, "Why not?"

Sinéad reached up to finger the cross around her neck and glanced at a passing ball of light, which floated past, whispering sadness. "When the shadow host came through here, many were slain. Even more were taken away. Many now haunt Rath Gealach down by the river. Too many souls already inhabit this place."

Aisling watched the globes of light, wondering what could have condemned their souls to remain here.

Fáelán stepped forward, looking intently at the Goth Fairy. "We've no intention of joining the souls that haunt this hill."

After a moment of thought, Sinéad glanced over her shoulder at the spirit orbs drifting over the tomb. She extended the palm of her hand and a ghostly white orb landed there. The area began to get colder and they could see Sinéad's breath fogging over. "A Circle of Containment cannot be broken, but it can be… modified."

"What do we have to do?" asked Aisling.

Sinéad pointed to the gray pillars on either side of the entrance. "Give me your names, and I will inscribe them here. This will allow you to pass into the circle."

Eileen gave their names, "My name is Eileen Bisset. This is Fáelán Anluain, Genevieve Sully, and Aisling. Erin O'Neil is the name of the girl that will be returning with us."

The Goth Fairy waved her arms at the stones, and writing appeared there, bearing their names. "What is Aisling's last name?"

Aisling shook her head. "I don't know it."

Sinéad tilted her head, as if she was listening to the spirits floating over the hill. "The magic controlling the Circle of Containment requires your surname. You may enter here, but without your last name, you cannot step out of the circle again."

Aisling hesitated, inundated with faint memories from the past. Turning towards Eileen, she asked, "How did you know my name was Aisling?"

Eileen returned Aisling's gaze. Her blue eyes were cold and unmoving. "My parents knew your mother and father. They were the ones that asked me to protect you."

Aisling raised her eyebrows, expectantly. "Where are your parents?"

Eileen looked away. "They didn't survive the war," she murmured. "I'm sorry, Aisling. They never told me your last name."

"Well then," said Genevieve. "I suppose we'll have to find another way."

Aisling wasn't sure if it was the Passion Stone in her satchel, or if she was just irritated at Genevieve, but she walked up to one of the pillars. She reached up to touch it. The gray stone was smooth and cool, except where their names were carved. Running a finger over her name, she wondered who she was or if it really mattered.

Genevieve yelled out, "No, Aisling!"

Without another word, Aisling walked through the gateway. As she passed over the Circle of Containment, she felt a sharp tingling sensation, like electricity, wash over her body. She glanced at her friends and said, "None of you has to come with me."

Fáelán walked through the gateway and stopped next to Aisling. "What, and give up the vacation of a lifetime?"

Eileen smiled and went through the barrier, followed by Genevieve.

Sinéad flew over to the other side of the barrow mound, landing in the shade of one of the tall birch trees next to the cairn of stones, seemingly unconcerned about the fate of her visitors. Spirit globes swirled around her like a bunch of lost kittens.

They walked the short distance to the other side of the grassy barrow. Cut into the side of the green hill was a path that led up to a gateway. A pair of large stones set into the hillside formed the walls of the entrance, which was capped by a large slab of gray rock. Darkness seeped out of the passage. Though there was no longer any breeze inside the circle of trees, Aisling felt something cold blowing against her face. A solitary ball of light came out of the tomb and flew up into the trees, vanishing into the sunlight.

Fáelán raised his hands and whispered, "Cur trí thine," and a pair of torches appeared. He gave one to Aisling and they went inside. The passage extended some forty feet under the mound. The walls and ceiling were lined in stone. Emptiness spilled out of four black arches on either side of the passage as they proceeded deeper into the tomb. At the far end of the hallway stood a stone doorway set into an archway. Fáelán set his torch into a sconce next to the arch. Aisling found a place for hers too.

Aisling took the Shadow Key from around her neck and examined the doorway. "There isn't any kind of keyhole that I see," she said.

Eileen looked at the Shadow Key and asked, "Where did you get that?"

Aisling remembered the day when Trista had been forced into the black whirlpool. "I took it off Ceridwen. She's one of the Shadow People that I saw hiding in the crowd when Trista was banished. When I was attacked after Conall's duel, I heard them talking about how they gained entrance into our world."

"How did they?" asked Genevieve.

Aisling ran a hand over the cold stone doorway, wondering if she had missed something. "They used this key. I also heard Ith's Lieutenant say that there was another secret gateway, but I haven't figured out where it is."

Eileen wondered aloud, "Do you think someone is helping them?"

"Who can say?" whispered Aisling. "Ith told me that King Skilia of the goblins opened this door for them."

"Enchanted doors like this one usually require a magic password," said Eileen. "But I'd rather not try to get it from the goblin king."

Genevieve said, "Take a moment to think about it and then guess."

Eileen gave her a dark look.

Suddenly, Fáelán said, "Give it to me. I want to try something."

Aisling handed him the Shadow Key.

Closing his eyes, Fáelán whispered soft words. He pressed the key against the surface of the stone. Nothing happened for a second, but then a faint glimmer of blue writing appeared over the archway. Growing with intensity, the inscription began to fill the passage with azure light:

Is tríomsa atá an bealach go dtí an scáth buan.
Muintir atá caillte iad, gan fiú dóchas an bháis acu.
In éad go brách le gach cinniúint eile a fhanann siad.
Is tríomsa atá tír na n-aislinglí dearmadta.

"Oh, much better!" said Eileen. Looking at the wall, she began to translate the words:

"Through me is the way to eternal shadow.

They are a lost people, without even the hope of death.

Forever envious of all other fates, they linger.

Through me is the Land of Forgotten Dreams."

Aisling wondered who had placed the inscription over the archway. Then, out of the darkness, uttered more words, echoing all around them, just beyond the light. Spoken in an ancient tongue, Aisling didn't understand it.

Fáelán tilted his head, intent on the whispering. He said, "It's a poem, very old."

"What does it say?" asked Aisling.

He shook his head. "I can't remember enough to repeat it, but I think it was written by a Milesian bard when they conquered the Tuatha Dé."

Genevieve said, "Amairgin."

The passageway was bathed in soft whispers, and a keyhole appeared in the wall. Fáelán inserted the Shadow Key and turned it. The doorway faded away. Beyond the archway they could see a bright world full of trees and dark wildflowers. A garden of mushrooms lay underfoot.

Eileen looked at Genevieve. "How did you know his name?"

Looking perturbed, Genevieve said, "I *read*. He's the poet that came with the Milesian invasion fleet to conquer Ireland. When the Tuatha Dé tried to destroy their ships with a magic storm, it was Amairgin's spell that calmed the winds."

They stepped through the archway into the Land of Shadows. Dim sunshine trickled down through a cloudy veil onto the hill. The air was full of the fresh smell of rain and wet grass, and the earth was damp. While the landscape was the same as where they had come from, there were no trees on the hill, and they could see clearly down to the river. Flowers and mushrooms were everywhere.

Eileen began to gather the wildflowers growing over the hillside.

Genevieve sniffed. "It doesn't seem so bad a place."

Fáelán chuckled. "Just don't eat any of the mushrooms."

Genevieve looked at him with disdain. "I still don't know why you all insist on using primitive weapons." She shook her head. "Swords!"

Fáelán did his best to ignore the remark, but Eileen wouldn't let it go. With a rather odd intensity in her face, she walked over to Genevieve. There was a small flash and a .45 ACP pistol appeared in her hand. She gave it to Genevieve.

Eileen walked over to one side of the hill. Taking the bunch of flowers, she did a slow pirouette in a circle, while scattering the flower petals into the wind and whispering an incantation. Aisling thought she saw a blue light surrounding her friend for a moment, but it went away as quickly as it had appeared. Eileen said, "Shoot me."

Genevieve ran a hand through her long brown hair. "What?"

"Shoot me!"

"I'm not going to shoot you, Eileen."

Aisling was about to intervene when Eileen walked over to Genevieve, took the pistol out of her hand and tossed it to Fáelán. Eileen walked back to where she had been standing and said, "Shoot me, Fáelán."

"Whatever you say, babe." With a bored expression on his face, Fáelán raised the pistol and fired three times. Tiny blue specks of light flashed in front of Eileen, but she remained unharmed. Aisling, not at all surprised that her friends were arguing again, simply sighed.

Genevieve, quickly covering up the look of shock on her face, crossed her arms. "If I had used my shotgun, would your magic shield have worked?"

Eileen smiled coyly. "That weapon was made by Finnian, one of the finest weapon-smiths among the Tuatha Dé. Only the Goibniu clan has ever succeeded in making better weapons, but their Sídhe, Brí na Slieve, was destroyed. They're all gone now. Although your shotgun is made for slaying Shadow People, it also has a *penetration* spell on it. Don't go pointing it at anything you don't want to shoot."

Genevieve wouldn't give in. "So my point is still valid. Why do you insist on using primitive weapons?"

Eileen, exasperated, walked over to Fáelán, took the pistol and gave it back to Genevieve. She pointed down towards the river. "See that large rock?"

Genevieve squinted, raised a hand over her eyes and nodded. "The one about a hundred yards away? Yes, I see it."

"Try to hit it."

With a wry smile on her face, Genevieve raised the .45 pistol, took aim and fired. A tiny puff of smoke appeared on the rock as the bullet struck it, not quite in the center. "So what's your point?"

Eileen raised her arm, took a calm breath and whispered, "Splanc thintrí." A bright blue fork of lightning shot out from her hand, accompanied by a thunderclap. The rock shattered in a cloud of smoke.

Genevieve's mouth dropped open. "Gloriofski!"

Eileen went back to gathering wildflowers. "Contrariwise, who is the one using primitive weapons?"

Aisling put her hands on her hips. "Are you two finished?"

Eileen and Genevieve turned shamefaced eyes towards Aisling.

Already furious with Genevieve, now she gave Eileen an equally fiery expression. "I'm glad you two understand the need to come into this world *quietly*."

"There's no one around." Genevieve gave Aisling a look up and down. "Come to think of it, shouldn't you dress in something darker? White isn't very stealthy."

Ignoring Genevieve, Aisling turned to Fáelán and said, "Erin is imprisoned in the Fortress of Árainn, in the San Juan Islands. We'll need to get to Vancouver first."

Fáelán went over to a bush and came back with several rushes. He handed one to each of them. Aisling, frowning, took the long stalk with skepticism. Fáelán put the rush between his legs and said, "Capall dubh."

A black horse appeared underneath him. It reared up, and neighed. Fáelán rode off down towards the river. Eileen said, "Capall Bán," and a white mare appeared.

"Isn't that the name of Rosheen's fairy Sídhe?" asked Aisling.

"Yes, that's where the Luchtaine clan lives, but it also means, 'white horse,'" explained Eileen.

Aisling duplicated the spell, and conjured up a white horse while Eileen created a brown colt for Genevieve to ride. After catching up to Fáelán, Aisling slowed her horse down so that she could ride next to him.

* * *

They rode down into the gathering darkness. The river alongside was a symphony of dark whispers bubbling out of the water. Ahead of them, an ancient cobblestone road swept down towards the sea, lined with silver fir trees.

Approaching an old willow tree, Aisling listened to the sad murmurs surrounding it, but the voices washed away into the river. Aisling closed her eyes, listening. After she passed under the branches, she felt someone watching her. Halting the horse, she gripped her sword hilt and looked around.

Cool sunshine dripped onto the grassy earth underneath the willow tree. Out of the shadows, something moved. The others had already ridden by, but Aisling didn't call out to them. A familiar voice rose out of the water, "What a shiny horse you have there, and your clothes all white."

Aisling turned her horse to face the river. The changeling Báirbre was walking up the riverbank, like a serpent coming out of the grass. Green reeds were wrapped around her black gothic dress. Desolate blue eyes looked up at the willow tree. She raised a finger to her lips, hushing silence.

Unable to resist, Aisling whispered, "Báirbre?"

"Shhhh."

Báirbre crept closer, barefoot over the green grass, until she stood next to the tree. "A willow nymph with a golden crown sleeps here." She pressed her hands against the bark, listening. "Pass gently through these trees. They call out to the shadows, whisper poison over you. Curses are no good to travelers."

Aisling glanced up at the willow tree, shuddering. What kind of shades lived inside these trees? For a moment, she caught sight of a metallic orb, meandering through the forest.

"Where is Siri?" asked Báirbre, in a dreary tone.

"She's in the Land of Dreams," whispered Aisling. "I'm going to the Fortress of Árainn. Can you help me?"

Báirbre walked up to the horse and placed a hand against its side. "An Chathair Dhubh, the Black City, lives just over that hill, next to the water. Ships go there, but you will never cross over." She dropped her hand away, smiling. "Try if you can."

Out of pity, Aisling offered her hand, but Báirbre backed away.

Aisling said, "Come with us."

Báirbre retreated until she bumped into the trunk of the tree. Her gaze slipped down into the river and her voice was faint, like a stone falling into a cold pond, settling against the bottom. "No." Her eyes drifted up into the dark branches. "My friends live here. They whisper sometimes, from their confinements." Báirbre began to fade away, bleeding into the shade covering the grass. "They whisper—"

Setting her jaw, Aisling kicked her horse into a gallop. It wasn't the first time she had watched Báirbre vanish into the shadows, but the sight of it was unnerving.

Coming out of the trees, Aisling caught up to the others. Eileen looked into her face and asked, "Are you alright, Aisling?"

Her hand was shaking, so she ran it through her hair, hoping Eileen wouldn't notice. Aisling inhaled a deep breath of cold air. "I'm fine."

After a time, they came to the crest of a hill overlooking a dreary town by the ocean. Metallic balls of light—gold, silver, gray and bronze went into and out of the buildings. Black-winged fairies swooped down from the skies, and the entire road was full of whispers. It was like riding into a graveyard, full of the restless dead.

Fáelán looked at Aisling as they went down. "You know, Genevieve is right," he said. "How are we going to sneak inside the fortress?"

Glancing down at her white clothes, Aisling said, "There's no reason to move stealthily. I have an invitation."

"How did you manage that?" he asked, incredulous.

"One of the Shadow People, Keir, has a crush on me," she said. "So I just . . . encouraged him a little bit, last night at the party."

Eileen looked back over her shoulder at Aisling and raised an eyebrow. "Would you tell me please, what you intend to do about Ith?"

Biting her lip, Aisling looked into the dark river. Lonely voices called out of the water, like ripples bouncing against a rock. "Ith won't be there."

Both Eileen and Genevieve brought their horses up short, blocking the road ahead. Fáelán halted too, with an unanswered question on his face.

Unable to continue, Aisling came to a stop. She took a deep breath. "Rath Gealach wasn't Ith's main objective in the attack," she said. "It was probably just a diversion."

"Nessa is gone, and the royal clan of Bodb Derg changed into trees and flowers, for no reason at all?" Eileen asked. "What could Ith have been looking for?"

"The Dream Crystal."

Suspicion began to creep into Eileen's face. "Aisling, you didn't!"

Aisling looked away.

"You told him where it was!" shouted Eileen. "How can you let Ith capture the Dream Crystal?"

"It isn't worth anything," said Aisling. "It doesn't really work."

Eileen screamed, "Aisling!"

Genevieve said in a matter-of-fact tone, "I don't know what this dream-thingy is, but you shouldn't have betrayed the queen, Aisling."

"You're one to talk!"

"What are you saying?"

Aisling let the anger spill out. "I saw you, last night, kissing Conall."

Genevieve laughed. "No you didn't!"

"I told you, I saw you!"

"Whatever you saw, Aisling, it wasn't me kissing your boyfriend." Genevieve brought her horse around, turned her back on Aisling, and rode away.

Aisling didn't answer. She kicked her horse into a trot until she caught up with Genevieve. She knew what she had seen. White fire burned the image into her mind. Slowing her horse to a walk, she closed her eyes, hoping to push the image out of her thoughts, but it remained there, simmering. Like sharks smelling blood in the water, the whispering voices began to call out, stoking the fires of her anger. Aisling began to think of revenge, ways to hurt—savage things. From the other side of reason, cruelties whispered out.

"Conall told me that you were dancing with some guy out by the pool," said Genevieve, over her shoulder. "He wasn't very happy about it either."

Shaking her head to clear away the murmuring voices, Aisling pushed away the anger for the present. "He was upset?"

"Yes," said Genevieve. "He made a pass at me, out of annoyance I suppose."

Aisling gazed hotly at her friend's back, but didn't say anything.

Genevieve turned around in her saddle, and glared back at Aisling. "I told him to get lost, and I left," she said. "But I didn't kiss him!"

"I know what I saw."

Eileen and Fáelán had also caught up to Genevieve. "Why were you dancing with another man?" asked Eileen.

Aisling ran a hand through her hair. "That was Keir. I got him to give me a pass to his fortress, where Erin is imprisoned."

Genevieve halted her horse and turned around. "You manipulated a guy because he likes you? That's a really low thing to do Aisling."

Eileen shook her head. "You should have trusted the queen Aisling."

Aisling didn't answer. After Gentle Annie had lied about Trista, she didn't think she could ever trust the queen again.

Eileen was still anxious. "This won't do," she said. "We have to go back!"

"I'm not going back without Erin," said Aisling.

Eileen frowned. "Then I'm going to send a message to Aoife. Maybe she can warn the queen about Ith."

Sadness welled out of Aisling. "Aoife can't help," she said. "She fell into the Land of Shadows last night."

Genevieve slowed her horse down and looked over her shoulder. "What? You're wrong Aisling! I saw her last night at the party. She was fine."

"That's right," said Eileen. "Aoife wasn't a proud person, so how could she fall?"

Fáelán said, "The only thing wrong with Aoife was that she was a bit aloof. All she cared about was having fun."

"Exactly so," said Aisling. "Aoife didn't care about anything or anyone else. All of the Tuatha Dé are like that. They're too frivolous."

"Being frivolous doesn't cause you to fall, certainly," protested Eileen. "The queen says pride is the reason for it."

"Maybe both things cause you to fall," said Genevieve.

Aisling wondered if anyone could stop the faeries from falling into the Land of Shadows. She turned towards Eileen and said, "You can go back if you want, but I'm going to get Erin before I return."

Eileen shook her head. "No. I'm your protector. I'm staying with you."

* * *

They finally reached the city. Tall gray buildings lurked on either side of the road now, and the street was full of metallic orbs. Dark figures leered out of the windows as they went by. Shadow People were everywhere, but they did nothing more than watch.

Aisling noticed a patch of black mist, swirling around an empty place in the street and she stopped to look at it. Purple and blue lights flashed inside. From the darkness came a low, mournful moan. She felt a dark presence around the whirlwind and discovered that there were several Shadow People standing by, waiting.

A flash shot out, so bright that everything vanished for a heartbeat, and all of the Shadow People faded away. The black fog swirled into a small funnel, reaching up into the clouds. There was another flash and Aisling saw a girl gradually appear in the street. The expression on her face made Aisling think of Brigitte—utterly lost, devoid of any semblance of caring, she stood there, waiting.

The Shadow People began to laugh. One of them grabbed the girl and held her while others placed a metal collar around her neck.

Aisling began to draw her sword, but Fáelán held her back. "We can't save her."

Gritting her teeth, Aisling turned her horse away and rode off towards the harbor.

Three tall sailing ships were anchored in the dark water. Dull sunlight marred the surface of the ocean, which reflected the mountains surrounding the city. A wood sidewalk ran in front of a line of buildings. They stopped in front of a place called 'The Green Heather Pub' and they got off their horses, which disappeared.

As soon as Aisling was standing on the ground she felt someone watching. She thought she saw something move out of the corner of her eyes. A steady drone of clanking chains drew her attention. Aisling saw a line of ragged souls come around the corner, chained together through a metal ring attached to collars around their necks. She noticed several of the collars had a Maltese Cross stamped on the metal. Several Shadow People, carrying clubs and spears, led them along towards one of the ships. One Shadow Person walked right in front of Aisling, leering at her with glowing red eyes.

"What now?" whispered Fáelán.

"We need to get onto a ship," muttered Aisling. "Wait here."

Aisling walked into the Green Heather Pub and stepped up to the bar. Shadows stood around the room, whispering. Some were corporeal, and others no more than a faint glimmer of darkness.

A man wearing a dark shirt with a red tie came over. A perpetual shadow covered his face, but he was otherwise solid looking. His raspy voice made her skin crawl. "Why have you come to An Chathair Dhubh?"

Aisling put a hand on the bar, grounding herself on the sturdy wood. It was smooth and cold to the touch. "I need a ship. Are any of these vessels headed for the San Juan Islands?"

"The Niamh is," he said. "You headed for the Fortress of Árainn?"

"Yes," she said. "Can you tell me where the captain might be?"

"Captain Fitzgerald doesn't take passengers."

Harsh laughter came from outside. Aisling saw a group of Shadow People standing next to her friends. One of the shadows clutched his hand, which was smoking as if it had just been burned. Fáelán's sword lay on the wood deck at the Shadow Person's feet.

Aisling rushed through the doors. Instantly, she felt someone grab her from behind, pulling her back against the wall. The man, completely invisible until he had appeared from behind, held her with an iron grip. She tried to break out of the hold, but he was non-corporeal, except for his hands. Aisling's friends were being restrained too.

Genevieve faced a woman with blonde hair pulled back into a pony-tail. She held a curved Shamshir sword at Genevieve's throat.

In front of Eileen stood a woman, with bright orange hair down to her shoulders. She held two curved short swords at Eileen's throat. She had painted her face with white makeup and blue eye-shadow. The effect made her look rather clownish.

A pale woman with long blonde hair and a proud look, wearing a loose white blouse exposing her shoulders, purple shorts, black tights, ankle boots, and a black newsboy cap, stood in front of Aisling, next to the man with the injured hand.

The one with the smoking hand yelled, "May the Devil swallow you sideways! It's a consecrated weapon!"

The Shadow People laughed.

The blonde haired girl called out, "You're getting careless Iarlugh. If you and Ith's Lieutenant didn't spend so much time toying with Milesian girls, this wouldn't have happened."

Iarlugh looked up and his face turned to shadow, except for a pair of glowing red eyes. "That's a lie, Laoise! His games are too cruel for me. But he has a Way Stone, and I like to watch them fall."

Laoise said, "Sucking down Milesian dreams is a waste of time, Iarlugh. You shouldn't spend so much time in their world."

"Your boyfriend likes to wander, doesn't he, Éile?" said the girl with the hat.

The orange haired girl shouted back. "Shut up, Dunfhlaith!"

Dunfhlaith crept closer to Aisling, moving like a panther. Raising a hand to touch Aisling's face, she said, "Out of the Heavens they came down, whispering thunder and fire and desolation. Who is this that without shadow passes through the lands of the forgotten?"

"My name is Aisling."

"Dia duit," she whispered. Dropping her hand, Dunfhlaith turned and stepped away, chuckling. "Hold this one tight, Scolaí. I've heard there's a curse ready to avenge her corpse."

"Let us go," demanded Aisling.

With one fluid motion, Dunfhlaith drew her sword and placed the tip an inch from Aisling's throat. "We'll take this one to Scáth Caisleán. Lord Ith should be pleased."

Aisling looked down the length of the blade, wondering if Dunfhlaith would tempt fate by killing her. Trying to ignore her pounding heart, she said, "I have a pass that guarantees safe passage to the Fortress of Árainn."

Dunfhlaith didn't move, but the shadow holding Aisling—Scolaí, reached into the bag at her side and withdrew the paper Keir had given to her. He looked at it while they waited. "It's true, but it only mentions her name, not any others."

Iarlugh laughed. "I've never fought left-handed before," he cried. Drawing his sword, he slashed out at Fáelán.

Fáelán jumped clear.

Iarlugh lunged and Fáelán dodged it.

There was a fast movement from the side, and Aisling saw Genevieve tumbling over the ground. Picking up the sword, she shouted, "Fáelán!" and threw it to him.

Fáelán spun around and slashed at his adversary, who ducked under the blade and counterattacked with a head strike. Fáelán parried it. "Clang!"

Dunfhlaith shook her head but she didn't turn around or move her sword point away from Aisling's throat. "As useless as a chocolate teapot, she is," said Dunfhlaith. "Laoise, how could you let one go?"

The blonde shadow leapt towards Genevieve, and pointed the Shamshir at her. Genevieve lay on the ground, looking up at the curved weapon.

Undeterred, Iarlugh feinted towards Fáelán's chest and tried to strike his head.

Fáelán parried it, retreating.

Iarlugh tried a head strike, with a left-handed slash, but Fáelán parried and ducked under the blade.

With every failed attack, Iarlugh became more determined. He lunged, feinted, whirled around in a furious strike, and lunged again.

Fáelán continued to retreat and parry, while looking for an opening. Unable to gain the initiative, he was being driven back. Avoiding a lunge, he spun around and tried a counterattack.

Iarlugh parried the strike and then delivered an overhand head strike.

Fáelán parried it and the two combatants stood facing each other for a moment.

Eileen, whose captor had turned slightly to watch the fight, drew her sword and ran between the two, knocking both of their swords aside.

Seeing that his opponent was distracted, Fáelán deftly disarmed Iarlugh and pointed his sword at his chest.

Iarlugh grew so dark that he nearly faded away. His red eyes burned hotly.

But it was Éile that shouted out in anger.

Raising two curved short swords, Éile jumped forward, aiming both blows at Eileen's neck.

Eileen, who had her back turned, deftly parried both of the attacks and then spun around to parry another attack aimed at her leg.

Éile tried a dual strike, slashing low with both weapons at once, but Eileen jumped over the pair of blades.

Aisling watched the fight, unable to do anything with Dunfhlaith's sword so close to her throat. Why had she brought her friends here? She didn't know what she would do if one of them got hurt.

Jumping forward, Éile slashed and lunged, but Eileen retreated out of the way.

The wind picked up and Aisling could sense an Air Elemental nearby. Éile began a series of spinning attacks, gaining momentum with each successive blow.

Eileen inhaled the cool air and spun aside, parrying as she went. Picking up speed, she whirled around and counterattacked.

Avoiding Eileen's sword strikes, Éile dropped down onto one leg, slashing out.

Eileen jumped to avoid the strike and had to retreat several paces, dodging more sword slashes.

The Air Elemental returned, and Éile began moving forward again, with dual spinning blade attacks. Although Eileen continued to retreat and parry, Aisling wondered if her friend knew what she was doing.

Éile lunged and then delivered a spinning attack.

Eileen dodged and jumped back.

Éile began striking out with her two swords while twirling around in a circle.

Eileen caught a gust of wind and spun around, dodging.

The wind knocked hair into Aisling's face and she had an urge to raise a hand to brush it away, but Dunfhlaith whispered, "Keep bloody still."

Through dark hair, Aisling saw Éile lunge. Eileen parried it. Éile whirled around, slashing, and Eileen was forced to jump back, parrying wildly. Éile changed direction, spun around and slashed again, but Eileen was too fast for her, dodging it.

"Yaaw!" Éile threw a head-shot.

Eileen parried the sword, and then pulled it aside, nearly knocking it out of Éile's hand.

Éile jumped forward, slashing with her other weapon.

Spinning around, Eileen parried the attack, kicked Éile's leg out, and knocked her down. Éile tried to regain her balance by spinning around and rising up for an attack, but it was too late.

Eileen slashed out, aiming at her opponent's neck, but she didn't follow through. She held her sword at Éile's throat.

Éile looked down at the blade, breathing hard.

Eileen waited.

With a yell, Éile knocked the sword away and attacked wildly, slashing with both of her swords.

Eileen calmly parried the blows without moving back.

Éile lunged.

Eileen deftly knocked one of the curved short swords out of Éile's hand and placed her sword at Éile's neck.

Again, Éile knocked Eileen's sword aside and slashed out.

Eileen parried the attack, stepped to the side and knocked Éile down. Éile's sword slipped out of her hand.

Eileen turned around and began to walk towards Aisling.

Éile got up and began to attack Eileen with her bare hands. "Yaw!"

Dunfhlaith said in an amused tone, "Éile stop! You're no match for her!"

Éile halted. Furious, she faded away into a shadow, eyes burning.

A smile crept into Dunfhlaith's face. She lowered her sword from Aisling's throat. "My ship is headed to the Fortress of Árainn," she said. "I'm Captain Dunfhlaith Fitzgerald."

* * *

Aisling and her friends stood on the deck of the ship, looking at the sunlight falling into the ocean. After sailing for a time, they saw the San Juan Islands appear, like green phantoms rising out of the sea. Not entirely certain that it was a good idea to trust Dunfhlaith, she breathed a sigh of relief at the sight of the island.

Throughout the journey over the sea, Aisling felt the Shadow People on board watching her. The crew of the ship moved around like specters. Most of the time, they held their corporeal form, but sometimes she caught one of them fading into the shadows, as if they had to concentrate to remain solid. The Niamh sailed into a quiet harbor, and docked next to another ship.

Dunfhlaith came down from the upper deck at the aft of the ship, moving with the calm certainty of one already condemned to oblivion. She smiled as she approached. "Follow that road. It leads to the fortress."

Aisling ran a hand through her hair. "Can I ask you something?"

"Yes?"

"What's a Way Stone?"

"Listening to us, were you?" said Dunfhlaith. "It's a magic crystal that allows us to travel into the Milesian world without needing to locate a Thin Place."

"Why do you visit the Milesian world?"

Dunfhlaith's explanation was simple and unsatisfying all at once. "They dream."

Frowning, Aisling asked, "Why are you helping us?"

"Your pass has been stamped with Keir's seal," said Dunfhlaith. "I'm not ready to discover what kind of curses he uses to enforce his will."

Aisling exchanged glances with Eileen, who stood quietly by.

Dunfhlaith raised a hand to touch the tip of her hat. "Slán leat."

As they debarked, Genevieve muttered, "Thanks for the ride."

Silhouetted against a cloudy sky, the castle stood on top of a high hill. A purple flag bearing a gold sixteen-pointed star flew on top of the highest tower. Rising up a steep road, they soon found themselves in front of the gatehouse.

A tall red-haired man stood guard, holding a spear in one hand. Aisling took out the scroll Keir had given to her and handed it over. He looked at it and asked, "What business do you have with King Eochaid Mac Eirc?"

Raising her eyebrows, Aisling said, "None at all. I'm here to see Keir."

His eyes whispered suspicion. "Who are these?"

Aisling glanced over her shoulder. "They're with me."

The man rolled the scroll up and gave it back. "Keir isn't here."

"We'll wait," she said.

The man called over his shoulder. "Gann, Rindail!"

Two men bearing spears and swords came out of a doorway on the other side of the gatehouse. At the sight of Aisling, they stopped short, surprise spilling into their faces. One of them recovered enough to speak. "Yes, Adar?"

The gatekeeper said, "Take these *visitors* into the castle."

As they went into the courtyard Aisling looked up at the main tower, which was attached to the rest of the fortress. Fading sunlight fell onto the cobblestones, and a dark fountain, murmuring quietly, stood next to an apple tree.

"This doesn't seem like so foul a place," said Fáelán.

"Who is this 'King Eochaid,' anyway?" asked Genevieve.

Eileen ran a hand along one stone wall, as if she was trying to gain a sense of what kind of dark earth spirits might live inside it. "He's the last King of the Fir Bolg. The Tuatha Dé conquered his people, but I never heard what became of them."

The guards led them into the great hall where a large fire burned inside a black stone hearth. Black marble pillars surrounded the room, and they were attached to a wooden latticework that ran between them. A long wood table stood next to the fireplace, flanked by smaller tables standing in front of the latticework. On the center table, a large bowl, made from quartz, was filled with red apples. Above the hearth hung a large round shield, painted purple and bearing a gold, sixteen-pointed star.

"You may remain here for now," said one of the guards.

Aisling was too stunned to move. The chamber was identical to the one she'd seen in the mirror hanging in her room back in Seattle. She whispered, "I've seen this place before."

Genevieve and Fáelán walked over to one of the side tables and sat down.

Eileen smiled at one of the guards. "Are you Rindail?"

He shook his head. "My name is Gann."

Running a hand through her long blonde hair, Eileen adopted a shy outlook. "Do you think we could get something to drink? We've come a long way."

Gann glanced at his companion, who was smiling. Gann looked uncertainly back at Eileen and said, "Very well. I'll send in a thrall."

Aisling hardly noticed that the guards had gone. Shaking her head, she walked into the room and ran a hand along the surface of a table. She could feel the heat of the fire on the wood. The room smelled of smoke and ale. Approaching the hearth, she noticed an inscription carved into the stone above it: Ní suaimhneach croí uasal cheal saoirse.

"What does it say?" asked Aisling.

Eileen looked up at the words carved into the stone and read them aloud, "A noble heart can have no ease if freedom fails."

"What do you suppose that means?" asked Fáelán.

Aisling shook her head. Ith had spoken highly of freedom, but his people kept slaves. "A man is either free or he is not," she said.

"Funny, isn't it?" said Genevieve. "They didn't take away our weapons. They're not even watching us!"

Eileen nodded her head and walked over to the side table. "Perhaps they have nothing to fear from us. After all, where have we to go? This place is darker than I had imagined it to be."

Genevieve chuckled. "It's sunny outside. They even have an apple tree! Okay, so there are lots of Shadow People around, but nobody—"

"What I meant," interrupted Eileen, "was that this is a world without hope. Truly, these people have abandoned their dreams."

A skinny girl came in, carrying a tray laden with four pewter goblets and a glass pitcher, seemingly full of water. She wore a white peasant blouse, a black vest embroidered with blue flowers, leather pants and thigh boots. Silver hair hung straight down past her shoulders. Her blue eyes held a lost, haunted look, tainted with ire. A metal collar with a ring in the front was clasped around her neck. She walked over to the table and put the tray down silently.

Fáelán stood up.

Aisling turned around and smiled.

The girl picked up a goblet and looked at Eileen. "What is your desire, mistress?"

Eileen raised her eyebrows and glanced at Aisling. "Why, I'll have a glass of red wine, please."

Whispering soft words, the girl began to pour, but wine came out instead of water.

Aisling ran a nervous hand through her hair. "Erin?"

The girl gave Aisling a suspicious look. "Yes?"

It was difficult to contain her excitement. Aisling whispered, "You're Erin O'Neil, aren't you?"

The girl tilted her head and a lock of silver hair fell into her eyes. Her response was cautious. "Yes." She picked up another goblet. "Will you have wine also?"

Aisling walked over and took the goblet out of Erin's hand, nodding her assent.

Erin poured wine.

Their eyes met. In Erin's eyes, years of loneliness and pain and an acceptance of her fate were blended together with a guarded curiosity.

"Erin, I've come to take you out of here."

Laughing, Erin turned around and began to pour wine into the other cups. Then she put the pitcher down and started to leave.

Aisling grabbed Erin's arm, "Wait."

With incredible speed, Erin pulled a stiletto knife out of one of her boots and raised it to Aisling's throat. "Let go of me!"

On pure reflex, Aisling sidestepped, grabbed Erin's wrist, turned and pulled.

Erin screamed and dropped the stiletto.

Aisling let go.

Erin leapt backwards, clutching her hand. "I'm not going anywhere with you!" she shouted.

Aisling took a step forward. "Let me explain," she whispered. "I'm—"

"I don't care who you are!"

Erin bolted down the hallway and out of sight.

*   *   *

Chapter Fourteen

Stolen Dreams

Out of the hearth, the crackling fire murmured. Erin had gone. Aisling had just lost all that she had and all that she would ever want to possess. Erin had just run away from what Aisling had so desperately wanted all of her life: Her parents' love. She began to understand what kind of life the Shadow People endured. It was like being roasted slowly—in a hell filled with nothing but whispers. Inside the bag at her side she could feel the fire emanating from the Passion Stone. Like a dry match, it waited, ready to ignite a firestorm, fueled by desire. Aisling felt the warmth of the hearth fire on her back, and with it, a grim determination settled into her skin.

"That went well," muttered Genevieve.

Eileen gave Genevieve a stern look and then turned to Aisling. "What now?"

Aisling brought up her knapsack and reached inside. "It's time to go."

Fáelán put his hands on his hips. "So you think we can just walk out of here?"

Aisling removed Nel's magic hat from the bag. "We should be able to travel in pairs," she said. "Who wants to go first?"

Fáelán nearly shouted. "So now we just leave, without Erin?"

A wry smile crept into Aisling's face. "Not exactly."

"We can't take her if she doesn't want to go," said Eileen.

"Don't worry," said Aisling. She threw the hat to Fáelán. "Take Genevieve back to the barrow tomb and return here for Eileen."

Fáelán shrugged. "Alright, it's your call."

He walked over to Genevieve, took her hand and said,

"By harebells and rue,

And a heart that is true,

Hie over to the Place of Returning!"

A sudden rush of air whooshed through the room, nearly blowing out the torches along the walls. Fáelán and Genevieve had vanished.

"Eileen, you wait here," said Aisling. "I'm going to have a talk with my sister."

Aisling ran down the corridor, hoping that she was still able to follow Erin through the labyrinth of passages. Luckily, she caught sight of her just around a corner. Erin went into a room, but before she could close the door, Aisling stepped inside.

Fading sunlight fell through an arched window into a lonely chamber. A simple bed lay along one wall, and an oak chest bound in iron stood at the foot of the bed. A long chain passed through a ring that was attached to a wall. The room was the same one that Aisling had seen through the mirror in the hallway of her parents' house.

Erin crossed her arms. "So, who do you work for? Lord Ith?"

"Nobody," said Aisling. "I'm your sister."

Erin laughed darkly and sat down onto the bed. "I don't have a sister."

"Well, I'm not your sister exactly," said Aisling. "I'm a *Síofra*—a changeling. Your parents—"

"My parents are dead," said Erin. She reached underneath a pillow and withdrew a doll, almost absentmindedly.

"No, they're not."

The sun had gone down, washing the hilltop with shadows. The mushrooms covering the hill caught the last of the light. It reminded Aisling of the fairy ring she and Genevieve had used to enter the Land of Dreams.

Using Nel's magic hat, Fáelán had brought everyone back to the barrow tomb at the Place of Returning. Eileen looked down on the river, sword in hand, while Genevieve stood next to Erin, talking quietly about her home. Fáelán walked over to Erin. He raised his hand and closed his eyes, speaking under his breath, "Saoraim thú."

There was a small click. Erin reached up and removed the steel collar from around her neck. For a time, she gazed down at the collar in her hands. Silver hair covered her face.

A chilly breeze washed over the grass, and small balls of light began to appear, darting over the field of mushrooms. The tiny spheres were mostly metallic colors; steel gray, gold, bronze, and silver. They whispered to one another, like lost souls. It was only a matter of time before one of the dark faeries changed into a Shadow Person.

Aisling watched a steel-colored orb hover nearby. It flickered and turned black. She could hear it whisper, "Stay with us."

Something burned inside, and Aisling felt the Passion Stone growing warm from inside the knapsack. She closed her eyes, unable to resist swimming in the dark current. Another whisper washed into her mind, "Stay!"

Aisling felt herself swaying slightly on her feet, and she opened her eyes. The clearing was full of black metallic spheres now, whispering...

Seeing the dark orbs, Genevieve took her shotgun out and pumped a round into the chamber.

Aisling put her hand on the barrel of the shotgun. "No wait," she said. "They're just lonely. They won't hurt us."

Genevieve lowered her shotgun, but didn't put it away either.

Aisling took the Shadow Key from around her neck and handed it to Genevieve. "Take her home, will you?" she said. "Give the key to Sinéad when you've gone through the doorway."

Genevieve was surprised. "You're not coming?"

Aisling shook her head. "No. Remember what the Goth Fairy said? I cannot leave the Circle of Containment without my last name."

Fáelán asked, "So you expect us to leave you here?"

"Yes."

Aisling turned away and took out her sword. "If I'm lucky, Ith will return through this door. When he comes through with the Dream Crystal, I'll stop him."

"We're not going without you," protested Fáelán.

Inhaling quiet air, Aisling smiled at Fáelán, knowing that he would go. Fáelán averted his eyes.

Genevieve called out nervously, "Eileen, you coming?"

Not taking her eyes off the dark river, Eileen said, "No, you go on ahead."

Aisling turned to Erin. "I'm sorry for what my parents put you through..."

Erin frowned, tilting her head slightly so that the wind caught her silvery hair. "You don't even know their names, do you?"

"No."

Erin spoke quietly, "My mother, or rather, your mother, was called, 'Ériu.'"

Aisling caught her breath. She had never thought of asking Erin about her parents. "And my father?"

"Elathan."

Aisling smiled into the fading light. She touched Erin's shoulder. "Thank you."

Eileen walked over to the barrow door, putting her sword away. She had a curious smile on her face. "Shall we go then?"

Aisling frowned. "What?"

"You can use your father's name as your surname," said Eileen. So that would make your full name Aisling Nic Elathan."

Aisling repeated her name out loud and smiled. "I like it."

*　*　*

Twilight had come.

Out of the darkening sky, stars began to appear. Their tiny lights reflected in an ocean of liquid glass stretching before the castle of Brú na Bodb. Bathed in sunshine all day, the earth poured out its heat, but little of its warmth reached the upper ramparts and towers of the fortress. A flash of lightning struck a tower.

Aisling landed on the top floor of the square tower next to the shattered remains of a stone gargoyle, its grim visage frozen in an expression of shock and surprise. Down on the upper courtyard, she heard the loud cry of birds, and as she moved over to the battlement she could see a flock of ring ouzels, black birds with a white ring around their necks, rising up into the sky. A cold breeze tossed hair into her eyes and sent a shiver over her skin.

Several soldiers were running over the cobblestones of the upper courtyard, towards the tower where Aisling had landed.

CRUMP!

A white flash erupted from below, shaking the tower and knocking Aisling off her feet. Getting up, she saw smoke rising from the bottom of the tower. She tried to see what was happening down below, but it was impossible.

Aisling took a deep breath and jumped off the tower, plunging down towards the upper courtyard. Cold air swept over her skin, blowing away the smoke, ash and heat of the fire below. At the last moment, she extended her wings and broke the fall. She landed gently on the cobblestones, which were littered with spears and swords and pieces of armor. Another ring ouzel hopped over a helmet, whistling angrily.

Click... click... click... click...

Smoke billowed over a stairwell that led to the square tower housing the Dream Crystal. Out of a hole in the wall of the tower, a figure emerged. Wearing a black suit, white gloves and a short Victorian top hat, Ith walked down the stone steps towards the upper courtyard. In one hand he carried a cane, tipped with silver. In his other hand he carried the Dream Crystal, the rainbow fires muted as if its brightness was being smothered by a solitary darkness. Not covered in shadows this time, he had a youthful face. He had short black hair, a sharp nose and eyes full of loneliness.

Click... click... click... click...

As Ith came out of the smoke, he slipped the Dream Crystal into one of his pockets, and his face darkened slightly. He raised the tip of his cane to the brim of his hat. "Good evening, Aisling."

Despite the smoke, Aisling detected the luxurious aroma of lotus flowers, dark violet, musk and a hint of mandarin. She could feel her heart beating with excitement. This was the first time she'd seen Ith in corporeal form. He was darkly handsome.

Now uncovered by shadows, Ith's eyes drew her in. They were like a still lake, hidden in the wilderness. Broken upon the rock of oblivion, darkness rippled out of them. Silent as the blackness between the stars in heaven, they were a wilderness of solitude, utterly lost—completely alone. Full of confined passion, his eyes were still bereft of love.

At the sight of his forlorn eyes, Aisling caught her breath. She licked her lips and said, "I can't allow you to take the Dream Crystal."

Ith smiled. "But you were the one that told me where it was—according to the leader of my bodyguard."

Aisling's mind reeled. *Keir was the head of Ith's bodyguard?*

"Have you changed your mind?" he asked.

"What do you mean?"

"I thought you wanted to end this war."

Aisling shook her head. "Not this way." She drew her sword. The sound shattered the silence covering the courtyard.

Ith placed his cane against the cobblestones with a click and put both hands on top of it. "Aisling, why don't you come with me? Live with me in the land of freedom."

His offer was tempting—to cover up those lonely eyes, to fill them with warmth. But something told her that they would never change. It would be like throwing a pebble into a lake, stirring the surface for a moment only, and then sinking down into the deep, to rest at the bottom with a thousand other abandoned pebbles.

Aisling glared at Ith. "If your world is so free, then why do you keep slaves?"

Ith tilted his head slightly. "Not all of us are at liberty, that's true. But those with the soul of a free man live free. Those that have the soul of a slave live as thralls."

Aisling shook her head. "How can you—"

Ith interrupted her. "As water seeks its level, the soul of a free man will always rise above others. The soul of a slave will always remain in the dirt. I'm not responsible for those too weak to control their own fates."

With every word uttered by the Lord of Shadows, Aisling felt herself slipping into agreement with him. Didn't every person determine their own fate? She knew how intoxicating freedom could be, especially after living under the queen's repression for so long. She closed her eyes, letting his words sink in.

Ith's words were coated in regret. "Everyone here is so frivolous—so *indifferent*. They're all just mindless vegetables living lives of escape," said Ith. "Are you so afraid to dream?"

Aisling opened her eyes. "I'm not."

"If you follow Queen Annan, you must abandon your dreams, your ambitions, your desires, your passions," whispered Ith. He offered his hand. "Come."

Slightly lightheaded, Aisling felt weakness in her knees. She put her sword away and ran unsteady hands through her hair. Ith was right about the Tuatha Dé. Indeed, they were terrified of dreams. She took a step in his direction...

"No. Leave your sword here," intoned Ith.

Without considering what she was doing, Aisling detached the scabbard from her belt and put her father's sword down on the stone.

Out of the corner of her eyes, Aisling saw Eileen fly out of the sky and land on the upper courtyard. Bringing a dark stormy whirlwind with her, Eileen's blonde hair flew into her face. Raising her arms, Eileen shouted, "Splanc thintrí." A bolt of lightning shot out at Ith, with a flash of thunder.

Ith spun around and swept his cane through the air in front of his face. The lightning hit the cane, but it reflected back and struck Eileen. She fell down onto the cold stone, unmoving. As the wind died down, red and purple geraniums fluttered to the ground around Eileen's body.

Aisling blinked. It was as if she had been underwater and had just come up for a breath of air. Shaking her head, she staggered on her feet and swallowed the pain of what she'd just seen. "Eileen!" But her words didn't revive her friend.

A dozen soldiers came down from the castle. Drawing swords, they advanced.

Ith twirled the cane around his head, reciting ancient words of power. A dark whirlwind of blue fire swept out, engulfing everyone in a fury of screaming flames.

To get away from the fire, Aisling jumped over the stone wall, and fell down onto the lower courtyard. The screams above her were quickly swallowed up the conflagration. Unfurling her wings at the last moment, she managed to break the fall. She landed hard on the stone, tumbled, rolled over and rose to her feet.

Two entities lingered in the shadows under the wall. Aisling could just hear the sound of swords being drawn and turned to see the shadows as they approached. For a moment, she stood there, wondering what to do without a weapon.

Two shotgun blasts rang out and the shadows screamed, fading away as they fell.

Aisling heard Genevieve pump another round into her shotgun. She looked up onto the staircase that connected the lower and upper courtyards and saw Genevieve raise her weapon again. She fired at Ith, just as he faded away. Genevieve cursed.

Surprisingly, Ith reappeared, becoming fully corporeal again. The look on his face was strained, as if it was difficult for him to concentrate.

Genevieve pumped a round into the chamber of her shotgun.

Sprouting black wings from his back, Ith flew up onto one of the towers connected to the gatehouse. Genevieve shot at him, but she missed.

Aisling sprinted through the gateway and flew up into the air outside the castle, hoping to head him off. Whirling around, she saw Fáelán standing in Ith's way on top of the tower, with his sword out. Fury swirled around Ith, and his eyes turned to hot coals. He swept his cane out and a bolt of fire erupted from it. Fáelán shouted a command word and instantly, the fire was extinguished. A thunderclap shook the fortress, and both he and Ith collapsed onto the gatehouse tower.

Fáelán lay on the cold stone, unmoving.

"No!" Aisling's shout fell into the black well of twilight.

Aisling landed behind Ith as he got to his feet unsteadily. His cane lay on the stone, burning with a violaceous fire and emitting acrid fumes. Ith tried to fade away into the shadows but he wasn't able to. Aisling put a hand on his chest. "You can't escape that way. Return the Dream Crystal and I'll let you go."

Ith laughed and turned away.

Aisling tried to grab Ith, but he knocked her hand out of the way, throwing a punch with his other hand. She blocked it.

Ith grabbed Aisling's arm but she slipped it out of the way, grabbed him and spun him around, hoping to restrain him. But he broke free and took off into the air, flying towards the town by the water.

For a moment, she wondered why he wasn't able to vanish into the shadows. "The Dream Crystal must be holding him to this world," she said.

Aisling glanced at her fallen friends, feeling a pang of guilt at not stopping to help them. She shot up into the air, flying towards Ith with all the speed that she could muster.

Flying over houses, Ith tried ducking down behind the rooftops, but he was unable to shake off his pursuer. Ith dropped down to the ground behind a building, and moved into the shadows.

Aisling came down and began to chase him on foot, running through an archway and into a courtyard. Ith took off into the air, flying over the rooftops. Aisling followed him, feeling the Passion Stone inside the bag at her side growing warm. The magic stone seemed to amplify whatever she did, and she used it to hunt him down. Ith glanced behind, perhaps sensing the stone, and he changed direction again, landing on the ground.

Aisling dove down out of the sky, striking a blow as she landed next to him, but Ith blocked it with a swift movement of his hand. She tried to grab him, but he crossed his arms, blocked it and pushed her away.

She pushed him back and tried grabbing him again, but he rolled his hands down, blocking again and he swung at her head. She blocked it just in time. He struck out with his other hand and she had to dodge out of the way.

Aisling delivered several elbow strikes to his face, but he blocked the attacks and tried to strike her in the throat. Aisling blocked his attack and counterattacked with a strike aimed at his chest.

Ith twirled around out of her reach, leapt into the air and flew away.

A black spirit swam in the twilight, just over the rooftops, watching.

Uncaring about the shadow, Aisling watched Ith fly into the air, more determined than ever. She could feel the Passion Stone throbbing against her side. "No you don't!"

Over the rooftops they flew, Ith always keeping just out of reach. Like a bloodhound, Aisling pursued him relentlessly. In the distance, she could see the tall spires of the cathedral standing like a sentinel at the entrance to the forest. Ith was headed straight for it.

Landing on a rooftop and closing her eyes, she drew strength from the Passion Stone. She felt a tingling sensation wash over her wings and, taking off again, she went after him, flying faster than she had ever flown before.

Overtaking Ith, she grabbed his leg and dropped, pulling him with her to the ground. Ith came down horizontal to the earth. Kicking off against her chest, he twirled around, spinning out of her grasp, and landed on the ground.

Ith chuckled. "I've fought battles a thousand years before you were born, Aisling. You can't defeat me!"

Aisling kicked at his chest. Ith blocked it with his hand and threw a punch at her face, which she blocked. Aisling tried a side kick, but Ith somersaulted out of the way. Furious, she attacked with several hand strikes followed by elbow blows.

Ith blocked all of her strikes. "You should go home," he said. "I have no wish to hurt you." He took off into the air.

Aisling leapt up, grabbed his jacket and threw him down to the ground. "Give back the Dream Crystal!"

Ith rolled onto his feet. "This war is going to end, just as you wished."

Ith began a series of strikes, moving forward. Aisling blocked the attacks, and grabbed his hand. Ith broke free, so she spun around and kicked at his head.

Ith ducked, flipped over and landed on the ground a few feet away. Steadying himself, he raised his hands in a defensive posture. The sorrow in his eyes grew darker, turning to fire. The shadows grew silently around Ith as the fading sunlight slipped away. "Very well," he whispered.

Aisling glared at him, and raised her hands in a fighting stance. It appeared that he was prepared to fight it out this time, without running. A gentle wind blew over the street while something lurking in the shadows watched.

Aisling's skin tingled with a gentle caress of the night. An immense feeling of loneliness came over her, reaching out with a feeling of exhaustion and despair. Mentally shaking herself awake, she pushed the strange sensations away and concentrated on Ith.

Aisling moved forward, delivering a spinning kick. Ith ducked, then countered with a spinning kick of his own. Aisling jumped up, over his attack, into a kick aimed at his head. He dropped down and kicked low. She jumped over it and landed on her feet.

Like a wave crashing against a shore, the feeling of dissolution brushed against Aisling and fell back against Ith. A desire to end the fight was over-powering. Again, she shoved the thought away into the fading light.

Ith narrowed his eyes, as if he was making a decision. "Your passion has made you powerful," he whispered. He took off, trying to fly away, but Aisling jumped up and kicked him, knocking him down.

Aisling smiled, realizing that he wanted to run, rather than fight. She moved forward and threw several strikes at him. He blocked her attacks and retreated. Ith reached up, caught her arm and tried to break it, but she broke free and shoved him back against a wall. As she moved closer, she struck out quickly, and he had to cross his arms in front of his face to ward off the blows. Aisling grabbed his arms.

Ith kicked up and spun around, breaking free of her grip, but as he turned, Aisling delivered a swift downward kick to his head and knocked him onto the ground. Reaching down, she took the Dream Crystal out of his pocket.

A rainbow of light exploded in the street, washing hopeful thoughts over the world. A thousand ideas, hopes and desires swept through her mind at once. Aisling could see Ith rolling over, his eyes ignited by the rainbow reflection surrounding the Dream Crystal. Aisling, swaying slightly on her feet as intense thoughts swept through her mind, looked down at him triumphantly. "I've beaten you," she whispered.

Ith looked past Aisling and then back into her eyes. Shaking his head, he smiled sadly. "No, you're mistaken," he whispered. His next words were full of sorrow. "I'm afraid I must say goodbye to you now, Aisling."

Pain pierced her side, knocking the wind out of her. Aisling looked down and saw an arrow protruding out of her side. Against an ocean of darkness filling her eyes, she felt herself striking the ground. The lake of sadness that she'd fallen into began to trickle away, and she felt something wet pooling around her body. Dimly, she saw Ith getting up, the Dream Crystal in his hand. Its light choked off again. The rainbow faded away. Ith put it back in his pocket.

In the distance she saw a woman standing on a rooftop, looking down at her soberly. It was Canlyn, the Shadow Person that Ith had rescued from the prison of the Eternal Flame. Her dark hair framed imperious eyes, full of calm resolution. She wore a white dress, belted in green, and she held a bow in her hands.

Fading sunshine washed over Aisling's body, and she could feel her dreams slipping away. She looked up at the emerging stars. Angels sang in the darkness. A tear fell from her eyes, and she whispered up at the night, "Forgive me, for what I've done."

Ith raised a hand to conjure up a new top hat and cane. He placed the hat onto his head, tapped it down and saluted her. "Oíche mhaith, codladh sámh," he said.

Canlyn's smooth voice drifted over the wind, "She doesn't speak Irish, my Lord."

Amidst Canlyn's laughter, the darkness rose up around Aisling.

Canlyn whispered, "Goodnight, sleep well."

*   *   *

Tangled trees blocked out the night, high above a dark forest. It was a place as remote as a dream lost in the echoes of eternity. Branches reached down, grabbing at her face. Tormented maledictions whispered from somewhere. A cold wind passed through the forest, spreading out icy fingers to grope and caress. The rush of air against the trees was like a wave breaking across a beach, so thunderous it was. Aisling dropped down to her knees, weary with the weight of the doom laid upon her: To wander dark pathways, forever lost in the whirlpool of infinity. A soft song followed the wind, seductive and alluring and terrifying all at once. The Shadow Witch, wrapped in desolate dreams, was coming...

Aisling awoke with a start. Cold sweat covered her face and matted down her hair. Dim light flitted in through the high windows of the long hallway, marking everything with shadows. Candles stood sentinel along the walls and in the windows. A girl was weeping nearby, and the air was heavy with the sweet scent of myrrh, tinged with blood. Exhaustion reached out, pulling her down back into oblivion.

Gentle hands touched the side of her face, and she heard a voice, calling out her name, but she couldn't keep her eyes open. It was like trying to stay awake after a long draught of wakefulness. The blackness called out from eternity with a silent voice; "Give up, surrender to your fate. Relinquish all of your dreams and hopes and thoughts of a life unfettered with mortal burdens."

"Aisling!" the voice repeated. "A Twilight Elemental has attached itself to your psyche. Wake up!"

Murmuring to herself as she rose out of dark dreams, Aisling opened her eyes, but she was unable to focus on the person speaking to her so, so urgently now. "Aisling! If you don't wake up now you'll be lost forever." A hand gently moved damp hair out of her eyes. "Wake up!"

It was a woman calling her name. Aisling licked her lips and struggled against the unseen tide of loneliness, which wanted to drag her down into despair. Near the bottom of an ocean of sorrow, she found something that gave her the strength to rise again: Contempt—scorn for the weak. Disdain against anyone that blandly gave up. She would never surrender. Fury against those that tried to pull her down ignited a will that helped her resist the nightmares that wanted to drag her down.

Aisling opened her eyes.

Morrigan sat by her bed, wringing out a damp cloth. She placed it on Aisling's forehead. Cool water, scented with mint and lavender mingled together, felt refreshing. Aisling blinked. "Morrigan? What are you—"

"Shhh!" Morrigan put her hand on Aisling's forehead. "You're lucky that Fintan found you lying in the street, and that I know how to de-energize elementals. If it is done too quickly, you could go mad—too slowly and you may never break their power over you."

Aisling sighed. Summoning elementals seemed to occur without her knowing it and without her control far too often. "What kind of spirit was it?"

"I'd call this one a 'Twilight Elemental.' They give you dreams of prophecy, and help you see in the darkness, but they will also make you surrender—give up. They're summoned by those seeking answers. Many have died under their silent influence, simply fading away."

Aisling closed her eyes, remembering the dark forest, the Shadow Witch, and a dark future... "Is that the kind of dream I was having?"

Morrigan didn't answer. Instead, she began to sing softly. Aisling felt warmth spreading throughout her body, reinvigorating and renewing her. Morrigan ran a surprisingly gentle hand against Aisling's cheek. The caress filled Aisling with hope and light. The chill seeping out of her body seemed to fade away, and her breath calmed.

Aisling shook her head, emerging from the nightmares crowding her mind. She grabbed Morrigan's wrist. "I thought you hated me," she said. "Why—"

Morrigan withdrew her hand, easily breaking out of Aisling's weak grip. "I am a *healer*," she said. "I guard your death."

Aisling shuddered at the phrase. "What do you have against change-lings anyway?" she grumbled.

Some of Morrigan's spite returned. "They're the children of the Lords of the Tuatha Dé and look at them! They can't even do magic here after their parents abandon them in the lands of our enemies. Changelings ignore their destiny. They're pathetic! Most die or fall into shadow so fast that it's a wonder their parents bothered to try to stop their assassination in the first place."

Sifu Yuen's words returned. *You have a destiny to fulfill.* Were her parents powerful lords? Why was Ith assassinating the children of the Tuatha Dé?

Aisling closed her eyes again, wondering if Morrigan held another kind of grudge against her. On sudden impulse, she said, "I'm sorry about Conall. I didn't know that you and he—"

Morrigan's laughter made Aisling open her eyes. For a heartbeat, Morrigan's green eyes were unmasked. They were full of pain and loss and... something else. Morrigan looked away. "I have no love for Conall. Take him."

Aisling didn't believe her rival.

Morrigan continued. "What you need now is sunlight, to drive away the remnants of the Twilight Elemental, and a change of your dressing."

Aisling looked down at her side where a bandage, made from leaves, covered her injury. She reached down to touch the slightly furry leaves. "What kind of herb is this?"

"Comfrey," said Morrigan. "We found it growing in this land when we arrived. It heals wounds quickly, and prevents scarring. You were pierced with a magic arrow. Whoever shot you wasn't trying to kill you, but the Twilight Elemental nearly finished you off. It's a lucky thing that Eileen was wearing a herbal talisman. Otherwise—"

"Eileen is alive?"

Morrigan tried to keep the irritation out of her voice. "Yes. Holly leaves deflect lightning. She was only stunned."

Aisling closed her eyes and breathed a sigh of relief. She was afraid to ask about Fáelán. "How long—?"

Morrigan leaned back, withdrawing her hands. "Too long." She began to wash her hands in a bowl resting on the table by the bed. "Ever since your act of *stupidity*, I've been stuck here in the hospital, treating the wounded and watching over you. Fifteen days and nights I've had to listen to your ravings and confessions and..." she wrinkled her nose, "Ooh! I hope I never have to look at you again!"

Cold hands wrapped themselves around Aisling's heart and she caught her breath. *They know!* Aisling blurted out words without thinking. "But I had to do it! Telling Ith where the Dream Crystal was hidden was the only way I could rescue my sister."

Morrigan looked into Aisling's eyes with cold surprise. Standing up, Morrigan ran her hands over her black dress and took out a pair of long gloves tucked into her belt. She began to put them on. "A fair exchange, I suppose. You get your Milesian sister back, and magic fades away from our world."

"What?"

"Oh yes, so silly of me. You don't believe in dreams, do you?"

"What do dreams have to do with magic?"

Morrigan raised her eyebrows. "Nothing—not anymore."

Aisling frowned. "But you used magic to heal me, didn't you?"

Morrigan picked up a black scarf and threw it over her shoulder. "I follow the old ways," she said. "After a few more days of rest, you should recover."

Aisling watched Morrigan walk off through the cloudy sunlight that fell through the windows of the hospital.

*   *   *

Cold sunlight fell into the music room, bathing the chamber with white radiance and making it hard to see. Red marble pillars, tipped in gold, held up the blue tiled arches that stood next to the windows, but they made no shadows to break up the brightness. A fresh breeze carrying a hint of roses from the garden came in through the windows along with the light.

Aisling sat behind the piano, with eyes closed against the brightness, playing Beethoven's Moonlight Sonata for her sister, who sat on a couch with Callix in her lap, next to Genevieve. In another chair, Hieronymus lay, asleep next to an open book. Eileen sat on the railing of an upper gallery by a blue pillar, legs dangling over the edge. Several other fairies reclined in the upper gallery, next to her. Eileen had white jasmine flowers woven into her hair. Their perfume mingled with the roses of the garden, like two lovers dancing in the sunshine.

No longer saturated with creativity, the Land of Dreams had become barren of some of the wonder that had made it so beautiful. Everyone said that magic was more difficult now, but Aisling hadn't noticed a change until she sat down in front of the piano. Unable to invent anything fresh, she had fallen back on what she knew well. But even the music of Beethoven sounded lifeless and empty.

Aisling's hands shook with the realization of the harm she had caused, but playing the piano seemed to help. She finished the piece, leaned back in her seat and sighed. "What have I done?" she whispered. Rubbing her hands together, she opened her eyes and glanced at her sister, who was scratching Calix behind his tiny dragon ears. Erin looked happy. Aisling realized that she would do it again, if given the choice. Smiling tears away, Aisling turned back to the piano.

Fáelán came in, wearing a white shirt with ruffles, a long black coat with the collar turned up, a red scarf, pants and shoes. He had also shaved off his goatee. Fáelán leaned on the edge of the piano and smiled down at Aisling.

Aisling gave him an appraisal up and down. "That's a new look for you."

"I thought I'd go with something more modern for a change," he said.

"I like it," said Aisling, returning his smile.

"You look tasty too, babe."

Aisling wore a white mini-skirt, a pair of matching sandals laced up to her knees, a white blouse and a rose colored, high-collared jacket with flared sleeves. Giggling, she began to play Beethoven's Für Elise. "I've wanted to ask you something... what happened the other night?"

A few of the fairies sitting up in the gallery giggled.

Ignoring them, Fáelán took off his jacket and scarf, laid them down on the back of a chair and took a seat. "I suppose I shouldn't have gotten in his way, but when Ith was about to cast that fire spell at me, I used a trick I learned from that old sorcerer, Fintan. I used a Counterspell."

Talking seemed to take the guilt away. "That still doesn't answer my question," said Aisling. "What happened?"

Fáelán rubbed his forehead. "Counterspells extinguish spells when an opponent is trying to cast them, but they have a tendency to burn out one's brain. I was lucky it only knocked me out. I bet Ith had trouble using magic after that."

Genevieve interjected a comment. "I thought he killed you. I don't understand how I could have missed him though."

From the railing above them, Eileen chided, "I daresay you're not as good a shot as you thought you were."

Aisling couldn't resist smiling.

Quite suddenly, the queen walked in, followed by Morrigan bearing a proud look, King Artrach, and a train of soldiers led by Marcus. Everyone stood up and bowed. Aisling stopped playing, got up, bowed and faced the queen.

Queen Annan wore a scarlet dress that shined in the sunlight. Hanging from a white belt, a jeweled scabbard held a Celtic Longsword. It was the first time Aisling had seen the queen without a gentle smile on her face. Annan walked up to Aisling and looked into her eyes. "Tell me that it isn't true."

Behind the queen, Morrigan had a satisfied look in her eyes.

Aisling met the queen's gaze. "I can't, Your Majesty. I've ended your war."

Queen Annan turned away and bowed her head. Her voice was covered in sorrow. "The damage is greater than you realize. You've doomed this world to extinction." She made a weak gesture towards Erin and Genevieve. "Their world also—will fade away and be forgotten. All of the world's dreams are about to die."

Aisling frowned. What could happen to the Milesian world? Was the Dream Crystal really that powerful? What could Ith do? But the Dream Crystal didn't work. Dreams had always lied.

A swift flash of steel—the queen's sword was laid against Aisling's heart before she could move.

King Artrach shouted, "No, Annie!"

Aisling didn't move. Part of her hoped the queen would do it. Death could take away her conscience.

Ask me why.

King Artrach's voice was fearful. "Annie, you can't!"

Queen Annan raised her voice slightly. "I have not drawn this sword in a thousand years. What do I care about curses now?"

The king moved forward delicately, as if he was walking on thin ice.

"A Fomorian curse protects her!" he whispered. "If you strike, it will affect the entire kingdom."

The queen raised her eyebrows. "So, this one's father is a Fomorian?" Lowering the sword, Queen Annan turned around. "Is that why you asked me to take her in?"

Marcus stepped forward. "What is your will, your majesty?"

Queen Annan looked askance at Aisling and whispered, "Get out."

Too stunned to move, Aisling simply stood there, reeling with the words of the queen. *This one's father was a Fomorian.*

Queen Annan whispered again, "Get out!"

Aisling backed up, stumbled against the stool of the piano and fell to the ground.

The queen repeated her demand, whispering forcefully, "Out, out, out, out, out!"

* * *

Chapter Fifteen

Without a Thought

Barren skies covered a city overcome with emptiness. As if eternity was holding its breath, a hush had fallen over the world. The streets were quiet, and not a single fairy flew over the town. Only a few orbs floated by, aimlessly.

From a stone bridge, Aisling looked up at the castle, whose walls were bathed in bleached sunlight. The tower by the gatehouse still bore the black scars of the fire that had nearly killed Fáelán. The queen had tried to cage dreams like they were a disease, and yet, the world had changed. Tír na nÓg was missing something now, but what it was, Aisling couldn't know. Had freedom won out today?

A blue and green orb floated down from the gatehouse and turned into Fáelán. He handed Aisling the case holding her sword and the small stone box, which her father had left for her. Aisling looked down at the carvings, running a finger across the sapphire dragon eyes. Who was her father? She looked at Erin, standing quietly with her hands in the pockets of her leather jacket. Sunglasses hid her eyes.

"Where to?" asked Genevieve.

Aisling shook her head. "I have no plans now, except to get Erin home." She looked at Eileen. "How can we return to the Milesian world?"

Eileen crossed her arms and looked away. "It isn't possible this time of year. We'll have to wait for an Áit Thanaí to appear."

"What's that?"

Eileen said, "A Thin Place. Don't you remember? There's one near my house, but Samhain is still four months away."

"Halloween," murmured Genevieve.

Fáelán sat on the stone wall of the bridge leading to the gatehouse of the castle. "Strange. Next week is the festival of Litha—the summer solstice. There should be people all around town, but it's as quiet as a deserted field down there."

"Let's go to my house," said Eileen.

Genevieve said, "Okay, but let's take a car this time."

Eileen shook her head. "What's wrong with using An Rí Bealach?"

Genevieve crossed her arms. "Besides my not being able to pronounce it, the last time we used the King's Road, we got caught in a snowstorm and attacked by those crazy changelings."

Sounding like he was trying to make conversation, Fáelán asked, with a trace of nervousness in his voice, "Is that where you met Siri?"

Aisling glanced at Erin, wondering why Fáelán was so afraid to talk to her. She held back a smile. "Yes, and Báirbre too."

At the mention of Báirbre, the changeling who fell into shadow, the conversation died. Barren heat seeped up out of the stone bridge, where they stood, filling the air with uncomfortable silence. After a moment, Eileen shrugged. "Alright, we'll go by car." She faced the road and waved a hand.

Nothing happened.

Genevieve raised her eyebrows. "Well?"

Eileen shook her head. "I can't seem to concentrate."

Aisling frowned. She, too, had trouble imagining what a car looked like. "Don't be silly," she muttered. Aisling closed her eyes and tried to imagine a car sitting in the road, but no image appeared in her mind. Her thoughts had drained away. It was like looking at a canvas, paint brush in hand, utterly lost in white oblivion.

Eileen's shout echoed the frustration in her face. "How could you have done this to us, Aisling?"

Opening her eyes, Aisling said, "I'm—I'm sorry. I didn't think—"

"Nobody's thinking much about anything now," said Eileen. "Don't you realize? Thoughts are the source of dreams and dreams are the source of magic."

"That can't be true," whispered Aisling.

Eileen shook her head and stepped up onto the stone wall of the bridge.

"Where are you going?" asked Aisling.

Eileen didn't seem to know. "Away!" She waved her arm, as if to brush them all out of her sight. "I'll see you later!" Eileen jumped off the bridge—without extending her wings. Screaming, she fell down into the river, splashing into cold water.

Everyone ran over to the wall and leaned over.

Erin said, "That was stupid."

They heard Eileen's angry shouts of frustration coming out of the river. Calix, who had been sitting on the wall, flew down and landed on a rock. His taunting cries only made Eileen angrier.

Fáelán got up onto the wall and began to jump down after her.

Aisling shouted, "Fáelán, wait! Where are your wings?"

With a shocked expression, Fáelán looked over his shoulder and flexed his back. Nothing happened. "I see why nobody is flying over the town today."

A blue ball of light rose out of the river, and ascended to the bridge, followed by the small purple fairy dragon. Silver light flashed and Eileen stood there, drenched. Bereft of jasmine, her wet blonde hair covered the fury in her eyes. Her long blue dress clung to her body. Shaking with cold wrath, Eileen pursed her lips. "Ooh!"

Genevieve and Erin exchanged smiles.

Aisling said, "You're lucky the river—"

"Don't say it!"

Aisling bit her lip.

Fáelán sat down on the wall. "What a great time of year for a hike. It's only a few hundred kilometers to Eileen's house. I say we walk."

Genevieve shook her head. "Be serious, Fáelán."

Fáelán looked wistful. "We should tell Nel where we're going before we head out. Let's stop by the cathedral."

Genevieve looked at Aisling. "You should tell Conall where we're going, too."

"Why don't you tell him?" Aisling turned away from Genevieve and closed her eyes. Using the anger inside, she ignited a warm draught of air and blew it towards Eileen. A hot breeze spun around her friend, and moments later, she was dry. Eileen sat down on the wall, conjured up a brush and began to straighten out the tangles.

"So what if it's harder than before?" said Fáelán. "Magic still works."

Aisling glared at him, swimming in guilt.

*　　*　　*

Birds sang from the bell tower of the cathedral. The building was awash in the shadows of the high birch trees that barred entry to the forest. Rather than standing around and admiring the architecture, Erin walked up to the doors and went inside.

Aisling glanced at the others. "She isn't afraid of anything, is she?"

"She looks like she's pissed off most of the time," grumbled Fáelán.

Aisling smiled. "Is that why you're afraid to talk to her?"

Fáelán didn't answer. He followed Erin inside the cathedral.

A cloud of frankincense, mixed with myrrh greeted them as they stepped inside. Summer fell through the stained glass windows, warming the empty pews that faced the large Celtic cross hanging over the white altar stone.

Dipping her finger into the stoup by the doorway, Aisling crossed herself with holy water, wondering if she would ever be forgiven for betraying the queen.

Fintan came walking up the nave with Nel. Fintan wore a white medieval tunic, an ornate belt with his Makhaira sword, and a crown of golden leaves on his head. Nel wore a black blouse, miniskirt, tights, ankle boots, and a white belt.

Fintan's expression was grave, but when he saw Aisling and her friends he brightened up considerably. "Genevieve!" He walked up and took her hand into his, kissing it. "Ah—the only thing that is humiliating is helplessness."

Shyly, Genevieve pulled her hand away from him, and looked over at the stony blue walls. The sunlight covering her face seemed to turn pink. "Hello Fintan."

Nel stopped next to Fáelán, glancing sideways at Erin. She crossed her arms and smiled thinly. "Dia daoibh."

Aisling walked over to meet them. She placed her father's sword case down on a pew. "Nel, Fintan, this here is my sister, Erin O'Neil."

Fintan reluctantly turned away from Genevieve and looked at Erin. His face filled up with wonder, and he whispered, "The child, arisen from shadow, has come."

Erin raised the dark sunglasses from her face and set them on top of her silver hair. Her blue eyes exuded silence.

Fintan threw Aisling a sidelong glance. "The price you paid for her release must have been dear."

Frowning, Aisling let hardness soak into her face. "I've ended the war, that's all. The queen has sent me away, so we're going to Eileen's house."

"Our wings are gone," said Eileen. "Have you noticed?"

"I'm afraid that without the Dream Crystal, we're reverting back to our old selves," said Fintan. "In Ireland, few of us had wings."

"What do you mean?" asked Eileen.

"The Tuatha Dé changed after coming to Tír na nÓg," said Fintan.

301

"In Ireland, we were altogether different kinds of faeries—wilder, darker, angrier, terrifying even, to the Milesians that banished us to this world. Like the Nix that nearly drowned you, Aisling, many of us have never forgotten their old enemies."

"But I'm only nineteen. I wasn't even born in Ireland," said Eileen. "I've always had wings."

Fintan shrugged. "Understanding develops by degrees," he said. "The Dream Crystal is in the Land of Shadows now, with Ith. That may be the reason our wings are gone. Quite frankly, I'm surprised that he hasn't destroyed us already."

Erin shivered, and looked over her shoulder into the recesses of the cathedral.

An uncomfortable silence followed. Aisling, hoping to change the subject, reached into her jacket, and removed Nel's magic hat. "I should return this."

Taking the hat, Nel murmured, "Thanks."

Nel looked at Fáelán and, taking his arm, she drew him aside. Aisling heard her whisper to him, "Take care on the journey. I doubt this war will end quietly."

As if she had been called away, Erin began to explore the cathedral. She went up into the organ loft, towards the whispering voices there. Genevieve and Eileen remained down in the pews.

Eileen sat down, dejected. "I miss my wings," she grumbled.

Genevieve looked on, pensively.

Aisling sighed, burning inside. The candles flared brighter with the arrival of a Fire Elemental. Reaching down to her father's sword case, she opened it and withdrew the sword. She walked out into the aisle between the pews and smiled at Fintan. "How about another go?"

Fintan raised his eyebrows. "In here?"

"I just want to see if I can beat you—that's all."

Fintan drew his Makhaira. "Five thousand years ago, I was an expert swordsman," he said. "There's little point to this, but I admire your ambition."

With a withering series of strikes, Aisling advanced—more determined than ever to beat Fintan. Retreating, he parried her blows with ease, but it seemed that it became more difficult as the fury arose within her. She breathed in the elemental's fierceness, allowing herself to be swept away with the power it gave her. Fintan had retreated to the end of the aisle, his back to the wall.

The Fire Elemental slipped into her muscles, burning with intensity. Her mind ignited into a thousand furies. Aisling saw an opening and lunged for his chest.

Swifter than ever, Fintan stepped aside, knocking the sword out of her hand. Then his sword was at her throat. Unable to move, she stood there until the fire inside had burned itself out.

Aisling returned her father's sword to the case, feeling a sudden chill.

Fintan put his hand on Aisling's shoulder. "There's an ancient Egyptian saying," he said. "You will free yourself when you learn to be neutral and follow the instructions of your heart without letting things perturb you."

Aisling had lost control. Perhaps to cover her embarrassment, she smiled. "You sound like my martial arts instructor," she whispered. "He's always talking about being 'centered' but I've never found the advice useful in a fight."

"The true reason you lost," he said, "is that you know it's impossible to defeat me." Fintan put his sword away. "Ith is not your greatest enemy."

Aisling felt like he was taunting her. Simmering, she turned away to go find Erin, but at the entrance to the staircase, Fintan held her back. "Aisling, your fate may involve more than simply ending this war."

"All I want now is to go home. I think I'll indulge in my passions for a change. I just want to have fun now." The words were an echo of what Aoife had said, just before she had fallen away.

A scream fell out of the organ loft.

Aisling ran up the stairs and found Erin kneeling on the floor, clutching her hand. Aisling thought of her father's sword and it appeared in her hand quite suddenly.

Whispers came from the darkness near the Mirror of Eternity. Out of the corner of her eye, she saw something black, moving. Twirling around, Aisling swung her sword and struck the Shadow Person. Wailing in agony, it fell down and evaporated as it died.

Fintan came up just as the shadow was slain, his Makhaira sword in hand. "How did it get in here, I wonder?"

Reflected in the Mirror of Eternity, the Fortress of Árainn looked down from the top of the island. Aisling scanned the rest of the balcony for Shadow People and helped her sister get up. An angry wound covered Erin's arm.

Fintan's face was full of surprise. "How did you summon your father's sword?"

Aisling shrugged. Lasarina had taught her how to conjure up swords and other things, but Summoning was a different kind of magic altogether. It never worked on magic swords. "I don't know. It was just an impulse..."

The others ran up the stairs. Eileen, seeing that it was safe, put her sword away. "What happened?"

Erin looked up at the Mirror of Eternity. "I heard them, whispering. They want me to return. One of them reached out—"

Nel leaned behind the Mirror of Eternity and withdrew a cloth, which she draped over the surface, covering it. "We're lucky that only one of them was hiding in the cathedral," she murmured. "I'll ask Father Harrigan to sanctify this place again."

Fintan knelt down by Erin. He had a small clay jar in his hand, which had the scent of eucalyptus, myrrh and goldenseal. He began to apply the salve to Erin's arm. He looked up at Aisling and said, "Take the King's Road. You should reach Eileen's house by nightfall. This war may be over, but there is still evil to come of it."

"I don't believe in evil," muttered Nel.

Aisling looked into Nel's eyes. "Neither do I."

* * *

They walked towards the entrance to the King's Road, but Aisling felt something, like a distant memory, nudging her in a different direction. She began to move into the forest, away from the road.

"Aisling, An Rí Bealach is this way," said Eileen.

Full of faint memories, Aisling said in a dreamy voice, "No, it isn't."

"Yes, it is."

"No, it's this way," insisted Aisling.

"Oh please!" Eileen looked at Genevieve. "Do something."

"She's still angry at me for what she thinks she saw at the party."

"I did see it. You were kissing Conall." Aisling shook her head. "I can't believe you're still lying about it."

"I'm not lying!"

Ignoring Genevieve, Aisling went into the trees. Ancient fir trees guarded an old, unused path through the forest. Hot sunbeams, filled with dust and pollen, covered the way. No sound made its way into the woods. It was as if all the wildlife had surrendered their sovereignty over this part of the earth.

After some time, they came to a clearing. White Puffball Caps, Red Fly Agaric mushrooms, and Brown-Topped Queen Bolete mushrooms littered the grass. Growing in a wide circle, the mushrooms surrounded a pale standing stone. Some twelve feet high, the stone was carved with ancient symbols. Sunlight reflected off the surface of the stone, which touched the earth in the center of the clearing.

Aisling felt a gentle movement swirling around the stone, like wind sighing across the grass. She went over to it, and placed the palm of her hand against the cool stone. Like a windstorm, flashes of distant places swept through her mind. Remembering the place where Trista had been banished, she saw a dark lake, inside a cave. Another image touched her mind—a grove of yew trees overlooking the ocean. She could see Irial walking through them, singing softly to herself. The fragrance of flowers pushed the view of her friend away and she saw a garden of roses, drenched in sunshine. Aisling smiled, wishing she could walk in that garden, if only for a moment.

Eileen shouted, "Aisling!"

A furious breeze swirled around Aisling and the world spun round. Dizziness made her sway on her feet and she opened her eyes. Brushing hair out of her face, Aisling saw that she was standing in the center of a circle of nine stones, arranged around a central pillar, overgrown with grass. A lovelorn birch tree stood next to the circle, bereft of bird songs. Nearby, the rose garden growing in her mind lay shining in the sunlight. She dropped her hand away, and looked around in alarm. The others were gone.

Aisling walked into the garden of roses and realized that she was on top of a hill, overlooking a river. A quaint town was nestled by the water. Although there were no bridges or major roads leading away, she recognized the place. She wondered aloud, "Portland. How did I get to Oregon?"

"Aisling?"

Conall had been kneeling in the garden by a chest made from polished oak. He shut the lid and stood up, surprise in his gorgeous eyes. "How did you get here?"

Aisling glanced over her shoulder at the circle of standing stones and shook her head. "I was in Vancouver, near the ancient forest beyond the cathedral. I found a tall white stone there—" She looked away.

His mouth dropped open. "How did you activate it?"

"What?"

Conall pointed at the circle of stones. "The Vortex. All over the world there is a network of sacred places—vortices—that are connected by Ley Lines. The ancient peoples traveled along them, but no one knows how to use them now."

"I thought Ley Lines ran under the King's Road."

"They do, and we move quickly along them, but the Ley Lines were meant for instantaneous travel. King Bodb Derg, Artrach's father, used them to bring us here from Sídhe Findabrach in Ireland, but the knowledge of how to use them died with him in the war. Now, only sorcerers can teleport."

Feeling her knees give way, Aisling sank down next to a rose bush. "What's wrong?"

She looked down at her hands. "I've made a real mess of things, Conall."

Conall picked a rose off a bush and sat down next to her. He laid the flower on her lap and brushed a strand of hair out of her face. He remained silent, seemingly aware of the pain tormenting her.

Aisling picked up the rose, breathing in its pink aroma. It warmed her heart just enough to ignite her anger. She looked up into his eyes. "What are you doing here, anyway?"

He looked down the hill and made a gesture. "Meadhar Grá has fallen into shadow. The Aoi clan is no more."

In a hushed whisper, Aisling asked, "All of them?"

Conall pulled a tuft of grass and tossed it into the wind. "Yes. It happened just yesterday. They've joined Maire, their ruler, in the Land of Shadows."

"But I saw Maire at your party!"

Leaning back onto his hands, Conall looked up at the sky. "Yeah, she was there. Thinking that I was attracted to your friend, Genevieve, she cast an illusion onto herself, hoping to seduce me."

The image of Conall and her best friend sent hot knives tearing into her heart. Aisling looked away, into the garden. "I saw you kissing her."

Conall laughed. "Not to worry, it wasn't Genevieve."

Aisling threw away the rose.

"I had to—"

Raising her eyebrows, she said, "Of course you did. Genevieve is very pretty."

Conall put his hand on her shoulder. "I needed to get information from Maire, Aisling. She's a Deceiver. Her illusions and phantasms have been wreaking havoc with the Fianna. Marcus has had quite a bit of trouble protecting the kingdom."

Shaking his hand off, she asked, "Did you get your information before you went to bed with her or after?"

Conall's laugh made her look up. "You're jealous!"

Aisling looked away. "What did she tell you?"

Conall reached over to the chest and opened it. Inside, a crystal sphere lay, pulsing with fire and lightning and ghostly images floating inside it. Something cool brushed against her face, where voices whispered next to her skin.

"What is it?"

"We call it a 'Concentration Focus.' Deceivers need to concentrate on their illusions, to keep them convincing. Otherwise an illusion would be discovered as soon as someone interacts with it. This artifact does all work for her when she's away."

"What's the difference between an illusion and a phantasm?"

"Illusions are static, and phantasms move," he explained. "But neither really exists, being no more than imaginary pictures."

All dreams are imaginary.

Aisling looked into his eyes. She wasn't sure if she wanted to forgive him. "What will you do with it?"

"I'll give it to Marcus and he'll probably smash it," he said. "When that happens, all of its secrets will be revealed."

Aisling let her gaze fall down into the town by the river. She saw dozens of illusionary faeries walking in the streets or flying over the buildings.

There was something else too: Hunger. Reaching into her pocket, she withdrew the Passion Stone. Desire burned within her, and she closed her eyes, letting herself go.

"Where did you get a Passion Stone?" he asked.

Aisling opened her eyes and tossed it to him, with a coy smile on her face.

Catching it, Conall caught his breath, as if he had just plunged his hand into icy water. "I haven't seen one of these in years, though sometimes they're found around the Eternal Flame."

"That's where I found it," she lied. "Sometimes, I use it to get what I want."

"What could an innocent girl like you possibly want?" he teased.

Biting her lip, she chose not to answer. Lying down on the grass, Aisling raised her arms over her head, stretching. Sunlight warmed her bare legs. *Love is something you take.* She wondered if he really believed that.

Conall moved over beside her, hefting the stone in one hand. As he changed position, his other hand brushed against her leg. "You shouldn't tease me," he whispered. "I'm very sensitive."

Warm sensations spread over her legs. She held her breath and let it out slowly. "Oh, really?" she whispered.

"Yes." Conall passed the Passion Stone along her thigh, and its touch sent tingling sensations all over her body.

Too intense to endure, she pulled away from contact with the magic stone and rolled onto her stomach. Aisling raised up onto her elbows, letting hair cover her face. Rose petals lay on the ground underneath her, stinging the air with a subtle aroma. She inhaled slowly, trying to calm herself down. "You love Morrigan, don't you?"

"I don't love anybody," he said.

Aisling felt his hand touch her hair, gently brushing it out of her face. She rolled onto her side, facing him. "I've never kissed anyone," she said.

Conall leaned back onto his hands. "I haven't either," he teased.

"Kiss me."

Taking her hand into his, he kissed it and smiled down at her.

"Ooh!" Frustration gushed out of her. Narrowing her eyes, she rose up and jumped on top of him, pushing him down into the grass.

He chuckled. "Say please."

"No." Aisling leaned down and kissed him.

They melted into one another in an eternity of bliss. Aisling found herself on her back as Conall took command. Passion began to turn into ecstasy. Heart pounding, she caught her breath.

Conall had pulled away, rolling onto his back.

Like a rising tide, emptiness began to wash over him.

Conall lay on the grass now, staring up at the sun.

Aisling rose into a sitting position, brushed a strand of hair out of her face and looked down. "What's wrong?"

Shadows began to slither around him. His face went pale. He reached up to touch her cheek, whispering breathlessly, "Aisling?"

Darkness came. Conall faded away into a black chasm.

Aisling screamed. She fell over backwards and scrambled away from where he had been. Rose thorns scratched her legs and caught against her jacket. Getting up, she ran back to the circle of stones. She dropped down to her knees and wept.

Something burned against the palm of her hand. Opening her eyes, she found the Passion Stone clutched tightly in her fingers. Overcome with revulsion, she threw it against one of the black stones, shattering it. A hissing sound, like steam, came from where it struck the rock.

Aisling screamed again, furious at Ith and all of the Shadow People.

The empty birch tree began to move, writhing and contracting in upon itself. Leaves rustled. Limbs vanished. Shimmering in the sunlight, the tree changed into a woman. Long blonde hair falling straight over her shoulders, she wore a short pink dress and white shoes. She calmly approached, not bothering to brush the windblown hair out of her face. She stopped just outside the circle, where she placed a hand on a tall stone. It was Maire. Her voice was covered in sadness. "He was destined to fall."

Rising to her feet, Aisling glared at the Shadow Person, who remained in corporeal form. "You don't know that."

"He didn't love anyone Aisling," said Maire in a clear, cold voice. "That's why he has come to us."

Aisling raised her hand and conjured up a hand crossbow.

Maire laughed, but the sorrow in her face pooled into darkness. It spread through her body until only a shadow remained. "You can't harm me with that, but go ahead if it makes you feel better."

Taking aim, Aisling fired the bolt into the Concentration Focus, not twenty yards away, shattering it. Ghostly images over the town whirled and danced and then the phantoms living in the town faded away.

Hissing angrily, Maire, too, dissolved into the shadows until only the cold wind remained, blowing through the rose garden.

* * *

Slipping into steaming water, Aisling spread out in the Jacuzzi, letting the heat cover her body. Through a warm haze, she looked out on the lake behind Eileen's house, hoping to wash away painful memories of betrayal and loss. Purple clouds covered the darkening sky. A green forest full of fairy lights, surrounded the lake. The fairy orbs looked like little fireflies dancing over the water and through the trees.

"I know that I shouldn't whine, but I really do miss flying," grumbled Eileen. She reclined in the Jacuzzi next to Genevieve and Fáelán. "I wonder how the faeries of Ireland got along without wings?"

Genevieve frowned and shot a glance in Aisling's direction. "It's not so bad. I've never had wings."

Aisling closed her eyes, hoping to shut out the guilt of what she had done. Could the world survive without thoughts? "I'm so sorry, Eileen. I never—"

"Did I ever tell you?" said Eileen. She pointed over across the lake. "There's a fine cedar tree over there, where there's a lot of sunshine. They say that an ancient nymph lives inside that tree, and that she's a healer."

Aisling smiled and looked into Eileen's blue eyes. The hot water lapped against the sides of the Jacuzzi, and steam blocked her view. Aisling knew how much she had hurt her friends, along with all of the other fairies too. "We should visit that tree nymph."

Erin came in, carrying a tray with glasses and a pitcher full of water. She kneeled down next to the Jacuzzi and set it down. "Anyone thirsty?"

Genevieve frowned at Erin. "Tell me, how can you do magic? Aren't you a Milesian, like me?"

The water coming from the pitcher turned into dark red wine, with an aroma hinting of violets. Erin shrugged. "I learned water transformation spells from my master Keir, but I also learned spiritualism, conjuration, and black magic from others."

"I guess that's what happens when you live here all of your life," said Genevieve.

Aisling looked at her sister. A locket hung around her neck. Aisling remembered seeing it before in the mirror of her room in Seattle. "Keir isn't your master anymore, Erin. You don't have to wait on us, either."

"Sometimes I miss him."

"Why?" asked Genevieve.

Erin looked out over the calm waters of the lake. "Many times, Shadow Lords wanted to take me away—they wanted to—use me… but Keir was always there, protecting me."

Aisling was surprised. Had she misjudged him? On impulse, she asked, "Do you remember when they took you?"

Erin ran a hand through her hair, her eyes downcast. "I heard a bird, singing. It was the most beautiful song I'd ever heard before. More beautiful even than your father when he was playing the harp," she said, glancing up into Aisling's eyes. "I went outside, to look for the bird, but just as I saw a blue jay sitting on a branch, it flew away. It landed on another tree, away from the house and began to sing again. His music was enchanting, and so I followed it." Erin hesitated, and Aisling could see a trace of pain in her eyes. "That's when they took me," she said.

Into the growing silence, Eileen said, "Why don't you join us?"

"I don't have a bathing suit," said Erin.

"Oh, is that all?" Aisling waved a hand and a bikini appeared on a chair by the deck, next to the pile of towels and robes. It was silver, like Erin's hair.

Eileen sighed. "It appears that I've forgotten how to make clothes too," she said. "You don't seem to have a problem, though."

"Making clothes is second nature to me," said Aisling.

Erin picked up the bikini and went into the house. Aisling saw her begin to remove her clothes in front of Hieronymus, who was sitting on a chair. He was watching Erin undress. For a moment, Aisling didn't think anything of it. Then she sat up in the Jacuzzi and shouted. "Hieronymus! Give her some privacy, will you!"

The cat flicked his tail and jumped off the chair.

Aisling shook her head. "Sometimes I forget that he isn't really a cat."

"I'm glad he's here, though," said Eileen. "He volunteered to reorganize my library. Genevieve has made a dreadful mess."

"Oh, so you wanted me to put them back in the same places I found them?" Genevieve looked at Fáelán. "You seem to be enjoying yourself."

"Why wouldn't I?" he said. "I'm sharing a Jacuzzi with the most beautiful women in the Land of Dreams. Fintan would be envious."

He thinks we're pretty? She frowned. "Did Fintan really have seventeen wives?" she asked.

"Yes," said Eileen. "But they were all killed in the flood."

"A flood in Ireland?" asked Genevieve.

"The great flood that covered the world," said Eileen. "He says he survived by changing into a fish."

Everyone grew silent for a time. Erin came outside, wearing the bikini. Fáelán's eyes were full of appreciation, but he looked away as she got in. Aisling smiled at his shyness, but she wondered if Nel was jealous of her sister. Erin moved over to the side of the Jacuzzi opposite Fáelán.

"Did I tell you?" said Eileen. "After you destroyed Maire's Concentration Focus, they discovered that three more Sídhe communities had already fallen into shadow. Apparently, they had set up illusions and phantasms around them, to hide the fact that they'd gone dark."

"Which ones?" asked Fáelán.

"Besides Meadhar Grá, the people from Sídhe an Domhan, Measarthachtshee, and Sid Imreas have all departed," said Eileen. "The Aoi, Creidhne, Iuchar and Ailill clans are all gone—or they had already vanished. No one knows for sure when they fell."

"So the people from eight fairy towns have disappeared. That's twice as many as we thought," whispered Fáelán. "My friend Tommy was from Sid Imreas."

Seeing the look in Aisling's eyes, Genevieve said, "Don't feel bad, it may not have been your fault."

Aisling moved over to the opposite side of the Jacuzzi, placed her arms up onto the rim and looked out over the lake. Bright fairy orbs floated over the water, mingling with the reflection of stars that were starting to appear. Already, the world was starting to die. Her eyes sank into the lake, swimming in its murky depths.

* * *

The old tree stood next to a field of grass, swimming in sunshine. With a trunk more than ten feet thick, its branches rose up in a confusion of twisted pathways. Green leaves covered part of the sky. Black birds sang from the branches.

Walking up to the trunk, Aisling pressed a hand against the twisted surface. She felt an earthy vibrancy there, like a quiet heartbeat. "What a beautiful tree, Eileen."

"I'd thank you for your flattery, if you would go back to wherever you came from," said a voice.

Standing among the grass where no one had been moments before was a tall girl with long dark hair, and an aroma of cedar and violets. Slender, she wore a long green dress with a belt of white cloth. Purple flowers were in her hair, and she went barefoot.

Eileen came forward. "Dia duit."

Aisling stepped back a pace. "You don't need to be unfriendly. We like trees."

"For nine hundred years this cedar has grown here. I am its guardian," said the girl. She gave them all a critical appraisal, up and down.

"What's your name?" asked Erin, in a rebellious tone.

Closing her eyes, the girl inhaled the breeze that flew over the field of grass. Turning towards Erin, she whispered, "Elsbeth."

"That doesn't sound like an Irish name," said Genevieve.

"Why, fairies don't have to have Irish names," said Eileen. "My last name is Bisset, which is French."

314

"I've never heard of a French fairy," Genevieve grumbled.

"There are lots of French fairies. Dames Blanches, or White Ladies, live there, along with several other—"

"So," Genevieve raised her eyebrows, "you're French?"

Eileen crossed her arms. "I grew up in Cnoc Firinn, which was near the Milesian town of New Orleans," she said. "But that Sídhe fell into shadow."

"So, *are* you, or *aren't* you?" asked Genevieve.

"Excuse me," said Elsbeth, looking down her nose. "Will you kindly depart?"

Aisling grinned. "Sorry. We just wanted to say hello."

Genevieve whispered, "That nymph is a little bit snippy snobby, but I like her."

They turned around and walked back towards the lake. Marcus appeared near the edge of the trees, along with two soldiers of the Fianna.

"Hello Marcus," said Eileen.

"I've brought you all something." Marcus waved a hand and one of the soldiers brought forth a small chest of oak, bound in iron. Opening it, he withdrew a silver collar with a ring around the front and a lock on the back. "Gentle Annie has ordered all of the Tuatha Dé to wear these Collars of Humility from now on."

Aisling heard Genevieve huff. "Fabulous. Sign me up."

Marcus continued, "Henceforth, we've been traveling all over the realm—"

Aisling interrupted him. "You've got to be kidding. We're not slaves."

"It's for your own good," said Marcus. "With these collars around your neck, we will be able to tell where you are, and if you're starting to fade into darkness. Once we know you're vulnerable, the queen will be able—"

"To banish us, like she did Trista," said Aisling. "Forget it, Marcus. We're not putting those things on."

Erin had a stiletto in her hand. She backed away.

Eileen drew her sword.

The two soldiers standing next to Marcus drew swords as well, stepping forward. Marcus raised his hand, holding them back. "There's no reason to draw your weapon, Eileen. I'm not your enemy."

"Then leave us alone," said Aisling.

Marcus gave Aisling a stern look. "The queen will not be pleased. If I were you, Aisling, I'd cooperate—especially after what you've done."

"Go tell the queen that we will not be bound, like slaves," said Aisling.

"Very well," said Marcus.

A golden fire erupted where he was standing, engulfing the three of them in a brilliant light. When it had died down, they were gone.

"That's done it," said Fáelán.

"This is dreadful!" said Eileen. "I can't believe the queen is doing this!"

Aisling looked at her sister.

Erin's hands were shaking as she put away her stiletto. She whispered, "Never again shall I suffer under collar or chain."

Aisling was reminded of the rebellious changelings who had been in her fashion show. She put her hand on Erin's shoulder. "Don't worry. Queen Annan has no authority over you."

"That's right," said Eileen. "But I wonder what she'll do now?"

"I know what I'm going to do from now on: Relax," said Aisling. "Anyway, that's how to avoid falling into shadow."

* * *

Chapter Sixteen

The Salamander

A field of golden yellow sunflowers covered the hill, swaying in the hot summer breeze. Like melted gold, light rain mizzled and drizzled out of the sky, rinsing the heat of the day into the ground. One fairy, four changelings, and a Milesian danced through the sunflowers, weaving in and out of the tall green stalks, laughing.

In a game of tag, running through stalks of sunflowers, Aisling and her sister Erin, along with Paola, Maija, and Siri tried to avoid getting caught by Fáelán. They had promised Fáelán a kiss if he could catch them. At first, he had tried desperately to catch Erin, but she was too wary for him.

Running into a clearing near the top of the hill, Aisling paused to catch her breath. She looked down into the field of yellow, and watched the changeling Paola try to hide from Fáelán. With long curly black hair and wearing a blue dress, she was easy to spot in the field of golden flowers. Aisling shook her head, muttering under her breath, "She'll never get away from him."

Feeling like a gypsy, Aisling wore a loose blouse of transparent flowery material over a blue shirt, a white cloth sash, a long yellow skirt, sandals, bracelets and earrings. Huffing, she leaned down and grabbed her knees, letting her breath out into the sunshine. With a cool touch, the misty rain refreshed her skin.

Genevieve had muttered something about bad omens from a dream and had chosen to remain at home with Eileen, who wanted to go swimming in the lake. Aisling grinned, wondering if the two realized that they had finally agreed on something.

Erin emerged from a bunch of flowers, and crept up the hill, towards Aisling. The last few weeks spent in the Land of Dreams had done wonders for her. Suspicious by nature, and quieter than most, Erin was now laughing with the others. Aisling smiled—glad to have rescued her sister from the Land of Shadows.

Maija came running out of the far side of the clearing. When she saw Aisling, she smiled and crept closer. "Where is he?" she whispered.

Aisling pointed to a clump of swaying sunflower stalks. Through golden flowers, they could see Fáelán creeping up on Siri, who was trying to hide on the other side of the field. Siri had distracted Fáelán from catching Paola, who had run off. Siri's red dress didn't blend in too well with the sea of green and gold. Moments later, Siri yelped as Fáelán caught up and tagged her. Aisling chuckled, wondering if Fáelán was going to dare offending Erin by kissing Siri.

With a violent crash, Paola rushed out into the clearing on the top of the hill, breaking stalks of sunflowers as she emerged. Her clear blue eyes were filled with terror. Paola stumbled and fell down. Rolling onto her back, she began to rise up.

A cherry-red bolt of fire shot out of the field of sunflowers, and struck Paola in the chest. Screaming, she disintegrated in a ball of crimson flame. A veil of silence fell over the hill, smothering the sunshine.

Aisling held her breath against the blowing wind.

A tall, thin fairy with long straight black hair, and silver makeup over delicate Japanese features emerged from the field of sunflowers. A blue stone hung from a chain around her neck. Hefting a black staff, tipped in fire, she halted and scanned the clearing with a predatory glance.

It was Kusanagi Gin, the Inferno Fairy.

Aisling shouted to the others, "Run!"

They scattered into the tall sunflowers, rushing and tumbling down the hill, going in different directions. The Inferno Fairy came after Aisling. She heard a loud whooshing sound and a hot bolt of fire shot past, igniting the flowers in front of her. Whirling around, Aisling conjured up a Dao sword. Just as Kusanagi Gin came into view, she ran off in another direction, hoping to hide in the tall green stalks.

Another flaming bolt whooshed by and Aisling had to tumble out of the way to avoid it. Fire was all around her. Remaining on the ground, she waited for the Inferno Fairy to approach. Heart pounding, she listened to the fire crackling in the wind.

Boots crunched on fallen flowers, as the Inferno Fairy appeared. Lowering her staff, she pointed it at Aisling. A thin trail of white smoke billowed off the tip, which held a scarlet flame. Aisling's heart skipped a beat.

With a fierce cry, Fáelán leapt out of the burning field, charging the Inferno Fairy.

Kusanagi Gin spun around and struck him in the head with the black staff. There was a bright flash and he fell to the ground.

Moving quickly, Aisling leapt to her feet and slashed down with her sword, cutting the staff in two. The world turned red and white as the elemental inside the staff was released in a blinding cascade of energy.

Aisling found herself lying on her back. Her conjured sword was now a twisted length of melted steel. Barely able to open her eyes against the heat, she lay there, gasping.

The Inferno Fairy stood in the same place, unmoved by the blast. The remnants of her staff lay on the ground, burning. Untouched by the flames, she looked closely at Aisling. Apparently satisfied, she stepped back and tapped the blue crystal on her necklace. There was a flash of sapphire and then she was gone.

Slowly, Aisling rose to her knees, gasping and coughing. Smoke and fire surrounded her, but she could feel the cold wind tickling the back of her neck. With her last remaining strength, Aisling summoned a Wind Elemental. The cold whirlwind blew away the firestorm. When the smoke cleared, she saw Fáelán lying in a pool of ash and blood. A charred sunflower lay against his face.

* * *

Under the fading light of the sun, the leaves in the great cedar tree rustled against the wind. Aisling kneeled on the ground next to Fáelán, eyes downcast.

Thoughts are things. Would this have happened if she had never tried to end the war? Her passion had done this. Maybe the queen was right about repressing desires and dreams?

Mingled with the scent of cedar, a cool breeze blew hair into Aisling's face. As the wind died down, she heard footsteps. The subtle aroma of violets touched Aisling on the nose. Barefoot, Elsbeth stepped out from behind the trunk, as if she had come out of the ancient tree itself. Kneeling down beside Fáelán, Elsbeth reached up to touch his bloody face. "He's badly burned. What happened to him?"

"Queen Annan sent an assassin to kill me," said Aisling. "I've heard that you're a healer."

Elsbeth gave her a thoughtful look. "I'm not certain that I can save his life, but I will try," she said. "Magic in the world has diminished, but some things remain true."

Biting her lip, Aisling sat down on her heels, submerged in the turbulent waters of conscience. Ever since the Dream Crystal had been taken, she had sustained herself on passion. She whispered, "I had a Passion Stone..." But her words faded away. She had destroyed it.

"Passion is no substitute for thoughts and ideas," Elsbeth said softly. "For this one, I need another kind of magic. Leave him with me. Go and rest now, changeling."

Rising out of the grass, Aisling went away, hoping that the nymph could help.

Aisling walked over to a fallen tree trunk and sat down. Red fire bathed the waters of the lake. The sun was going down. Drawing a deep breath, she closed her eyes. Her mind was in utter and impenetrable darkness. Not since her life in Seattle had she known such emptiness, but now it was deeper and denser. There, there were at least ideas moving, and echoes of dreams, and a sense of reaching out for desires, however futile those goals seemed to be. But now all thought had become stagnant and still, like the smooth surface of a lake, and ideas fell dead. The Sídhe now swam in a motionless lake of black vapors that emptied dead dreams into the night. The mind had become blind to thoughts, and even the memory of dreams had faded away into the shadows of eternity. Empty shadows had overtaken dreams. Shadows had always been, night was all there was, and darkness would last forevermore.

Shaking her head, Aisling opened her eyes. "What have I done?"

With a trembling voice, she whispered a message to Nel, casting it into the wind. Aisling hoped Nel could help, but she wondered how her friend would react to the news about Fáelán.

Against the promise of more assassins, Aisling hoped that her submission to the queen would save her friends. Queen Annan was right after all. Her words of caution echoed in Aisling's mind: *Be careful what you wish for.*

Caged dreams were better than empty shadows.

* * *

The whisper of falling water spread itself over the clearing. Untouched by the birdsongs up in the trees, Aisling sat, with her face resting on her knees. Hoping to cool some of the passions that had taken the world's dreams away, she had come to a waterfall near Eileen's house. Hot sunshine caressed her arms, but it only reminded her of the fire that had consumed her friends. Paola's screams still burned her memories.

Through a curtain of silver pearls, a voice whispered, "Aisling?"

Looking into the waterfall, a rippling image appeared. It was Nel.

"Aisling? I need to speak with you."

For a moment, Aisling sat, staring at the wonder of how fairies communicated. She stood up, smoothed out her short white dress and looked into the waterfall. "Nel? You received my message..." but she didn't finish. Her words fell into the pool of silent water.

Nel spoke with a voice cold and warm altogether—veiled anger mixed with fiery concern. "Are you alright?"

Aisling felt her legs weaken in dismay. "Oh Nel! The queen sent an assassin to kill us. The Inferno Fairy murdered Paola!"

"Wasn't Paola one of Siri's friends?"

"Yes, but—"

"Siri was cursed, Aisling. It wasn't your fault."

Aisling remembered how Siri had killed Laigne in the duel. They had placed the Friendslayer curse on Siri. Aisling remained silent.

"How is Fáelán?" asked Nel.

"He's in a terrible way," said Aisling. "I gave him to the nymph Elsbeth, but I don't think he'll recover."

A moment of silence filled the clearing. Silver water drowned out the expression in Nel's face, but Aisling knew what her friend was feeling. Nel loved Fáelán. When Nel spoke, her words were too gentle. "Would you like me to speak to the queen?"

Aisling sat down on a rock covered with moss. "I don't know what else to do," she said. "You think it will help?"

"No lamp burns till morning."

"What do you mean?"

Rippling pearls of water washed over Nel, cooling her smile. "The fire in the queen's heart will fade."

A breeze carried a chill into the clearing, and a few green leaves fell out of the trees, landing in the pool and in her hair. Aisling brushed the leaf away. "I sent a message to Queen Annan, but she didn't respond. I should never have let Ith—"

"Annan shouldn't have sent an assassin," said Nel. "A curse isn't the only thing that will avenge you."

Unsure that she wanted to know what Nel was talking about, Aisling remained silent. Nel was one of the oldest fairies, and the magic she wielded might prove too terrible for anyone to withstand.

Nel was looking into her eyes, with a thoughtful expression in her face. "I think King Artrach will force the queen to withdraw her assassins if we could bring it out into the open, but the queen is away from Brú na Bodb. She's avoiding you, hoping that her assassins will get to you before you can reach her," said Nel. "The queen is traveling through Tír na nÓg, so there's no way to get in touch with her."

"How do you mean?"

"We can only travel so fast along the King's Road. I've heard she's traveling to her clan's Sídhe, Na Teach Cúirtéis, but it's on the east coast, in a place the Milesians call North Carolina. It will take me several hours—"

Aisling interrupted. "What about your magic hat?"

"The magic has faded away from it," said Nel.

Aisling asked, "But if you can get there before she does, could you talk to the queen for me?"

"Do you have a way?"

Nodding, Aisling said, "I think so."

* * *

Aisling stepped over a red-capped mushroom and walked up to the tall stone, which marked the entrance to the vortex leading to the world energy grid. The sunlight had nearly faded, and tall shadows spread into the trees at the edge of the clearing. The stone was twice as tall as a man, and it was covered in ancient symbols in a swirling pattern.

"This is a bad idea," muttered Eileen.

Glancing over her shoulder, Aisling asked, "Why do you say that?"

"I know your father was a Fomorian, but it's not safe playing around with ancient magic," said Eileen. "Are you sure you can use the Ley Lines like you did before?"

Aisling crossed her arms. "I don't see why not."

Eileen put her hands on her hips. "Just how do you plan on convincing the queen to call off her assassins?"

Aisling shrugged. "Why not ask Nel when she gets here?" Her eyes darted over to the path that led back to the cathedral near Vancouver. "I wonder what's keeping her."

Genevieve emerged from the forest path. She wrinkled her nose. "Nel was cleaning out a flask of unicorn blood when I saw her at the cathedral. She said that she was finishing up a spell. She'll catch up with us."

Aisling frowned, as a memory tugged at her mind.

Genevieve chuckled and fingered the shotgun case around her shoulder. "Hey, if you trust Nel's diplomacy skills so much, then why are you armed?"

Aisling wore a white silk Nehru shirt embroidered with gold dragons, a pair of white leggings, and ankle boots. Her father's sword hung from a black leather belt around her waist. She smiled wryly, but didn't answer.

Erin followed Genevieve out of the forest. She looked up into the sky. "The sun's going down," she whispered. Dropping her eyes onto the path, she tilted her head slightly, as if she was listening to something.

"What is it?" asked Aisling.

Erin remained still for a moment, and then she shrugged. "I thought there was...something there." She let her words fade away into silence.

"I suppose we can all agree to wear those Collars of Humility," murmured Eileen.

Genevieve huffed. "What a marvelous idea!"

Eileen frowned. "Queen Annan is only trying to prevent more people from falling away. So many people have been lost already."

"You're talking about trusting Gentle Annie," said Genevieve, "the woman that banished Trista—who was innocent—to the Land of Shadows."

Erin, who had remained where she was, staring into the trees, turned around and approached the tall stone. "In the Land of Shadows, they say that slaves choose their own fate," she said. "People are always too eager to give up their freedoms."

"Trust me, Eileen," said Genevieve. "I'm usually right about these things."

Eileen looked doubtful. "Indeed?"

As if out of an ancient fable, a winged lioness appeared in the sky. It came down slowly, gliding along the wind currents. Flapping its great wings, the lioness descended, landing in the clearing by a tall birch tree. Purple light, mingled with silver, flashed out like a fallen star, spilling brilliant incandescence over the clearing for an instant.

Among the trees, Aisling thought she could see a great host of warriors, waiting. But then the light was gone, and the winged lioness had changed into Nel. The moment she appeared, all trace of the figures vanished, as if they had existed only in a fleeting flash. She could no longer hold onto the thought of them.

Walking swiftly, Nel approached as a cold wind brushed against the treetops. She wore a white blouse, black leggings, boots, and a red vest, embroidered with winged lions in gold. Her Palarak sword hung from a black belt around her waist.

A strange sensation accompanied Nel into the clearing. It was as if the world was watching, from some hidden place. Aisling found herself looking around into the trees again. Shaking herself free of the impulse to look over her shoulder, Aisling glanced down at the sword by Nel's side. Biting her lip, she withheld a growing sense of trepidation and asked, "So you really think you can help us—you've come to talk?"

Nel nodded silently and then looked up at the stone. Placing a hand on the smooth surface, she whispered, "I haven't seen one of these since King Bodb Derg brought us out of Ireland."

Dropping her hand away, Nel looked at Aisling with wonder in her eyes. "Stone circles like these were found in Babel, Uruk, Akkad, and Calneh in the land of Shinar by Lord Nimrod. The Fomorians built them a long time ago, but nobody remembers them now."

Aisling raised her eyebrows. "Nimrod?"

Nel looked away, as if she were remembering an ancient ambition.

325

"A man of great power, who founded Babylon," she whispered. "He told me once, how he had persuaded his people to abandon their dreams, and to seek happiness through deeds of passion and courage instead. Nimrod believed that only cowards submitted to the will of God. Truly, he was a hater of dreams..."

Inhaling cold air, Nel's green eyes focused on the present once more. She met Aisling's gaze. "So how does it work?"

Aisling looked at the stone, remembering the vision of the rose garden above Meadhar Grá. "I put my hand on it, and then images come to me, of places far away..."

Nel interrupted, "Instead of allowing your desire to take you there, you should call for a doorway instead, so that we can all move through it."

Aisling laughed. "Yes, but you read my mind. I didn't mention my desire to go to the garden I saw."

"Meadhar Grá has a beautiful flower garden," murmured Nel. "The roses there are as fine as the flowers that grew in the Hanging Gardens of Babylon."

Stunned, Aisling whispered, "You can read minds?"

Nodding, Nel laughed.

Genevieve said, "Wow, you'd make a great spy. Maybe you should take over Conall's job?"

Eileen's rebuke was a harsh one, "Genevieve!"

At the mention of Conall, a dark well of night threatened to overtake Aisling. She missed the way he teased her, his playful antics, the feel of his hand on her thigh...

Genevieve interrupted her dark memories with a touch. "I'm sorry."

Aisling surfaced from the waters of sorrow and inhaled the clear air. She smiled at her best friend.

"Look for a mountain standing against a forest," said Nel. The Aed Ernmas clan lives near a mountain of quartz. Their Sídhe, Na Teach Cúirtéis, lies near it."

Nodding her head, Aisling looked around at the others. Suddenly, she missed Fáelán's impulsive optimism. Wondering if he was dead, she placed a hand on the stone. Images began to whirl around in her mind. Taking a deep breath, she asked the others, "Ready?"

* * *

Emerging from a line of standing stones that faced a wall of black granite, Aisling felt like she had just stepped into a warm sauna. There was a pleasant breeze, tinged with the sweet aroma of wildflowers. The sun had gone down, plunging the rocky clearing at the base of the cliff into purple shadows. A silver moon made the black rocks glow, like ghostly sentinels standing guard over the mountain. Trickling water erupted silently from springs buried deep within the cliff, dripping moonlight over the surface of the rocks.

Erin's voice came out of the blackness. "I don't like this place."

Eileen laughed. "How can you say that? It's beautiful here!" Dimly, Aisling could see Eileen step over to one of the standing stones, which was twice her height. Shyly, she put her hand against it, as if she were hesitant to touch the ancient lines of force that connected the world in a mystical energy grid. Eileen whispered an incantation and silver moonlight flared up from the stone, illuminating the base of the cliff.

No longer hidden in the dark, tiny white flowers grew in tufts of grass at the base of the nine standing stones. Between the stones and the cliff face a large pillar of black quartz lay at an angle, pointing away from the mountain.

Nel walked over to the pillar and knelt down. Closing her eyes, she began to whisper in an ancient tongue, "Sapti sui nasu tabuli. Lu us hal liqma al kat sunu lu saap piih. Enûma shaplish ammatum lä shüpû, mariu tu rështû nabû. Umma hu burpa ti qat kalamu."

Although Aisling couldn't understand the words, she thought they were full of pride and fury.

Inside the crystal, a deep scarlet flame began to glow, in the shape of a lizard. At once Aisling felt the presence of a fire elemental of immense power. A feverish wave of fury washed over the clearing, and she swayed

327

on her feet. An aggressive rush of desire and passion spread through her body, filling her limbs with strength and vigor. Unable to resist smiling, she watched Nel get to her feet. "What kind of elemental is this?"

Nel took a deep breath and turned to face Aisling. "I've summoned a salamander. The black quartz will magnify his powers, but his influence on this world is still fragile."

Nel waved a hand and a red candle appeared on the ground next to the stone. The salamander inside the stone glowed brighter. Aisling could feel the whirling storm of fury around her solidify into a steady stream of warmth, filling her with desire. "Do not allow this candle to go out," said Nel. "Otherwise, the salamander will fall back into the earth, and I will no longer be able to draw strength from it."

"Just what are you trying to do?" asked Genevieve, hotly. She, too, felt the touch of the elemental.

Nel smiled. "The salamander will give me great presence and magnetism, which will help me influence the queen."

Remembering the power that had always threatened to overwhelm her when elementals were involved, Aisling frowned against the force of its attention. An urge to fight, a desire to exact vengeance, was growing within her mind. "But it can also magnify your aggression, can't it? Hot tempers aren't conducive to making peace."

Nel laughed. "Don't worry," she whispered. "Trust me."

A sudden unwillingness swept over Aisling. "I'll come with you."

"No, Aisling," said Eileen. "You need to stay here."

Aisling put her hands on her hips. "Tell me why."

"It's too dangerous, certainly," said Eileen. "Let Nel talk to the queen first."

Dropping her hands, Aisling began to pace. A moment later, she stopped and looked into Nel's eyes. Something fierce lay there, just under the surface.

Nel glanced over her shoulder, as if she was listening to something. "I need to go now, before the queen arrives," she said. "Stay or go—I don't care."

Aisling moved to follow Nel, but Eileen stepped in front of her. Placing a hand on Aisling's shoulder, Eileen whispered, "Please Aisling..."

It was the look in Eileen's eyes that stayed Aisling's feet. Over Eileen's shoulder, she watched Nel walk towards a trail leading into the forest. A delicate breeze swept through the glade, knocking the hair into Aisling's face. The further Nel went away, the more deflated she felt, like a balloon losing its air. But the fire remained inside, ready tinder for something to ignite it. Aisling turned around and sat down underneath the pillar of black quartz, hugging her knees to her chest. She felt the heat of the candlelight flickering in her face.

The forest took another breath of wind, and they listened to the long exhalation, washed in silver moonlight. When it had faded away, silence stood between them until Genevieve spoke. "I had a dream last night: I saw an army of bees flying over a great field, gathering riches from the flowers as it went by."

"Another one of your visions?" asked Aisling.

Genevieve didn't answer. Instead, she took out her shotgun and pumped a round into the chamber. She went over to a standing stone and leaned against it.

Eileen walked over to the cliff face, searching the sky above it. Placing a hand against the wet wall, she remained there, waiting. Erin stood between the standing stones and the cliff face, staring into the forest. Her silver hair fell down past her shoulders, and it caught the moonlight. She seemed to be listening to something.

An hour later, Aisling felt the quartz at her back grow hot. A rush of aggression began to seep into her skin. The candle flared, giving off a brilliant light.

Erin reached down and drew a stiletto out of one of her boots.

Genevieve asked, "What is it?"

Erin's voice was soft, almost like a caress. "They come..."

The sky ignited with a brilliant flash, which was quickly swallowed up by the darkness. Moments later, the earth shook. Lightning came down.

Aisling got to her feet.

Like a thunderstorm, the horizon erupted with dozens of flashes, spreading crimson fires into the darkness. Distant thunder roared, and a fiery glow appeared on the horizon, growing larger with every flash.

"So much for the negotiations," grumbled Genevieve.

Erin glanced over at Genevieve. "Shhh!"

The salamander danced inside crystalline darkness.

Another white flash, as bright as daylight, lit up the sky.

"I'm going to find Nel," said Aisling.

Eileen called out, "No, wait!"

Out of the corner of her eye, something moved.

Eileen drew her sword.

With a deep exhalation, like the last breath of a dying man, a Shadow Person came swiftly out of the darkness. It reached out for Genevieve. Raising her shotgun, Genevieve fired into the shadow. Screaming, it faded out of sight.

Another flash lit the sky. In the brief illumination, they spied dozens of Shadow People coming out of the trees.

Firing several blasts, Genevieve retreated. "We need to get out of here."

Eileen went into a furious attack, whirling round the standing stones, striking shadows down. Their screams sent shivers down Aisling's spine.

Erin held her ground, stabbing any Shadow Person that came near. Cries came out of the darkness around her.

Since they were so difficult to see, especially at night, Aisling pushed away the concern for her sister and closed her eyes, waiting and listening.

Something dark approached.

Drawing her sword and slashing out in the same motion, Aisling twirled around and struck three times. A trio of screams indicated that she had struck home.

Moonlight glinted off of a sword as it lunged towards her chest.

Stepping to the side, Aisling counterattacked.

The dim figure choked off a scream and faded away.

White fire ignited her heart. A hunger burned inside, and she began to wish more of the shadows would come out of the trees. Aisling went on the offensive, striking them down wherever she found one. She was on fire. Strength and agility rushed through her body. Against the fury of her attack, the Shadow People retreated back into the forest.

Dimly, she heard Genevieve's shout, "Where are you going? Stay with us!"

But the fire would not go out. Soon, Aisling found herself in the middle of the forest, listening for the whispers of her enemies. Distant thunder roared, and hot flashes rose into the night. Something stirred in the trees.

Two shadows leapt out of the branches, brandishing spears.

Unable to parry either of them, Aisling dropped her sword. Deftly stepping between the two spear points, she grabbed the shafts. Using the spears as a springboard, she jumped into the air and kicked, striking them both in the head.

Aisling fell onto her back, just as another Shadow Person leapt out from behind a tree, aiming a spear at her chest.

Rolling out of the way, the spear struck the earth. Retrieving her sword, she grabbed the shaft of the spear with her left hand, and used it to rise to her feet. She slashed out, striking the shadow. He fell away into the night.

With a shout, another shadow lunged from the side. Turning, Aisling grabbed the spear and dropped onto her back, pulling her attacker overhead and throwing him. He struck a tree trunk and was silent.

As she got to her feet, she became aware of several Shadow People to her front, holding spears. One of them whistled a signal and they all threw their spears at once.

Aisling sliced out with her sword, cutting the spears in two as they came at her.

The Shadow People drew their swords, circling around her.

Aisling took up a fighting stance, holding the sword out in front with the blade up, and with her other arm upraised, palm-up behind her head.

331

Her body was washed in resplendent energy, an insatiable fire. Daring them to strike, she called out in a coy voice, "Come on!"

The shadows attacked.

A raging fire, Aisling twirled around, striking the shadows as they came. She parried two sword strikes, moving between a pair of shadows. Spinning around, she killed them before they could turn around. More of them advanced and she swept them aside, like fire burning through a dry field of grass. She lost count of how many she killed, feeling only the intense energy of the Fire Elemental, as it ignited her anger. Their screams passed through the trees like a cold gale.

She was too fast for them. They recoiled, melting back into the darkness.

Moments later, she stood, panting next to a tree, wishing they would return. Shaking herself out of the hot delirium, she glanced down at her sword and found that it was covered with blood.

Once again, she had failed to control an elemental. She had become an animal, driven by an insatiable lust for blood. A wave of revulsion washed over her and she nearly dropped the sword. Her disgust turned to anger. Gripping her sword tightly in her hand, Aisling's rage turned into a scream.

"I can't do this anymore," she muttered.

Returning to the standing stones, she found the others resting after their fight. She walked up to the pillar of black quartz where the candle burned. Kneeling down, she looked up into the crystal, where the light of the salamander flared.

"What are you doing?" asked Eileen, out of breath.

"Some of the elementals I've encountered are difficult to master, but this one is impossible," said Aisling. "I don't think Nel can control it."

"You think the salamander has taken command of Nel?" asked Genevieve.

Aisling looked towards the Sídhe, where the sky burned. "Isn't that obvious?"

Eileen put her hand on Aisling's shoulder. "Don't blow out the candle."

"You don't understand," said Aisling. "These elementals can make you do things, terrible things."

"What happened?" asked Genevieve.

"I... lost control," whispered Aisling. She shuddered. "I should never have come here."

"Don't be so critical of yourself," said Eileen. "How can you expect to gain mastery over your powers if you quit at the first sign of trouble?"

Aisling didn't answer. When she made mistakes, people died. She looked up at the red horizon, where fires raged against the night.

"Why don't we just get out of here?" said Erin.

"Great idea," said Genevieve. "I'm running out of ammunition."

"I won't abandon a friend so easily." Aisling closed her eyes in concentration. Moments later, several boxes of shotgun shells lay next to her.

With a shrug, Genevieve knelt down and began to reload.

Aisling put one hand behind the flame, intending to extinguish the candle.

"Isn't it dangerous to put that out?" asked Eileen. "Nel told us to leave it alone."

Aisling looked towards Na Teach Cúirtéis.

Another flash lit the horizon.

It was hard to know what to do, but she came to a decision just the same. "I fear the salamander more than any other consequence."

Aisling blew out the candle.

The distant conflagration seemed to subside, and the night fell into darkness, except for a red stain burning on the horizon.

Rising to her feet, Aisling said, "All of you stay here and guard the vortex. I'm going to get Nel."

Before any of them could protest, Aisling changed into a ball of light and zipped off through the forest, heading into Na Teach Cúirtéis.

*   *   *

Chapter Seventeen

Gateway to Shadow

Cold moonlight, mingling with fire, glittered off of the river that Aisling flew over. The sphere of gold and silver surrounding her bounced a tiny reflection off the water. On the far side of the river, a once beautiful town lay burning. Fairy lights scattered into the night, fleeing the turmoil down in the streets.

Aisling flew down a wide road bordered with oak trees. On either side, magnificent houses with white pillars stood in ruins. It was as if a marauding army had just swept through the town.

A scream erupted from a house. Turning to look, Aisling saw a little fairy girl cowering before a pair of Shadow People. Changing direction, Aisling materialized beside them, sword in hand. With one swift motion, she slew the shadows. They faded away as they died.

Holding a hand out, Aisling smiled at the girl. "Are you okay?"

The little fairy girl nodded, but she didn't take Aisling's hand.

There is no way I can take a child into the fight that's waiting for me.

Aisling lowered her hand.

Another scream came from down the street. Aisling glanced over her shoulder and there was a flash of lightning.

Turning back to the little girl, she said, "I have to go. Turn into a sphere and fly away from here. It should be safe to return in the morning."

"I'm afraid."

Aisling knelt down beside the girl. "Think of it as a game. Your part is to go hide in the forest."

A little smile crept onto the girl's face. "Like hide and seek?"

"Yes."

Pink and silver light covered the porch as the small girl changed into a fairy orb. She sped off into the night. Aisling watched her go, hoping that she would find her parents. Full of guilt, Aisling whispered, "You shouldn't leave her."

A low rumble swept through the oak trees. Aisling took off, changing back into an orb, speeding towards the source of the tumult. Some of the houses along either side of the road burned, and everywhere Shadow People crept, like hungry wolves.

The road opened up onto a wide plain, where a nineteenth-century southern mansion stood at the end of a long grassy field, lined with ash trees. The mansion was burning. Across the field of grass lay the bodies of the slain.

Among the dead and injured fairies, Aisling found Lasarina and knelt beside her, taking her hand. Blood dripped from a wound in her friend's temple. Lasarina opened her eyes. "So you've finally come to visit me?" she murmured, a wry smile tugging at her lips.

Biting her lip, Aisling simply nodded.

Lasarina turned her blue eyes towards the mansion. "I've been the high priestess of the Sídhe and the leader of the Aed Ernmas clan ever since we came from Sídhe Finnachaidh in Ireland," she said. "How could this have happened, Aisling?"

Aisling looked up at the burning mansion. An impossibly bright light shone from the main entrance and she had to turn away from it. "It was a salamander—" but her explanation died away, empty. *What had happened here?*

"We've done battle with more than a salamander tonight," said Lasarina. "Ancient powers have been awakened. A star came down from heaven and struck the palace. I had to summon an angel..."

"Where is Nel?"

The light in Lasarina's eyes darkened. "Nel drew her sword and struck the queen," she said. "Annie fell..."

Aisling whispered, "The queen is dead?"

Lasarina shrugged. "Nel was about to strike again, but the fires in the city went out suddenly and she dropped to her knees," she said. "It was as if the fire had been fueling the fury in her soul."

Aisling realized that moment must have been when she blew out the candle.

"I don't know if the queen lives," said Lasarina. "They came upon us..."

Aisling looked over the field of dead fairies.

Lasarina's voice was soft, like a breeze against a field of flowers. "There are shadows here..."

Lasarina had fallen unconscious. Aisling closed her eyes and placed a hand against her friend's forehead, conjuring up a bandage for her injury. Aisling got to her feet, wishing that she could do more for her friend, but she had to find Nel.

Approaching the entrance to the palace, Aisling encountered the brightest light she had ever seen. Materializing from her faerie sphere, she walked into the rays, squinting against the glare. The source of brilliance was an incredibly handsome man, wearing a white tunic and a belt of gold. White feathered wings sprouted from his back. A flaming sword was in his hand. As she drew near, the man shook his head and waved her off with the sword.

Overcome with fear and awe, her knees felt weak. Aisling turned and fled. Deluged by the guilt of what she had wrought here tonight, she had an uncontrollable impulse to get away.

It was some time later that she found herself among a field of flowers in a garden below the mansion, shaking. The fires had gone out, and a black smoke was rising into the night. The sounds of strife and pain had faded away from the Sídhe, but a great weight had fallen on her shoulders. Was she responsible for what had happened?

Aisling took a deep breath, catching a whiff of smoke, mingled with the aroma of tulips that grew in the garden about her. It seemed that everything she did had led to more despair and suffering. Shaking her head, she whispered to herself, "No. I was right getting Erin out of that place."

A groan emerged from a garden of flowers, not twenty paces away. She heard a voice murmuring, "We shall not lie down in peace, but I will destroy their way, I will..."

It was Nel, lying face-down on the earth. Rushing over to her friend, Aisling gently turned her over. Blood covered her face, and her white blouse was burned in several places. Nel opened her green eyes and smiled.

"Oh Nel!" said Aisling. "What have you done?"

Nel's smile faded away. Her eyes filled with a cold obsession. "I called down the wrath of God, to smite them," she whispered.

Aisling shook her head. "I sent you to talk!"

Closing her eyes, Nel began to shake. She was crying. "Why has God abandoned me Aisling?"

Aisling shook her head, but before she could answer, she heard a voice, coming from a stone landing above the garden. It was Marcus, with his back turned, facing a soldier. "Nel has deceived us all. Alert the soldiers of the Fianna. She and Aisling are in league with Ith. When you find them, kill them if you can, or send word to us so that we can send aid."

A fairy with a stern face saluted Marcus and went away. Marcus faced the garden and looked down into it silently. Aisling saw him gaze directly at her, but he didn't move. She held her breath. A slight grin touched his face. Then, Marcus turned and walked away slowly, as if he was deep in thought.

Aisling wondered if he had seen her. But if he had, why didn't he call the soldiers? Indeed, it was dark, but the garden was bathed in moonlight.

She leaned down to Nel and whispered, "We have to get away from here. Can you travel?"

The cold glare in Nel's eyes went away, as if she had just put a mask back on. She smiled. "Yes, I think so."

* * *

Shadowed by moonlight, birch trees towered over their heads. Cold air washed over the forest, and it blew Aisling's hair into her face. An owl hooted in the darkness. Shivering, a part of Aisling wished she was back in Na Teach Cúirtéis, where the air was warmer. Brushing the hair out of her eyes, she looked out of the forest, tensely.

"Do you think there are any more of them?" asked Erin.

Aisling shrugged. They had been ambushed several times by Shadow People in their retreat from the Sídhe where the queen's clan had lived.

Having made their way down from the vortex site near Vancouver, Aisling leaned against an ancient fir tree, watching Nel, who sat with her back to the trunk. Nel's face was covered in blood from a head wound and her clothes had been blackened by fire and lightning, but she suffered from more than pain and fatigue.

"I know she's hurt, but I think something else is wrong with her," said Genevieve.

"You're right." Aisling shook her head. "It's as if her spirit is fading away."

A lonely blue sphere came up the road, stopping at the tree line. Flashing silver, the orb changed into Eileen. She held a sword in her hand, and threw a furtive glance into the forest. This time, the shadows remained still.

Putting her sword away, Eileen said, "The road is clear."

Aisling knelt down and helped Nel to her feet. "Come on, it's not too far."

Eileen looked at Genevieve. "You and Erin take up the rear. I'll go first."

For once, Genevieve didn't argue.

339

Moving through the cold night, they passed through fields of moonlit wildflowers and tall grass towards the one place they knew was empty of Shadow People: The cathedral. In the distance, they could see orange torchlight illuminating the arched stone entryway. A welcoming glow spilled out of the stained glass windows.

Breathing a sigh of relief, they went through the oak doors of the church. At once, Aisling felt a presence surrounding her, like a warm blanket. Myrrh and frankincense mingled with the aroma of flowers. Bunches of candles illuminated the sides of the hall, spilling golden light into the white archways.

Aisling moved towards a pew close to the chancel, but Nel shook her head and pointed up the nave towards the rear of the cathedral. It was as if she couldn't find rest so close to the sanctuary. Finally settling down in a pew just under the organ gallery, Aisling breathed a sigh of relief.

Genevieve remained by the closed oak doors while the others collapsed into pews in the center of the cathedral. She called out, "What now? It's only a matter of time until the queen's men find us here."

Bewildered, Aisling shrugged. "I have no idea, really."

Genevieve huffed. "What a mess you've made of things, Aisling!"

"Excuse me?"

"Why did you have to interfere with this world? You should have left the Dream Crystal alone," grumbled Genevieve. "How many have died because of your impulsiveness?"

Simmering in silence for a moment, Aisling considered her best friend's words. She glanced over her shoulder at Erin, who was leaning against a pew under the organ loft, looking at her mother's locket. "So you think I should have condemned my sister to dark oblivion?"

"No, but you should have thought of a better way to save her," said Genevieve.

Sighing, Aisling shook her head. "I'm not responsible for their war."

"No, you're not," said Genevieve. "You're responsible for ending it."

"Yes," whispered Aisling. "They were fighting over a lie."

"Were they?"

The thought lingered: *Do dreams really come true?*

Silence covered the cathedral. Aisling stared at the play of candlelight against the red marble pillars supporting the white arches. The Celtic cross stood under a garden of stained glass, now full of moonlight. The only illumination came from the quiet flicker of burning candles—the only sound was a delicate tracery of something, like leaves falling onto a forest floor.

Whispers were floating down out of the organ loft.

Aisling noticed a darkness clouding over Nel's green eyes, turning them black. Tilting her head slightly, Nel said, "Was it hard for you, living among the Milesians?"

Wrinkling her nose, Aisling remembered the distant eyes, the furtive glances when she came near them, the hushed whispers and the polite, withdrawn smiles. "They didn't like me very much. I guess they could feel that I was... different."

Nel looked away. "Then you know what it's like—being alone."

"Yes."

Nel glanced up at the Mirror of Eternity in the organ loft. "Sometimes I wonder what fate brought me here to guard this place."

A black mist emanated from the mirror. Distant voices chanted a haunted melody. Aisling found herself staring at the reflection of the organ pipes, imprisoned in the glass. The memory of their music was lost in the reflection. Candlelight flickered against the vaulted roof, throwing shadows into all of the arches. Nel smiled. "But I was never really alone. They whisper to me, occasionally, from the dark."

For an instant, Aisling wondered how difficult it must have been, guarding such an accursed thing. Nel must have endured a thousand nights of solitude, standing watch, with no company except shadowy whispers. The thought of it made Aisling's skin crawl. Had Nel always lived a life of solitude? On impulse Aisling asked, "Has Ith ever spoken to you?"

Nel's voice became a low murmur. "Yes."

Aisling frowned. Ith had a seductive way about him, with cloying

341

ideas that slipped into the mind and found a home there, next to a place where doubt lingered. She wondered how long Nel had been listening to his words of poison. What dark promises did he offer? Did he speak about freedom?

Abruptly, Nel asked, "Do you think I'm evil, Aisling?"

Aisling frowned. "I thought you didn't believe in evil."

Nel's words were distant, as if she was reliving an old memory. "I did—one time, long ago, before God abandoned me. When I came here, I began to talk to Ith, who sat in his fortress, Scáth Caisleán, mocking me. He said that he was looking forward to the day when I would come to him. I told him that only evil people fall into the darkness. He said that there's no such thing as evil. He said that anyone can fall into the Land of Shadows."

Aisling licked her lips and threw a glance into the mirror, where something stirred. Was it pride, or passion or frivolity that had caused people to descend into shadow? But how could these traits be evil?

Nel interrupted Aisling's reverie with a dark admission. "I've been testing the Sídhe, to see if they would fall. I made them angry and passionate—I aroused their pride."

Aghast, Aisling asked in a harsh whisper, "You've been helping Ith wage war against the Tuatha Dé Danann?"

Nel looked away at the Mirror of Eternity. "I wanted to know—I had to know, that Ith was wrong about evil, but they were all the same... They all fell away."

Aisling shook her head as if she was trying to wake up from a bad dream. "But you helped defeat Ith's army at Rath Gealach. You found Morrigan..."

Nel's smile revealed a ruthless kind of pride. It was as if a mask had dropped away from her face. But her eyes were empty, indifferent. "When I read your mind, I knew how you felt about Conall, so I used the enchanted oranges to make them fight. Morrigan was distracted while Rath Gealach was attacked. After Ith's army had destroyed the Sídhe and had slipped back into the Land of Shadows with their captives, I brought Morrigan back."

Too stunned to react, Aisling sat there with her mouth open.

"You shouldn't have extinguished the salamander," murmured Nel. "The queen was *mine*, but then the fire inside me went out. Now, Fáelán will never be avenged."

Aisling's eyes turned cold as it became plain that Nel had orchestrated a coup against the queen. "There were Shadow People at Na Teach Cúirtéis..."

"Yes," Nel said in a spiritless tone. "The doorway only worked one way, until I used the black unicorn blood to strengthen it." Her eyes drifted up to the organ loft. "Now it's a door—a gateway to shadow..."

Aisling looked up at the Mirror of Eternity with a sinking feeling in the pit of her stomach. The Shadow People had secretly gathered in the forest, coming out of the cathedral and hiding among the standing stones while Aisling had activated the ancient Fomorian Ley Lines. Nel had brought an army of shadows with them to Na Teach Cúirtéis. Nel never had any intention of talking to the queen.

The silence ended with the sound of a sword being drawn.

As quick as a lioness, Nel leapt to her feet, just as a sword slammed into the pew next to Aisling. Eileen withdrew her weapon from the wood.

Aisling shouted, "What are you doing?"

Through clenched teeth, Eileen said, "Everyone from Rath Gealach is dead or enslaved. She helped the shadows kill them all."

Nel backed into the aisle between the pews and drew her Palarak sword.

Before Aisling could say anything, Eileen leapt into a spinning sword attack, aiming three blows at Nel, who backed away, parrying. The clangs from the swords striking against each other shattered the peace in the cathedral.

For a moment, Aisling was too shocked to intervene. As much as she wanted to, she could not make her legs move.

Eileen lunged and Nel parried the attack, retreating. Eileen ran down the aisle and tried several overhead strikes, but Nel blocked them all. Eileen spun around, delivering a series of quick slashes, and then twirled around in the opposite direction to attack from the other side, but Nel parried the strikes.

A second later, Aisling was able to move. She got up and began to run.

Eileen gave out a fierce yell and lunged forward, aiming her sword at Nel's chest.

This time, Nel didn't retreat. Deftly, she disarmed Eileen, sending her sword clattering across the stone floor. Nel jumped up and delivered a spinning kick to the side of Eileen's head and she collapsed.

Smoothly advancing toward her fallen adversary, Nel raised her sword...

"Nel!" Aisling's scream stopped her cold, as if she had been struck with a bolt of lightning. Aisling stopped just in front of the altar, which was now bathed in brilliant silver moonlight. Aisling looked into Nel's impassive eyes and said in a calmer voice, "She's your friend..."

Nel blinked, as if she had just awoken from a dream. Dropping her sword, she sank down onto her knees. A wave of despair washed over her, and she began to shake.

Approaching slowly, Aisling knelt down.

"None of my dreams have ever come true," said Nel.

"Is that why you think God has forsaken you?"

Nel nodded, slipping down onto the floor. "Evil does exist," she whispered, "and I have become wicked."

Darkness gathered around her.

Aisling felt a peculiar sinking sensation, as if she was rapidly descending in an elevator. Blackness began to pool on the floor as if it was blood draining out of a corpse.

Nel's voice began to fade. "Forgive me!"

Aisling reached out, hoping against fate to catch Nel, but her hand swept through empty air. Sighing into oblivion, Nel fell into the empty darkness.

She was gone.

Aisling held her breath, trying to keep her emotions inside. A cold shiver ran through her body. There was a movement to the side and she turned to see Genevieve kneeling down beside Eileen, whose face was now covered in blood.

"We need to get help," said Genevieve.

Something angry whispered from the blackness. All of the fear in the world spilled into the moonlight covering the altar. Just out of the light, the place where Nel had lain moments before brooded in a whirlpool of shadow. There was a motion to the right, just out of sight. Hate spilled onto the floor of the cathedral.

With one swift motion, Aisling drew her sword and struck out in a wide arc, spinning around. A trio of screams pierced the gentle twilight inside the cathedral. Dimly, Aisling could see three Shadow People falling down. As they dissolved in the moonlight, Aisling caught a glimpse of a symbol embroidered on their black tunics: A white tower.

Erin screamed.

Whirling around, Aisling looked over to where Erin had been sitting, next to the shrine of Saint Joseph. Two Shadow People were dragging her away towards the staircase leading up to the organ loft. Aisling began to run, but she was seized by a pair of hands around the waist. Slipping out of the tight grip, Aisling spun around and dropped to the floor. The Shadow Person let go. Rolling onto her back, she flipped onto her feet. Aisling swung her sword, striking her captor, who screamed and faded away.

Aisling began to run towards the staircase at the rear of the cathedral. Up in the organ loft, darkness seeped out of the Mirror of Eternity, sending ripples through the glass, as if a match had been dropped into a lake, leaving a thin trail of smoke in its wake.

Aisling saw Erin, screaming, being dragged into the mirror, which now looked like the surface of a pool. Plunging into the gateway, Erin's voice vanished as she disappeared. The reflection in the glass flickered and danced and then lay still, frozen into lifelessness. Aisling stopped in her tracks as if she had struck a brick wall. She stared up at the gateway.

Silence.

The scent of flowers mingled with frankincense and myrrh, touching her nose. The delicate tracery of a song whispered away into silence. The cathedral had become a tomb, the melody a funeral dirge that faded away into nothing.

Furious, Aisling screamed.

All of her efforts had been in vain. Erin was lost, the Dream Crystal had been taken, her friends were either gone or badly hurt, and she was a renegade. Just as her life had been in the Milesian world, any dream that she might have had was a lie. Like Nel, none of her dreams would ever come true. Would she be the next one to fall into the Land of Shadows?

Erin's locket lay on the floor. Aisling picked it up and opened it. There was a tiny photograph of her mother inside. Aisling closed her fist around the locket and looked into the Mirror of Eternity.

The doors of the cathedral crashed open. Soldiers of the Fianna stormed in, led by Marcus. They spread out into the sides of the cathedral, blocking the other doors and surrounding Aisling. Marcus stepped into the moonlight that pooled in front of the altar, his hand on the hilt of his sword.

Queen Annan walked into the cathedral, leaning upon a staff of oak and wearing a long white dress stained in blood. A bandage was wrapped around her side. Painfully, she stepped in front of the altar.

Turning her back on the Mirror of Eternity, Aisling spun around to face the queen, her mind awhirl with conflicting emotions. A part of her wanted to strike out at the queen, but there was something else too. Inside, she hoped to see an end to the violence. The calmer side won out. Aisling sheathed her sword, and put her hands on her hips.

Covered in majestic moonlight, Queen Annan looked down at Eileen. In a gentle voice she said, "Take this one to Morrigan."

Marcus apparently hadn't noticed Eileen lying on the floor, but when he saw her, he moved quickly. Kneeling down, he picked her up and in a flash of fire, they were gone.

Queen Annan stepped out of the moonlight, and came towards Aisling.

Rising from between the pews, Genevieve appeared next to the queen. Pumping a round into the chamber of her shotgun, she aimed it at Annie. "That's far enough," she warned.

Queen Annan looked with disdain at Genevieve. She whispered, "Kindly lower your weapon, mortal."

Genevieve glanced at Aisling, who nodded her assent. Genevieve withdrew her shotgun and leaned against a pew, apprehension covering her face.

The queen didn't come closer. She looked at Aisling as if it was the first time she had really seen her. Gentle Annie's face was filled with mixed portions of wonder, admiration, and caution. It seemed that she was trying to decide what to do.

The queen glanced around the cathedral. "Where is Nel?"

Crossing her arms, Aisling looked away. Slightly shaking her head, she whispered, "Fallen into shadow—she's one of the forsaken ones now."

Queen Annan seemed to sway on her feet. Clutching her side, she leaned against a pew. Sadness began to seep out of her body. "So many of my people have fallen..."

Aisling thought of Conall as he faded into darkness. His kiss had been empty. "Love, bereft of passion, is just as evil as passion without love."

The queen shook her head. "And yet, passion caused Nel to fall."

"*Indifference* caused Nel to fall into shadow," said Aisling. "I looked into her eyes as she faded away. They were full of apathy."

The queen closed her eyes and grabbed the edge of the pew. Shaking her head, she wondered aloud, "Why haven't you fallen? Changelings never survive so long."

Impatience began to tug at Aisling. She threw a glance up into the organ loft. Could she help Erin? The Mirror of Eternity remained passive—even the whispers had stopped. Turning to look at the queen, Aisling brushed a strand of hair out of her face. "Better to fight for something than to live for nothing."

The queen's eyes hardened. "Don't let your passions destroy you, Aisling."

Aisling met the queen's gaze. "But that isn't what this war is about. It's about choosing to live a life of freedom or a life of restraint," she said. "Perhaps Ith is right. You shouldn't be afraid of dreams."

For a moment, the queen's smile returned. She laughed, and the sound of it was like a waterfall splashing over rocks. "But you don't believe in dreams. What do you care about selfish desires? That kind of freedom leads to ambition, cruelty and tyranny."

"So your answer is to remain weak and unfulfilled?"

"You can't always have what you want," said the queen. "If you walk down the path of pride, you will become powerful and evil."

Aisling shook her head. "I don't believe that. We always have a choice."

The queen sighed, as if she was letting go of a great burden after having tried to drag it up a mountainside. Queen Annan released her staff and drew herself up to her full height. She whispered, "Then I am sorry I must do this."

Before Aisling could react, the queen raised her hands and shouted a command word. Whatever it was, the sound of it was drowned out by a thunderclap. A bolt of lightning shot out from Queen Annan's hand, striking Aisling squarely in the chest. There was a flash of white.

Blue electricity washed over Aisling's body, surrounding her in a globe of scintillating brilliance. For an instant, Aisling felt the jolt, but then it slipped away, and she felt the presence of an elemental, gathering its strength.

Raising her arms, Aisling brought the energy into a ball of electricity, resting it in her cupped hands. Sensing the Electricity Elemental's desire to escape, she tossed it into the air, and it vanished in a sparkle of light. Blinking away the bright spots in her eyes, Aisling brushed a strand of dark hair out of her face, wondering how she had absorbed a bolt of lightning.

The queen's eyes were full of surprise. She took a step back, clutched her staff and exclaimed, "Ní chreidim é!"

Genevieve had been too astonished to react, but now she raised her shotgun and pointed it at the queen.

"No!" shouted Aisling. "Put that away, Gen."

Genevieve didn't lower the shotgun. "In case you haven't noticed, Aisling, she just tried to kill you."

"I'm perfectly fine," said Aisling. She softened her voice, "Please put it down."

Genevieve lowered her weapon.

Queen Annan stumbled and fell down, like a leaf falling out of a tree. The wound in her chest had begun to bleed, turning her bandage red.

Aisling looked down at the queen. "Why have you lost your fear of the curse protecting me?"

Queen Annan closed her eyes. Her words were bitter. "Because it doesn't matter anymore—we're all lost without the Dream Crystal. Thought creates reality. Ith will soon gain a mastery over all three of our worlds."

Two soldiers came forward cautiously and helped the queen to her feet.

The idea of Ith using the Dream Crystal to control the source of thoughts and ideas would have been terrifying if she had believed it to be true, but Aisling refused to accept it. She put Erin's locket around her neck. "I'm going back for her," she whispered.

"Are you crazy?" asked Genevieve. "That's the wackiest idea I've ever heard."

"They've taken Erin," said Aisling. "I won't let them enslave her again."

"I can't allow it," said the queen. With a glance at the soldiers, she motioned to the Mirror of Eternity. "Destroy it."

"No, wait!"

Queen Annan raised a hand and the soldiers halted.

Aisling glanced into Genevieve's eyes. "It's true. I've made some mistakes here, but I can still fix them." She turned towards the queen and said, "I'll bring it back—I'll bring the Dream Crystal back."

"That isn't possible," said Annan. "Ith will slay you as soon as you cross over."

Aisling tilted her head, a grim smile on her lips. "What a strange thing to say for someone who just tried to kill me."

The queen waved towards the gateway. "Go then."

Genevieve shouted, "No, Aisling!"

Aisling looked into her best friend's blue eyes, a coy smile on her lips. "Take care of Eileen for me, will you?"

Before Genevieve could stop her, Aisling ran up the stairs to the organ loft.

The Mirror of Eternity stood over six feet tall, whispering poison. She looked into her own reflection, wondering how a mirror could have become a gateway to the Land of Shadows. An empty flask of black unicorn blood sat on the bench in front of the pipe organ, grim evidence of the evil wrought by Nel.

"No," she whispered. "Ith is the cause of all this trouble."

Silver engravings set into the frame bore leaves and flowers, but beneath the pretty foliage, a grim landscape of bones and skulls looked out. It reminded her of something...

There was a shout from below, and Aisling heard Genevieve running up the staircase. "No, my friend, you can't follow me this time," she murmured.

Looking into the mirror, she whispered, "I choose freedom."

Aisling stepped into the Mirror of Eternity.

* * *

The touch of it was like an erotic dream. Intensely pleasurable, Aisling's entire body tingled in ecstasy. At the same time, a cold breeze spread icy tendrils over her figure, gently caressing, but freezing her soul. It was daring and forbidden all at once, like skinny dipping in a cool river in front of a crowd. Aisling closed her eyes and smiled at the sensations spreading over her body. The world whirled around, and she felt herself falling. A moment later, the sensation changed, and she realized that she was flying. Aisling opened her eyes as she swept down onto the ground, swirling in exquisite ecstasy.

Aisling looked down and noticed that her clothes had changed. Now she wore a pair of shiny black leggings and her silk Nehru shirt had changed from white to black, but the golden dragons embroidered on it had remained unchanged. Her father's sword hung from a golden belt at her waist, and she wore a pair of black patent leather boots laced up the front. Almost forgotten, her white wings, edged in silver, were extended from her back.

Inhaling the cool air around her, Aisling looked around and found that she was standing in a cavern, lit from behind. Glancing over her shoulder, she saw a scintillating wall of glass set into a silver frame. Although brilliant light came out of it, the surface of the glass was lustrous black.

With an earsplitting crash, the glass shattered. Aisling was blasted onto her back with a violent force. Angry whispers pooled in the darkness around her and mingled with the tinkling sounds of broken glass falling.

Sitting up on her elbows, Aisling listened. Like a tide washing away, the whispering departed. The chamber had become a solitary prison. All hope of Aisling's return to the Land of Dreams had vanished with the broken mirror. The queen, perhaps glad to be rid of her, had destroyed the gateway.

The cave filled up with silence.

Standing up, Aisling said, "Solas."

A globe of light appeared, just over her head. Brushing herself off, Aisling found that the chamber was made out of a curtain of limestone columns that formed a cage. Through openings between the pillars, she could see a dark cavern. To one side, there was an opening that twisted through the earth, as if a giant snake had slithered out of the prison where she stood.

Moving forward, Aisling crept through the passage, which went down,

down, into the earth. Aisling thought better of drawing her sword, realizing that she would need her hands free in case she came across a slippery patch of rock or a sudden chasm. Dripping water came from the roof, and everything was wet. After awhile she became disoriented in the darkness, and she lost track of time.

After walking down a long stretch of tunnel, she began to hear the sounds of flowing water, forever calling her onwards. Like the Shadow People, it whispered, drawing her close. Before long, she encountered the underground river, which flowed out of a wide hole in the rock face. The water ran alongside the passage for over a mile, always the sound of it calling, whispering, luring. Aisling began to derive pleasure from the sound of it. The melody caressed the senses and she found it strangely alluring.

The path went down into the river and across it, but Aisling also found another passage, smaller, rising up and away. Too modest to walk upright in, she realized that she would have to crawl if she chose the upward path. A moment of decision halted her, but the river continued to whisper, seductively luring her down. Her nose twitched, and she looked down at her clothes. "Too dirty, that way," she muttered.

Dizzy abandonment swept over her mind, and she plunged through the river and onto the other side. As she went down, she began to be aware of a presence, always watching, always listening—studying every movement she made. Several times she tried to catch sight of whatever it was, swiftly looking over her shoulder or twirling around, but there was no one there. The silent watcher was different from a Shadow Person, somehow—earthy, but more menacing.

A large cavern opened up before her, abruptly ending her journey. Shadowy images danced upon the huge wall of the cave. Aisling became aware of hundreds upon hundreds of people sitting in iron chairs, staring at the shadows along the wall.

Cautiously moving forward, Aisling could see that they had been bound to the chairs with chains of iron. The chairs had high backs. It was impossible for a person to see what was behind them while sitting in the chair. A beam of light passed over their heads, casting the shadows on the wall. Aisling turned around and saw a gallery, high up in the opposite side of the cave. The small passageway she had encountered probably led there.

A bright ball of light hovered in the air above the high chamber, throwing rays of light into the cavern. Several figures moved there, illuminated by the globe of light, and their shadows were thrown onto the wall in front of the viewers. It was like a theater for the damned.

"This is a strange place," she whispered.

A lock of blonde hair caught her attention. The clanking of chains moved with the girl's arm. A dreamy voice called out, "Aisling?"

Moving swiftly to the side of the chair, Aisling saw that it was her friend—one of the changelings from her fashion show. The last time she had seen her was in the field of sunflowers near Eileen's house, the day of the attack. "Maija! What are you—?"

"Aisling, it is you! Why have you come?"

Shaking her head, Aisling wasn't sure how to respond.

"I've finally found a home, Aisling," said Maija. "My family, the Ailil clan from Síd Imreas has found me."

Aisling looked down at the chains that bound her friend to the chair, but Maija didn't seem to even notice them. "Who brought you here?"

"The leader of my clan, Rhona helped me find this place." Maija shifted in her seat. "Where are you? I can't see you."

Aisling stepped in front of her friend, but Maija's eyes didn't focus on her. She was looking up, over Aisling's head, at the wall of the cavern, where shadows danced. The smile faded from Aisling's lips. "I'm getting you out of here."

Closing her eyes, Aisling let her senses travel through earth and stone. Warm, dry, stubborn rock lay hidden in the dark. At first the elemental spirit did not want to move, but with slow, consistent pressure, it finally came forth, grating and grinding softly in the cavern. Although no solid mass stood there in front of her, she could sense the Earth Elemental. She breathed in the scent of clay and salt and limestone.

Licking her lips, Aisling concentrated on the chains, imagining them dissolving, cracking, rusting away. She whispered, "Dust..." The Earth Elemental slid closer, grinding out a low rumble that echoed throughout the cavern. Voiceless, it cried out...

Steel cracked, chain dissolved into powder.

Maija stirred, but didn't make any other move to escape.

Aisling felt the presence of something moving in the darkness, approaching...

Her mind began to stagnate into boredom. She felt herself wanting to slow down. Threatening to overwhelm her, an impulsive desire appeared—to look for secret treasures, hidden in the earth, to gather gold and jewels from the rocks.

Aisling shook her head, realizing that the elemental was starting to take over her mind. She stepped back, and nearly fell over. Remembering the words of her mentors, Aisling realized that the way to de-energize an elemental was to use something inimical to it. While Marcus had taught her about fire and Rosheen had taught her about air and wind elementals, Aisling thought she understood how to detach an elemental from her psyche. At least she hoped so.

Shaking her head again, Aisling cleared her mind of all sense of practicality, responsibility, and strength. She conjured up a cup of water and poured it onto the ground, breathing deeply.

With a grumble and a rumble, the Earth Elemental sank into the stone, dissipating into the rocks. Aisling felt it recede like a stone falling into a pit.

Dark figures, holding spears and swords that glinted in the light coming from the sphere of brilliance, moved into the cavern, but no one came near Aisling. The dark figures began to go through the seated crowd, testing the chains that bound them in place.

With one eye on the figures, Aisling reached down and helped her friend to her feet. Maija was unsteady, and she resisted every move that Aisling made to help her.

Aisling whispered, "Come on, Maija! Don't you want to get out of here?"

Listless, as if another world held a tight grip on her spirit, Maija stopped struggling. It seemed that the energy it took to fight off Aisling was more than she could bear. Maija stared meekly at the wall of the cave, where shadows danced.

Aisling had to help Maija up and drag her along. Her friend finally relented, but she remained spiritless and docile. There was an opening in the far wall of the cave and she made her way to it, pulling Maija along.

Aisling couldn't shake the feeling that something—an invisible menace lurking in the darkness had followed them out of the cave...

The river flowed away and down from the chamber, accompanying them on their way out of the cavern full of chained shadows. After a time, a beam of moonlight washed into the passage ahead.

Aisling stepped outside into a wilderness of tall trees, showered with silver. The river tumbled down a steep slope in the side of a hill, cutting a swath through a forest. The globe of light flying in front of her sped up into the night's sky, as if it was glad to be free of the cave.

Maija stirred, waking from some kind of dream. She looked around, her eyes full of confusion. In a dreary voice, she asked, "Where have you brought me, Aisling?"

"I'm going to take you home, back to the Land of Dreams."

Fear slipped into Maija's face. "I can't see you—where are you?"

"I'm right here, in front of you, Maija." Aisling waved a hand in front of her face, but Maija's eyes didn't move. Aisling thought of conjuring up a bright light or a fire, but there was plenty of moonlight covering the hillside.

Maija began to shake. Backing away, she reached out, as if she was trying to touch the light. She screamed, "The world is gone!"

Stepping close and gripping her friend by the shoulders, Aisling said in a calm voice, "No, Maija. The world is right here. We're standing on a hillside by a forest." She smiled. "You have a pretty blue dress on. Moonlight is in your hair..."

"Take me back! I want to go back!"

Frowning, Aisling shook her head. "You don't know what you're saying, Maija. Come with me, I'll—"

Someone grabbed Aisling by the shoulder and wrenched her away. Aisling felt herself being thrown across the grassy slope. Tumbling, she rolled onto her feet, but her adversary was faster.

Fire rippled up the blade of a sword, and it was swiftly brought up close to her chest. Aisling made a move to draw her sword, but her enemy raised the flaming sword higher up, and advanced to press it against her throat. Aisling backed away until she bumped into a tree trunk. She could feel the heat radiating out of the point of the sword. Unable to see her foe clearly because of the fire so close to her face, Aisling thought it was a woman. Long black hair blew in the wind.

A cool voice said, "What brings you to Uaimh Fírinne?"

The heat of the fire reflected in Aisling's eyes. "Lower your sword," she demanded.

Laughing, the woman took down her sword, and the flames went out. Silver moonlight glittered off of the steel. Aisling recognized Rhona, one of the Shadow People that Ith had released from the prison within the Eternal Flame. It was hard to believe that she had been walking through the wilderness, or a cave. Nearby, Maija stood under the moon, her eyes lost in dark dreams. She was shaking.

Aisling asked, "Where did you say we are?"

Rhona tilted her head slightly. "Uaimh Fírinne—The Cave of Truth, where the Shadow People walk through the dreams of men," said Rhona. She glanced back towards the cave entrance. "You've awakened the guardian, a Shadow Witch who devours dreams."

Aisling thought of the silent watcher, lurking in the dark. The shattering of the gateway must have drawn its attention. Running a nervous hand through her hair, she said, "I followed the Shadow People through the Mirror of Eternity."

For a moment, Rhona faded into a shadow. Her eyes turned into glowing coals. "Why have you taken Maija out of the cave?"

"She's my friend. I'm taking her back, to the Land of Dreams." But Aisling's voice was full of doubt. She didn't know how to get back. Wrinkling her face, Aisling asked, "Why do you keep them chained so?"

"Whoever has walked with truth generates life. One man's truth is different from another's. We help them see one kind of reality—the dreams we project upon the wall," said Rhona. "They are full of images and miseries, loves, tragedies, griefs and sorrows."

Aisling shook her head. "What miserable madness this is!"

"Why do you say that?" said Rhona. "They're spared from the pain of suffering these things while they learn the truth of the reality we give them."

Aisling shook her head. "True suffering causes a person to change, to become a better person, and compassion towards others is a mercy, but if you're watching it from a distance, you gain nothing and you help no one," she said. "You're making them numb to the truth."

Maija called out, "Take me back, Rhona!"

"No!" Aisling drew her sword.

Fading into shadow, Maija dropped to her knees. She began to cry mournfully. "I don't know this place. Please, take me back!"

Rhona put her sword away and grasped Maija's hand to help her get to her feet. With an expression bereft of hope, Rhona said, "She's from my clan." She waved her hand towards the forest. "Go where you will, but do not trouble us again."

Aisling felt hope slipping away. There was no way ever to return to the Land of Dreams. Truly, she and Maija were both lost—sentenced to spend the rest of eternity wandering through the Land of Shadows. She glanced over her shoulder, down to a path leading into the forest. "Where does this lead?"

"Away—"

* * *

Chapter Eighteen

The Haunted Forest

Tangled trees blocked out the night, high above a dark forest. It was a place as remote as a dream lost in the echoes of eternity. Branches reached down, grabbing at her face. Tormented maledictions whispered from somewhere. A cold wind passed through the forest, spreading out icy fingers to grope and caress. The rush of air against the trees was like a wave breaking across a beach, so thunderous it was. Aisling dropped down to her knees, weary with the weight of the doom laid upon her: To wander dark pathways, forever lost in the whirlpool of infinity. A soft song followed the wind, seductive and alluring, and terrifying all at once. The Shadow Witch, wrapped in desolate dreams, was coming...

Inhaling cold air to calm down, Aisling breathed in the scent of night flowers. Opening her eyes, she saw that she was kneeling next to a tall pine tree, bathed in pale moonlight. Inkwell mushrooms grew all around her, along with the white twirls of gardenias, pink and yellow evening primrose, pale moonflowers and sweet night phlox, dripping with dew. Tangled branches covered the sky but there was still enough moonlight to see by. Glowing white and pale yellow, dozens of luminous orbs floated through the trees. They mingled with the flowers, seeming to breathe in their delicate aroma, and then moved on, as if they had not yet found what they were looking for.

Drifting through the trees, a vague, misty vapor, glowing with a pale light of its own, came into view. Aisling thought she could hear a mournful child's voice calling out. Cold surrounded the fog, and her breath began to cloud over into a white steam.

Aisling felt something being drawn out of her heart, like thin threads of fine cloth—a breath of sweet air, long forgotten—but now uncovered by the ectoplasmic mist. It was about to slip away forever, drawn into the cloud, which glowed brighter.

Aisling drew her sword. "Yah!" Shouting out a defiant protest, she swung the sword wildly through the air, slicing the misty vapor in two.

A child giggled, and the smoky cloud reformed. A pale blue tendril of mist reached out again...

A quiet rhythm of twinkling bells chimed far away, lost in the darkness. A melody, no more than a gentle sighing against the forest canopy, wafted overhead.

The child shrieked out in terror. The misty vapor whooshed away, followed by all of the orbs. Cold malice caressed the wind, and Aisling knew that she was being hunted too. The presence that she had awakened inside the Cave of Truth was approaching.

Hardening her eyes, Aisling stood up as the Shadow Witch entered the clearing. Tangled locks of black hair curled around a pale face, white with envy. Her eyes reeked with dark hatred and an unquenchable thirst. She wore a purple dress with a belt of black cloth, and silver sandals were on her feet. Wrapped about her shoulders was a cloak of utter darkness, sprinkled with stars that seemed to twinkle out from the depths of night.

The Shadow Witch sniffed the air, and turning towards Aisling, raised a white hand. She beckoned Aisling to come near. Her voice was a whisper, smooth as a cat's purr. "Faint they are, but you have them still..."

Gripping her sword, Aisling asked, "What do you speak of?"

"Dreams..." The Shadow Witch pointed a pale arm in her direction and whispered, "Give them to me!"

For an instant, Aisling was ready to give in, as if a magical force compelled her to do so, but something touched her deep inside, where white fire burned. Shaking her head, she mentally pushed away the ghostly impulse. Somehow, Aisling knew that reason would be useless against this one, so dark she was, full of savage hunger and malice. With one swift stroke, Aisling slashed out with her sword.

Whooshing through emptiness, the blade met no resistance. Moonflowers and white jasmine spilled into the air in the place where the Shadow Witch had stood. Gently, ever so gently, the flower petals drifted to the earth, to lie under a moonlit canopy, breathing in the dew of night.

Turning, Aisling fled into the gloom, pursued by the lyrical laughter of the Shadow Witch. Brambles and briars pricked and cut, and dark roots appeared out of nowhere, tripping her as she ran. Aisling could feel her heart pounding. Dark branches reached down, groping and clutching.

Breaking out of a grove of blackthorn trees, she came to a stop, listening. No one came after her through the haunted forest. Catching her breath, Aisling looked about her. A path, unnoticed at first, wound off in one direction, next to a stream of cold water. Putting her sword away, Aisling conjured up a wood cup, and kneeling down, dipped it into the water and drank deeply of it. But the chilly draft sapped her strength, draining away the last vestiges of hope within her heart. Aisling lay down by the stream and wept.

After a time, shaking, Aisling reached up to hold the cross around her neck, and she whispered a prayer. "God, look with pity upon the soul of Thy handmaid, and grant me courage against terrors and darkness and false lights, and strengthen my spirit to persist on to the end of my journey."

Through a reflection in the flowing water, Aisling saw a beam of silver moonlight shining off of her father's ring. Sitting up, she looked at the delicate tracery of silver dragons there, whose blue sapphire eyes glared back at her through a maze of Celtic knotwork. Ith had murdered her father and mother, and had taken her sister away to be a slave here in the Land of Shadows. Cold determination gave Aisling the energy to rise up again.

Shaking off fear, she began to walk down the path, wondering how long it would take to get clear of the forest. The moon marked the passage of time as she walked, and when the moonbeams were low over the trees, she came into a clearing.

A tatterdemalion cottage leaned against a magnolia tree, as if it were a crutch. White saucer-shaped flowers caught the remaining moonlight that spilled over the leaf-strewn earth. Pale smoke drifted out of a crooked chimney, spreading strange perfumes into the night.

While Aisling was considering what to do, she noticed a movement out of the corner of her eye. Turning to face the Shadow Person, she confronted a pair of red eyes in the darkness. Wind blew through the forest, a wave across a beach. Forming out of darkness, the Shadow Witch materialized, laughing.

Aisling drew her sword, but the Shadow Witch uttered a command, "Stad."

As if she had been plunged into water—or thick mud, Aisling found it difficult to move. Unable to even step forward or raise her sword into a defensive posture, Aisling stood there in the clearing, surrounded by fading moonlight.

The Shadow Witch stepped forward slowly, as if she had been wandering in the woods and had caught sight of a passing frivolity. Gently, she brushed a strand of dark hair out of Aisling's eyes. Walking behind her, she ran an icy finger along Aisling's arm and up to her wrist. Taking the sword out of Aisling's hand, the Shadow Witch looked at the weapon curiously. "How quaint," she purred. "A Fomorian weapon."

A tingling sensation ran down Aisling's spine. Fighting to move proved utterly useless, and she was unable to do anything except wait.

The Shadow Witch walked around in front of Aisling and asked, "Why won't you relinquish your dreams?"

Aisling was unable to answer.

Irritated, the Shadow Witch waved her hand. "Tá cead agat labhairt."

Still unable to move, Aisling found that she could speak. Glaring at the Shadow Witch, she said, "Because my dreams belong to me alone."

Tilting her head slightly, the Shadow Witch commanded, "Tell me your dreams."

Aisling hesitated, afraid to speak of her dreams, as if saying them aloud would doom them to utter oblivion, but a fire raged inside, forcing words into her mouth. She whispered, "To fill the world with pretty clothes, to bring forth beauty."

The Shadow Witch smiled, turned around and stepped away. "Beauty is a mighty weapon. Its magic can turn people into subservient fools," she said. "I too, seek power, but of much another sort. I wish to become beautiful and glorious—not to give it away. Your dreams will serve me well."

When the Shadow Witch raised her hand, Aisling felt a fine tendril being drawn forth, out of her heart. The sweet aroma of roses began to pervade the air. Aisling had to fight to catch her breath. Intensely sensual and exciting at once, the sensations made her dizzy. Her skin tingled with exhilaration even as she began to lose consciousness.

Abruptly, the feeling stopped. Able to breathe clearly again, Aisling blinked. Her head began to clear.

The Shadow Witch was looking off into the forest with a look of astonishment.

A child stood at the end of the path, and hunger was in her eyes. For a moment, she waited there, and then she dissolved into a white mist. The vapor drifted forward slowly, stopping only a few paces away from Aisling.

As if she wanted her words to reach far away and to remain quiet all at once, the Shadow Witch's hoarse whisper rang out: "Drust! Heulfryn!" Muttering under her breath, "Where are those Hobgoblins?"

A pair of short figures emerged from the cottage. They had sharp features, long noses, and pointy ears. They wore tunics of blue and green, embroidered in silver and gold. Moving speedily, they began to run, but the Shadow Witch waved at them. "Shh! Slowly! Bring the caighean an spioraid—be quick!"

One of the Hobgoblins, turned around and went back into the house, while the other stopped. He looked longingly at Aisling, who was still frozen in place. Moments later, the second Hobgoblin returned, carrying a golden cage almost as tall as he was. Throwing a critical gaze at his companion, he came forward cautiously, set the cage down on the ground and opened a small door with a golden key.

Returning the sword to Aisling's hand, the Shadow Witch smiled at the vaporous child, which had remained in place. Aisling sensed the child's eyes on her. She felt like a piece of candy.

In a friendly, motherly voice, the Shadow Witch said, "Hello there. What's your name?"

A child's voice emanated from the mist, "Fionna."

The Shadow Witch purred, "Are you hungry? Would you like to feel dreams again? Come with me and I'll give you something."

Hesitating for a moment only, the mist floated forward.

As if she was trying to catch a skittish animal, the Shadow Witch intoned sweet sounds, and gestured towards the cage. The child stopped just outside the golden doors, and looked longingly at Aisling.

The Shadow Witch whispered, "Go inside dear. I'll bring her along and then you and I can dine together in my house."

The mist went inside the cage and twirled into a globe of pink light.

Gently, the Shadow Witch closed the door to the cage, locking it securely behind the child. Picking up the cage, she handed it to the Hobgoblin standing by. "Heulfryn, take this one inside," she ordered.

Heulfryn picked up the golden cage and went into the house while the Shadow Witch threw a sidelong glance at Aisling. "Perhaps you might be useful for a time." She waved her hand.

Aisling felt the iron grip that was holding her body in place, release her. She was able to move. Unsure if she liked the idea of being used as bait to catch errant spirits, Aisling sheathed her sword and glanced at one of the paths leading out of the clearing.

Chuckling, the Shadow Witch said, "All paths in the forest lead here. There is no escape that way. Come inside."

Reluctantly, Aisling followed the Shadow Witch. Next to her, walked the curious Hobgoblin Drust, who kept glancing at her with poorly concealed admiration. Sensing an opportunity, she ran a hand through her hair, flirting with him. Slowing down, she spoke in a friendly tone, "I've never met a Hobgoblin before."

"Hello." Drust smiled shyly. "You're even lovelier than my mistress."

As the Shadow Witch moved out of earshot, Aisling whispered, "Tell me about this place, Drust."

Happy to hear Aisling use his name in such an intimate manner, he said, "This forest is a place where forgotten dreams linger, hunted by spirits of the dead," he said. Drust looked her up and down. "You don't belong here."

Aisling stifled a giggle, placing a hand up to her mouth. "Of course not, silly! I'm still alive," she said. A sidelong glance at Drust told her that her act was working well. "What does your mistress want with me?"

"To put you to sleep—she'll give you a potion when you go inside," he said. "Gathering your dreams, she'll spin them into her magic cloak—it's the source of her enchantment."

The Shadow Witch paused at the doorway, and Aisling noticed the cloak reflecting the stars overhead. "The Cloak of Dreams," she whispered.

A friendly fireplace dominated one wall, and the fire threw amber light into the house. A small iron cauldron was suspended over the fire from a metal hook, spilling out an inviting aroma. An oak table stood to one side of the main room of the cottage. Dried herbs hung from the sturdy beams that held up the ceiling. A large mirror stood in the adjacent room, next to a bed covered with fine linen blankets. A loom sat in the corner next to a long shelf that supported dozens of crystal chalices. These held varying amounts of liquid. Above the chalices were hung a long row of golden cages, each holding a small globe of light—spirits of children. Sad sounds came from the souls inside the cages. They were weeping.

The Shadow Witch took off her cloak and hung it up on a peg by the door. Running her hands through tangled black hair, she stepped over to the row of golden cages, admiring her collection for a moment before moving away. Heulfryn was just finishing the installation of Fionna's cage next to the others, and then he went through a doorway. Drust remained in the room, sitting down on a stool next to the fire, his eyes straying over to Aisling, as if drawn there by magic. Drust picked up a wooden spoon and began to stir the liquid brewing in the cauldron.

The Shadow Witch behaved as if Aisling were a guest, and smiling, she went over to a cupboard. Withdrawing a pair of silver goblets, and a bottle, she asked in a mirthful tone, "What do you seek, in the Land of Shadows?"

Not sure that she wanted to drop her guard so quickly, Aisling was evasive. "I'm looking for my sister."

Two goblets were now sitting on the table. "Your sister?"

Aisling nodded. "You know, we haven't been properly introduced— what's your name?"

Pouring crimson liquid into goblets, the Shadow Witch smiled. "I didn't give it."

Aisling didn't pick up the goblet. "No."

The Shadow Witch tilted her head coyly. "Spells of enchantment are made powerful with a person's true name. You didn't give yours."

Aisling smiled. "Enchantment is not my area of expertise."

Tossing a glance over at Drust, the Shadow Witch laughed. "Oh, you already have enchantments of your own, like any girl," she said. A hint of envy reflected in her eyes. "Such a pretty thing you are."

Fionna, still a little sphere of pink, began to weep. The Shadow Witch stood up and adjusted the crystal chalice underneath the cage so that it would catch the girl's tears. Appalled, Aisling watched as a steady stream of tears trickled into the vessel. The Shadow Witch cooed and purred, while raising a finger to caress the golden cage. "Don't feel bad, dear. I'm here to help you," she whispered. "Cry your dreams away..."

Unable to remain silent any longer, Aisling asked, "What are you doing?"

The Shadow Witch pursed her lips as if she wanted to kiss the child inside the cage. Taking up one of the crystal chalices, which was nearly full, and replacing it with an empty one, she walked over to the cauldron and began to pour. "I gather liquid dreams for an Elixir of Exquisite Beauty." Her eyes darted over to Aisling and she whispered, "Perhaps one day I will be as stunning as you are now."

"You're attractive, in a dreamy sort of way."

The Shadow Witch sat down across from Aisling. "Once, long ago, before I fell into shadow, I knew a girl; Helen of Sparta. A great war was fought over her beauty. You are such a girl, though I sense reluctance in you to use it so."

"You would take a fair thing and turn it into something ugly," said Aisling. "I'm not a monster."

The Shadow Witch leaned back in her chair, bearing the insult with a smile. "Come now, aren't you going to drink?"

Picking up the goblet, Aisling swirled the liquid around, gazing into it. With one swift motion, she tossed the potion into the Shadow Witch's face. "I've no interest in sleeping tonight," she said. "And I'll keep my dreams to myself."

Crimson liquid dripped from the face of the Shadow Witch, whose eyes smoldered. Getting up and walking into the bedroom, she washed the potion away. Drying her face off with a towel, indignation was in her voice. "You seem to have no qualms about manipulating my servants with your... *ugliness*."

Aisling watched her captor as she gazed in the mirror. To her astonishment, the glass returned a familiar reflection: Morrigan.

Walking back into the room where Aisling sat, the Shadow Witch said, "Who is the real monster?"

Before Aisling could reply, Heulfryn bolted into the room. "Mistress, more child spirits have come!"

Looking through a window, Aisling saw a dozen small orbs floating into the clearing.

The argument with Aisling forgotten, the Shadow Witch commanded her servants, "Quickly, bring the cages." Moving to the doorway, she gave one last look at Aisling. "You must have sweet dreams, indeed, to draw them to you so."

The Shadow Witch went out the door, followed by the two Hobgoblins. Drust gave Aisling a final look, as if he was looking at the last remnant of loveliness in the world, just before it was gone.

Aisling sighed, glancing into the gallery of trapped souls, weeping their dreams away. An idea came. Aisling licked her lips at the audacity of the thought swimming around her mind. Did she dare? With head tilted, lips pursed, she embodied the image of a girl planning mischief.

Quietly, silently, she stood up and crept to the door. Outside, the Shadow Witch was busy trapping children. A pair of cages had already found residents, pale orbs, flickering sadness. Around Heulfryn's neck, a golden key glittered. Unused to summoning charms, Aisling had to concentrate. Was it even possible? Perhaps this kind of magic was alien to her? Closing her eyes, she imagined the key resting in the palm of her hand.

A tiny flash, and she felt the weight of a quarter ounce of gold in her hand. Moving swiftly through the gallery, she unlocked all of the cages, though most of the children seemed afraid to leave their prisons. Aisling ran to the door just as she heard an angry shout outside. With an impish smile, she reached up and took down the Cloak of Dreams, forgotten for only a moment, from the peg by the doorway. With a final glance outside, she noticed that the Shadow Witch had her attention diverted elsewhere, into a forest lit with glowing orbs. Slipping outside, she crept around the magnolia tree to the other side of the house.

Glancing over her shoulder, she noticed that all of the children had followed her, a line of pretty lights. Impulsively, Aisling threw the cloak around her shoulders, hoping to hide from the lights. A world of images opened up before her eyes. Voices cried and laughed and sang in her ears.

All at once, she could smell hundreds of flowers, and a banquet of flavors touched her lips. Her skin tingled with a thousand exciting caresses, and hope lingered in a place next to her heart. Dreams lived and breathed next to her greatest desires.

Dizzy, Aisling shook her head. With one swift motion, she imagined a pathway out of the clearing. A tree lined path appeared, leading into the forest. Aisling ran down the trail, followed by a hundred lost souls, children, chasing after dreams.

* * *

The moon had fallen below the horizon, plunging the forest into night, but silver light still wandered through the trees, reflected by the dark clouds overhead. The forest floor seemed to open up before her as she moved through the woods, with a dizzying array of trails leading away in multiple directions. It was as if the Cloak of Dreams had opened up myriads of possibilities, but there were too many to comprehend. Soon, Aisling became hopelessly lost. All along the way, she was trailed by the little spheres, like wayward cats following after their master.

Aisling stepped into an open area, exhausted. A rocky outcropping dominated one side of the clearing, while pine trees growing over thick underbrush formed an impenetrable wall around the rest of the area. Three new paths led away, back into a labyrinth of trees. The spheres gathered around her. Some of them dared an approach, whispering. Sitting down on a rock, Aisling raised a hand. A silver ball of light touched down. It was icy cold, and she quickly withdrew her hand.

Aisling took off her cloak, and fingered the silky fabric. An ocean of stars twinkled out of blackness. Running a hand along the surface, she thought she could hear faint whispers—of dreams long ago, forgotten. The cold globe of silver came forth again. She had an urge to drive them all away. Waving her hand, as if she was trying to swat away an annoying bee, the spirits retreated for a moment, only to come back.

"Enough of this!"

Standing up, she found a loose thread in the fabric. She pulled it until she had a small coil, which she wrapped around her hand. With one swift motion, she threw the cloak up into the air, allowing it to unravel. The Cloak of Dreams dissolved into a thousand sparkling colors, ascending into the sky. All of the spirits went after it, like cats chasing after birds, and they flew up—away into the night. A pang of guilt touched her heart: she still might realize her dreams, but these spirits would remain unfulfilled, forever. Aisling whispered a prayer as they vanished into the darkness.

A chilly breeze swept over the forest, tossing her hair about. Wondering idly if the Shadow Witch would find her, Aisling trudged off into the maze of trees. She wandered the rest of the night away, tangled up in a sea of green shadows.

*   *   *

Just as the sun appeared over the tips of the trees, an expansive clearing opened up before her. Aisling inhaled the fresh scent of grass, mingled with the dark aroma of wildflowers. A stream trickled out of the forest and wound its way through fields of purple mimosa flowers, pink purslane, white ramsons and a host of other flowers that Aisling couldn't hope to identify. On the far side of the clearing, a trail led through a carpet of bluebells. Hummingbirds flitted over the fields, hovering now and again over a flower. "The Land of Shadows doesn't seem so bad," she murmured. A lonely memory came forth: *That's what Genevieve had said once.*

Stepping into the sunlight, Aisling looked down at her attire and wrinkled her nose. "I need to clean up," she muttered. Walking over to the stream and climbing down over wet rocks, she shed her clothes and jumped into the cold water. Kicking about in the stream, she listened to the sounds of running water, and of birds, which had come down to watch her bathe.

Emerging from the stream, Aisling conjured up a towel, along with a warm draft of air. Moments later, she was wearing a black blouse with flared sleeves, bound with a purple cloth belt, a black miniskirt, purple and black striped tights and a pair of black leather boots with buckles down the side. Her father's sword hung from a black belt over the sash. Sitting on a mossy rock, she was brushing tangles out of her hair, while listening to a black-capped chickadee, which had just landed on a nearby branch. Aisling stopped to watch the bird, while it pecked at a tree. "I'm hungry," she grumbled.

About to conjure up a meal, she felt someone watching her. Out of the corner of her eye, she noticed a Shadow Person, standing in the field of bluebells. Closing her eyes for a moment, she took a deep breath. "Here we go again," she said. Standing up, she placed her hands on her hips and looked at the Shadow Person, whose eyes burned cherry red. "How long have you been standing there?"

The Shadow Person stepped out from the cover of the trees, into the sunshine, which made him fade slightly. A menacing whisper revealed his identity, "You're such a tease," said Ith's Lieutenant. "What brings you to the Land of Shadows, Exile?"

Her brown eyes caught the red glow of his, burning with fury at the sight of him. "My business," she said, "is with the Lord of Shadows."

Ith's Lieutenant shook his head. "Go back to the Land of Dreams."

Crossing her arms, Aisling asked, "Why do you care where I go?"

Slowly, he approached, moving like a panther. Sunbeams hid his shadowy form as he came through the clearing, treading over flowers. Aisling felt his gaze, but there seemed to be a lack of hate in his red eyes. For an instant, she thought he wanted to embrace her. The effect was unsettling, and she took a step back as he came close.

A familiar aroma, lavender, patchouli, and musk, with a trace of vanilla, touched her nose. "Canlyn tells me that she shot you with my magic arrow," he said. "How disappointed she was, not to have slain you..."

The duel with Ith still troubled her thoughts. She had been one step away from stopping him from stealing the Dream Crystal, and then, pain had exploded in her side. Aisling raised a hand to touch the place where she had been pierced, but put her hand on the hilt of her sword instead. "She was a long distance away," she said. "Are you disappointed?"

He chuckled. "Not at all. My charm prevented the arrow from killing

371

you."

Aisling wondered if he was toying with her. Narrowing her eyes, she said, "I still have to repay you, for killing my parents." Swiftly, she drew her sword, but he didn't respond in kind. It was as if he didn't really care what she did to him.

His voice filled with sorrow. "I didn't kill your parents."

Their duel by the fountain was still fresh in her mind. "But you told me—"

"I lied."

Aisling lowered her sword slightly. "Why would you lie to me?"

"I was hoping you would kill me," he said. "Why did you hesitate?"

Now, her hand wavered, and she nearly lowered her weapon entirely. One of the Shadow People—Iarlugh, had said that Ith's Lieutenant enjoyed playing cruel games. "What trick is this?"

His tone was curious, even conversational—not like a mortal enemy. "It would have been your first time—killing me, or was it because you had just disarmed me and I was helpless?"

"I'm not an animal."

"You will become a rapacious beast, if you remain here in the Land of Shadows," he said. "Like me." His voice turned into cold steel. "Go back."

Aisling lowered her sword. "I can't."

His glowing, red eyes began to fade. Shadows dissolved and he began to appear before her. He wore a leather jacket with chains attached to it, black leather pants, and a gray t-shirt. Rings were on his fingers, and a silver cross hung around his neck. His black hair caught the sunlight. Beautiful, warm brown eyes, full of youthful mystery, sent a jolt of electricity through her body.

Aisling nearly dropped her sword—"Keir!"

"When I first saw you in the coffee house, a dream touched my soul. I heard voices, shadows, whispering old dreams that I had thought long dead. I found that my heart was filled with remorse, and the pain of it troubled me, propelling me upwards. I found myself wanting to shake off my sensuality, to abandon my cruel games. I wanted to become a better man, as I once had been."

His voice became distant. Stepping close, he took Aisling's hands gently into his own. Warmth tingled over her body at the touch. Her sword fell onto the grass. "An echo of a dream—a shadow, whispering into silence, was all it was, but I want you to know that it was inspired by the sight of you."

The world spun around. It was hard to catch her breath. She, too, had felt the electricity in his eyes, pooled into dreams long forgotten. A flood of loneliness threatened to spill out of the darkness, to carry her soul away, but a steady rock stood before her, anchoring the warm glow burning in her heart. It seemed like she could lose herself, forever, in those warm brown eyes.

Keir smiled. "When Lord Ith commanded me to murder you, I could not. When I learned that Ith wanted you at his side, a fire burned within my heart, and I wanted to slay you, but again, I could not. So I hoped you might kill me instead."

"That's why you attacked me by the fountain..." she whispered.

"Yes." Keir leaned down and kissed her, gently. Warm electricity melted into sweet fantasies, and mingled with the flowers growing around them. Then he pulled away. Aisling felt a desolation smothering the sunshine. He let go of her and stepped back. Reaching out, her outstretched hands met emptiness. He had faded into a Shadow Person again, though his eyes remained dark and did not glow.

"I'm sorry," he whispered.

Keir turned around and walked over a carpet of bluebells.

"Wait!"

For a moment, he continued on, but then he stopped next to a pine tree. He placed a hand on it, leaning against the tree, as if he was too weak to resist her voice. The shadow became solid once more. He stood there, with his back to her, listening.

Now that he had stopped, Aisling wasn't sure what to say. She reached up to hold the locket resting against her heart. "They've taken Erin."

Keir bowed his head. "Ith is using her to draw you to his side," he said. "You shouldn't try to help her."

Aisling looked through the trees. "Is there no end to this forest?"

Turning around, Keir chuckled. "A week from now, I will be standing in front of the tree by my fortress, eating an apple. Imagine where you will be and it will be so."

Aisling could feel her life slipping away into shadow. "Stay with me."

He shook his head. "I am a lost soul, Aisling."

Keir faded into shadow and went into the forest.

At his going, anger burned in her heart. "Go then," she whispered.

Aisling didn't know how long she stood there, gazing into the trees. But when the fire inside had cooled down, she looked around at the many paths leading out of the clearing. She shook her head in exasperation, and closing her eyes, she imagined herself standing in one of the streets of the Black City—Cathair Dhubh.

Aisling opened her eyes, and shook her head again. What kind of magic was this? She had never been able to learn Sorcery from Marcus, and so she didn't expect teleportation to work, but still... Kier's words had been as useless as a dream in the Milesian world. Aisling's eyes drifted up into the sky.

Suddenly, she laughed. "Of course, silly!"

Extending white wings, edged in silver, she took off into the air, flying out of the Haunted Forest.

* * *

For a long while Aisling flew, without any thought of where she was going. Up in the sky, she looked down at the earth, like a hawk. The wind blew through her hair, and she could feel the heat of the sun against her skin, high up over the clouds. Pulling her wings in, she let herself fall, feeling weightless in a steep descent. Extending them again, she climbed up, turned in the air, and twirled into a spin. It was exhilarating to be able to fly again. The taste of freedom swirled around her on a gentle breeze.

Late she came to the Black City, now gleaming orange with the setting sun. The fading light tingled over the ocean, blending into the water. Like a lightning storm, dark cyclones dropped out of the sky. They ignited flashes of light when a new soul fell into the Land of Shadows. A thousand Dark Faeries flew over the town like a flock of crows over a battlefield. Aisling could see them scanning the earth, hungry for the remnants of dreams from the newly fallen souls.

Aisling licked her lips with a strange anticipation, like a hunger for something long forgotten. It was like smelling chocolate for the first time. As she drew closer she could feel her heart racing with excitement.

Heels clicking against pavement, she landed in the street amid the laughter of a group of Shadow People. Continuing to walk after she landed, she retracted her white wings, and looked over at the Shadow People. One man held a group of complacent souls chained together in a line, their dull eyes echoing indifference. More Shadow People went about, gathering up people that appeared at the end of the black twisters. It was like watching someone collect a group of lost kittens.

One Shadow Person turned to look at her with glowing red eyes. As their eyes met, he materialized into solid form, and she found that he was rather attractive, with cold blue eyes and a smile on his face. She couldn't keep herself from flirting with a smile, but before he could say anything, she turned away. It felt good to tease him so.

Cathair Dhubh was a cauldron of unholy loves, and Aisling discovered that she longed to become ensnared, to fall headlong into temptation. It was like being away from home for the first time, unwatched and ungoverned by any kind of authority. There was something else too: The joy of freedom, unrestrained by conscience. She whispered to herself, "Here, anything goes."

Walking down the street, she noticed that there were signs hanging from the buildings: Gunther's Goblin Emporium; Killeen's Candles; Quillan's House of Mysteries; Draighean's Fabrics—We import spider silk from Measarthachtshee; Gobán's Armory - The finest weapons of the

Goibniu Clan; Doran's House of Exiles...

Hesitating outside a shop, Aisling read a sign: "Fina's Charm Shop: Amulets, talismans, herbal charms and magic squares." She thought of the Holly charm that Eileen had used to deflect a bolt of lightning. The queen had just tried to kill her with lightning, but she hadn't had a charm... Shaking her head, she continued on, wondering.

A Shadow Person appeared outside an Alchemist's shop, whispering invitingly as she walked by; "Come inside my friend. We have the very best potions, powders, dusts, elixirs, balms, salves, suffumigations, and constructs."

Curious, Aisling stopped and turned towards the shopkeeper. "What are suffumigations?" she asked.

Forming out of shadow, he now appeared in a finely made green tunic, and he opened the door for her. Raising a hand, an atomizer appeared and he began to pump sweet smelling aromas into the air. "Suffumigations are magic gases. I can place them inside of perfumes, and colognes, or if you like, the spell may be suspended inside a suitable container."

A wave of desire swept through her and Aisling felt an overwhelming urge to purchase something. She wondered if he had just cast a spell on her. Steadying herself, Aisling muttered a question: "Spell?"

"Whatever you like," he said. "How about a perfume that makes you irresistible to men? Not that you aren't already quite popular." He smiled. "Or I could place a Wind Elemental inside a box, so that you may talk to others from afar."

She raised her eyebrows. "A cell phone?"

"Ah, I see that you've come from the Milesian world. Yes, it works like one, but it can also—"

Aisling shook off the impulse to shop. "No thanks, I'd better be on my way."

The man faded into shadow, his eyes glowing red. "Very well, but be sure to think of me, the next time you take a drink."

Moving down the street was like walking down a gauntlet full of a hundred temptations. More than once, she had to resist purchasing some-thing. "I'm not here for that," she muttered.

Nearing the docks, Aisling recognized a familiar place: The Green Heather Pub. Music came from inside. Ships were anchored in the bay, but Aisling wasn't sure if it was a good idea to simply go to Ith's fortress. She thought it might be better to do some scouting first. Three horses stood outside. Aisling recognized the sign of a white tower stamped onto the saddlebags. She ran her hand along the leather, wondering if this was one of the shadows who had taken her sister.

Wishing she had acquired one of the magic perfumes, she glanced down at her attire, and she had an idea. Closing her eyes, she imagined herself wearing a new outfit: A scarlet mini-dress, fishnet stockings and patent leather boots. Smiling to herself, she thought how easy it would be to acquire information now.

There was a crash from inside the bar, and Aisling heard the sound of someone getting punched. A man fell backwards through the doorway. A bald man, wearing a black tunic with an emblem of a white tower on it, sauntered outside and kicked the man on the ground, who rolled onto his back, groaning. Straddling his prey, the bald man began to strike the man repeatedly. Aisling walked past, ignoring the bald man, who dropped his victim and looked up at her as she went inside.

Glancing around, she noticed a band playing a song from a stage. Most of the Shadow People were corporeal, but a few of them remained as shadows, lurking in the corners. Aisling recognized one of them. Scolaí stood at the bar, nursing a drink. A vase holding a bouquet of withered roses rested on a shelf, unloved, next to a row of bottles. Aisling walked up to the bar and ran a hand over the smooth mahogany, trying to get Keir out of her mind. The bartender, in a dark shirt and red tie, came over, his face full of shadow. "What'll you have?"

"Mint tea."

The bartender chuckled and went over to the other end of the bar. Aisling glanced at Scolaí, who was looking at her. She ran a hand through her hair and turned away. Two Shadow People, both wearing black tunics with the sign of a white tower, were beating another patron, who had fallen down to the floor.

Scolaí walked over, his face full of appreciation. "I see that you've returned."

"Yes."

"Sorry to hold you last time, but your friends didn't need any help, did they?"

Aisling remembered how he had blindsided her, appearing out of nowhere and grabbing her from behind. "I don't always mind someone holding me," she said, smiling.

The bartender returned with the tea, glancing at the fighting soldiers and muttering to himself, "Is minic a bhris béal duine a shrón."

Scolaí waited for him to leave before speaking. "Returning to the Fortress of Árainn?"

At the mention of Keir's fortress, she winced inside. "No. I'm looking for a way into Ith's fortress—what was it called?"

His voice dropped to a whisper. "Scáth Caisleán, but why would you want to go there?"

Pushing away the guilt at manipulating him so easily, she said, "I'm looking for someone, a girl with silver hair. She was taken by those bearing a symbol like theirs."

"The tower guard," he said, glancing at the two soldiers.

Out of the corner of her eye, she saw that they had taken notice of her. The bald man had also followed her inside and he positioned himself to her back. Ignoring them, she said, "Do you think Captain Fitzgerald—"

One of the soldiers tapped Scolaí on the back. "Get out."

Scolaí backed away and went out the door.

Aisling turned to the soldier. "Not very polite of you."

The second soldier said, "What kind of drink is that?"

"Mint tea."

The three laughed. One said, "Let me buy you a real drink."

"No, thank you. I prefer tea."

The first soldier said, "Now wait a minute, friend. You're not going to drink tea while I'm offering something better. That's not too friendly, is it, Ultán?"

The second soldier smiled. "No, Fial. It isn't."

Aisling wondered if it was really a good idea to have changed her clothes. She realized that it probably wouldn't have made much difference—her other outfit was almost as sexy as this one. She said, "Excuse me, please. I just came in here for a quiet drink."

"Now look, when a man offers you a drink, you're obligated to accept it. That's only *polite*," said Fial, mocking her words. "Isn't that right, Ultán?"

The bald man stepped behind the bar and retrieved a bottle, and put it on the counter. Fial leaned close. "You're a polite girl, aren't you?"

Aisling smiled, but didn't answer. These Shadow People were the haters of dreams. She wondered how many they had slain or enslaved. How many had they caused to fall into shadow?

The bald man retrieved a hand crossbow from under the counter. "You have just one minute to drink that bottle down. After that..." he smiled at the others.

She glared at him until his eyes began to burn red.

With his free hand, the bald man grabbed her on the shoulder. "I said, drink!"

Grabbing his hand and wrist, Aisling turned his wrist up in a painful hold. He dropped to his knees with a cry. "Aaw!"

Pulling him up to his feet, Aisling threw him back against the wall and he fell to the ground. The music stopped and everyone in the bar looked on.

Fial tried to punch her, but she caught his wrist and turned it up forcing him onto his knees. Ultán tried to strike her twice. Not letting go of Fial, Aisling blocked the blows with her free arm and kicked Ultán in the chest. He fell backwards onto a table.

379

The bald man got to his feet, raising the crossbow.

Aisling let go of Fial and with one swift motion, drew her sword and slashed out at the bald man, who screamed and faded away. Fial and Ultán drew swords, but she was too quick. With a single blow, she had killed them both. They vanished before they hit the floor.

Feeling a rush of power, Aisling smiled. She wasn't sure which she had enjoyed more: Teasing and controlling Scolaí, or destroying the others who had gotten in her way. She glared at the bouquet of withered roses, as if they had accused her of infidelity. "I won't play your games anymore, Keir," she whispered. "I'm getting my sister and then we're out of this place."

Something dark inside hoped that more of them would get in her way.

* * *

Chapter Nineteen

The Hat Man

Night had come again, blanketing the city in eternal gloom. Cold moonlight swept over the streets like a slow searchlight, drifting with the clouds. The streets of Cathair Dhubh were full of many kinds of music, all jumbled together in the darkness. Every door promised another kind of sensual delight, inviting, enchanting, and beguiling all at once.

Aisling stepped outside the Green Heather Pub, inhaling the chilly air—and freedom. Sheathing her sword, she glanced up and down the street. Metallic orbs drifted to and fro, into doorways and over the water. Occasionally, a winged faerie would drop out of the sky, blending into the darkness as they abandoned corporeal form. Some of them turned to gaze at her with red-glowing eyes. Laughter drifted down from someplace higher up, tumbling out of a window. As always in the Land of Shadows, a sense of being watched predominated.

A silent voice whispered, "Don't let them find me."

A caress curled around her ankles. Tiny bells tinkled. Looking down, Aisling saw a shadow, in the form of a cat, encircling her legs. A cold purr wound up her legs, but its touch made her tremble. She took a step back. No more than a shadow, the cat faded away. A pair of small red eyes remained, suspended in midair, looking up.

A voice came from one side, "Oh, fiddle! Where is that cat?"

Looking down the street, Aisling saw a pair of Shadow People, one with a familiar voice, calling out, "Vailintín! Here, kitty, kitty!"

Aisling looked down but the cat wasn't there any longer. She heard a voice from somewhere, *Oh, please! I never get out!*

A tiny flash of blue and gold came from a horse chestnut tree across the street. Aisling noticed a pair of glowing-red eyes peering out of the leaves from a branch.

Laughter. Another voice, more familiar, came from the other Shadow Person. "I can't imagine why you choose to bring your cat along on a shopping trip."

Giggling, the other said, "I like to see how long Gordon will carry him around—he's always acting so tough. It's fun to make him hold my kitty, especially in front of his friends."

Aisling approached the two Shadow People. "Aoife?"

One of the figures took on corporeal form, materializing out of the blackness. It was indeed her friend, fallen so long ago, though her red hair was longer than Aisling had remembered. Aoife wore a pink dress with a white leather jacket, cream-colored tights and pink shoes with diamonds. A small purse with a golden chain hung from her shoulder. "Aisling!"

The second figure materialized. It was Maire, wearing a gray tunic, black tights and sandals. Tilting her head so that her long blonde hair fell into her eyes, she said, "Come to join us, have you?"

Unsure whether to smile or draw her sword, Aisling raised her eyebrows. "Hello. I saw a cat, in that tree over there."

Aoife went over to the horse chestnut tree and began calling up into the branches. "Vailintín! Come down from there!"

Chuckling, Maire walked over to Aisling and handed her a golden brooch. "Pin this on your dress," she whispered. Then she turned around, raised a hand and whistled.

Aisling noticed that there had been dark forms moving through the streets, almost invisible in the gloom. One of them slowed down and materialized out of shadow. Six black horses drew a coach. The driver was headless, but she sensed his attention on her. The coachman reminded Aisling of the dark faerie that had whisked Genevieve away from the coffee house on Halloween.

Aoife returned with the shadow cat in her arms. "Oh good, you've called a taxi."

Another disembodied voice hissed at Aisling: *Traitor.*

"Hush Vailintín!" said Aoife. "Why don't you come and stay with me, Aisling?"

Maire whispered, "Don't worry, the Dullahan won't harm you if you wear that pin—they're afraid of gold."

Cautiously boarding the coach, Aisling sat down across from Maire, and from Aoife, who was running her hand along the shadow in her lap. A pair of glowing-red eyes glanced in her direction, and Aisling thought she saw a tail twitching.

Maire called up to the driver, "13 Angus Drive."

"I absolutely love the attire," said Aoife. "Sexy!"

Aisling crossed her legs, but the gesture only made her more uncomfortable. She looked outside at the row of nightclubs they were passing by. "Quite a lot of bars..."

"We do love to party!" said Aoife. "That's all anyone does here, aside from dueling."

The steady drone of the coach began to lull Aisling to sleep. With some difficulty, she managed to fight off the urge to let herself drift away into dreams, if dreams were possible in the Land of Shadows.

As they pulled into a circular driveway by a large house, Aoife said, "You look exhausted, Aisling."

Aisling gave a faint smile. "I've never had a finer day."

Through an arched door of carved oak, they made their way into a

Tudor-styled house, made of brick, with a gabled roof. The entry foyer had openings to either side, with a large sitting room to the right, dominated by a huge fireplace, and a formal dining hall to the left. A staircase led upstairs, with paintings hanging upon the wall.

A bare-chested man, wearing dark pants and a wide red belt of cloth, greeted them as they entered the house. A ring of steel, stamped with a Maltese cross, went round his neck. A small ring was attached to the front of the collar and a lock secured it in the back. "Good evening, mistress."

"Hello, Lonán," said Aoife, dropping her shadow cat onto the floor, to the tinkle of tiny bells. "Kindly prepare rooms upstairs for my two guests, and tell Jago to bring dinner into the dining room."

Lonán bowed and faded into shadow.

As they moved into the sitting room, a chime sounded.

Reaching into her purse, Aoife withdrew a cell phone, glanced at who was calling and then answered it in a friendly tone, "Hi, Sean."

Unused to seeing a cell phone in the hands of a fairy, Aisling tried not to listen to the conversation, which seemed rather intimate. She sat down on a leather couch, crossed her legs and looked out of the large window, upon a garden.

Night blossoms began to open up: Moon Frolics and Night Gladiolus, White Bleeding Heart blossoms and Moonflowers. Moths darted about, and bats dropped down out of the air, too. Dimly, she could see Gnomes creeping through the garden, carrying atomizers. Small globes of light floated by, seemingly attracted to the fragrance of the garden, and then—whoosh!—One of the gnomes would spray something into the air. Engulfed in a gray cloud, the lights would blink and splutter and then go out, dropping onto the earth.

After Aoife hung up, Maire asked, in a voice full of amusement, "Your phone is always ringing, Aoife. How many boyfriends do you have, anyway?"

"I can't help it if men love me," said Aoife. "Besides, I like it when they buy me things—and there are so many things to buy!"

"I just don't see why you seem to think you need to sleep with every man in Tír na nAislingí Dearmadta," grumbled Maire. "Don't your servants keep you satisfied?"

A bland expression made its way into Aoife's face. "They have begun to bore me. Perhaps I should go with you when you return to Meadhar Grá. There are so many new men there, to entice, since the fall..."

"My clansmen aren't so easily distracted." Maire leaned towards Aisling and in a mock whisper, added, "Unlike you and me, she doesn't believe in love."

"I love," protested Aoife. "I love to love. I'm in love with loving! To love and then to be beloved, is sweet to me." She threw a sidelong glance at Aisling. "Why not take a few of my servants to bed with you, Aisling? They can be quite entertaining."

For a moment, Aisling considered the idea, but then she remembered the steel collars. She shook her head. "I think sleep will be enough for me." Aisling bit her lip, but couldn't resist asking. "Why do you keep slaves, Aoife?"

"Fettered with the joyful bonds of desire, they serve me," said Aoife. "Without their servitude, they would suffer the burning pains of jealousy. They'd be full of suspicions, fears, and angers." Leaning forward, Aoife whispered conspiratorially. "Sometimes, I let them quarrel over me. It's quite fun."

For a moment, Aisling tried to contain her shock, but then let it slip out, shaking her head. "You've changed, Aoife..."

"So have you," retorted Aoife, "or you wouldn't be here." She laughed. "Come on, admit it: What's more beautiful than an attractive woman in sexy clothes? Nothing is more powerful."

Aisling frowned, sensing something wrong with that statement.

Maire interrupted her thoughts. "Have you seen Keir?"

Crossing her arms, Aisling debated how to answer.

"Come now, after all the trouble I went through, using an illusion to appear as Marcus, while I was in Na Teach Cúirtéis," said Maire. "Would you have come here, if the queen wasn't trying to kill you?"

"What do you care about my relationship with Keir?"

"He is... infatuated with you, Aisling," said Maire.

"He told me to go home," she whispered.

A stunned silence filled the sitting room, punctuated by the steady clicking of a clock on the mantelpiece. Aoife and Maire exchanged glances and then Aoife said, "You just let him walk away?"

"What choice did I have?"

To her surprise, Aoife and Maire broke out in laughter.

Aisling simmered in silence.

"Enchantment," said Maire, "is all about sex, power and control. You have to use his passion against him. Anyone that dares to dream is easy to dominate."

"As I've said to others," said Aisling, "I'm not that kind of person."

At that moment, another man, also bare-chested, came into the sitting room. "Dinner is ready, mistress."

"Thank you, Jago." Aoife stood up and motioned for them to go into the dining room. An intoxicating blend of roast beef, potatoes, and cabbage struck Aisling's senses. Not realizing how hungry she was, she began to eat, forgetting her troubles. The night wore on, and Aisling soon found herself resting in an upstairs bed, dreaming, while the rest of the world lay barren.

*   *   *

Bird songs drifted in through the window. Aisling awoke and found herself staring into a pair of red eyes. A small shadow lay next to her on the bed. "Meow!"

Sitting up in bed, Aisling reached out, paused only a moment, and then stroked Aoife's cat. His fur was icy cold to the touch, but he purred nonetheless. He wore a collar, with a bell attached to it. A voice appeared inside her mind: *You should have left me alone in that tree. She never lets me outside.*

"I'm sorry, Vailintín."

The shadow cat—no more than a stain of black against white linen,

386

stood up and stretched. Aisling got up and walked over to the shower. Removing her white gown, she stepped inside and washed off the stain of hopelessness. It was hard to believe that she was in the Land of Shadows—everything seemed like it was in the Land of Dreams, except for—everything! Drying off, she conjured up a pair of black leather leggings, a white peasant blouse, a purple cloth belt and ankle boots that zipped up the front, along with a short black leather jacket. Fastening her father's sword onto a leather belt, she smiled. "I must look like my sister now."

Vailintín meowed while she was brushing her hair. *Hurry up.*

Still not used to the idea of a telepathic kitty, she continued to brush her hair. "Why?"

They're coming.

"They?"

The Tower Guard, thought Vailintín. *They're here to arrest you.*

Still brushing her hair, Aisling grumbled aloud. "What, before breakfast?"

Vailintín jumped up onto the nightstand and sat down in front of the mirror. His eyes were radiating crimson light, he flicked his tail in annoyance.

Taking a deep breath, Aisling paused to look at her reflection. They were grooming her to be a proud tyrant over those that dared to dream. Was beauty really the greatest source of power? But why would Maire help Keir, if her allegiance was to Ith? "I'm never going to get these tangles out," she complained. Putting the brush down next to Vailintín, she asked, "How do you know all this?"

I'm lucky.

There was a hard knock on the bedroom door.

Vailintín faded away entirely, except for his glowing eyes, which remained to glare at her with impatience.

Another knock came, louder this time. "Open up in the name of Ith, the Lord of Shadows!"

Aisling reached out to pet Vailintín, who materialized, as a shadow,

387

to accommodate her. Scratching the cat behind the ears, she whispered, "Give Aoife my thanks for letting me stay here, and say goodbye for me, will you?"

Yes.

The door crashed open and Vailintín vanished, the bells on his collar tinkling.

*   *   *

White sunshine bled through a window high up in the stone wall, scattering the shadows into the corners of the prison cell. Cold iron lay against Aisling's neck, and she could feel the weight of the chain dangling from the ring attached to the collar. As they had fastened it around her neck at Aoife's house, she had noticed that the collar was stamped with the symbol of a Maltese Cross. "The mark of a slave," she muttered.

A choir of voices—distant, no more than a quiet murmur—rang out in her mind. Aisling gasped at the beauty and majesty and power of the music, but it faded away. She found herself wondering about it. She resisted an impulse to shake her head, not wanting to disturb the echo of music, but it slipped away into silence.

Unnoticed until now, a shadow stood motionless in the adjacent cell, silhouetted by the sunlight. It was a girl, gazing out of the barred window of her own prison. Far off, the ocean sighed sadness.

At the sight of the sea, memories of Aisling's recent voyage bobbed up and down, making her stomach churn. "Not much to see there," said Aisling.

The shadow, whose nose, silhouetted against the light, looked familiar, turned away. Chains clinked slightly at the motion, like a slap in the face, demanding silence.

Aisling bit her lip. Although they had placed a bag over her head, she knew she had been on a ship, had been carried down a gangplank, walked and walked, up a steep hill, down into an echoing courtyard, through a maze of passages and up a circular stairway. Her captors had removed the black covering from her head moments after they had fed a chain through the ring attached to her steel collar. The door screeched shut. Aisling had remained silent until they were gone.

Dropping to her knees, Aisling closed her eyes against the darkness. It was hard to resist an urge to cry away what little hope she had left. She wondered at the title Keir had given her: Exile. But what had she returned to?

Sitting onto the stone floor, she looked up at her dark companion. "What is the name of this place?"

The shadow continued to gaze outside at the ocean, with her back turned to Aisling, silent.

Aisling grasped the chain which bound her to the wall of the cell. There was something strange—earthy, about the metal. Thoughts called out from the steel...

The shadow turned her head. A whisper: "Why have you come here?"

Letting go of the chain, which settled to the floor, clinking, Aisling brought her hand up to her sister's locket. It lay against the cross necklace she wore. "No one deserves to live as a slave..."

An angry hiss came from the shadow, and she turned away from the window, moving into the darkness and disappearing altogether. The silence began to overflow with gentle sobbing.

Aisling stood up and walked over to the bars separating the two cells. Her hands grasped cold steel. The touch sent a chill up her arms. "Are you alright?"

"Leave me alone!'

"What—"

A shout, "You never should have come for me!"

Aisling gasped. She thought she had been speaking to a Shadow Person. "Erin?"

"I was doing alright, before you came!"

"You were a slave."

"I *am* a slave."

"I'm here, Erin. I've come to take you home."

"I have no home," Erin's voice became softer. "Not anymore."

"Let me take you away," whispered Aisling.

Silence.

Her fists clenched around the steel bars. Aisling began to burn. Slowly, she removed the locket from around her neck. "I suppose I should return this." She threw the necklace at Erin and turned away, dragging the chain which bound her to the wall. She sat down in a pool of sunlight and hugged her knees in silence.

After a moment, there was a tiny click, as Erin opened the locket and held it up. The photograph of her mother inside the locket caught the light.

Aisling whispered, "Every time they look at me—" Cold memories came flooding back. "They don't even want me around! Fintan told me that they're under an enchantment—they think I'm their daughter, but they *know*. They can sense I don't belong there."

Erin brushed a strand of silver hair out of her face.

"I'm sorry, Erin," Aisling said, "but their pain is greater than yours."

"Is it?"

Aisling looked through the barred window, into an ocean of blue.

Like a whisper, a chorus of enchanting voices sang out from somewhere distant. Aisling found herself straining to hear the music, but it drifted away as the sun began to go down.

Calmer now, Erin smiled. "I can't believe you let them capture you."

Forgetting the music, Aisling raised her eyebrows. "To tell you the truth, I couldn't think of another way to get inside this place."

"It's called, 'Scáth Caisleán'—the Fortress of Shadow." Standing up, Erin stepped into the setting sun and looked outside. "There is a Dark Sídhe nearby called, 'Brugh na Bás,' of the clan of Brian. Their ruler is Bryce."

A tall blonde man wearing a tuxedo came to mind. His eyes, full of cold indifference, had once looked on while Keir had kicked her in the head. The promise of meeting him again wasn't very inviting.

Aisling took the chain up into her hands, feeling the cold steel against her skin. Something stirred within the metal, like a stream of water rushing by. Biting her lip, she closed her eyes, reaching out with her mind, in search of an Earth Elemental. Through rock and earth, Aisling let her mind wander, but the entity within the chains held her back. Blood and steel, bound together long ago, lay in the palm of her hand. She opened her eyes. "A spirit of some kind has been trapped here, inside the metal," she said. "I can't break these chains."

"You faeries are too dependent on magic," Erin huffed. "A fine rescue this is!"

Holding back an angry remark, Aisling bit her lip.

Once more, faint music rustled against the walls of her mind. The choir of voices returned, calling out, inviting.

Erin began to say something, but Aisling interrupted. "Shh! Do you hear that?"

"I don't hear anything," said Erin, glancing outside, "except for the call of the ocean and the birds above it."

Rising in power and majesty, the voices were still very faint. As Aisling was listening, the choir was drowned out by the steady march of boots, approaching. Shadows moved outside their cells. She heard clanking keys, and the door to her cell opened, screeching. Strong hands grabbed her as others detached the chain from the wall. The guards dragged the two of them outside of their cells, into the stone hallway.

She heard Erin shout an angry protest, and Aisling smiled at her sister's defiance. "I see you're not entirely ready to surrender," she said.

Erin returned her smile.

A painful slap against Aisling's face brought her attention around to the Shadow Person in front of her. He was the one that brought her here from Aoife's house. In a voice, cold with menace he whispered, "Silence, Exile!"

He glanced at the other guards, "Bring them."

Turning around, he marched off down the corridor. They were pulled along at a swift pace, to the steady marching of boots against stone. They turned down a new hallway which, if Aisling hadn't been a prisoner, would have filled her with awe.

Lined in black marble, streaked with white, it was adorned with exquisite artwork, and embellished with gold. A line of ornate benches, black and gold, stood to either side next to a line of statues. Overhead, the curved hallway was hung with crystal chandeliers and painted with fine art. A long line of candles burned from gold mountings along the walls. Candles also burned from the chandeliers, rippling light against the black stone floor.

At the end of the hallway, they came to a grand hall with a wide marble stairway. A remnant of sunlight fell through windows high up in the walls. Aisling noticed that the floor in front of the stairway was covered with finely drawn symbols. As they were brought to a halt in front of the doors, Erin said in a quiet voice, "Aisling, be careful when you're speaking to Ith!"

"What do you mean?"

"They say his words have the power to control the mind and ensnare the senses," Erin whispered. "It's his greatest weapon."

The guard standing next to Erin struck her in the face. "Keep silent!"

Aisling had to restrain her temper, and she caught Erin's hot gaze, hoping her sister would also remain calm. The leader planted his spear on the floor in front of him, and he began to whisper arcane words in an ancient tongue. The symbols glittered for an instant and then went dark.

Aisling felt herself being yanked up the wide staircase. At the top, lay a huge set of doors made of black marble. A symbol of a tower, made from gold, was etched into the stone. A pair of shadowy guards stood at either side, nearly invisible against the black stone walls.

Breathless with anticipation, Aisling sensed a power like a raging fire behind the massive doors. Strangely enthralling, she felt her heart beating rapidly. It was as if she was about to greet the most desirable man in the world. She couldn't wait for them to open the doors. Shaking her head, she wondered if the enchantments of Ith were already affecting her.

Aisling stepped into a grand throne room. Made of black marble, a line of archways encircled the oval chamber, creating a courtyard with a domed roof sixty feet over her head. Greek pillars stood on top of the archways, encircling the hall with majesty and awe. More a temple than a throne room, the magnificent chamber was lit with fading sunlight and fires burning from a pair of braziers flanking a throne of gold, to the right of the entrance. Facing the throne, beyond an archway open to the outside, an arched stone bridge led up to a black tower, surmounted by a plume of dark smoke. Gentle music descended from the tower, barely audible against the wind.

No more than a faint apparition, the Lord of Shadows stood in the center of the throne room, beyond a tall archway carved with the images of proud angels. His hands rested upon his cane, and he was gazing up at the tower.

As the soldiers brought them into his presence, the Shadow Person holding Aisling tried to force her to kneel down, but she threw him onto the ground. To her surprise, Erin knelt down submissively.

Aisling narrowed her eyes. "You once told me that slaves choose their own fate. So how can you accept this?"

"There's no escape from this place," whispered Erin.

"Fear is the only shadow here," she said.

The soldier got up and pointed his spear at Aisling's chest, barking out a command. "Bow down to the Lord of Shadows!"

Aisling raised her eyebrows at the Shadow Person, refusing to submit.

Ith removed his gaze from the tower outside and as he turned, his eyes ignited into hot coals. Slowly, he began to walk forward, his cane clicking across the marble floor, until he was only a few paces away. Aisling breathed in the aroma of mandarin, lotus flowers, musk, and dark violet. Ith glanced at the guard. "What is your name, soldier?"

Lowering the spear, the shadow stepped back a pace. "I am Felic, Lord."

"Where is Keir, my Lieutenant?"

"He remains at the Fortress of Árainn, Lord, with the Firbolg King."

Ith raised his cane and caught the chain attached to Aisling's collar.

His voice dropped to a whisper. "And why does she wear the collar of a slave?"

"Lord, she murdered three soldiers of the tower guard!"

Like a snake striking out, Ith turned swiftly, and swept out with his cane. There was a flash of light and a clap of thunder. Blue lightning struck the soldier, who flashed away into darkness, screaming as he died. The rest of the guards stood motionless, transfixed. Ith glared at them. "Leave us!"

Quickly, the soldiers retreated out the door from whence they came.

Ith moved behind Aisling. She felt an exquisite touch on her neck, cold and inviting. Pleasurable sensations washed over her body, which tingled with excitement. Aisling caught her breath, closing her eyes involuntarily. The weight of the collar was lifted and she opened her eyes to see it tossed onto the ground, along with the chain, clinking.

Walking a few paces away, Ith turned to face Aisling once more. He raised his Victorian top hat in greeting. The shadows engulfing his body faded, and he materialized into a darkly handsome man, just as he placed his hat back onto his head. He wore a black suit and a white pair of gloves. Fire illuminated the side of his face. "My apologies," he said.

Aisling glanced down at Erin. "What about her?"

Smiling thinly, Ith looked down at Erin. "But of course." With a motion of his cane, he whispered, "Saoraim thú."

The collar around Erin's neck opened and fell off. She got to her feet, but she didn't raise her eyes from the floor. Aisling noticed that her sister was trembling. Uncertainty covered Erin's face. Aisling had seen the same look in King Artrach's eyes. He too, was enslaved by doubt.

Ith waved his cane, and a formal dining table appeared across the hall. Golden candlesticks held up a line of white candles, and their sumptuous scent mingled with the aroma of a bouquet of roses in alabaster vases. A set of crystal goblets stood by a silver carafe. Ith walked into the room. "Magic has become so easy for my subjects, since the end of the war," he said. "Some of them have even begun to fly."

Aisling went into the throne room, followed by Erin. As she approached the table, Ith picked up the carafe and began to pour scarlet wine into crystal. Ith handed a goblet to Erin, who took it silently. As he moved to pick up the carafe again, Aisling stepped closer, and gently took his cane out of his other hand. "But you're having trouble using the Dream Crystal," she said.

Ith's smile was unresponsive. Picking up both carafe and goblet, he poured a glass for Aisling and held it out.

Taking the crystal goblet, Aisling turned her back to him and she walked towards the golden throne, twirling the cane in her other hand like a cat twitching her tail. She heard Erin gasp as she took a seat on the throne. Aisling crossed her legs, rested the cane in her lap and looked outside at the tower before taking a sip. Full-bodied, its supple flavor prickled slightly against her tongue. Generous warmth spread through her body at the taste, and she found herself thinking of more sensual delights.

Ith poured a glass for himself and turned away from her, returning his gaze to the tower once again. "I was once a man of dreams," he said. "Breoghan, my father, was the king of Iberia. He erected a tower such as this, overlooking the ocean. There, he placed sentinels to watch for invaders. One night, as I stood in that tower watching the sun fall into the sea, I saw a shadow of an island, bathed in sparkling green. The island began to whisper to me in my dreams, and the druid Caicher prophesied that my people would rule the land of emerald shadows one day."

"Queen Annan told me that you brought dangerous ideas with you when you came," she said, "about unrestrained freedom and pride, which leads to cruelty and tyranny over others."

"*Gentle* Annie," snapped Ith, "was not the queen of the Tuatha Dé Danaan when I arrived." His face faded into shadow, and his eyes burned for an instant before he returned to solid form. "Three kings they had: Mac Cuill, Mac Cecht, and Mac Greine. Perceiving me as a threat to their power, they sent warriors after me when I left their hall at Ailech Neid, and they tried to slay me on the plain of Mag Itha. Wounded, I returned to my ship, bleeding out my dreams of friendship with a dishonorable people.

While on my ship, darkness began to surround me, and I found myself here in this land."

So strange to hear a tale of treachery from the one who murdered her parents, Aisling narrowed her eyes and looked away. But a lonely wall seemed to slip away from Ith as he spoke. She remembered his desolate eyes, full of empty sorrow, and the deep lake of loneliness surrounding him. Music came down from the tower, a beautiful choir of voices, chanting a melody of sadness.

Ith whispered, as if he feared her response, "I shall make you a queen, Aisling."

Stunned, Aisling turned to look at him, wondering if she had heard his words correctly. She put the crystal goblet down on a table by the throne. "What did you say?"

At that moment, an exquisite voice began to sing from the tower. More beautiful than any other song she could remember, the melody was a breath of hope and love and light. With a choir of angels, the voice sang out, familiar at last. Aisling stood, and looked up at the tower. "Trista!"

"Angels sing from the Dream Crystal." Ith turned to face Aisling. "You hear the music too."

A fire ignited inside Aisling, and she threw his cane onto the floor. Outside, the wind began to rise, causing the fires in the room to flicker.

Chuckling, Ith turned around and walked over to the end of the table, where a sword lay, next to a vase of flowers, unnoticed. As he picked it up, red sunlight glinted off the blade. It was her father's sword. "A fine weapon, don't you think?" he said. "Did you know that the Fomorians were conquered by the Firbolg King, Eochaid Mac Eirc? He is a servant of mine. I've given him the town of Sídh ar Saoirse and the Fortress of Árainn."

At the sight of Ith holding her father's sword, Aisling fumed. "Put that down," she demanded.

Ith threw the sword down onto the floor, next to his cane. Reaching over to the table once again, he withdrew a Celtic Longsword, which had lain next to her father's sword. "I, too, have an enchanted weapon," he said, "a newer model, but just as effective."

Aisling felt her father's ring tingle against her finger. Inhaling cool air, she felt the wind rising into a whirlwind outside. Walking calmly up to her sword, she picked it up and raised it in a salute.

Ith took off his black top hat and placed it on the table. "Tell me, what's wrong with freedom?" he asked.

With a glance at Erin, who had gotten to her feet, Aisling said, "Not everyone is free in your world."

"Not all souls are equal, Aisling," said Ith. "But everyone in the Land of Shadows is free to pursue their own destiny."

"You just want people to follow their dreams because you know they'll fall into shadow, out of pride," said Aisling. "You're just looking for more people to dominate."

Ith smiled. "Thralls are in such great demand in my realm."

Air Elementals swirled around just outside. Aisling caught one, inhaling it like a breath of clean air, and spun around into an attack, slashing at Ith, who retreated. Aisling lunged and slashed out several times, while Ith continued to back up through the black marble archway, onto the bridge.

Aisling paused at the arch, breathing in the fury on the wind.

Ith lowered his sword. "Why do you resist me?"

"I stand against you because the Shadow People are the haters of dreams," said Aisling, "and because *you* seek power over those that dare to dream."

Ith leapt forward, aiming a slash at her leg and then delivering an overhead slash.

Aisling parried the strikes, but did not retreat back inside the throne room.

Ith slashed out again, and then tried a lunge, aimed at her chest.

A gust of wind blew across the bridge, and Aisling began to spin, while parrying his strikes. Her speed increased until she was too fast for him. She began a spinning counterattack, forcing Ith to retreat to the center of the bridge, out of range.

Aisling smiled at the sight of Ith backing away. En guard, she pointed her sword directly at Ith, who once again, lowered his weapon.

"You do not yet understand your importance, Aisling," said Ith. "Milesius was my nephew, and when he heard of the treachery against me, his sons raised an army and returned."

Aisling had caught her breath now, and was about to spin into another attack, but her curiosity made her hesitate. "I already know that the Milesians defeated the Sídhe, and they were banished to the Land of Dreams."

Ith nodded. "Yes, but before the battle, my kinsman, the poet Amairgin met with the three queens of the Tuatha Dé Danaan. They blessed him, and foretold that his descendants would prosper in Ireland. Amairgin promised that the land would be named after the queens. Their names were Fodla, Banbha, and Ériu."

Aisling nearly dropped her sword.

"Ireland was named after Queen Ériu, your mother," said Ith. "You're a princess, Aisling."

Descending out of the sky, lightning struck her sword, sending tingling sensations all over her body, but she was unhurt. With a cry, Aisling spun into another series of attacks, striking at his head.

Ith parried the blows.

The wind swirled around the black tower, and Aisling flipped over Ith in a cartwheel, slashing at his head. He ducked under the attack and turned around to face her and the tower. Twirling into another attack, Aisling tried to strike him, but he jumped back out of the way.

Landing on her feet, she took up a fighting stance again, with two fingers of her left hand held up in front of her face. "So that's why you've been assassinating the children of the Tuatha Dé. You were trying to kill me," said Aisling. "It's why I'm a changeling."

"Yes." Ith pointed his sword at the ground contemptuously. "*Gentle* Annie didn't tell you, did she? That one day, you will have greater magic than anyone else in Tír na nÓg."

The Air Elemental swirled around Aisling, throwing hair into her face. Taking a deep breath, she gathered all of the speed and power from the elemental. She could feel the whirlwind building up inside her. In the back of her mind, she felt another elemental—a spirit of fire—gathering force, behind Ith.

"Yaaah!"

With a fierce yell, she twirled into a rapid series of spinning strikes, and it forced Ith to retreat quickly, while parrying in a figure eight pattern. As he reached the end of the bridge, he faded into the shadows.

Aisling spun down and shrieked away her frustration.

Ith's voice came out of the darkness, and he began to materialize in front of her. Fire was in his eyes. "Very well," he whispered, "I shall burn you and scatter your ashes in the darkness."

Still in touch with the Air Elemental, Aisling extended her wings and twirled up in a spinning pirouette, out of the way of a violent conflagration of fire and fury below her. Rising up, she landed on top of the black tower.

A choir of angels sang from a dense cloud of black smoke, which surrounded a marble pillar sprouting from the roof of the tower. Bound to the base of the pillar with a rope of gold and silver, was her friend Trista, her blonde hair covering her face. She wore a black sleeveless tunic and gray tights. Looking up with exhausted eyes, she smiled. "Aisling! What are you—"

"Shhh!" Rushing over to her friend, Aisling swiftly cut the ropes and caught Trista as she fell. The choir of voices died down into silence, leaving nothing but the sound of the wind blowing.

"He made me sing to it, to make it come alive." Trista pointed into the top of the pillar inside the billowing smoke. "But he can't use it anymore."

"Can you fly?"

"I think so, yes."

"Then go," said Aisling. "Find Erin if you can. She's down in the throne room. Take her away from here."

Trista nodded and then grinned. "It's good to see you, Aisling."

Returning the smile, Aisling helped Trista to her feet and led her over to the battlements. Trista shook her head, as if she were waking up from a deep slumber. Then, extending her wings, she dove off the tower.

Turning around, Aisling stepped into the billowing smoke. A brief flash of light illuminated the Dream Crystal resting atop the pillar. Licking her lips, she removed the gem—more beautiful in its loneliness than ever before. Untouched by the denizens of the Land of Shadows, it lay dormant, calling out with a choir of angels in search of a lonely dreamer. But the Land of Shadows lay desolate beneath the tower.

A flash of rainbow colors swirled around the tower, causing Aisling to close her eyes for a moment. A bouquet of beautiful fantasies and desires swept through her mind, enticing and inviting and full of love.

Flapping wings were at her back, and she turned to see Ith landing on top of the tower. Retracting his dark wings, he came forward slowly, circling around the pillar.

Lowering her sword, she watched Ith as if he were a snake slithering at her feet.

Waving his arms, he began to gather fire into his hands.

Calling the Air Elemental, Aisling surrounded herself with a whirlwind.

Fire ignited against the storm. Its tendrils reached out, to touch, to grasp, to burn, but they were blown away in the violent storm. It took all of her strength to maintain the windstorm, and she felt her sword dropping from her hands. The conflagration raged around her, and she felt her knees give way. Falling to the stone, she summoned the last of her strength to maintain the storm. Dimly, she saw Ith falling, too, onto his knees. At last, the firestorm withered and went out. Both of them lay panting against the stone.

Ith spoke first, "Do you still believe that our war was fought over a lie?"

Aisling glanced down into the crystalline ocean, swimming in dreams. "Two kinds of dreams there are: Those inspired by pride, selfish, glorifying the dreamer; and those kinds of dreams that whisper with the love of truth."

Ith looked up from the stone roof of the tower where he lay. "What is the truth?"

The rainbow of light diminished slightly, like a lover scorned. Aisling was silent.

Chuckling, Ith rolled onto his back, "You and I are much alike, Aisling. We're both too proud to admit that we've abandoned our dreams. We no longer believe in them."

The cool crystal resting in her hand whispered, with promises too dear to accept, granting impossible dreams. Like a lover, it sang with the hope of eternal bliss. Aisling gripped the Dream Crystal tight in her hand, unwilling to ever let go of it again. *If you can dream it, you can do it.*

"Maybe the queen was right to hide this from you," she said.

Ith crawled forward, and he placed a gentle hand on top of hers. He said in a quiet voice, "To cage a dream of pride is to ignite the flames of anger. To imprison dreams of truth is to defile the love of God. Queen Annan is no better than I." Ith smiled darkly, his voice a whisper. "Join me! Together, we shall bring freedom to all three of our worlds."

Against a life of abandonment and loss, his offer was enchanting.

Aisling brought her lips up to his, and she kissed him. Sensual dreams exploded in her mind, touched by a rainbow of colors. Melting together, they writhed on the roof of the tower, full of passion. Aisling began to moan with exalted delight, and she rolled Ith onto his back and let all self-control slip away in an ecstasy of dreams. Her hands loosened, and she heard the Dream Crystal rolling away from them.

Breaking contact, she sat up and gazed down into his lonely eyes. Oceans of emptiness awaited her there. She wondered if passion, unrestrained, would lead to tyranny, as the Queen had said. All he could ever give was a chasm of despair. Ith lay there, with solitary eyes staring up into hers.

"No. The freedom you offer is empty." Aisling stood up, glancing at the Dream Crystal, which lay nearby, its light purring softly. "Both you and the queen want to control everyone's dreams. No one has the right to play God."

With a thought, her father's sword appeared in her hand, and she struck down at the Dream Crystal. A shattered ocean of light flashed over the Land of Shadows and dimly, she thought she could hear Ith screaming. She felt herself flying through the air, thrown far away from the tower. Swirling colors blended with passions and fantasies, and at last, the love of God went out.

Aisling found herself lying on the earth in a field of flowers, bathed in moonlight. Tears fell from her eyes. She looked up and saw the ruins of the tower of Caisleán na Scáthannain in the distance, a shadow against the blue light. The Land of Shadows lay dim before her, a hopeless world of forgotten dreams.

Soft winds swept over her face. Aisling looked up and saw Trista landing next to her, followed by a globe of silver and metallic black. With a flash, the orb changed into her sister. Trista looked up at the tower while Erin knelt down beside her.

"What happened?" asked Erin.

"I destroyed it," whispered Aisling. She glanced down at her father's sword, still tingling with a fading rainbow. "All we have left now are shattered dreams..."

Erin said, "The queen's going to be pissed..."

"Yes."

*   *   *

Chapter Twenty

The Land of Dreams

Cold moonlight evaporated into mist rising from the earth. The world lay empty, dark—full of shadows. Still languishing in the memory of the music of the Dream Crystal, Aisling lay on the ground next to Trista, whose songs had gone out too. Erin stood next to an oak tree, looking down at the ocean.

Too numb with the realization of what she had done, Aisling lay, stunned, on the grass, trembling in silence. Today was the day where all of the world's music lay dead, extinguished into eternity. The whirlwind of energy from the night before had swirled away into a tomb of silence, leaving Aisling exhausted.

Like a distant fire rising on the horizon, the world ignited with warmth, and a ray of light fell onto the grass where they lay. Presently, a blue jay landed on the oak tree next to Erin, and it began to sing.

Aisling had never heard a bird sing so sweetly. Lonely, the song called out, and it was inviting, like a cool lake on a summer's day. Refreshing and invigorating, the pure melody filled Aisling with hope. She stood up. But just as she caught sight of the bird, it took off, flying to a faraway tree across a field of daisies still damp with the breath of night.

Both Erin and Trista had noticed the bird too, and all three of them walked over to the ash tree where it had landed. The bird sang more sweetly than before, and Aisling found herself wishing she could stand and listen to it all day, but the bird took off again, flying off into a grove of hawthorn trees. Pausing to eat from clumps of red berries, the bird stopped singing for a moment.

The silence was like the blackness between the stars.

As they drew near, the bird sang out again for an instant, and then it took off again, enticing. Thirsting for more, Aisling began to follow the bird, but she felt Erin's hand on her arm. Turning, she saw wariness in her sister's eyes. "What is it?"

Erin whispered, "The night your parents were murdered, I followed a bird like this into the trees outside the house."

Trista shook her head. "This bird is not an evil thing."

"Maybe the bird you followed wasn't sent by the Shadow People," said Aisling. "I should think their magic would be of a darker sort."

"Come on!" said Trista.

Too enthralled to resist, they followed the bird deeper into the forest. The blue jay stopped only long enough to serenade them for a moment before flying off again, always leading them further away.

As they entered a grove of birch trees, everything turned to white sunlight, shadowed in green. Moving through the shade of the trees, they found themselves looking down on the ruins of Rath Gealach from the edge of the forest.

The bird chirped out a final merry tune and then happily flew away, up into the sky. Aisling looked at the others. "How can we have returned to Tír na nÓg? I thought all of the gateways to the Land of Dreams were sealed."

Trista thought for a moment before speaking. "We've been following an angel."

Aisling looked out over a field of grass leading down to the river. Rath Gealach stood deserted across the water, its ring of mushrooms abandoned by the Sídhe. The wind came up, blowing hair into her face.

Along with the breeze came an argument:

In an exasperated tone, a voice asked, "Would you tell me please, why we've come here?"

"I told you, I've had a vision of Aisling appearing from this forest," said the second voice. "I'm usually right about these things."

Grinning, Aisling threw a glance at her sister and walked up behind her friends, who were standing by a tree, with their backs turned. It looked like they were about to get into a fight.

"You should stop pretending that you can tell the future," said Eileen. "You're not even a fairy."

Genevieve brought up a pair of sunglasses to the top of her head. "Magic isn't exclusive to the Sídhe," she said. "I've been telling fortunes all of my life."

Eileen huffed. "Oh please! That doesn't mean you have the right to drag me off into the forest every time you start seeing things!"

Erin crossed her arms. "Why do you put up with them?"

Aisling sighed. "They have more need of me than I of them."

Turning around, Eileen shrieked.

Genevieve took a step back and glowered at Eileen, whose face had turned pink. Addressing Aisling, Genevieve said in a wispy voice, "A fine thing you've done! You go off seeking glory for yourself and leave me alone with her!"

Aisling laughed. "Sorry."

"How'd you get back?" asked Genevieve.

"We followed a little bird," said Trista.

Genevieve frowned and was about to ask a question when Eileen shouted out with glee. "Trista!"

Genevieve gave Eileen another dark look.

Eileen stared back at Genevieve with her blue eyes. "I was startled."

"That's what I do when I'm surprised," said Genevieve. "I scream."

"Maybe we should go back to the castle," said Erin, "and leave them here."

Trista giggled. "Come on!" Extending her wings, she leapt into the air and began to fly off towards Brú na Bodb, singing as she went.

Eileen's mouth dropped open. "We can fly again?" Extending a beautiful pair of transparent blue wings, Eileen took off into the air. "Fantastic!"

Genevieve crossed her arms as she watched Eileen fly after Trista. "Just like a fairy," she grumbled. "She's left us mortals here... to walk."

Erin laughed.

"No need for that," said Aisling. "Give me your hands."

*   *   *

Three orbs; one metallic black and silver, the second pink and white, and the third silver and gold, descended out of clear summer breezes, dropping down to the palace of Brú na Bodb, which stood brooding in the sunshine. In front of the gatehouse, next to a pair of soldiers, Eileen and Trista awaited their arrival.

As Aisling materialized next to Genevieve and her sister, she noticed that Eileen had her arms crossed, anxiously tapping her foot. But before Eileen could complain, Genevieve went on the offensive. "It's nice to see that you can still fly."

Before Eileen could respond, Aisling walked over to one of the guards, who held a halberd in his hand. "I don't suppose you can let us in?"

The soldier raised his eyebrows. "You're expected."

Not entirely sure if she liked the implicit invitation, Aisling went through the gatehouse, followed by the others, and stepped onto the lower courtyard. High up, above the upper courtyard, she could see the palace. King Artrach stood on the highest balcony, looking down. Smiling she resisted an urge to wave at him and went up the staircase that ascended from the left of the gatehouse. As she reached the upper courtyard, she glanced at the square tower which had housed the Dream Crystal. No trace of fire or fury remained to blacken the white stone. She couldn't spot any of the gargoyles and wondered if all of the stone guardians had been destroyed by Ith in the attack. Walking up the long stairway leading to the palace entrance, Aisling glanced over her shoulder at Trista, and wondered what the queen would do when she saw her.

Through ornate corridors, heavy with silence, they made their way to the grand hall leading to the balcony over the courtyard. The peaked roof was made of sturdy oak, finely carved into woodland scenes. Golden candelabrums, six feet tall, lined the hall, their candles extinguished. A line of exquisite chandeliers hung from the gabled roof. Bright sunlight shone through stained glass windows over the balcony, and through windows along the side of the hall. Bright and airy, the hall could have held several hundred of the Sídhe, but it was empty now, save for the king, whose back was turned. He remained looking out of the balcony for a time after they had arrived.

King Artrach, in a black tunic embroidered in gold and wearing a crown of leaves and flowers, turned around. "Dia daoibh," he said. "Fáilte ar ais, Aisling."

Aisling, along with the others, bowed to the king.

King Artrach came closer and stopped a few paces from them, hands behind his back. "Tell me, why has magic not returned?"

"It has, your majesty," said Eileen. "We can fly."

"Not all magic has come back," said the king, "only some of it."

Aisling took a deep breath and she drew herself up to her full height. "I've destroyed the Dream Crystal."

As if his legs could no longer support him, the king turned around and staggered over to a chair by the wall. "Then we must all return to the old ways," he said. The king looked into Aisling's eyes.

Unable to bear his gaze, she looked away. "I couldn't defeat him," she whispered. "I—"

"We will all fall into shadow now." Silence covered the hall, as if his pronouncement had transformed the palace into a tomb.

"No, your majesty," Aisling shook her head and looked deeply into the

King's eyes, "I think I know why people have been falling into the Land of Shadows."

The king raised his eyebrows. "Indeed?"

"Their souls have died."

Erin echoed the thought in a whisper, "Dead souls—"

"Think about it," said Aisling. "The proud, the indifferent—they don't care about anyone but themselves. They've forgotten how to love."

"When love dies, so does the soul." King Artrach nodded to himself. "Yes! That's the secret I've been looking for." Standing up, he waved to an attendant. "Bring Marcus to me."

Eileen looked dubiously at the king. "What are you going to do, your majesty?"

Artrach smiled. "Something dangerous."

As the man went out, the King glanced outside. "I've been swimming in a lake of uncertainty for too long," he murmured. He gave Aisling a look of relief. "Doubt is the first cause of slavery."

Aisling remembered how angry she was with herself for failing to control elementals. Too often, they had dominated her actions, turning her into a killer. But she needed to keep trying, or quit altogether. "Self-judgment destroys faith, and leads to failure."

Momentarily, Marcus came down the long hallway, his boots echoing off the walls. He wore a short tunic, breastplate, sandals, and he had a Gladius in a scabbard at his side. Without glancing at Aisling or the others, he stopped in front of the king and bowed. "What is it you wish, majesty?"

"I command," said Artrach, "that all Collars of Humility are to be removed from my subjects. No longer shall anyone have to guard their thoughts."

Marcus was appalled. "But my Lord—"

"A leader is not a tyrant, but shows others how to dream," he said. Then the King laughed out loud. "Tír na nÓg will become a place of freedom," he said, with a glance at Aisling. "Guarded freedom."

Aisling began to understand. "The best way to live life is by being

408

neutral."

The King nodded. "Do not be proud of your successes; do not be angry at your failures: Passion with moral responsibility."

Genevieve huffed. "Sifu Yuen could have told you that," she said.

"Yes," said Aisling, "he already did."

Marcus bowed and went out of the hall.

The king turned toward Trista. "You shall remain here in the Land of Dreams." He lowered his voice and put his hand on her shoulder. "I've always liked your music."

Aisling was still nervous. "What of the queen? Has she recovered?"

King Artrach grew quiet. He gestured towards a doorway. "She's in the next chamber."

With a backwards glance at Genevieve, Aisling walked through an ornate door. In a room adorned with resplendent paintings and one large standing mirror, the queen stood, looking at her reflection. When Aisling walked in, the queen said in a distracted tone, "Hello, Aisling."

Aisling had forgotten how beautiful the queen's eyes were. Brown pools of mirth, coupled with an irresistible smile, she looked at Aisling through the reflection in the glass. Despite what had happened between them, Aisling couldn't resist a smile of her own. She bowed her head, "Hello, your majesty."

The queen wore a dress of purple silk. White gardenias were woven into her hair, and she had matching shoes. A tiny frown made its way into the queen's face, but only for an instant. "This dress," Annan shook her head, "just won't do." Glancing around at Aisling, she raised her eyebrows plaintively. "I need to find something suitable for the festival of Litha." Again, she faced the mirror, sighing audibly. "Can you help?"

Aisling examined the dress with a critical eye. "The color isn't right," she said. "Litha is the summer solstice party, isn't it? Something brighter would work better."

With a wave of her hand, Aisling conjured up a yellow dress with white flowers woven into the fabric. "Try this."

A smile as bright as the dress burst into Queen Annie's face. Gently, she picked up the dress. "This is exquisite!" Holding it up to herself, she turned to the mirror once more. Her eyes fell, and she whispered, "Some of the events of the past few days have been... regrettable."

It was a subtle apology, but Aisling knew she was talking to a queen, unused to making excuses. "Yes."

"Although you're a changeling," murmured the queen, "I would have wanted you here anyway—your designs are quite beautiful." Queen Annan straightened up with an imperious air. "In any case, my husband did ask me to look after you."

"You knew that my mother was Queen Ériu," said Aisling.

"Of course," said Queen Annan. Her voice took on a more formal tone, and she put the dress down on the table. "I'm certainly not going to tell you anything until I think you're ready to know it."

Aisling raised her eyebrows. "All for the good of the kingdom?"

Apparently too weak to stand, Queen Annan sank down onto a seat by the mirror. She lit a white candle on the table and a cool light began to illuminate the chamber. "Did you know that before you came here, a third of my people had fallen into shadow?"

"No, majesty."

Obviously in pain, the queen closed her eyes. "Now, half of them are gone—eight of our cities now lay barren..."

"I've spoken to the king about that," said Aisling. "Controlling the dreams of others causes their souls to die."

"Yes," whispered Annan. "I was listening." Through the mirror, the queen looked into Aisling's eyes, this time simply curious. "How could you destroy such a beautiful thing?"

Suffering under those eyes, Aisling turned away. "It wasn't easy," she whispered. "Ith had beaten me..."

The candle went out. Morrigan walked into the chamber, carrying a satchel. She wore a tight, cherry-red dress, a black leather corset and ankle boots. Stopping short at the sight of Aisling, she chose to ignore her and looked at the queen. "Are you in pain, your majesty?"

The queen opened her eyes and, displaying a weak smile, nodded her head. Clutching her side, she glanced at Aisling and said, "Nel's sword was an ancient weapon. Morrigan has had some difficulty countering its magic."

"You are unkind, your majesty," said Morrigan. She sat down by the queen, and took out a pair of red candles. Placing them on the table, she ignited the candles and began to sing in an ancient tongue. Their spicy aroma began to fill the air with warmth.

The pain in the queen's eyes began to fade, and she looked up at Aisling again. "Please continue."

Aisling began to think of how Aoife had changed. She thought she heard the tinkle of bells nearby, and Aisling found herself looking around the room for a pair of red eyes, and a small shadow. But it was only the sound of wind chimes hanging from the balcony outside. "I was afraid of what Ith might do if he began to use the Dream Crystal. The thought of him gaining control over the realities of three worlds...." Aisling shook her head and whispered, "Also, I was afraid of what I might become, if I remained at his side."

Morrigan began to chuckle.

Both Aisling and the queen looked on inquisitively.

Morrigan had stopped chanting. With a wicked smile on her lips, she said, "He kissed you!"

Aisling bit her lip.

Morrigan was undeterred. "Or did you kiss him?"

"What does it matter?" asked Aisling.

"It matters a great deal," said Morrigan. "The Lord of Shadows is a master of enchantment, but he also has formidable powers with the Black Arts."

"You think he cursed me?"

Morrigan laughed softly and shook her head. "I have no idea, really."

"Enough!" said the queen. "How do you know so much about Ith?"

411

Still smiling, Morrigan said, "My sister, Macha, lives in the Land of Shadows. We talk to each other sometimes, through the glass."

Aisling thought of Morrigan's reflection in the mirror of the Shadow Witch. She shouted, "Oh, she's a horrid person!"

"Silence!" Queen Annan stood up. "If you two aren't going to be civil to one another, then get out!"

Collecting the candles with a wave of her hand, Morrigan stood up, bowed and went out of the chamber, smirking at Aisling.

Standing, Aisling began to leave, but she noticed the queen looking at her in the mirror's reflection.

Queen Annan whispered, "Some fairies should never have been banished."

Aisling knew the queen was talking about Trista. "None of them should have been banished."

The smile slipped out of the queen's face for an instant. "Don't be contrary," she chided. Queen Annan picked up a gold brush and began to run it through her hair. "What will you do now?"

"I'm going to take Erin home," said Aisling. "One queen is enough for the Land of Dreams."

The queen looked away. "Take care of yourself, Aisling."

Aisling whispered, "I will, your majesty."

*　*　*

Not too hot, the day, when a cool breeze blew over the lake, sending goose bumps up arms and legs. Scattered globes of light swept over the water, fairy wings barely discernible in the afternoon brightness. The forest was illuminated in sunshine, except for the most ancient of places, where shadows pushed back against the heat.

Aisling ran her hands across her bare arms, wishing she had chosen to wear tights under her white sun dress and gold sandals.

Erin was wandering through the trees nearby, with her arms outstretched. Now and again, she brushed her hands against a wild clutter of flowers or a trunk of wood. Sometimes it was smooth, like birch, but more often rough, like the magnificent cedar tree Aisling was approaching.

Eileen came out of the sky, landing nearby, but she didn't retract her wings after she was on the ground.

Genevieve grinned. "She's been flying every minute since you came back. You may have destroyed the Dream Crystal, Aisling, but magic still seems to work here."

Will it ever be like it was before? A frown slipped across Aisling's face. "You may not notice it, but magic is decidedly difficult now that dreams have died."

They came near the ancient cedar, whose branches twisted up into the sky over their heads. Without warning, a low moaning sound, full of pain, rang out through the clearing. Aisling and Genevieve stopped in their tracks, listening. The groan came over a breeze that whispered on leaves, and its touch sent chills over Aisling's skin.

Eileen nearly bumped into them. "What's wrong?"

Aisling threw a glance over her shoulder. "Shh!"

Again, a long utterance came out of the clearing by the old cedar tree, to languish in the shade like a wounded animal.

Genevieve gave Aisling a critical look. "Just why did you choose to leave Fáelán with this...this nymph?" she said. "We don't really know her, do we?"

"Nonsense!" clucked Eileen. "Elsbeth comes highly recommended around these parts. Certainly she wouldn't—"

This time the groan was accompanied by an ecstatic giggle, as if the nymph was toying with a caged beast. Smooth as honey, cold words drizzled over the clearing. "Your kind is weak. How much longer will you be able to endure my attentions, I wonder?"

Another moan, louder this time, emanated from the huge cedar tree.

The nymph giggled. "Ooh, what a sniffler you are!"

Erin had come up behind. Aisling felt her sister pushing her forward and she heard Erin's whisper, "You go first."

Aisling shook her head and looked at Eileen. "You're the one with the sword," she whispered. "I didn't bring mine."

Eileen choked down a giggle and whispered back, "I can't believe you're afraid of a tree nymph, especially after—"

"Okay, okay!" said Aisling.

Shaking her head, Aisling cautiously approached the ancient cedar tree. Walking at a slight angle, she looked around the other side, but didn't see anyone there. At that point, she heard Fáelán's voice. "No, please! I can't take it anymore!"

Biting her lip, Aisling walked up to the tree and, not knowing what else to do, knocked on the trunk, as if it was a wooden door.

There came a rustling and tumbling from somewhere, and then silence.

Aisling raised her eyebrows. "Hello?" Again she knocked on the trunk of the tree. "Hello, Elsbeth?"

Out of nowhere, a smooth imperious voice came from behind the thick trunk of cedar. "Go away."

"I won't." Aisling stepped back and looked up into the branches. Countless leaves hid most of the sunlight. "Not without Fáelán."

Elsbeth stepped out from behind the tree. She wore a short burgundy dress with a belt of purple cloth. Red Dianthus and magenta Firewitch flowers were woven into her hair, and she was barefoot. The scent of cedar filled the air, along with the sweet aroma of Dianthus. "How presumptuous of you," she purred. "Fáelán has not... fully recovered yet."

Eileen came forward, but the others remained where they stood, still under the cover of sunshine. "How can that be?" she asked. "Is it because magic has diminished?"

Looking down her nose at Eileen, Elsbeth laughed. The sound was quite different from the giggles they had been listening to. "Faeries are such upstarts," she muttered. "I follow the old ways."

Genevieve put her hands on her hips. "So you're unable to cure our friend?"

Elsbeth crossed her arms. "I didn't say that." Her eyes drifted over to the ancient cedar, and for a moment, her face was full of longing.

At that instant, Fáelán stepped out from behind the tree, sipping from a goblet of wine. Although he wore black pants and shoes, his shirt was off. In a mellow tone, he said, "Elsbeth, are you coming back inside? I still have a kink in my shoulder."

The nymph's face turned a deep shade of pink.

Aisling shouted, "Fáelán!"

Fáelán turned a pair of sleepy eyes in their direction. "Oh, hello!"

Moving around the nymph, Aisling grabbed Fáelán's arm and began to lead him away from the tree. "Just how long were you planning on keeping him?"

Eileen and Genevieve giggled.

At first, Fáelán began to protest against Aisling's guiding hands, but then he saw Erin standing in the sunshine, with an irritated look in her eyes. For a moment he stopped, dumbstruck. As if waking from an enchantment, he shook himself. With a glance at the tree, he waved a hand. A black shirt appeared and he hastily put it on. He stepped ahead of Aisling, muttering aloud, "It's, um... great to see you girls."

Erin turned around and began to walk away, and Fáelán hesitated, as if all the leaves had just fallen from the trees. Turning round, he gave the nymph a shy smile. "Thanks for everything, Elsbeth."

The memory of a beautiful man standing in front of an oak tree came to mind. Fintan had told Aisling that she might have been trapped for a hundred years inside the tree, whose spirit had tried to kiss her nearly a year ago. With a sigh, Aisling led Fáelán away from the tree nymph.

With a regretful look at Erin, Fáelán said, "So, have I missed much?"

They all laughed.

Fáelán gave them a curious look. "What?"

* * *

Chilly sunshine fell through the tall windows of Eileen's living room. Mingling with the melody of Trista's song out in the garden, the light filled the room with cheer. A brick fireplace held a fire, and its warmth drove away the morning cold. Genevieve and Hieronymus sat near the fire,

415

reading from the same book. Fáelán and Aisling sat on chairs, drinking tea.

"I'm not used to this—doing nothing," said Erin. She lay on one of the couches, with Calix perched on top of her chest. The fairy dragon was enjoying a scratch behind the ears.

"You'll have plenty to do once we get home," said Aisling. Her voice fell to a whisper, "Freedom is better than slavery."

"I'm not so sure..." muttered Erin, but she smiled just the same.

Hieronymus put a paw on the book, preventing Genevieve from turning the page. Genevieve stopped herself so that he could finish reading it. "Sorry, Hieronymus," she said. "For a librarian, it's hard to believe that you read so slowly."

Hieronymus didn't look up, but he flicked his tail.

Genevieve sighed. "To think that you can make things happen just by thinking about it is... childish."

"That's how magic works," said Fáelán.

"But you're a faerie," said Genevieve. "It won't work for us mortals."

Fáelán chuckled. "Milesians don't believe in anything."

Aisling turned to look at her best friend. "So, what does it say?"

Genevieve glanced down at the book. "It just talks about the 'cycle of creation'—whatever that is."

"Queen Annan told me about that," whispered Aisling. "She talked about visualizing your dreams to make them come true."

Hieronymus removed his paw and meowed. Genevieve turned the page, but didn't continue reading. "This book says that the Dream Crystal took the place of faith, so that magic was easier."

Aisling murmured, "So it created thoughts and it also helped you believe...."

Once again, there was a knock on the door of Eileen's house. With a wry smile, Aisling glanced over at Genevieve, who made a face.

Heading for the door, Eileen walked out of the adjacent room, wearing a t-shirt, jeans, and an artist's smock, covered in paint.

"Tell him I'm not here," whispered Genevieve.

With a naughty smile, Eileen glanced over her shoulder and answered the door. A pleasant exchange occurred and then Eileen said, "Why yes, she's right here."

Fintan came in. He knelt down by Genevieve and took her hand into his. "Sadness fills my heart at the prospect of losing you so soon," he said.

Genevieve raised her eyebrows.

"What do you mean?" asked Aisling. "We're still waiting for Samhain, two months away. That's when the next Thin Place will appear, isn't it?"

Fintan dropped Genevieve's hand and stood up. He turned a playful smile towards Eileen. "You didn't tell them?"

Eileen bit her lip.

"What didn't she tell us?" asked Aisling.

Eileen ran out of the room.

Aisling followed her into a room full of windows that looked out over the lake. Paintings of beautiful landscapes covered the walls. Eileen sat in front of an easel with a partially finished painting of the lake. Aisling sat down onto a stool.

"I'm so sorry, Aisling."

Holding back a tide of anger, Aisling said, "We could have gone home anytime we liked?"

Eileen nodded. "All you need to do is find another Thin Place."

* * *

The world held its breath where a stream came out of the forest, to tumble down a series of rocks and then to fall, down, down, into a pool of cold water. Mist rose from the waterfall, which hid a ledge underneath it. The rocky path led to an Áit Thanaí—a Thin Place, where the veil between worlds could be drawn aside.

Aisling stood on a hill overlooking the path leading down into the gorge and underneath the waterfall. She wore a white peasant blouse with a purple belt of cloth, black leggings and boots.

"I don't see what the problem is," said Genevieve.

"What would Calix do in our world?" asked Aisling. "Nobody's ever seen a fairy dragon there."

"His name is Calixtus," said Genevieve. She held the small dragon in her arms.

Aisling thought how well his purple scales went with Genevieve's green blouse, white jeans and hiking boots. Brushing a strand of dark hair out of her eyes, Aisling smiled. "I'm sure that if Hieronymus were here, you'd want to bring him along too."

"I know." Genevieve frowned, scratched the dragon behind the ears and whispered, "See you, Calixtus."

Breathing a little puff of fire, Calix took off into the air, flying over the spray of the waterfall and up into the sky. Genevieve watched him go, until his calls could no longer be heard over the roar of water.

Fáelán came out of the forest and took a deep breath. "What an enchanting place this is," he said. "Has anyone seen Eileen?"

Aisling shook her head. "She wouldn't come."

Erin was sitting on a rock overlooking the path, her arms wrapped around her knees. "Should we wait for her?"

"I said," hissed Aisling, "that she doesn't want to say goodbye to us."

Erin looked away at the waterfall.

Genevieve put her hand on Aisling's shoulder. "Don't be angry," she said. "Remember, her entire clan fell into shadow, and her parents are dead."

Aisling let the anger slip away into a pool of sadness. "I know. She doesn't have any family."

"I'll always consider her part of my family," said Genevieve. "I wish she'd come with us."

Smiling, Aisling looked up. "What's this? You're sticking up for her?"

"Well...."

Erin brushed a strand of silver hair out of her eyes. "What's that in your hands?"

Aisling looked down. "It's something my father left for me."

The stone box with the carved dragons rattled as she shook it. Aisling whispered her name and opened the magic box. She put the gold medallion, which Genevieve had returned to her, back inside the box, but she continued to wear her father's ring on her forefinger. A third item, forgotten, lay inside. Aisling picked up the stone, which caught the light dancing over the waterfall. It looked like a large diamond. The stone caught the glittering light of the rainbow hovering over the waterfall.

After leading them here, Fintan had remained standing on the hill, unwilling to go down under the falls. He looked at the stone with wonder in his eyes and smiled. "That's a Fomorian power crystal," he said.

"What does it do?" she asked.

Fintan held out his hand. She gave it to him and he lifted it up to the light. A million colors danced inside its crystalline landscape. "Each one is different." Returning it to Aisling, he added, "Their magic blossoms, like a flower, becoming something beautiful or terrible, depending on the character of those who possess it. This is a rare treasure."

Aisling put the crystal back inside the stone box and closed it. She looked down into the gorge, inhaling the damp mist, and she closed her eyes. Soon, she would return Erin to her parents.

A bird sang out from the forest and she saw Eileen standing by a pine tree, far down by the pool of water. She wore a long blue dress embroidered in white, a silver belt, and white sandals. Daisies were woven into her hair, and her sword hung from a black scabbard.

Aisling put the stone box down next to her other belongings and flew down to Eileen, whose blue eyes were damp with the rising mist at the bottom of the waterfall.

Suddenly nervous, Aisling ran a hand through her hair. "Thanks for coming."

"Don't go."

"I have to," said Aisling. She glanced up at her sister, who sat talking to the others. "I have to take her home. Erin's never really known her parents."

Eileen nodded and looked into Aisling's eyes. "Alright," she whispered. "Keep Genevieve out of trouble for me, will you?"

Before Aisling could answer, Eileen changed into a blue and silver sphere of light and flew off into the forest. Aisling stood looking into the trees for a time before she rejoined the others.

Fintan was telling them a story about the wars of Alexander when Aisling landed on the hilltop. He looked longingly into Genevieve's eyes for a moment and then he turned to Aisling. "So, are you ready to go?"

A mischievous smile crept into Aisling's face. "Not yet. I'd like a final match, if you don't mind."

Raising his eyebrows, Fintan smiled and stepped back several paces. He drew his sword and waited.

Closing her eyes, Aisling imagined herself in the upcoming duel— what strikes she would make, his counterattacks, how the sunshine would shine off their blades—the entire feel of it. The duel was a choreographed dance of beauty in her mind.

Opening her eyes, Aisling took a deep breath and drew her sword.

Fintan saluted her with his Makhaira sword.

Not bothering to summon any elementals this time, Aisling leapt into an attack, furiously striking out while advancing.

Fintan calmly parried every blow, retreating through the grass towards the forest. Stepping aside to dodge an overextended strike, he began a swift counterattack.

Aisling barely had time to get out of the way. Off balance, she retreated.

Fintan had to get closer, since his weapon wasn't as long as hers, and so he advanced aggressively, striking as he came on.

As she neared the edge of the cliff overlooking the gorge, Aisling stepped aside and brought the flat side of her sword down against his wrist to loosen his grip. Then, catching his weapon with her sword, she twisted her wrist and sent the blade flying down far below into the water, where it landed with a splash.

Fintan put his hands on his hips. In a distracted tone, he said under his breath, "Now I've got to go down there."

Surprising herself, Aisling began to laugh. "I can't believe it," she said.

"I beat you!"

Irritation in his voice, Fintan said, "Why is it so hard to believe? You set a goal, imagined yourself winning, took action again and again, and again, and you refused to quit until you had finally beaten me." He looked into her eyes. "It's really impossible to fail if you stick to the old ways of practicing magic."

Aisling stopped laughing.

Fintan threw a lusty pair of eyes towards Genevieve. "It's why I know that one day, I shall have you, my dear."

Genevieve frowned and looked away. She was blushing.

Fintan made a move towards the edge of the cliff, but Aisling caught his arm. "I'll get it."

Diving down into the icy water, Aisling swam deep, looking through the clear pool. A golden glint of sunlight caught steel, and she reached out to retrieve the sword. Breaking over the surface of the water, she caught her breath and ran a hand over her face. Extending her white wings, she took off into the air and flew up to where the others waited. Handing the weapon back to Fintan, she said, "Thank you for the lessons, sir."

Genevieve hefted a large satchel over her shoulder and looked down at the path, which went down under the waterfall, and into another world: Home. "I suppose," she said, "that magic can work for us mortals too, if we stick to the old ways."

Drying herself off with a warm gust of air, Aisling felt the chill of damp clothes evaporate, replaced by the warm sunshine. "If you ask me," she said, "I'd say that imagination rules the world."

Erin stood up and threw a conspiratorial glance at Genevieve. "Can we go now?"

Frowning at her sister's sudden impatience, Aisling watched as they went down the trail. The satchel at Genevieve's side quivered slightly as she stepped in front of Erin and out of sight. A muffled meow was drowned out by the roaring water.

Aisling shook her head in exasperation and turned to look at Fintan

421

and Fáelán. "You know," she said, "I'm always getting your names mixed up."

Fáelán gave a short bow. "Goodbye, Aisling." He smiled impishly and whispered, "You mind if I come round sometime? I'd like to see your sister again."

Aisling giggled and punched his arm. "It's about time you asked her out." She gave them both a hug and she even kissed Fintan on the cheek. "So long," she said.

Fintan, his eyes full of longing, watched Genevieve disappear under the waterfall. "Go n-éirí an bóthar leat!" he said. Then he extended a pair of beautiful red and white wings and took off into the sky.

"It means," said Fáelán, "to have a good journey." There was a flash as he changed into a blue and green sphere, which drifted away into the forest.

A pretty song descended out of the sky.

Aisling looked up to see a pair of blue-white wings circling overhead. It was Trista, coming to sing a farewell song. Aisling waved and shouted, "Goodbye, Trista!"

Aisling inhaled a warm summer's breeze, which caught her hair and threw it into her face. Brushing it out of her eyes, she whispered, "There's no reason that the Milesian world can't also be a Land of Dreams."

Turning down the steep path, Aisling went quickly, hoping to catch up to the others. A cool breath of mist washed over her skin as she stepped behind the waterfall and into another world.

Darting out of the trees, a little blue sphere, tingling with silver light, flew out. It went through the waterfall after the others.

THE END

Appendix A

Faerie Mounds of Tír na nÓg

Brí na Slieve – Mountain of Power. Home of the Goibniu clan, ruled by Sean.

Brugh na Bás – Palace of Death. Home of the Brian clan, ruled by Bryce.

Capall Bán – White Horse. Home of the Luchtaine clan, ruled by Rosheen.

Cnoc Firinn – Hill of Truth. Home of the Donn clan, ruled by Donn.

Cnoc Síoraíocht – Hill of Eternity. Home of the Trogain clan, ruled by Irial.

Lismore – Home of the Danand clan.

Meadhar Grá – Dizzy Love. Home of the Aoi clan, ruled by Maire.

Measarthachtshee – Sidhe of Moderation. Home of the Iuchar clan, ruled by Canlyn.

Na Teach Cúirtéis – House of Courtesy. Home of the Aed Ernmas clan, ruled by Lasarina.

Rath Gealach – Fortress of the Moon. Home of the Bodb Derg clan, ruled by Nessa.

Roth Cinniúint – Wheel of Fate. Home of the Éogan clan, ruled by Finnian.

Síd Imreas – Sidhe of Strife. Home of the Ailill clan, ruled by Rhona.

Sidh ar Saoirse – Sidhe of Freedom. Home of the Eochaid clan, ruled by Eochaid mac Eirc.

Sidhe an Domhan – Sidhe of the Earth. Home of the Creidhne clan, ruled by Ceridwen.

Slieve Críonnacht – Mountain of Wisdom. Home of the Iucharba clan, ruled by Marcus.

Svartálfaheimar – Home of the Dvergar clan, ruled by Mótsognir.

Appendix B

Irish Words & Phrases

I'd like to thank the community on the Irish Translation Forum and my Irish teacher, Shanti Hofshi, for help in translating English words and phrases into Irish Gaelic.

CHAPTER FOUR

Dia daoibh (Djia deev) – Hello (to more than one person).

Fáilte ar ais! – Welcome home!

Síofra (Sheefra) – Changeling.

Tuatha Dé Danaan – The people of Danu.

Dia duit (Djia gwich) – Hello (to one person).

Tír na nÓg – The Land of Eternal Youth.

Slán agus beannacht leat. – Goodbye and blessings with you.

CHAPTER FIVE

Linn na Cinniúna – The Pool of Destiny.

Sídhe – Faerie mound or hill. It's also a loose term for the Faeries.

CHAPTER SIX
An Rí Bealach – The King's Road.
Brú na Bodb – The Palace of Bodb Dearg.

CHAPTER SEVEN
Síoraí Bladhm – The Eternal Flame.

CHAPTER NINE
Lebor Gabála Érenn – The Book of Takings.
Comhrac Aonair – Single combat.

CHAPTER ELEVEN
Áit an Fhillidh – The Place of Returning.
Cuilithe – A vortex or a Thin Place.
Áit Thanaí – A Thin Place, which is a doorway to another world.
Nach breá an lá é – What a lovely day.
Dragan Sídhe – A Fairy dragon.

CHAPTER TWELVE
Glaine ár gcroí; Neart ár ngéag; Beart de réir ár mbriathar – Purity of heart, strength of limb, and deeds to match our words.

CHAPTER THIRTEEN
Cur trí thine – Set on fire.
Is tríomsa atá an bealach go dtí an scáth buan – Through me is the way to eternal shadow.
Muintir atá caillte iad, gan fiú dóchas an bháis acu – They are a lost people, without even the hope of death.
In éad go brách le gach cinniúint eile a fhanann said – Forever envious of all other fates, they linger.
Is tríomsa atá tír na n-aislinglí dearmadta – Through me is the Land of Forgotten Dreams.

Splanc thintrí – Flash of lightning.

Capall dubh – black horse.

Capall bán – white horse.

Cathair Dhubh – The Black City.

Slán leat – Goodbye.

CHAPTER FOURTEEN

Oíche mhaith, codladh sámh – Goodnight, sleep well.

Saoraim thú – I release you.

CHAPTER SEVENTEEN

Ní chreidim é! – I don't believe it!

CHAPTER EIGHTEEN

Stad – Halt.

Tá cead agat labhairt – You have permission to speak.

Is minic a bhris béal duine a shrón – Many a time a man's mouth broke his nose.

CHAPTER NINETEEN

Tír na nAislingí Dearmadta – Land of Forgotten Dreams.

Caisleán na Scáthanna – the Fortress of Shadow.

Appendix C

Cast of Characters

Main Characters are in *italics*.

Adar: The Firbolg gatekeeper to the Fortress of Árainn.

Aisling (ASH ling): A Changeling faerie. Her Milesian name is Erin O'Neil.

Alaiya: The Style fairy.

Amairgin: A Milesian poet.

Aoife Kippen (EE fa): A frivolous changeling faerie with red hair.

Báirbre (BOI breh): A changeling outcast.

Brigitte: A Milesian fashion student that fell into the Land of Shadows.

Bryce: A Shadow Person/Necromancer from Brugh na Bás.

Calix / Calixtus: A Dragan Sidhe – a fairy dragon.

Canlyn: The leader of the Iuchar clan, she is an expert with a bow.

Ceridwen: A shadow from Sidhe an Domhan, she holds the Shadow Key.

Chocolate Fairy: Another popular fairy.

Conall Cernach: A smooth talking faerie that's trying to seduce Aisling.

Drust: A Hobgoblin.

Dunfhlaith Fitzgerald (DUN a la): The captain of the ship, Niamh.

Éile (AYL yeh): One of the Shadow People crewing the Niamh.

Eileen Bisset: Aisling's faerie protector.

Electricity Fairy: She sells Electricity Elementals.

Elsbeth: A Nymph that guards an ancient cedar tree, she is a healer.

Eochaid Mac Eirc: King of the Firbolg, he rules from the Fortress of Árainn.

Erin O'Neil: The girl who was kidnapped by Aisling's faerie parents.

Fáelán Anluain (FWAY lawn): An impulsive faerie that befriends Aisling.

Father Harrigan: The Milesian priest of the cathedral near Rath Gealach.

Felic: One of the Tower Guard, residing in Caisleán na Scáthanna.

Fial: A member of the Tower Guard, from Caisleán na Scáthanna.

Fina: The owner of a charm shop in the Land of Shadows.

Finnian (FIN yan): Mystic ruler of Roth Cinniúint, the home of the Éogan clan.

Fintan Mac Bóchra: The most ancient of the faeries, he is attracted to Genevieve.

Fionna: A child lost in the Land of Shadows.

Gann: A Firbolg guard stationed at the Fortress of Árainn.

Genevieve Sully: Aisling's best friend, a Milesian.

Hulegu Khan: A king that conquered Persia. He gave his sword to Nel.

Heulfryn: A Hobgoblin.

Hieronymus: The librarian, cursed to live as a cat after losing a duel.

Iarlugh (EER loo): One of the Shadow People crewing the Niamh.

Ice Cream Fairy: A popular fairy, even in the winter.

Irial (IR eeal): Enchantress that rules Cnoc Síoraíocht, and the Trogain clan.

Ith, the Hat Man: The Lord of Shadows. Identified by the top hat he wears.

Ith's Lieutenant: Ith's cruel champion and second in command.

Jago: A house servant in the Land of Shadows.

Keir: A Shadow person that lives in the Fortress of Árainn.

Kerrin (KER in): Morrigan's handmaiden.

King Artrach: The king of the Tuatha Dé Danaan.

Kusanagi Gin: The Inferno Fairy.

Kylie (KYE lee): A faerie that likes to play pranks on Aisling.

Laigne (LAH neh): Morrigan's boyfriend.

Laoise (LEE sha): One of the Shadow People crewing the Niamh.

Lasarina: High Priestess of the Sídhe, she is from Na Teach Cúirtéis.

Lonán: A house servant in the Land of Shadows.

Macha: Morrigan's sister.

Maija (MY uh): A friend of Aisling, she was in her fashion show.

Maire (MOI reh): A dark enchantress that wants to teach Aisling about love.

Marcus: Sorceror and Fire Elementalist from Slieve Críonnacht.

Mrs. Whitaker: The Milesian fashion director at the school Aisling is attending.

Mil, Milesius: A Celtic king, whose sons invaded Ireland.

Miss Bentley: One of Aisling's fashion instructors in Seattle.

Morrigan: A powerful faerie, she is a jealous rival of Aisling.

Mótsognir: King of the Dvergar.

Nel: A faerie from Babylon, she guards the Mirror of Eternity.

Nessa: A friend of Eileen's, she is a spiritualist and Water Elementalist that rules Rath Gealach.

Nimrod: A man of great power who founded Babylon.

Paola (pah OH la): A friend of Aisling, she was in her fashion show.

Queen Annan: The repressive Faerie Queen, also known as "Gentle Annie."

Rhona (ROH nah): A Fire Elementalist from Síd Imreas.

Rindail: A Firbolg guard stationed at the Fortress of Árainn.

Rosheen: Air Elementalist from Capall Bán, she rules the Luchtaine clan.

Scolaí (SKUL lee): One of the Shadow People crewing the Niamh.

Sean: The shadow ruler of the Goibniu clan.

Shadow Witch: A witch living in the Haunted Forest in the Land of Shadows.

Sifu Yuen: The director of Aisling's Kung Fu school.

Sinéad (shin ADE): The Goth fairy that guards the Place of Returning.

Siri (SEE ree): A changeling faerie.

Skilia: King of the Goblins.

Snorri: A Dvergar (Dwarf) guarding the entrance to Svartálfaheimar.

Tómmán Mac Craith (TOW awn): The bartender at the Green Heather Pub.

Tommy: A friend of Fáelán's from Sid Imreas.

Trista: A faerie that loves to sing.

Ultán: A member of the Tower Guard, from Caisleán na Scáthanna.

Vailintín: A Shadow Cat.

MARK O'BANNON
Biography

Mark O'Bannon is an American novelist, screenwriter, and game designer best known as the author of the science fiction series *Imperium* and for three fantasy series: *Whiskers*, *Aia the Barbarian*, and *Shadows and Dreams*.

O'Bannon is the CEO of Shadowstar Games, which publishes the Interactive Storytelling Game (a Pen & Paper Role Playing Game), "Fantasy Imperium."

O'Bannon is an advocate of Self-Publishing and teaches workshops to aspiring authors on how to publish, market and promote their work.

Born in San Diego, California, O'Bannon is the grandson of the famous aviation pioneer, Reuben H. Fleet (who acquired the Wright Brother's airplane company Dayton-Wright along with Gallaudet Aircraft and formed Consolidated Aircraft, the makers of the famous B-24 Liberator bombers and the PB-Y Catalina flying boats from WWII).

O'Bannon is a registered Libertarian and runs a non-profit, Mapping Freedom, which teaches Free World Theory (FWT), an exploration of the freedoms protected by the U.S. Constitution, and new scientific discoveries of freedom, coercion, property, slavery and intellectual property.

www.ingramcontent.com/pod-product-compliance
Lightning Source LLC
Chambersburg PA
CBHW020503020726
47493CB00001B/150